PAPAVER SOMNIFERUM (Book 2)

K.M.KNIGHT

PAPAVER SOMNIFERUM

DEDICATED TO THE REAL VILLAGERS AND
THEIR ANCESTERS

IT support by Zachary Ulm
Painting by K M Knight
Photographs by Zoe F Knight

Chapter 1

Eve watched the darkening sky. It was 3 o'clock in the afternoon and a storm was approaching from the North, hovering menacingly above the ominously dark estuary. Her fingers trembled as she drew the heavy curtains, unwilling to be startled by the inevitable lightening. She had feared storms since early childhood, when she had witnessed her grandfather struck dead on the marshes. She could still remember the scent of charred, smoking flesh and the horrific expression on his face. He had made her lie flat on the grass and told her to remain still whilst he calmed the agitated dogs. She had shut her eyes in terror as the billowing black clouds and deafening thunder rolled above her head. A seismic crash accompanied by a blinding flash, still visible though her tightly closed eyelids, ended her grandfather's life. Eve lay there until the storm passed trying not to look at her blackened grandfather and listening to the pitiful whining of the dogs. She had run across the marshes, sobbing in the quiet drizzle that followed the path of the storm. Her father and brother found her just outside of the village, muddy and retching and struck dumb. Eve was four years old and remained mute and tormented by nightmares, until her mother, against the wishes of her father, took her to see a tall, thin man with a long beard and strange clothes. He was called Mustapha the Magician and had kind eyes that could see right inside her head. Eve listened to her mother explaining as best she could what had happened, although as Eve had not spoken, nobody knew the details. Mustapha lifted Eve onto his lap, enclosed her in his arms, stoked her hair and sang quietly as he rocked her gently. Eve snuggled into his chest and put her small arms around him and began to cry. Her alarmed mother moved toward them but Mustapha smiled and shook his head.

'She needs to do this, the tears will heal her soul.' He whispered with such conviction that her mother sat down again.

Eve cried herself to sleep on Mustapha's lap and awoke with a small smile. She looked up into Mustapha's eyes and in a tiny voice she whispered.

'Granddad got burned up.'

Her mother began to cry as she listened to the child's quivering voice relate the incident on the marshes, encouraged and reassured by Mustapha, who continued to rock her gently.

Mustapha gave Eve's mother a bottle containing a pale gold liquid and instructions to mix a teaspoonful into warm milk and give to Eve at night to relieve the nightmares. To Eve he gave a small, bright, soft cushion that smelled of flowers and told her to take it to bed with her and sniff it if she felt sad or frightened. Eve's father forgave his wife for disobeying him as soon as he heard his little daughter speak again. Eve's nightmares stopped but her fear of storms remained and she would bury her face in the little cushion. The smell of flowers gradually faded and in the end it just smelled like Mustapha. Over fifty years later she still had the little cushion.

Eve had attended the local school, one of the first village girls to learn to read and write. She had married and had three children, the first two with the help of Mustapha and Mary. When her children grew up she had worked at the big house next to the woods at Christmas and the harvest parties. She had watched Mustapha during the passing years, his hair growing whiter. She had rejoiced at his marriages and the births of his descendants. He had given her a safe place when her little world had become too terrifying to talk about and when he finally died she felt the loss keenly. She visited his grave whenever she needed to, and was comforted by the smell that enveloped her when she knelt beside his grave. Eve would shut her eyes and return to the safety of Mustapha's lap, lulled by his peaceful rocking.

Mustapha and Mary's simultaneous deaths left the family and the village bereft, in a web of vague confusion, like a beehive without a queen. The old couple's famous skills had been passed on and the garden flourished under the watchful eyes of Mustapha's grandson and his wife Isabella, but the sense of loss was palpable. Little Mustapha, old Mustapha's great-grandson was the only one who still sang and laughed and bore no scar of bereavement. He had no concept of death, so he still saw them, talked to them and walked in the woods with them. He slept in their bed at night and often walked with old Mustapha around the house at night. His mother, believing him to be sleepwalking, would lead him back to bed where he and Mustapha would dissolve into a fit of giggling due to Mustapha's invisibility magic.

At the age of four, little Mustapha announced that he wanted to be a sea captain when he grew up. Mustapha and Isabella were initially dismayed, having expected him to follow in the Mustapha's tradition of healing and they prayed for a change of heart. Paulo had also hoped his youngest sons Edmundo and Estavo would reassess their intention to go to sea like their uncles. But at fifteen years old they remained intransigent. They had no interest in following Paulo in his carpentry business, neither one could knock a nail straight without bruising a thumb. They had managed to convince their uncles, Sam and Sal that as the grandsons of Aziz Shadi Rashad Salamar Badr al din the sea was in their blood. Sam and Sal were now in their early fifties and Sam continued to spend most of his time at sea with his eldest son Khalid, who was an excellent navigator but remained reluctant to travel far from the ship. He had never recovered from the trauma caused by flies, heat, filth and relentless diarrhoea experienced whilst visiting his mother's home village in India.

As Sam and Sal had matured their characters slowly diverged. Sam remained the more adventurous, impulsive, vociferous twin, whilst the gentler Sal had become more introspective and sensitive, content to remain in the village with his family. Following the death of his father-in–law Mustapha Sal shouldered the responsibility as head of the family. His wife Maria was quietly ecstatic. She had lived in fear every moment he was away at sea, and now with her father dead, she had dreaded her husband's departure.

Edmundo and Estavo jubilantly sailed away with Sam and Khalid in the late summer. Paulo watched sadly from the dock, his dream of building his own family business in tatters. His eldest son George, now in his early twenties had successfully managed the family's finances for the last ten years having turned his back on the carpentry workshop and his only other child was an impractical, beautiful young woman with dark curly hair and violet eyes who spent her days with her head in a book. His wife Rose, sensing his disappointment, took his hand and kissed his cheek.

'I think it best that you bequeath the business to Harry and Big Ern, they are like sons to you anyway.' She laughed.

By the time they had returned to the big house, Paulo had warmed to the idea and found George and had him make up the necessary paperwork.

Mina, Sam's wife, coped well with her husband's absence. She was a stoic woman with few expectations and eternally grateful to have a roof over her head and food every day. Her time was consumed with Joey, her lively erratic son who was banned from sailing due to his disruptive boundless energy, dissuaded from the carpentry workshop for the safety of the carpenters and sent packing from Gabriel's farm to protect the horses from insanity. He loved animals but the feeling was not mutual. He agitated horses to nervous exhaustion, caused sheep to stampede wildly and irritated to violence the most genial of dogs. Even Bill the monkey became uneasy when he approached.

Paulo and Rose sat at the long kitchen table, waiting for the pot of tea to brew, enjoying the peace that had descended on the house after the departure of its four noisiest inhabitants. It was evening and the perfume of the lavender bushes pervaded the kitchen. They had been planted along the path from the kitchen door by Mary many years ago and had grown to the size of fully-grown sheep. They provided local bees with sustenance and Maria with enough lavender bags to keep the linen fresh. The couple took their tea outside and sat on the bench in front of the house catching the last rays of the sun. The large meadow bore the brown, dusty scars of a long sunny summer. To the right of the meadow Mustapha's garden was flourishing, a patch of vivid colour contrasting starkly against the parched vegetation. Mustapha, Isabella and little Mustapha were perched in the tree house watching the sunset. Rose watched them as Mustapha helped his heavily pregnant wife down the steps from the tree house, followed by little Mustapha and the chattering Bill. At a distance Mustapha looked just like his grandfather had when Rose was a tiny child over forty years before. He possessed the same lithe, elegant, easy gait of a cat in no hurry. He wore the same long trousers and knee length shirt but without the headscarves and his long dark curls glowed bronze in the sun. Isabella was laughing at her own laborious descent and inability to see where she was placing her feet. Her long pale hair, bleached white by the sun, was in two thick plaits. They walked through the garden, stopping to assess the health of the plants and instructing little Mustapha to water them now the sun was losing heat. Little Mustapha scurried off to find the can that he filled from the water tank in the corner of the garden, closely followed by Bill. Isabella sat down on the bench beside Paulo, her cheeks red from the effort. Rose watched Mustapha watching his wife and sensed his trepidation. His grandfather and Mary had delivered her first child with great skill. This time it would be down to him alone and he prayed fervently for the ability to succeed.

'There is a baby in there!' Little Mustapha announced loudly, pointing towards his mother's belly. 'That's why she is so fat!'

'Yes, we know.' Rose laughed.

'Apparently, I was in there a long time ago, but I don't remember.'

Chapter 2

The following week was a busy one. The family and half of the villagers were busy preparing for the big party held at the end of the harvest. Sal attempted to organise the event but everyone was so adept at parties that everyone already knew their role. Harry and Big Ern set up the spits and the seating. Women from the village arrived three days before to start the mammoth task in the kitchen. Men arrived with freshly butchered carcasses and crates of vegetables, George had ordered the fireworks and even Joey had managed to harvest and build a huge woodpile behind the spits and build the bonfire in the centre of the field. Gabriel and Paulo had made ready the clearing in the woods where Aziz Shadi Rashad Salamar Badr al din and Elijah had died. Musicians practiced in the stables and Sal was reduced to quietly ticking off the items on his list.

The villagers began to arrive in the early afternoon on the Saturday, scrubbed and dressed in their best clothes for the occasion. The fires for the spit roasts had been lit at dawn and Big Ern had enlisted the help of his wife Beth's younger brothers who were in charge of turning the carcasses. By midafternoon the first mouth-watering aromas began to invade the growing tumult, coinciding with the onset of Isabella's labour pains. She tried to convince herself that it was more likely to be wind or cramp. Little Mustapha and Maria discovered her sitting on the stairs, clutching the banister rail with one hand and her belly with the other and before they could stop him little Mustapha had run off to find his father. He eventually found his father talking to Big Ern and Beth.

'Mother has a bellyache!' he shouted as soon as he saw him.

Mustapha leapt to his feet and ran through the startled crowd and into the house, closely followed by Beth. Isabella was still at the bottom of the stairs, the pain had subsided and she tried to apologise for her timing. Maria had already lit the bathhouse fires and arrived with a tray of tea. Isabella's pains, timed by Mustapha, were about ten minutes apart. Beth disbursed the clamouring crowd that had instantly gathered at the front door. She explained that Isabella's pains had begun and that they would be kept informed of any developments. The crowd meandered away informing anyone that remained ignorant of the news that old Mustapha the Magician's great-grandchild had decided to join the party.

Mustapha had prepared everything, as his grandfather always did. He gave his wife a mild potion and attempted to persuade little Mustapha to return to the party. Little Mustapha refused to leave his mother's side. Beth and Maria filled the bath when the water was hot, listening to the musicians and the laughter of the crowd. The delicious smell of roasting meat and hot bread made them feel hungry. Beth went out and asked one of her brothers to bring in a plate of food. He arrived with a tray packed with chunks of roast lamb and beef, a succulent spit-roasted chicken, hot bread and roast potatoes. Beth carried the tray of food into the bathhouse as Mustapha and Maria supervised Isabella getting into the warm water. She relaxed into the water, a piece of chicken in one hand and a slice of thickly buttered bread in the other. The three women and little Mustapha managed to eat most of the food and no one noticed that Mustapha had been unable to partake. Isabella's pains increased in intensity after a cup of hot sweet tea and Mustapha administered a stronger potion that made her laugh and sing along to the music from outside. Little Mustapha once again declined the suggestion to leave his mother and go and play with the other children at the party.

The party was in full swing. The villagers, dancing full of roast meat, were attempting to keep up with the musician's increasing tempo. The children had organised themselves into a complex game of chase at the bottom of the field, in order to pass the time until someone lit the bonfire.

When Isabella had reached the pushing stage Mustapha spoke sternly to his son, telling him it was time to leave, but was demolished by his calm response.

'Granddaddy told me that I should be here to welcome my sister!'

Beth and Maria looked at each other, then at Mustapha, who was lost for words. At that moment he would have given his life to have his grandfather by his side. The deadlock was interrupted by Isabella asking for help to reach a kneeling position. Beth and Maria lifted her and she knelt and faced her husband as he encouraged her to push long and hard. Beth, who had attended numerous deliveries with Anna, put her arm in the water to feel Isabella's progress and was astonished to discover the baby's head almost out. She smiled at Mustapha, who thought he felt his grandfather's hands on his shoulders, just for a moment. Beth caught the baby as it wriggled free and passed it between Isabella's legs so that she could sit back and hold her baby. Mustapha leant his head on the edge of the bath and cried. His mother stroked his heaving shoulders.

'I thought, just for a moment, that granddaddy was here.' He sobbed.

'Of course he was, silly!' piped little Mustapha with a snort. 'He was here all the time and he said you would name her Bella Mary and that she will be a great healer.'

Isabella lifted the child out of the water and she was definitely a Bella Mary. She was utterly bald with white eyebrows and the black eyes of the Mustapha's. Beth ran outside and told one person the news, confident that the whole village would know by the time she got back to help in the bathhouse.

The bonfire was lit as Mustapha and his son made their way through the crowd with Bella Mary wrapped in a towel. The crowd was utterly silent as he held his tiny daughter aloft and offered her with the usual unintelligible prayer to the sky. Few villagers had witnessed the event before, but they were all aware that it happened. One by one the men took off their caps and one by one the villagers knelt down in the field and when Mustapha had finished, a quiet 'Amen' wafted up from the bowed heads.

Then everyone jumped out of their skins when Harry set off a huge firework that exploded into a thousand glittering stars above the rapt gathering and initiated an enthusiastic bout of applause and cheering as Mustapha returned Bella Mary to her mother.

Big Ern knocked at the door in search of his wife and was welcomed in to have tea and see the new baby. The family sat watching little Mustapha as he held his sister for the first time. She Stared into his eyes and held tightly to his finger and he was delighted. He looked at his father.

'Granddaddy is always here, but he invisibles himself with magic. I can see him because I am four and he says my mind is not clouded by reality. But I can give him a message if you like.' He whispered.

With tears in his eyes, Mustapha said.

'Tell him that I miss him and that I love him very much.'

'He knows that, silly!'

Meanwhile, children began to fall asleep on the piles of hay in the field and small groups began to make their way through the woods, the pathway lit by lanterns, on route to pay their respects to Aziz Shadi Rashad Salamar Badr al din.

Little Mustapha peered out of the window and waved to Mustapha and Mary who were watching the last of the festivities from the tree house, and then he climbed into the big bed and waited for them to join him.

Chapter 3

A week after the party little Mustapha started school, he was less than keen but finally persuaded that he needed to learn geography and history if he intended to be a ship's captain. Mustapha walked with him to the school on his way to the sick house. On route they met with Harry, his children Gabriel and Daisy perched high on his massive shoulders, causing little Mustapha to plead with his father for the same mode of transportation. The men followed the footpath that led to Lily Lane as the children of the farm workers swarmed from the houses in a tumult and chased each other to school. The men delivered their children at the school and returned to the main street, passing Harry's mother's cottage where his brother still lived with his wife Beth. It was a warm morning, the sun was shining and the first of the leaves on the horse chestnut trees were turning brown. Mustapha walked quickly to keep up with Harry's long strides. He moved like a powerful horse, his head high, his hair bouncing like a mane and he never appeared to be out of breath.

Paulo's workshop was on the left, just before the Bull Inn, Mustapha joined them for a welcome cup of tea and then turned right into the hill that led to the marshes and opened the door of the sick house. Beth was tidying the cupboards and Maud, now a young woman, was mopping the floor and the kettle was singing on the stove. Mustapha sat at his desk with a fresh cup of tea and was aware that he was extraordinarily happy. He watched Matthew arrive and put his horse in the stable at the back and called to Maud to pour Matthew's tea. They discussed their forthcoming visit to the London Hospital in Whitechapel where Matthew had been a student. Mustapha had never been to London or set foot in a hospital. Sophia, Mustapha's younger sister had expressed an interest in accompanying them. They intended to stay for two nights at the lodgings where Matthew had lived during his training.

Matthew, well aware of the snobbery rife amongst the powerful surgeons at the London, insisted that he lend Mustapha a set of suitable clothes to wear, rather than allow him to arrive in his usual attire that could be mistaken for pyjamas. Mustapha was reluctant and wore his own clothes on the thirty-mile journey to London, taking Matthew's clothes in a bag. The following morning they had breakfast listening to Matthew and his landlady reminiscing about the past. Sophia had a fit of the giggles at the expression on her brother's face as she and Matthew helped him dress for the visit. He looked impressive in breeches, shirt, waistcoat and frock coat but felt uncomfortable and restricted, and constantly fiddled with the stiff collar. Matthew insisted that he tie his long curls in a tight knot at the back of his head with a black ribbon. Mustapha loathed the top hat, which he knocked off his head twice before getting outside of the lodgings and spent the rest of the day carrying it. Sophia, in purple and black silk looked stunning as usual.

Mustapha had always imagined the London Hospital to resemble a larger version of the sick house. He was astonished at the sheer size of the building and the daunting façade with huge archways and too many windows to count. The three of them waited in a dark, over-furnished room until a young man arrived. He was a former student named James Miller who had studied with Matthew and had arranged the visit. The tour began with a visit to one of the wards. Mustapha was horrified by the smell of vomit, rotting wounds and excrement, the crowded conditions and the general unspeakable filth. Sophia put her handkerchief to her nose and did her utmost to appear calm. Several patients were screaming and writhing in agony whilst the aged nurses were attending to their dressings. Some were liberally covered in open sores and scabs. Others were crying pitifully and pleading for help or roaring incoherently with delirium. Men with long, heavy leather aprons, smeared with a sickening conglomeration of human debris were dragging the emaciated dead from their beds. The floor was littered with piles of stained, discarded bedding and bloody dressings, Mustapha fled through the nearest door and leant against the cold, white tiled wall trembling and sweating. Sophia joined him, her eyes wide with shock. Matthew and James, accustomed to the conditions, ushered them to a quiet room where tea was served. It took Mustapha some considerable time to regain the power of speech, his teacup rattled in his shaking hands and there were tears in his eyes.

'Why?' was all he could manage to say.

'We do the best we can.' Explained James. 'There are so many sick and injured, amongst the poor in this area, those are the lucky ones.'

'The *lucky* ones?' Mustapha shouted, suddenly overcome with uncontrollable, exasperated rage. He would have continued to rant but Matthew grabbed his arm and silenced him with a shake of his head.

'It's not James fault, it's just the way it is. This is why I work with you and not here! I vowed to your grandfather that I would not become a surgeon until I could cut a patient without pain.'

'But we can manage pain, why don't you tell them that we have potions and remedies!'

Matthew and James shared a glance.

'We have tried, many times.'

A deep bell tolled in the vicinity, loud enough to resonate in Mustapha's stomach. James ran from the room.

'It's the operations bell, he has to help hold down a patient whilst the surgeons operate.' Matthew explained.

Sophia's mouth dropped open and Mustapha broke down and cried.

Matthew guided the distraught pair from the hospital into the busy street for fresh air and lunch but neither of them wanted anything to eat. In actual fact the air was colder but not a great deal fresher than inside the hospital, due to the open sewers and decomposing debris that lined the roads. That afternoon they were due to meet two of the rather eminent surgeons, to whom Matthew had been assigned during his time as a student. Mustapha was less than enthusiastic, particularly when Matthew made it clear that they would not be mentioning potions. He tried to convince Mustapha that these doctors were dedicated men, who occasionally saved a life, and that they could have no understanding of old Mustapha's extraordinary abilities.

'Mustapha, you are a very fortunate man, the world is not yet ready to accept your skills, but one day it will be!'

Sophia stared into space listening to the haunting echo of the operations bell.

The meeting with the doctors did not go well. They were pleased enough to see Matthew, although one persisted in calling him Maurice. They looked down their noses at Mustapha and declined to shake his hand and he sat mutely dejected, hearing the randomly spaced but regular muffled screams emanating from the depths of the hospital. The surgeons were far more taken with Sophia. Matthew attempted to engage them in discussing their latest successes and any new developments, but they preferred to flirt like schoolboys and even had the audacity to stroke Sophia's behind as she took her leave. Matthew was embarrassed, Mustapha was silently fuming and Sophia could not stop the ghostly bell from ringing inside her head.

When they returned to their lodgings, Mustapha insisted that he was returning home that afternoon. He had lost the top hat somewhere in the hospital and he threw off Matthew's clothes and put on his own familiar garb in a desperate attempt to remember who he was. They paid for the two nights they had booked at the lodgings and set off home in silence.

It was late in the evening when Mustapha and Sophia rode up to the house. They retired directly to bed, explaining to the surprised family that they were very tired.

Chapter 4

Mustapha and Sophia never forgot their visit to the London Hospital. It was several days before they were even able to talk about what they had seen. Mustapha was unable to comprehend how Matthew could have withstood the daily relentless onslaught of extreme human suffering during the years of his studies. Sophia eventually stopped hearing the bell but was haunted by the small, thin, dirty children she had seen everywhere in the streets of London. They had been clamouring to run errands, or begging for money. She asked Matthew about them and he said they were often orphans or children that had escaped from the poorhouses or the Foundling Hospitals. They lived on the streets, sleeping in alleys and doorways and many froze to death in winter. Their life expectancy was short. Sophia was horrified that they chose the streets above the institutions provided for them. Then she remembered the hospital and the conditions there. The village had its share of poor families, but no one lived on the streets, apart from the odd travelling vagrant who passed through the village. The Parish Relief fund helped to support the poorest families and the school made sure the children all had a breakfast and a good hot meal at lunchtime.

Maria was taken aback when her daughter announced that she wanted to provide a home for orphaned children. Maria urged caution and warned Sophia that she knew nothing about raising uncivilised, wild children. They would have fleas and lice and may be infected with any number of serious diseases. Sophia reminded her mother that Isabella had been a foundling.

'Sophia.' Maria said, taking her hand. 'You have little knowledge of real poverty and suffering, you and your brother have wanted for nothing, you have been surrounded by some wonderful individuals that love you. This village, by and large, is a happy place to be. It was not always like this.'

Sophia looked woefully at her mother.

'If your grandmother Lily had not married a very rich, successful and generous man, and your grandfather Mustapha had not been the man he was, with his knowledge and skills, this village would still have children starving to death, families living in filth and dying of the cold in winter and the sick and dying would still be screaming just as loud at those you witnessed in London.'

'But mother, you did not see them, some were as young as four or five.'

'Sophia, even I remember how different it was when I was a little girl. Before I lived here I lived next door to the school when it opened. The few children who were permitted to attend were filthy dirty, starving hungry and had been worked almost to death by their desperate families. That's why the school started to provide them with food.'

Sophia bowed her head, the wind taken out of her sails.

'Your grandfather Aziz Shadi Rashad Salamar Badr al din was a very wealthy man and his fortune transformed this village. He bought farms, employed labourers, paid for the school, built this house and supported everyone in it. This family now employs farm labourers, teachers, carpenters, domestic help and nurses at the sick house. It has built houses for the workers and has plans for more. But, do not forget that all of this is only possible due to the men of this family continually risking their lives at sea. Without the profits from their voyages none of this would be possible.'

Sophia nodded her head slowly. Maria put the kettle on for tea.

'Remember Sophia, this family has made a difference to the lives of everyone in this village, but it is not able to help everyone, everywhere.'

Mother and daughter sat drinking their tea.

'Perhaps you could think of a way to help some of the less fortunate children in this village? By the way, how is your brother?'

'I'm not sure, he was very upset by the conditions at the hospital, which were truly awful mother!'

Sophia was determined to do something and by Christmas she was hatching a plan to open a clothing shop and train the dressmakers and tailors. She had already visited the school in search of suitable candidates.

By Christmas, Bella Mary remained completely bald and had developed an engaging smile and a ready chuckle. Little Mustapha had settled well in the school, largely due to the presence of a globe, depicting where all the countries of the world lay. Following the usual sumptuous feast, Sophia unveiled her plan to train six children who had expressed an interest in tailoring and dressmaking, with the eventual aim of opening the first shop to provide a made to measure service in the village. Maria and Sal glanced at each other and breathed a sigh of relief. Everyone clapped and cheered and Sophia blushed profusely.

'Talking of plans.' Interjected the smiling Paulo. 'I too have an announcement to make. Due to the appalling lack of interest in the illustrious art of carpentry shown by my three sons.'

It was George's turn to blush.

'I have decided, with the support and agreement of my lovely wife Rose, to hand the entire business over to my loyal, capable and trusted employees Harry and Big Ern!'

Paulo jumped up, nodded to George and they left the room, returning with a length of wood covered by a sheet. Everyone was looking at the brothers who sat like statues with their mouths agape. They propped the object on the chair and invited Elsie, mother of Harry and Big Ern, to unveil it. The flustered, confused woman staggered to her feet. Paulo took her hand and told her to pull away the sheet. Elsie pulled aside the sheet, revealing a sign that read.

Richards Bros: & Son. Carpenters and Joiners.

The brothers rose slowly, shakily to their feet amidst another round of applause. They gaped in disbelief at Paulo who smiled warmly and shook their hands and told them that there were papers to sign. They were not listening, they continued to stare at him and then suddenly Harry flung his great arms around Paulo and lifted him into the air, Big Ern jumped about causing the cutlery to vibrate wildly on the wooden table. When the commotion eventually died down, it was little Mustapha who noticed poor Elsie prostrate on the floor in a swoon that required the swift attention of Mustapha and the smelling salts. Throughout the afternoon, Elsie sat beside the sign, sniffing and smiling and rubbing at every tiny speck of dust with her handkerchief and spittle. Paulo then explained that he and Rose, freed from their responsibilities, intended to hitch a lift on the ship on its next voyage. They were going to visit Portugal, his home where they met and had never been back to for some twenty-five years.

The snow began to fall on Boxing Day, much to the excited delight of little Mustapha, who carried in a snowball and explained in great detail to Bella Mary that snow was just very, very cold water. The following day at breakfast little Mustapha unexpectedly proclaimed that the sheep needed to be brought in from the marshes.

'Why is that?' asked Isabella.

Little Mustapha shrugged.

'I do not know, I just know they have to because of the snow that's coming.'

The family were unsure of what action to take. Had old Mustapha told them to bring in the sheep they would have had no doubts, but little Mustapha was just a child? Sal took the news to the villagers, he told them that it was up to them, but his own sheep would be brought in just in case. The news spread through the village and every shepherd gathered his dogs and set off to collect his flock as the rest of the villagers built the fences around the village green.

The following morning the inhabitants awoke to an ominous silence and a sky so low that it rested stealthily on the rooftops. That night it imperceptibly collapsed into large, silent crystallised flakes, the size of saucers, and quietly submerged the village under three feet of snow. It snowed for weeks and by mid-January the heavy horses were delivering sledges full of wood. Joey spent his days chopping down dead trees, which would foster in him a love of visionary woodcarving that remained with him until his death fifty years later. Harry and Big Ern delivered the food from the school to the villagers unable to get out. The school once again transformed into the heart of the village, supplying piping hot drinks and food to anyone who arrived. Little Mustapha knelt on the sofa

beside the window and pulled aside the heavy curtain, squinting at the blinding white landscape.
    'Granddaddy was right!'

Chapter 5

The Reverend Knightly suffered periodic crises of conscience relating to the death of his youngest son James. The shame and guilt left him wallowing helplessly in a swamp of deep depression that prevailed despite his most fervent prayers. During his bleakest hours he believed that God had deserted him and he began to seek temporary respite in half a bottle of communion wine. The amount increased to a whole bottle and when the realisation disturbed him he opened another. There were nights following the choir practice when the villagers heard the Reverend's deep baritone hymns echoing through the village on his way to the rectory. Most of them attributed this to a sudden attack of devout piety. On those nights he walked home leading his horse due to his inability to persuade his apprehensive horse to stand still enough to mount and also to delay his arrival at home.

The Reverend elicited the support of the young curate. He was a large flabby man with the slow movements of a beast of burden and an unpleasant, humid aroma that clung to his cassock. His voice was querulous and his pale eyes darted nervously, like a well-kicked dog. His name was William. It was William who slipped surreptitiously in the back door of the Inn and purchased the cheap spirit, risking sullying his own good character, that the Reverend discovered brought oblivion faster and without the acid bile following a surfeit of the communion wine.

The Reverend's decline was swift. Although he continued to deliver a reasonable sermon on a Sunday morning, the rest of his behaviour became more erratic as the week progressed. William was stunned to discover the Reverend, laughing like a drain and wildly chasing the choirboys around the church during Tuesday evening choir practice. The startled boys were squealing, giggling hysterically, jumping the pews and trying to find safety by scrambling up the woodcarvings and seeking refuge on the sills of the stained glass windows. William ushered the boys out of the church and sent them home, still dressed in their cassocks and surplices. The Reverend had grabbed the unsuspecting elderly spinster who played the organ and was forcing her to dance with him up the central aisle on William's return. William grabbed the Reverend from behind, allowing the discombobulated spinster to make her frantic escape, violated by her first, unwelcome close contact with a man. With a resounding bout of hearty laughter the Reverend fell to the floor unconscious, lost control of his bladder and began to snore peacefully. William placed a jug of water beside him and locked him in the church.

William returned to the church at six o'clock in the morning to discover the Reverend much improved. He had washed in the font and dressed in clean clothes and appeared to have no recollection of the events of the previous evening. He greeted William warmly and trotted off to the rectory, unaware that he had been locked in. Faith was grateful for his plausible story of a grieving parishioner, unwilling to entertain the terrible mounting fear of an alternative explanation. The Innkeeper, the choirboys and their families, the organist and William, were well aware of the Reverend's crisis with the drink and yet the news failed to spread to the wider population. Like Faith, they were uncomfortable and disinclined to know the truth. But when William discovered the Reverend, drunk and naked in the vestry valiantly chasing a bleating sheep on a Thursday afternoon, he locked the church door, and too embarrassed to talk to Faith, went to the sick house in search of Matthew and told him everything.

Matthew stared at William, whose big, flaccid face glowed scarlet with mortification, particularly when it involved revealing the presence of the sheep. Matthew put his head in his hands as the past few months flashed into unfavourable focus. It was Mustapha who motivated him into action, and armed with a sedative and a horse and trap, set off with

William to the church. They found the Reverend, still naked and in the vestry, reading the twenty-third psalm to the mystified sheep. Mustapha persuaded the Reverend to swallow the sedative as William shooed the sheep to freedom. Then they wrapped him in an altar cloth and laid him in the trap where he fell asleep. Matthew shook hands with William and asked him to take charge of the church and tell the congregation that the Reverend was currently indisposed. Faith was dumbstruck when Mustapha and her son lugged her portly, unconscious, naked husband through the kitchen and into the sitting room. Anna made tea and sat with her husband, Faith and Mustapha and heard the unwelcome news.

John was sent for. He was the eldest son and working as a vicar in a large parish in the city. Matthew took charge of his father, having dealt with patients suffering from a prolonged diet of alcohol. He knew the worst was still to come. With the aid of the gardener, he and Mustapha managed to drag the dead weight of the smiling Reverend upstairs and put him in James's old room, to spare Faith from witnessing her husband's undignified recovery. In the hospital patients were strapped to their beds, but Matthew was loath to subject his poor father to physical restraint, so he locked him in the bedroom. He changed his mind early on the following morning, when the Reverend tried to gain his freedom by smashing at the door with a heavy wooden chair, waking everyone and frightening the children. At first he pleaded with Matthew and when that tactic failed he became angry and abusive. The gardener was once again summoned to help and with great difficulty they managed to tie the thrashing, bellowing Reverend to the iron bedstead.

Matthew explained to the distressed children that their grandfather was very sick, but that he would be well again. In the meantime they must try not to worry and ignore what they heard. Mustapha arrived with a collection of remedies. He had read old Mustapha's notes revealing the ominous observation that sometimes people died suddenly during the alcohol weaning process. He had brought mild sedatives, emetics and a pale, cloudy liquid for settling stomachs. By the afternoon, the poor Reverend had begun to sweat profusely and within a few hours the alarming trembling began. Matthew administered a sedative but it was ejected along with the vomit. He tried the stomach settler but it failed to remain inside the Reverend long enough to achieve the desired result. Mustapha arrived after his day at the sick house to find the family outdoors in their coats trying not to hear or smell the Reverend. When he entered the sickroom he was overpowered by the smell of the London hospital and his eyes watered. Matthew was up to his knees in soiled linen. The Reverend continued to retch, producing a trickle of bile but had now lost control of his bowels. Matthew had untied him as he lacked the strength to raise his head, yet alone escape from the bed. Mustapha helped the exhausted Matthew to wash his father and place him on a wad of old linen and then he sent Matthew out to wash and to rest for a while. Mustapha opened the window and threw a pillowcase stuffed with soiled linen to the gardener with instructions to burn it. He left the window open to dilute the foul air and covered the shivering Reverend with an extra blanket. His energy depleted, the unfortunate old man slept for almost an hour, until his incoherent rambling woke him up. He mistook Mustapha for his grandfather and burst into tears, begging forgiveness from the man he had loved most in this world. Then he grimaced with pain, drew up his knees, shit himself and sobbed with humiliation and despair. Mustapha removed the top layer of linen and cleaned him up, noticing the bright blood present in the frothy excrement. He gave him a few spoonsful of the stomach settling remedy with extra sugar and salt and held his hand and stroked his forehead until he dozed off into a fitful sleep. Matthew, having slept soundly for several hours in the armchair beside the fire, returned to find the room transformed. The opened window and lit candles had almost obliterated the ghastly smell, his father was asleep and the room smelled of fresh herbs with a hint of jasmine. Unspeakably grateful, Matthew hugged his compatriot. Mustapha told him of the blood in the excrement and instructed him to administer small amounts of the stomach settling liquid each time his father awoke. They bid each other goodnight and Mustapha set off home and Matthew sat beside his sleeping father and cried quietly.

  The Reverend spent a fitful night, he woke frequently, babbling and crying for Mustapha. Matthew had the good sense to tell him that he had just stepped out and would return soon, which satisfied his father enough to allow him to sleep aga

Chapter 6

On Sunday morning William opened the church as the first of the congregation arrived. He had pleaded with Miss Carter to return and play the organ with assurances that the Reverend was too ill to attend. There was no sermon that morning, just a shy curate with clammy, shaking hands, explaining that the Reverend was indisposed and, his voice even more querulous that usual, asked the congregation to say the Lord's Prayer and ask God for a swift recovery. Miss Carter chose several hymns that were the most popular and the villagers sang their hearts out. The choirboys were absent.

The sick house being closed on Sundays, Mustapha went to the rectory to assist Matthew, who he found fast asleep in the chair beside his father who was delivering a sermon to an imaginary congregation and scratching himself to the point of drawing blood. Mustapha managed to coax him to take a sedative and a glassful of the stomach settling liquid and whilst the Reverend dreamt of sheep he smeared his deep scratches with a healing ointment.

By the time John had arrived on Wednesday, the Reverend's vomiting and diarrhoea had dissipated, but his grasp of reality had not improved. He continued to hallucinate and scratch himself to shreds. He recognised no one except Mustapha, firmly believing him to be his old friend. John shouldered the responsibility for the parish and at his first sermon he warned of the dangers of drink. He had learned from William that his father's drinking had been regular and excessive and assumed the whole village knew. The majority did not. The astounded congregation sat with their mouths open, stunned by the news that the Reverend had succumbed to the evil drink that John asserted was put on earth by the Devil.

'Then why did our Lord turn water into wine?' demanded a particularly contentious man in the back row.

John was unable to offer an explanation.

The Reverend began to regain a little of his vigour and was managing to retain the chicken soup recommended and administered by Mustapha. His delirium persisted and he began to see his son James, which caused him so much torment and wretchedness that it became necessary to lash him to the bedstead again. He pleaded for a bottle of spirit, he sobbed, he demanded and finally he begged for death. Mustapha and Matthew discussed their alternatives. Mustapha was wary of continuing with the sedatives aware that prolonged use was beset with problems. After much deliberation and against the backdrop of harrowing cries, they decided on the sedatives that could be gradually diluted when the Reverend showed signs of improvement. Mustapha provided a strong sedative for the nights, which allowed the Reverend to sleep without the persistent interruptions and malicious accusations from his dead son James. A milder dose in the morning maintained a tenuous calm but failed to heal his disordered mind. Matthew and Mustapha began to suspect that he might be suffering from a condition seen occasionally in the elderly, where their reason and memory appears to unobtrusively trickle away.

The Reverend recovered some of his memories and began to recognise members of his family, to the great relief of Faith. But each time they reduced the strength of his sedative his obsession for the bottle that gave him oblivion returned. He was not allowed out unaccompanied and all of the Innkeepers had instructions never to sell him alcohol. He lived the remainder of his life only half alive, but with a peaceful mind, in the gentle haze produced by Mustapha's potions.

John stayed in the village as the new vicar but not well liked. Villagers arrived at the rectory at random intervals, often with flowers for the Reverend. They continued to regard him as their spiritual leader, more fervently due in part to his well-known human weaknesses. Despite his dilapidated memory he was always delighted to see them and unfailingly able to recall all of their names. Mustapha became accustomed to alternating between being himself or his own grandfather, dependent upon the fluid whim of the Reverend James Knightly. They talked of different things relative to which Mustapha he was on that day. Over time Mustapha began to believe that whatever had happened between the Reverend and his son James, it had so irreparably scarred the mind of the old man that he was left with an unendurable, pestilential wound that never healed.

Faith had never been happier. Secretly she loved her husband more than she ever had in all of their life together. He was more amiable and content to spend his afternoons in her company, riding the horses or walking in the countryside. Sometimes he even held her hand. He listened to her relate mundane stories of the grandchildren's latest endeavours with interest. He was never in a hurry and laughed a great deal more than he had in the preceding years. His rotund belly and double chin receded and he appeared more youthful. More importantly, the troubled, haunted look in his eyes, present since the death of James, had vanished.

John however, demonstrated a suspicious antipathy toward Mustapha, reminiscent of many former vicars. Matthew, on the other hand, compared his father's current quality of life with the abysmal fate that would have awaited him in the London hospital and was eternally grateful to Mustapha and loved him more than a brother.

Matthew and Mustapha spent their quiet hours playing chess at the sick house and discussing advances in medicine. Matthew told Mustapha that there had been some successful operations to remove the appendix from the abdomen. Matthew had witnessed the procedure and believed he could perform it. He was familiar with the symptoms of a swollen, acutely painful abdomen, generally accompanied by vomiting. The patient invariably died with no intervention and post mortem examinations revealed a swollen, inflamed or ruptured appendix. Mustapha was confident that he could induce sleep in the patient and render them pain free with his potions. They laid in wait for the first case of appendicitis in the village. Unbeknown to both of them, Friedrich Wilhelm Adam Serturner, a twenty-one year old pharmaceutical assistant in Germany, had just isolated the alkaloid compound from the resinous gum of the opium poppy. He named it Morphine, after Morpheus the god of dreams.

Chapter 7

In the spring the ship returned with Edmundo and Estavo. Their first trip had done nothing to dampen their enthusiasm for a life at sea. The ship also returned with a gift for little Mustapha, a large tortoise from Morocco called Thomas. Nobody in the village had ever seen a tortoise and he received daily visits from curious onlookers, some of whom waited around to see if he would ever come out of his shell. He decimated the vegetable plot and Paulo built him a fenced enclosure with a garden of his own.

Sophia had enlisted the help of her Aunt Rose and they were busy teaching the six children she had selected from the school, in the finer arts of sewing. The three boys and three girls, aged between twelve and fourteen, spent their Saturday mornings honing their skills, surrounded by sawdust as Big Ern built cupboards, shelves and sewing tables for the new shop. Each was given a task to complete at home during the week and they received a wage at the end of each month. The youngest, a quiet timid child called Esther, proved able to sew tiny, neat stitches more accurately and faster than either Rose or Sophia and she blushed profusely when they congratulated her on her skill. The children learned to understand a pattern, cut material and measure people. They were soon making nightshirts and nightdresses, embroidered by Sally and Emily. Once the boys had mastered the basic skills, Sophia arranged for them to serve a six-month apprenticeship to a tailor in the nearest town. The boys left by cart on Monday mornings and returned to the village on Friday evenings. The tailor, Mr Josiah Heath was a jolly rotund character with an even more rotund wife Effie. They were childless and delighted to have the boys lodging with them. One of the boys, Freddie, had no mother and a drunken father and at the end of the six months failed to return home. His father barely noticed and Freddie lived very happily with the Heaths until their deaths and inherited the thriving business. Jack and Frank did return to the village with a sound knowledge of collars, cuffs and frock coats.

By the time the ship sailed away in the autumn, carrying Paulo, Rose and Olivia, Sophia's shop had opened. The large front window contained a tasteful display of clothing worn by life-sized wooden models carved by Joey. Nobody had seen anything like it and within a week the order book was filling up. The news travelled fast and they soon received visits from some wealthy customers from surrounding villages. The women were impressed by the illustrated pattern books with drawings of the latest London fashions and the vast array of vibrant silks, cottons and soft wool fabrics to choose from and began to order their winter wardrobes. The sign above the door read,

Exclusive Fashions.
Made to Measure Clothing Suppliers.
Proprietor. Miss Sophia Badr al din.

One of the first customers to order a variety of dresses and nightgowns was a haughty, rather loud woman in her late forties, whose sharp features betrayed a lifelong habit of looking down her nose at others, and whose family owned a considerable portion of the land in the county. The family had lived on the estate for generations in a very substantial mansion with countless servants. Their family name was Lyle. Sophia was beside herself with excitement to have received such a large order from such an influential family, who led where others would undoubtedly follow and poor little Esther had to be coaxed out from under the table where she had taken refuge ever since the hawk-faced Mrs Lyle had soared into the shop.

When the time came for the first fittings of the partially made dresses arrived, Mrs Lyle expected Sophia and an assistant to transport the garments to their estate on a particular date. A carriage arrived for them and the mound of half-finished dresses was loaded aboard. Esther refused to go, so Sophia took Emily. The nightgowns were completed and needed no fittings. They were in various pastel shades of fine silk with delicate embroidery in a matching silk thread. Mrs Lyle approved of them and summoned her two daughters for the dress fittings. Mrs Lyle had ordered two dresses, one in silk and the other in soft wool, both in a rather sombre shade of oatmeal. Her daughters' dresses were in shades of green and blue silk and the woollen ones in deep burgundy and a heathery pink. The dresses fitted and Emily pinned the hems and cuffs and showed them a variety of lace trimmings. Mrs Lyle studied the workmanship in the clothing and found no fault with Esther's tiny meticulous stitches. Mrs Lyle's daughters were affable, plain girls with light grey eyes and pale hair and their complexions had the unfortunate pallor of never venturing outside in the sunlight. The girls giggled with pleasure at the colours of their dresses, but were effectively silenced by a stern glance from their mother.

Sophia and Emily piled up the dresses and promised delivery of the finished articles in a week's time. They chatted happily as the elderly carriage driver helped them load the garments. At a first floor window Mrs Lyle's son only Hugh watched in awe as the most stunning creature he had ever seen, tripped lightly down the steps to the carriage, her long dark curls cascading down her crimson silk dress. As she was about to enter the carriage, she stopped and turned and slowly surveyed the elegant building.

He tried to step back in case she saw him, but was unable to move. Her beautiful smiling face was framed by her unruly hair and he was instantly smitten. Oblivious, Sophia turned and hoisted up her crimson dress and skipped up into the carriage, revealing her ankles and a froth of white lace.

The girls worked long hours to neatly hem the dresses and attach the delicate lace trimmings, they gave the garments the last press and hung them on carved wooden hangers with Exclusive Fashions lightly branded on the front and Richards Bros. & Son on the rear. They covered the dresses with a thin white voile dust cover with Exclusive Fashions embroidered in rich cream silk thread on the top right-hand corner. The woollen dresses were priced at five pounds and the silk ones at six pounds and ten shillings and the nightgowns at one guinea each. Sophia's girls and boys had never seen so much money, and as they had worked so hard and so skilfully, she gave then all a bonus of a whole pound each that caused Emily and Sally to jump up and down and Esther to burst into uncontrollable tears. Within a week, an order came from Mrs Lyle for a dozen silk shirts in appropriate colours for her son. Sophia was uncertain what Mrs Lyle viewed as 'appropriate'. The following afternoon, when Sophia returned to the shop with more coat hangers from the carpentry workshop, Jack and Frank were already measuring lengths of silk and said that a gentleman had been in and chosen the colours himself. He had asked to see the proprietor, but they had explained that she had stepped out. Sophia shrugged and smiled, gladly relieved of the responsibility.

The frustrated Hugh Lyle rode slowly out of the village. He had ridden to the shop, using the pretence of choosing colours for his shirts, with a burning desire to see Miss Sophia Badr al din at close quarters. He had taken his time choosing colours, hoping she would return, but in the end he felt like a fool and left. A mile out of the village he stopped his horse and, throwing caution and his pride to the wind, galloped back to the shop. Sophia was seated at a table with a tray of tea as he entered the shop and she rose and came forward to meet him with a devastating smile.

'It's the gentleman.' Whispered Emily.

'Ah, Mr Lyle, I hope you found our colours to your liking.' Said Sophia, shaking his hand. 'I've just made tea, perhaps you would like some?'

Hugh nodded and sat in the chair offered him by Emily. He watched Sophia as she took a blue and gold glass from the shelf and poured his tea, then he realised that he had failed to speak.

'Thank you.' He said with a voice he did not recognise.

Sophia was oblivious to his discomfort and watched him sip his tea. It was different to the tea he was accustomed to, much sweeter and with no milk.

'I hope it is to your taste.'

'It's very nice.'

'Oh, I do beg your pardon Mr Lyle, I have omitted to ask what it is I can do for you!' She laughed, her dark eyes shining.

Cornered, he felt a blush creeping up from his collar. Several excuses presented themselves but were dismissed.

'I just wanted to meet the person who had made my sisters so joyful.' He managed at last.

'I am so pleased that your sisters are happy with our work, Mr Lyle. Our little shop is new and we aim to please, did you hear that girls?'

Emily and Sally smiled and nodded and Esther blushed.

'I must say,' ventured Hugh, 'I have rarely seen such a wide choice of colours.'

'My family are merchants and they bring the cloth from India, China and Turkey. Our ship is currently on a voyage that will take two years and will visit East Africa, India and China. They also trade in tea, porcelain, hides, spices and many exotic items that are now very popular in this country and Europe.'

Sophia continued to talk about her family. She explained that her father, who had sailed the seas with his twin brother for many years, now chose to remain at home. She told him that her grandfather had come from Iran, her other grandfather from Afghanistan and her grandmothers were from the village. Hugh listened, fascinated by the information, charmed by her natural, relaxed, easy manner and transfixed by her beauty. She was a stark contrast to the pale, primped, powdered, insipid gaggle of young women with no conversation, no charm and no elegance, continually presented to him by his impatient mother, expecting him to choose a suitable wife. Hugh was twenty-seven years old, tall and slim, with long fair hair and hazel eyes. He lacked the sharp features of his mother and possessed a pleasant disposition and he was the heir to the largest estate in the county. He was accustomed to people bowing and scraping to him. He was unable to imagine Miss Sophia Badr al din bowing and scraping to anyone!

When Hugh took his leave, Sophia said that he would be more than welcome to drop in for tea anytime he was passing and that a shirt should be ready for fitting in a few days. He left the shop with a spring in his step, leapt on his horse and forced the reluctant animal to gallop like the wind.

Chapter 8

The weather was pleasantly warm and the sea calm when the ship sailed in late August. Their first port of call was Portugal, where Paulo, Rose and Olivia disembarked. The ship was not expected to return for two years so Paulo would arrange their trip home when they felt homesick. Paulo purchased a horse and cart for their transport and they set off to explore Portugal as, although it was his home he had seen little of the country himself. Their intention was to head north in a meandering journey towards the mountainous region where Paulo was born. He had no idea if his parents were still alive, but was confident that he would still have some family there. Overnight they found lodgings in farmhouses and Rose and Olivia spent their time practising their Portuguese on their amused hosts. It took them almost a month, averaging about ten miles a day, to reach Paulo's home village in the mountains. His sister Cristiana saw the horse and cart slowly mounting the hill as she was hanging her washing to dry. She walked to the gate with her washing basket balanced on her broad hip as the cart approached. She shielded her eyes from the sun in an attempt to see who was arriving, shrieked and dropped the basket when she recognised her brother. Paulo knew it was his sister due to her striking resemblance to his mother when he left over twenty years ago. He jumped down and embraced his sister who chattered so quickly that Rose and Olivia had no chance of understanding a word.

Eager to take them to see the rest of the family and tell Paulo who was still alive, Cristiana climbed up into the cart, flushed with extreme excitement, jabbered constantly and persistently stroked Rose and Olivia as big tears rolled down her plump, ruddy, smiling face. Paulo's mother was still alive and had evolved into a stooped, wrinkled, jolly old lady, dressed all in black, smelling of lavender and with the laugh of a crow. She was sitting in the garden peeling vegetables when they arrived and Cristiana jumped down from the cart and ran to her mother, shouting and gesticulating wildly, causing the poor startled old woman to drop her bowl of vegetables and clutch her chest. Then she slowly rose to her feet with the help of her daughter and stood and watched in amazement as Paulo approached her.

'Meu filho, meu filho. ' She whispered.

'Mae.' He answered.

Rose and Olivia watched the scene. Rose had tears in her eyes, wondering what it was like for a mother and son not to have met in over twenty years.

Paulo's father was still alive but virtually bedridden due to breaking his leg badly whilst leading his sheep and goats down from a day's grazing on the mountain slopes. He was beside himself with joy at the return of his son, delighted to meet Rose and Olivia, and even more delighted that Paulo had three sons of his own to carry the name of Salazar into the new century. Paulo's brother was still alive and out with the animals. Paulo's sister had three children. The entire family gathered for dinner. Everyone wanted to know what Paulo had been doing. They were impressed to discover that he had built up a thriving carpentry business, disappointed that his sons were not following in his footsteps and immensely proud that he was rich enough to give the business away. Rose gave her mother-in-law a small crate of Chinese porcelain containing plates, bowls, cups and saucers and a teapot. The old woman gently lifted each piece from the straw one by one. The china was so fine that the light from the window shone through each piece. She dusted it with her apron and carefully set it on the shelf on the dresser. It took her all morning to arrange it all and find new homes for the displaced ornaments. She dusted the pieces once a week for the rest of her life and forbade anyone from ever touching it, let alone using it. She invited neighbours in to look at it and when she died, her daughter put the unused teapot in the coffin with her. Paulo and Rose had also brought Turkish lanterns for candles with blue and red glass, that his mother did use and a substantial amount of escudos to keep them free from worry in their last years. They stayed for six months. Rose learned to cook some new dishes and Paulo spent his days with his brother in the mountains with the sheep and goats and a cloth containing bread and cheese, as he had done as a child. Olivia was fluent in Portuguese by the time they left. It was a tearful parting, as the old couple knew it was for them the final farewell to their son. Mr Salazar died later that year and old Mrs Salazar found great comfort in her tea service and the lanterns as it was tangible proof that her son had returned and when she sat looking at them during her solitary evenings she felt closer to Paulo.

Paulo, Rose and Olivia travelled slowly back to the coast to await a vessel bound for England. It was early summer and their twin sons Edmundo and Estavo were somewhere in the Indian Ocean watching the shoals of fish, dolphins and whales in the clear emerald waters, bound for India. The size of the world and the distance between her and her three sons made Rose experience a sense of fragmentation and she felt a great empathy with Paulo's poor mother.

Chapter 9

It proved a hectic autumn for Sophia and her workforce and they were obliged to enlist the temporary help of a few women in the village with good needle skills. The rush was due to the Christmas Ball at the Lyle estate. Numerous young women from wealthy families, expecting invitations to the Ball, were clamouring for silk dresses in the latest fashion and brightest colours, with the aim of outdoing their rivals and catching the eye of the most eligible bachelor in the county. Sophia had so many orders that she demanded that the young women come into the shop to choose their designs and fabrics and return for their fittings, as visits to their homes were out of the question due to the volume of work. They were so desperate for her dresses that they agreed. Sophia converted an upstairs room for fittings and collected a cartful of bolts of material, cottons and haberdashery from the big house. Shiny carriages with perfectly matching snorting horses became a common sight outside of Sophia's shop.

Hugh had returned for his fitting and then again to collect his completed shirts. He invariably stayed and had tea with Sophia. He learned that she had opened the shop following her visit to London, in order to give some of the children a chance to improve their lives and the lives of their families. He learned that her family had opened the school and the sick house and built new homes for their workers.

'Mother, I think we should invite Miss Sophia Badr al din to the Christmas Ball!'

'I *beg* your pardon!'

'You heard what I said Mother!'

'You expect me to invite a *shopkeeper* to the ball? Never!'

'Mother, she is not a shopkeeper, she is from a wealthy family that do a great deal of good for the poor in their village!'

'*And* she has a foreign name!'

'That's because her grandfather was a very wealthy merchant form Iran!'

'*A foreign merchant*? Now I've heard everything!' Shrieked Mrs Lyle. 'And, may I ask, how do you know so much about her?'

'Because I have spoken to her when I collected my shirts, and she is a well-educated, well-mannered young woman of means and I don't see why she shouldn't be invited to the Ball.'

Mr Lyle, considerably older than his wife, tall, thin and somewhat deaf, pottered unsteadily into the room leaning on his walking stick and wearing his usual inane smile as a mask for the pain in his legs. Largely ignored since his mobility dwindled and only summoned when Mrs Lyle required backup.

'Oswald! Hugh wants to invite a shopkeeper to the Ball!' Bellowed his wife to be certain he heard her.

Oswald jumped.

'What ho?' he responded.

'Hugh'. Shouted Mrs Lyle. 'Thinks I should invite *that Sophia, from a family of foreign merchants* to my Ball!'

'Ah! The pretty girl with the dresses what? Yes, why not! The more the merrier what?' Mr Lyle shuffled off to get out of range, still smiling and the thought crossed Hugh's mind that his father might not be as daft as everyone assumed he was.

'That's it then, Father approves, so you should send her an invitation.'

Mrs Lyle, with a great deal of rancour, sent the invitation.

The ball was held on the Saturday before Christmas and Hugh sent the carriage for Sophia. She wore a simple, but very elegant dress in black silk embroidered with silver thread and tiny pearls and her favourite shawl of white silk embroidered with tiny mirrors that sparkled in the lights, brought back from India by her father. She wore her hair loose in ringlets that reached almost to her waist and adorned with a white silk flower. At the last moment she added a necklace, two long strings of simple pearls and jasmine perfume. She inadvertently ruined the evening. The Ball was in full swing when she arrived and the dance-floor was awash with colour and music. She was noticed by several people immediately and by Hugh within minutes. He had been lying in wait for her arrival. She took his breath away. Her appearance was cool, elegant and dramatic as she moved into the room gracefully, reducing the heavily powdered, brightly dressed young women to gaudy subordination. He asked her to dance and the gaudy brigade's faces fell in mute exasperation as they saw the couple move on to the dance-floor, they had spent the last hour lurking near Hugh hoping to be the first he asked to dance. Sophia's shawl glittered brightly under the chandeliers endowing her with an ethereal quality. Hugh was mesmerised by her lightness and the subtle but enthralling smell of jasmine. The men watched with a smile on their faces, the young women watched with clenched jaws and the older women wondered who on earth she was. Old Mr Lyle approached them, eyes twinkling, his constant pain temporarily pacified by a large quantity of brandy, as the dance ended.

'She's a pretty mare, this one, what?' He winked at his son.

'Good evening my dear, I must say, you are a sight for sore eyes, what ho!'

'Why thank you Mr Lyle, you are very kind.' Answered Sophia with a slight curtsy.

'Nonsense, you are undoubtedly the most beautiful woman in the room, what,' he giggled. 'And you've put a few long noses out of joint, what, what?'

'Father!'

'Shut up Hugh.' He muttered happily, he was thoroughly enjoying himself as he kissed Sophia's hand, chuckled and wandered away waving his walking stick in the air.

The young men asked Sophia to dance and she accepted one or two. She danced with Hugh again and then she danced a slow waltz with old Mr Lyle, and twice it was necessary for her to move his hand back up to her waist while the old man smiled innocently. Hugh watched them and smiled at his father's masterly camouflaged audacity.

Sophia left early as she was tired and Hugh escorted her to the carriage. He kissed her hand and thanked her for coming. Then he quietly escaped to bed, leaving the frustrated young women, full of rum punch, their powdered faces streaked with sweat, avidly searching for him. The Ball descended into little groups gossiping about who the young woman was. A few of the older couples took to the dance-floor in an effort to bring the evening alive again. Old Mr Lyle meandered about with a full glass of his favoured tipple French brandy in his hand and his usual lop-sided smile, convinced that it was the best Christmas Ball they had ever held. A considerable number of guests became noisily inebriated, for various personal reasons, and were removed and pushed into carriages by their nearest and dearest. Although Sophia was at home in bed, her presence continued to permeate the Ball, as did the lingering smell of jasmine.

Chapter 10

The big house felt empty, with only eight adults and two children left at home, so Maria invited Gabriel and family, Big Ern and family and the Knightly family for Christmas Day. Sophia had given her workers a large hamper of food each to share with their parents at Christmas, as well as a generous bonus. The day was a success, the food delicious and everyone seemed to enjoy themselves, but Maria remembered the magical Christmases when she was a child, with the glorious surprises arranged by the extravagant, boisterous Aziz Shadi Rashad Salamar Badr al din and the kitchen dominated by Mary and Aunt Isabel's raucous laughter. She missed them all, but then she realised that more than anyone she desperately missed Rose. They had been together all of their lives and were closer than sisters.

Hugh Lyle became a regular visitor to Sophie's shop and one afternoon in February she took him to the sick house to meet her brother. Mustapha stood up to shake his hand and Hugh was surprised by his height, at least two of three inches taller than himself. The resemblance to his sister was striking, the same long curling, almost black hair, the fine arched eyebrows, but Mustapha's eyes were blacker than his sister's and Hugh experienced a fleeting moment of vulnerability when he realised that the smiling eyes could see what he was thinking. He assumed that Mustapha's long white pyjamas were something to do with treating the sick, until Doctor Matthew Knightly arrived in normal attire. Sophia and Beth made tea. Hugh was fascinated with the sick house, impressed with their stories and staggered by the remedies and potions. The three men remained talking for so long that it was necessary to make a further pot of tea. When Hugh walked with Sophia back to her shop he expressed his admiration for the work at the sick house and his wonder at the claims Mustapha had made regarding his remedies. Mustapha had invited Hugh to visit the big house on Sunday, so that he could see the garden, the microscope room and the variety of potions.

Mrs Lyle snorted in disapproval and shook her head woefully when Hugh mentioned his plan to visit Sophia's brother, but old Mr Lyle listened attentively to his son as he related the stories from the sick house. Hugh was unsure about how much his father actually understood until he asked two very astute, relevant questions. On the Sunday, as Hugh was mounting his horse, his father appeared at the front door.

'Ask him about my knees boy, what?' he shouted.

Hugh arrived in time for Sunday lunch. Nothing could have prepared him for that afternoon. There was no butler, and the front door led directly into a spacious room that smelled of jasmine. Large windows on two of the walls provided light and the coloured glass lanterns, hung inside them threw patches of colour on the walls and furniture. The floor was gleaming polished wood, scattered with soft thick rugs in brilliant colours that matched the low, hide sofas and the vast array of silk cushions. He understood why Sophia was so beautiful when he met her mother and father. Maria's beauty had not faded as the years passed it had intensified. Sal presented a fine figure of a man. He was tall like Mustapha, but had a heavier build and broad shoulders. His skin was darker than Sophia's, his hair was black, long and straighter than hers and his eyes were a soft deep brown that lacked the piercing intensity of Mustapha's. As they seated themselves ready for lunch, Mustapha joined them, with Isabella and the children, coinciding with the arrival of George, Joey and Mina. Hugh had never been in the presence of such attractive people. Isabella's delicate build, so light that she could blow away, her long, straight hair the colour of ivory, her pale skin and smiling hazel eyes were in stark contrast to her husband's colouring. George was not quite as tall as the other men and had a head covered in thick black ringlets and the brightest blue eyes that Hugh had rarely seen. Joey was tall and dark and his mother Mina had long dark hair that reached below her waist and amber eyes and she wore a sky-blue sari. A colourful family, Hugh thought, in a colourful room, full of purples, reds, cerise and sunlight. Then little Mustapha climbed into a chair directly opposite Hugh and fixed him with the same smiling, piercing gaze as his father. Hugh was momentarily shaken when the two young women who had served the food sat down at the table and began to help themselves to a meal. Maria noticed his poorly concealed alarm and explained that it was customary for the women from the village to eat with the family. The food was unusual, but delicious. Consisting of roasted meats and peppery sauces and the puddings tasted like flowers. Hugh shook his head and smiled, imagining his mother's reaction to dining at the same table as the servants. The 'servants' were introduced to him as Betty and Jane, and he to them as Hugh, which he found disconcerting. But after discovering that the rock he thought he saw move of its own accord, was in fact a creature named Thomas, Hugh was prepared for anything. So he was not at all surprised when Maria, Sophia and Sal helped to transport the chaos of the table to the kitchen and clatter about helping Betty and Jane, laughing and singing. Tea arrived in a tall glass pot and a dozen or more glasses in a dark raspberry colour, liberally decorated in gold and on an ornate silver tray edged with jewels that resembled rubies. Little Bella Mary climbed onto Hugh's lap. She had the same black eyes as her father and brother, with the pale skin of her mother. Her hair was just beginning to grow and her little head was covered in tight, pale curls, like the fleece of a newly born lamb. Hugh tried to imagine what she would look like as a young woman and was defeated, but he knew she would be utterly captivating.

After tea, Mustapha and Sophia took Hugh to see the garden, currently displaying the early spring phase. Fresh green shoots were emerging from the soil and the larger plants were coming back to vigour after their winter rest. Hugh listened as they gave names to the shoots and random clumps. When they adjourned upstairs to the microscope room, where the shelves were full of labelled glass bottles, Hugh remembered his father's knees. Mustapha subjected him to a barrage of questions concerning his father's knees. Then he explained that it was likely to be a condition of his aging joints, commonly seen in the elderly. The condition could not be cured, but the disabling symptoms could be alleviated. He prescribed a mild pain reliever, and the daily application of a sticky, greenish brown balm to the affected area. He instructed Hugh to monitor his father's progress as the dosage may require adjustments and improvement would not be immediate, but he should notice some relief within a week. The consultation was rudely interrupted by excessive squealing and shouting from the rooms below.

'Granddaddy says that Aunt Rose is home!' shouted little Mustapha as he ran off. 'I knew she was coming today!'

Mustapha, Sophia and Hugh made their way downstairs to the homecoming. Maria and Rose were in an embrace and sobbing loudly. George was hugging his father Paulo and Olivia was smiling, having collapsed into a soft sofa. She jumped up as Sophia entered the room and they embraced warmly. Sophia introduced them, and as Olivia turned and smiled her astonishing violet eyes caused Hugh to instantaneously forget her name. He bowed and kissed her hand. He took his leave shortly after their arrival, not wishing either to outstay his welcome or intrude upon a family event. He asked Mustapha to send the bill for the medication and Mustapha just laughed and explained that all of the remedies were free of charge.

On the journey home, Hugh's head was in disarray, never having experienced an afternoon like that before. Everything about the family was unbelievable, and reminded him of the fairy tales told to him by his nanny. Fortunately, his horse knew the way home.

Mustapha's potions were such a success, that after three days old Oswald Lyle, pain free for the first time in years, trotted to and fro like a foal let into the meadow for the first time, and insisted that he make the acquaintance of the young man who had miraculously provided him with new legs! Mrs Lyle raised her eyebrows ferociously when she heard her son offer to bring Mustapha to see him, and lowered them with relief when her husband shouted.

'Nonsense boy, I want to visit this sick house, what?'

Sir Oswald Lyle for the first time in years, mounted his large, black stallion named Bones and lovingly stroked the animal's neck.

'Never thought I'd see the day, what?'

Hugh watched his father stroke his beloved horse. Over the years that he had been unable to ride, he had continued to visit Bones regularly in the stables, despite the difficulty of negotiating the route with his painful knees and a walking stick. His father's inane smile had disappeared and there were tears in his eyes. Hugh rode in front during the journey, harbouring the fear that his father might gallop off and take a fall. Old Mr Lyle happily watched the countryside pass and talked incessantly to Bones who responded with that soft noise that horses make when they agree with you.

Hugh introduced Mustapha and his father.

'How do you do Sir, I am delighted to make your acquaintance.' Said Mustapha shaking his hand.

'Oswald, it's Oswald to the man who made it possible for me to ride again!' shouted Mr Lyle, whose deafness remained unaffected by the potion.

Mustapha examined Mr Lyle's knees, listened to his heart, looked into his eyes and when he looked in his ears and was not surprised that the old man was hard of hearing. His ears were full of crusty, hard wax. With Mr Lyle's permission, Mustapha filled his ears with gently warmed oil, explaining that he would be unable to hear while the oil did its job of softening the wax. Mr Lyle would have trusted Mustapha to remove his head if he had asked, and he sat happily grinning and drinking the unfamiliar tea.

Carefully, with a bowl of warm water that smelled of mint and tiny sticks bound with a layer of cotton, Mustapha removed the clods of wax from Mr Lyle's congested ears, then he gently poured warm water into his ears as he lay on the couch. Beth held a towel to catch the drips. The treatment caused Mr Lyle to spend days jumping out of his skin at the slightest sound. Mr Lyle wanted to pay Mustapha handsomely for his service. Mustapha explained firmly that his grandfather had never charged the potions, as they were gifts from God, and that on no account would he accept money for them. Mr Lyle wandered around the sick house. He looked at the kitchen area, the room with the freshly made beds for treating the more serious problems and out of the window at the little stable.

'I trust that your grandfather would have no objection to a donation to the sick house, what?' He said with a crafty smile.

'No Sir, I don't think he would.' Chuckled Mustapha.

'Oswald, please call me Oswald.' The old man smiled. 'I will be forever in your debt my young friend'.

'Oswald.' Answered Mustapha.

Hugh had only ever heard two people allowed to call his father Oswald, his mother and old Aunt Jemima who smelled of urine and mothballs.

Mustapha gave Oswald some drops for his ears, to prevent a reoccurrence of the earwax, another bottle of the pain relief and a pot of balm and instructions not to stop using the potions, even if he felt better.

'I have heard that your grandfather was referred to as Mustapha the Magician. Sadly, I never knew you grandfather, but I shall always think of *you* as Mustapha the Magician, what?'

Mustapha was embarrassed to receive a substantial donation from Oswald. So substantial that they were able to knock down the old stables and build a new one, as well as building a whole new room, with a large window in the roof, at the rear of the sick house, that Mustapha and Matthew equipped with new surgical instruments and new linen and a stove for boiling the instruments. This room would be for the sole use of the treatment of serious injuries and the long anticipated appendix removal.

Old Mr Lyle's only slight regret with regard to his new ability to hear a pin drop, clothes rustle and clocks tick, was that his wife's shrill voice was a great deal louder, but with his new legs he could at least retreat out of earshot faster than before.

Chapter 11

Maria was eternally grateful for the return of Rose, to listen to Paulo playing his guitar and to have Olivia draped over the sofa, reading her books. Maria took Rose and Bella Mary to visit the new shop. Rose was impressed and offered to help anytime she was needed. Esther fell in love with little Bella Mary and asked Sophia if she could design and make a little dress for her out of the scraps of material, during the brief times when they were unoccupied. Sophia said she could, and she could use any materials that she wanted to. Esther insisted on using the scraps, she cut small squares of silk in all of the shades of purple and all the pinks from the palest to deep cerise. The dress was a tantalising patchwork, with appliqued poppies around the bottom of the skirt in all their different shades, cream, pink, lavender-blue, purple and deep red. She trimmed the neckline and cuffs with black lace to match her eyes and embroidered 𝔅𝔢𝔩𝔩𝔞 𝔐𝔞𝔯𝔶 all the way around the hem of the skirt.

Sophia had to sit down quickly when Esther shyly presented her with the dress. It was truly the most beautiful garment she had ever seen. Esther was not just a skilled needlewoman she was also an outstanding designer.

'Oh Esther, this is so beautiful!'

'Do you think she will like it?'

'Everyone will love it Esther, did you enjoy making it?'

Esther nodded and blushed slightly.

'Well then, I want you to know that you are exceptionally clever and you are free to make any garment you want to, for anyone that you want to. You must make a paper pattern, a representation of your designs and you alone will own those designs, because I believe you will be a great success one day.'

Esther went very red, and without warning, flung her arms around Sophia. Sophia hugged her.

'I am so very proud of you.' She whispered to Esther.

Everyone did love that dress. Bella Mary loved it so much that she would wear nothing else and Isabella washed and dried it overnight when it became soiled, until the delighted Esther made her another one in all the shades of green, turquoise and blue with black and white lambs running around the hemline. Then Bella Mary decided each morning whether to have a poppy day or a lamb day, depending on how she felt. Isabella and Bella Mary sent Esther a note of sincere thanks and a little package containing a delicate necklace and bracelet in silver and what Esther thought was beautiful, sparking blue glass to match her eyes. It was definitely not blue glass.

Old Mr Lyle went riding with Bones most afternoons, partly to avoid Mrs Lyle and mostly because he enjoyed it so much. He asked Hugh if he thought it would be alright to visit Mustapha's family at their home and Hugh said he would arrange which day would suit them best. The following Sunday, in early summer, Hugh and his father rode to the big house to meet the family. Hugh watched in amusement at the expressions changing on his father's face, responding to the countless surprises of the afternoon. The old man sprawled contentedly on one of the sofas drinking tea, squinting in the sunlight that streamed through the windows, and gazed at the six most beautiful women he had ever seen. The pale one reminded him of a fragile butterfly and the others of beautiful, elegant, spirited fillies.

Mustapha took Oswald upstairs and introduced him to the microscopes and the old man spent over an hour gasping in amazement at his finger tip, the hem of his shirt, a hair, a passing spider and anything else he could find, under the microscope. As he followed Mustapha downstairs, he paused. The whole house smelled of fresh flowers and the women flitted about placing food on the large dining table. He could hear laughter and the giggling of children. The happiness in these people was palpable and he had the uneasy feeling that somewhere in life, he must have made the wrong decision and embarked on the wrong path. Like his son, he was initially disconcerted by the crawling rock, but little Mustapha formally introduced him to Thomas who was a tortoise all the way from Morocco. He did not bat and eyelid when the women from the village joined them to eat.

'By God!' he barked in appreciation. 'Even the servants in this house are jolly attractive young mares!'

Betty and Jane blushed in unison.

Mr Lyle watched Bella Mary skipping around in her poppy dress, a more exotic butterfly than her mother. She saw him watching and walked over and leant against his legs and scrutinised him with her extraordinary eyes.

'Are you my grandfather?' she asked.

'No my dearest, I am not, but I fervently wish I was! What?'

'Are you anyone's grandfather?'

'Sadly, I am not.'

'Then I would really like you to be mine, if you don't mind.'

Before he was able to answer her, the momentary delay caused by the lump in his throat, Bella Mary had announced to the crowded room that she would like to introduce her new grandfather and she would call him Grandy, so as not to confuse him with her other Grandfather. She turned to Mr Lyle and explained that she was very happy, as she now had two grandfathers, and children were supposed to have two, and up until now she only had the one.

He looked up at Mustapha who shrugged and grinned by way of an apology for his daughter's behaviour. Oswald smiled.

'Thank you Bella Mary, I can think of nothing more wonderful than being your grandfather.'

From that moment Mr Lyle became known as Grandy by everyone in the family, and he became a regular visitor, invariably armed with gifts for the children.

Mr Lyle began to live two lives, one at the estate with a shrill, objectionable wife, a musty house full of the belongings of his ancestors, who glowered menacingly at him from portraits, where he consumed bland, predictable food and where he was known as Oswald! Sir and other less favourable names whispered by the servants. The other life was as Grandy, a carefree happy old man sharing life with the fillies and the butterflies, where he drank strange tea, ate mouth-watering food, encountered a monkey called Bill whose erratic and at times shameful antics resulted in his sudden removal from the room and where he frequently tripped over an unpredictable, ambulatory rock known as Thomas.

One afternoon he arrived unannounced as he had special presents for the children. For little Mustapha he brought a globe of the world, even bigger and better than the school's globe. For Bella Mary he brought a cream Shetland pony with a long mane and tail the colour of her hair. She loved him and called him Moonshine. The old man arrived each afternoon to teach her to ride. He attached Moonshine to Bones and they circumvented the meadow. To his horror, Bella Mary fell off, but before he could dismount to pick her up, she had jumped up laughing, dusted off her dress and climbed back on. She fell off several times, but she was fearless and within a week was cantering about as though she and Moonshine was one creature. They were the happiest days of his long life and he wondered why he had hardly ever seen his own children when they were small. The children had lived in the nursery, cared for by a fierce nanny, who unveiled them occasionally, always in their best clothes, to say Good Evening Papa just before they retired to bed. The nanny had made it clear that his presence in the nursery was unwelcome at it disrupted the children's routine and that was not good for a child. His wife had little interest in the children and believed they were the sole property of the nanny until they were young adults, and she insisted that he stop disturbing the nanny's routine, she had threatened to withdraw her services if the Master persisted in ruining her routine with children at such an impressionable age. He realised sadly that he had never heard his children laugh when they were young and he hoped that at times that had laughed, even if he had failed to hear them. He told Maria as they drank tea on the bench outside the front door, watching Bella Mary trot around the meadow chattering to Moonshine. Maria held his hand.

'That custom is normal in wealthy families. The grandmothers in this family had been from poor village families and the grandfathers were from cultures where children represented the heart of the family. The family was rich by the time I was born, but we kept our traditions. We have never considered employing a nanny.' Maria thought for a moment and then laughed. 'Actually, I think we are just poor people with money!'

'Then I envy you my dear.' And he squeezed her hand affectionately.' Thank you for allowing me to share your lives.'

'Grandy, you are more than welcome, we look forward to seeing you and the children adore you.' She said, and she meant it. 'My own father died a few years ago, Rose and Sal's father died prematurely and Paulo and Mina's families are in other countries. To be honest, we were all in desperate need of a grandfather!'

Thomas clonked laboriously past their feet, he had escaped his enclosure with nothing but dogged determination, in search of dandelions.

Bella Mary and Moonshine interrupted the quiet discussion.

'Grandy, Moonshine did a poop in the meadow and now he's gone and trod in it!' She giggled helplessly in the saddle.

Sir Oswald Lyle was experiencing true happiness, a previously undiscovered, uncharted emotion. He was unsure whether to laugh or cry. He looked at Bella Mary, her pale curls shimmering in the evening sunshine, and he chose laughter.

Chapter 12

During that mild, fine summer, Grandy built friendships. He and Gabriel both loved horses and Grandy laughed till he cried at the story of Henry the bronze horse. He spend time listening to Mina's account of her life in India, of her rescue from poverty by a man who valued love and beauty above money. He liked Harry and Big Ern and re-named them Hercules and Colossus or 'the giants, what, what?' if they arrived together.

Hugh and his father attended the harvest party a few days after Bella Mary's fourth birthday. Nobody recognised who they were, or if they did, nobody cared. Grandy watched the swarm of children playing at the bottom of the field, passing time until the food was ready. He thought that the relationship between the family and the villagers was extraordinarily egalitarian, but wonderful. Isabella told him that Bella Mary had been born during the harvest party and how the villagers had all knelt down in the field whilst her husband gave thanks to God and offered her to the sky. After the meal, the dancing began and Grandy retired to the tree house for a rest. He experienced a calm presence, the aroma of jasmine and thought he felt a leaf landing on his left shoulder.

Small groups of people began to meander below the tree house and head into the woods. Curious, Grandy came down from the tree house. Little Mustapha walked past.

'I saw you with my granddaddy and granny Mary, they told me that they have been waiting for you to join us.'

Little Mustapha took his hand and led him into the woods. The path was illuminated by dozens of different coloured lanterns. He explained that it was time to visit Aziz Shadi Rashad Salamar Badr al din's shrine. That he was the rich merchant who fell in love with a shepherd's beautiful daughter, and he broke his neck against a tree when his horse Elijah died underneath him. Mustapha went on to explain that his grave was in the churchyard, but Elijah had been buried where he fell by Uncle Gabriel, and this is where everyone brings the party as Aziz Shadi Rashad Salamar Badr al din always invited the entire village to his birthday parties. As they reached the clearing, the musicians were tuning up and they started their performance with slow melodies and the amassed crowd sang quietly. Rose stepped onto the musician's platform and explained that she was going to attempt to sing her father's favourite song, in his native tongue. Accompanied by a solitary violin, she closed her eyes and sang an unintelligible haunting ballad. Some of the crowd lit candles and held them aloft. A number of the women wiped their eyes on their sleeves. The villagers erupted into deafening applause and appreciative whistles, as Rose curtsied and left the stage. Grandy found it very moving. He offered his own silent prayer of thanks to Aziz Shadi Rashad Salamar Badr al din for travelling so far from his home and falling in love with a shepherd's daughter and this village. Then he offered another, for Sophia, for opening her little shop. The last one was for Mustapha and his potions. Without those three individuals, Grandy would not exist. He would have been only Oswald, trapped in his great, sad, dark mausoleum of a house, unable to escape because of his painful knees. Marooned with a wife he intensely disliked in an increasingly silent, isolated world.

'Don't worry Grandy, it gets better soon!' whispered little Mustapha.

The music speeded up and the audience began to dance and Grandy and little Mustapha decided to return to the tree house where they could still hear the music without getting trodden on. Maria arrived with mugs of steaming hot chocolate and reminded little Mustapha that it was bedtime in half an hour.

'I am going to be a sea captain when I grow up.' he said, sipping his chocolate. 'My great grandfather was a sea captain, so is my grandfather and my uncle and three of my cousins, and it is in my blood, it is my destiny. My other great grandfather did not like the sea so much. That was granddaddy and he had the magic of the potions. My father has the magic too and my sister will have the magic when she is older, but not me as I shall go to sea!'

Grandy watched the young boy's animated face in the moonlight.

'The sea.' Continued little Mustapha. 'Is different in other places. Our sea is cold and grey but my grandfather's favourite sea is warm, clear and green and you can see the fishes, which are not silver like our fishes, but all the colours of the rainbow, and you can hear the whales, the biggest things in the sea, singing to each other at night. My great-granddaddy's favourite sea was the deep blue one near a place called China. I will show you where they are on my globe tomorrow if you like?'

'Thank you Mustapha, I would like that very much.'

Little Mustapha hugged Grandy and kissed him of the cheek, picked up the empty cups and ran down the steps from the tree house.

'Goodnight Grandy!'

Grandy climbed down the steps to find Esther struggling to carry a sleeping Bella Mary who she had discovered fast asleep on the hay at the bottom of the field with some of the village children, rendered comatose after a surfeit of food and chasing about. Together they manhandled the child through the front door and onto a sofa.

'I love that dress.' Stated Grandy. 'The colours make me feel so very happy! Nobody could feel sad wearing colours like that! In fact, I'd like a jacket like that! What ho? Are you the famous Esther?'

'Yes Sir.' And Esther curtsied.

'I am not Sir, I am Grandy and I am very delighted to meet you and I hear you are a very clever young woman.

'Thank you, erm, Grandy' answered Esther with a shy smile.

Hugh and Grandy spent the night at the big house. They slept in Edmundo and Estavo's spacious room, with fresh sheets that smelled of lavender and blue silk bedspreads. Grandy woke first and lay listening to his son's quiet snore. The sun flickered through the blue silk curtains and he could smell warm bread. The walls were covered in maps of the world. The quiet tap on the door heralded the arrival of Rose with a tray of tea, hot bread, butter and an orange coloured jam. The smell woke Hugh and father and son enjoyed breakfast in bed for the first time in their lives.

Little Mustapha was lying in wait with his globe downstairs and he and Grandy spent an hour slowly turning the globe, whilst little Mustapha retold the adventures of his family and pointed to where they had actually happened.

If Sir Oswald Lyle had been a younger man, the servants on his estate would have believed that he was up to no good with a woman. It would have accounted for the spring in his step, the sparkle in his eyes and his general good humour. As it was, they decided he must have been overtaken by madness. Mrs Lyle failed to notice his absence, having primarily overlooked him throughout the bulk of their marriage. Christmas was a sombre affair on the estate. Mrs Lyle disapproved of the silly habit of giving presents and was preoccupied with an extreme sulk, adopted since Oswald had had the audacity to refuse to pay for another Christmas Ball. Hugh and his father had been invited to the big house for Christmas and they had every intention of accepting.

Meanwhile, at Exclusive Fashions, Esther had told Sophia that Grandy wanted a jacket like Bella Mary's poppy dress. Sophia thought it was a wonderful idea and Emily and Sally helped Esther cut the squares of silk in the colours of the poppy dress. Esther chose the positioning of the various shades and the girls sewed them together. Jack and Frank cut a paper pattern made from one of Grandy's jackets that Hugh had provided them with. The boys demonstrated their skills in collar and cuff construction and made a splendid lining in royal blue satin. Esther added large pockets at the front and a smaller breast pocket on the top left. She appliqued dark purple poppies on the big pockets and embroidered a rearing black horse on the breast pocket. On the inside of the back of the jacket, just below the collar, Esther embroidered 𝕲𝖗𝖆𝖓𝖉𝖞'𝖘 𝕳𝖆𝖕𝖕𝖞 𝕵𝖆𝖈𝖐𝖊𝖙 in ivory silk thread. The finished article was majestic and everyone was proud. Harry and Big Ern contributed an elegant hanger made from ebony. Sophia wanted the little team to see Grandy's face when he saw his happy jacket so she invited them all for Christmas lunch.

Big Ern, Beth and Elsie collected the excited team from the village green on the bright, crisp Christmas morning. Esther carried her precious parcel on her lap in the back of the cart. The house smelled of roasted meat and the women were setting the table. The children were playing with the simple gifts they had opened earlier. Esther was thrilled to see that Bella Mary was wearing her poppy dress. Dinner was due in less than an hour, so there was time for the little team to present Grandy with his jacket. Everyone came in to watch as the trembling Esther gave the brown paper parcel to Grandy where he sat on the sofa. Unprepared for the surprise, Grandy was lost for words.

'Come on Grandy, open it up, it's Christmas!' shouted Bella Mary.

'It's from all of us.' Explained the shy Esther, pointing to her friends, who were grinning with expectation.

Grandy untied the string to the rhythmic clapping of the entire family. He was struck dumb as he unfolded the enchanting jacket. He saw the delicate ivory embroidery of 𝔊𝔯𝔞𝔫𝔡𝔶'𝔰 𝔥𝔞𝔭𝔭𝔶 𝔍𝔞𝔠𝔨𝔢𝔱 and looked up at the smiling, triumphant Esther.

'Oh my dear one, you made this for *me*?' Grandy's voice trembled.

'We all did Grandy and we hope you like it.'

Bella Mary pulled the disconcerted old man to his feet and almost shook him out of his grey jacket and with the assistance of Esther they held up the happy jacket and he slowly pushed his arms into the sleeves. It was a magnificent garment and received a round of applause.

'See Grandy, I have a poppy dress and now you have a poppy coat and we match!' shouted Bella

Mary. 'I knew about your jacket, didn't I Esther? But I didn't tell!'

Sophia wheeled in the long mirror so that Grandy could see himself in his happy jacket. They left him preening whilst they presented Sophia's team with gifts. For the young women it was their own needlework sets. Sturdy polished wooden boxes with each of their names painted on the lid, filled with needles of every size, pins, scissors, thimbles, tape measures and reels of silks and cottons in a rainbow of colours. For the young men, their own tailoring equipment, neatly stored in similar boxes.

'I also have something for you all, what?' Grandy announced to the team. He had bought them all a pair of new boots. For the young men, soft, dark brown leather and for the young women he had chosen three different shades of beige.

'I have never, ever had a pair of new boots!' whispered Sally.

'Nor have I!' echoed another couple of voices.

'Thank you Sir!'

'He not Sir, he's Grandy!' hissed Bella Mary.

'Thank you Grandy!' they shouted in unison, but he had resumed admiring his happy jacket in the mirror. Then the children put on their new boots and squeaked up and down the room until dinner was served.

Grandy took off his happy jacket to eat his meal and hung it where he could still see it from the table.

'Bit of a sloppy eater, what?' he offered by way of explanation.

Dinner was roasted beef, lamb and chickens, roast potatoes, parsnips, carrots and onions and steamed winter cabbage. There was a choice of sauces, a creamy-coloured one that was peppery and rich, a darker one with garlic and mint and a rust coloured one that was spicy and best consumed with the chicken. There was a pile of puffy batter puddings, mint sauce, mustard and horseradish. The four women from the village sat down and everyone began passing dishes, plates and serving spoons, mouths watering in anticipation. Hugh watched his father glancing at the cheerful faces around the table and then up at his happy jacket. He caught his glance and father and son smiled at each other and Hugh was grateful to see the old man so happy. In keeping with tradition it was the women in the family who cleared the table and brought in the puddings and the village women who remained seated. The puddings were made to old Mustapha's recipes and disappeared quickly. Sophia's girls insisted in clearing the table and helping their neighbours with the clearing up in the decimated kitchen, which offered them another opportunity to squeak about in their new boots. Paulo made the tea and even Hugh helped to carry in the plates of cheeses and crisp biscuits. Grandy donned his happy jacket as soon as the potentially messy food was cleared way.

Big Ern drove Sophia's happy little team and the exhausted village women home during the evening, laden with parcels of food for their families.

Grandy sat on the sofa, reading a fairy tale to Bella Mary.

'Grandy, you do look very dashing in your poppy coat!'

Dashing was an adjective he had never been accused of, not even in his prime and he suffered a prolonged outbreak of uncharacteristic giggling, exacerbated by Bella Mary's puzzled, probing frown.

Chapter 13

Khalid declined to go ashore when the ship reached India. The smells from the dock was reminder enough of his last harrowing visit. He swatted the inevitable fly and retired below deck to study charts. Edmundo and Estavo couldn't wait to run down the gangplank and Sam was reminded of when he and Sal first arrived with Aziz Shadi Rashad Salamar Badr al din. They hired a donkey cart and set off inland to purchase sacks of ginger, turmeric, chillies, peppercorns, coriander and cumin seeds, tamarind and garlic. The twins watched the dry, dusty landscape that is India waiting for the monsoon rains. They arrived at the village in the late afternoon and the old men instantly recognised the tall, dark man from England who always paid a fair price for their purchases. The little village sprung into life, the women lit the fires and peeled vegetables, they chased the chickens and chopped their heads off and the men cut the throat of an unfortunate goat that failed to run as fast as the others. There would be a feast that night and tomorrow the men would set off in different directions and collect the best spices from the surrounding area. The women fussed over the twins, who, with their skins darkened by months at sea, were indistinguishable from the locals. By the time the sunset cloaked the village in a red glow, the tantalising food smells made the twins ravenously hungry and they sat outside on rush mats in the soft warm breeze and watched the stars, their bellies rumbling. The women served drinks of buffalo yoghurt, bhang and water that put a wide smile on peoples' faces and increased their appetite. Sam watched the twins as they tucked into their meal, eating with their fingers and scooping up the sauce with the chapattis. After the meal, Sam sat talking to the men and the twins slung their hammocks under the trees and lay down to digest their meal. They were soon asleep and the women covered them up with a thin cotton sheet.

    They were woken by the bright sunlight that flickered through the leaves of the palm trees and the smell of fresh chapattis. Many of the men had already left to coordinate the delivery of the spices. Sam informed the twins that they would need the little spade to dig a latrine away from the village, and anything they left there should be well buried. The undaunted twins loped off to find themselves a relatively private spot amongst the bushes. They returned laughing merrily and remarked that the food was almost as hot on the way out as it had been on the way in! They astonished the women when they offered to help with chores and they insisted on collecting the water from the stream. They tried to carry the large jars of water on their heads and failed miserably, reducing the women and children to hysteria. Sam was proud of them. He had been sorely embarrassed by Khalid's blatant discord and whining complaints at his mother's village. When the twins had finally finished collecting water they devised a fly swatting game, first one to a hundred! Following lunch of dhal with green chillies and chapattis they watched in awe as a young man tied a string around his ankles, held a machete in his teeth and ascended with bewildering speed up the long thin trunk of a nearby cocoanut palm. He shouted a warning as he chopped through the tough stalk of the cocoanut that promptly hurtled to the ground, landing with a resounding thud. For the rest of the time at the village, almost two weeks, Edmundo and Estavo struggled valiantly to master the skill. They mastered the machete holding technique immediately, but the rest of the task proved more taxing. The following morning the muscles in their arms and legs were stiff and sore and they jumped about stretching and laughing, warming up for the conquering of the cocoanut palm. Edmundo was first to achieve a few feet up the trunk before he fell off, but Estavo made little progress, until he tried without the string around his ankles. He held the trunk and placed the soles of his feet against the trunk. Then he moved one foot at a time and began to walk up the tree. He could have got to the top but his legs and arms refused to go one step further, consumed by a tremendous, burning ache and Estavo tumbled into a heap in the dust, sweating and rubbing his thighs.

At the end of the first week, the cart was half full of sacks of spices, plus several sacks of bhang, that Sam was convinced Mustapha would find a use for and Estavo had devised a way of getting higher up the tree. He put a rope across his back, under his arms and tied and two the ends together behind the trunk, adjusting it so that it was loose enough for him to move freely and tight enough so the he could lean back against it to rest his limbs. Sam watched them and realised that they were beginning to achieve an altitude that was inconsistent with a safe landing. The following morning, one of the young locals scaled the two nearest trees and attached a strong rope to the top of each one and left it dangling to the ground. They were very long ropes and the remaining yards lay coiled on the dust. Sam explained to the twins that they could either use the attached rope to climb the tree, or their previous method with the rope attached to their belt in order to break their fall. He reminded them that he had already lost a member of the family on a previous voyage and he did not intend to have to face his sister with bad news. They understood and took the necessary precautions, and when the cart was finally full, they could both get to the top with the safety rope attached. Edmundo and Estavo, unlike their cousin Khalid, were reluctant to leave the village and would have been happy to stay. They had learned to climb a cocoanut palm, to cut the top off a cocoanut with a machete, kill and gut a goat and almost mastered balancing jars of water on their heads. The happy memories stayed with them and they would continue to return there for the rest of their lives.

Khalid was relieved when they returned safely but felt slightly crestfallen due to the twins' robust health and apparent lack of any sort of disabling discomfort after enduring two whole weeks in an Indian village.

The next day, Sam and the twins visited the local market. Khalid politely declined the invitation to join them. Estavo wanted to get a new sari for Aunt Mina and chose one the colour of saffron with gold embroidery. Sam purchased fresh meat, fruit and vegetables for the ship's cook. The fresh meat consisted of two crates of squawking white chickens that occasionally quietened down into a commiserating, mournful whine.

The following day they set sail and headed south along the Indian coastline and when the most southern tip of India was left behind they sailed east and made for the South China Sea. The ocean was littered with islands and they regularly dropped anchor and rowed into the small islands in search of fresh provisions. Sam and Khalid had timed the journey well and they were in China in time for the new-year celebrations. The twelve days of celebrations inevitably caused some delays in business matters, but was worth the sacrifice. Edmundo and Estavo saw themselves as seasoned travellers as they sat at a long table in the street, surrounded by firecrackers and dragons, sampling lizard, snake and fried insects and improving their skills with chopsticks. Khalid ate his bowl of noodles, avoiding looking at whatever creepy-crawly the twins were currently devouring with gusto. Edmundo held aloft a crisp, fried spider and then, to Khalid's horror, ate it. Khalid turned his back on the twins and Sam laughed heartily and put his arm around his son's shoulder and gave him a reassuring shake.

Sam and the crew filled the remaining spaces in the hold with crates of porcelain, bolts of silk and wooden chests full of tea. Then they weighed anchor and sailed westward for the first time on their long journey and headed for home.

Chapter 14

Mustapha and Matthew continued to wait for a case of appendicitis to present itself. News had disseminated its way around the village, that the doctors at the sick house had found a miraculous cure for a particularly vicious bellyache that proved fatal if untreated. A glut of patients with stomach problems arrived at the sick house, keen to be the first to undergo the new procedure. Nobody presented with all of the necessary symptoms, their pain had not originated in the centre of the belly and moved to the right of the abdomen, and none experienced the sharp increase in pain when pressure on the area was suddenly removed. They did not have high temperatures and only one reported feeling a bit sick. Mustapha and Matthew diagnosed muscle strain, cramp, a great deal of constipation and numerous cases of trapped wind.

'Sorry Doc.' the potential patients said, more downhearted than relieved, as they left with their relevant potions and a clearer knowledge of the symptoms of the fatal bellyache.

The new room was used for the first time when a commotion arrived at the sick house carrying a young man with terrible injuries who had been gored by a bull. His body had been ripped open by the bull's horns and when they removed the bloody cloth that someone had rolled him in, his intestines threatened to fall to the floor. He was barely conscious and, fearing death from shock, Mustapha immediately gave him a strong dose of his best pain relief and a strong sedative. Beth and Maud put on gallons of water to boil. They boiled the knives, the scissors, needles and thread. Matthew and Mustapha washed their hands and arms with soap and the hottest water they could bear and scrubbed their nails with stiff brushes. The young man was quickly comatose and Beth and Maud had cut off his clothing, taking care not to touch the wounds. Mustapha asked for a bowl of warm salted water, and he gently washed every inch of the exposed intestine by immersing it in the water as Matthew searched for any laceration in the viscera. He discovered two small ones and a larger one. He stitched the torn areas with thin boiled cotton and his finest needle. Beth replaced the salted water and they checked again for any tiny holes. They balanced the exposed gut on a clean cloth and Beth and Maud held it aloft whilst Mustapha and Matthew cleaned the abdomen of any unwanted debris. They poured pints of warm salted water into the cavity and let it run out. When they were satisfied that they had removed every blade of grass and speck of soil they washed their hands again. Then they gently began to replace the poor man's guts. Mustapha, Beth and Maud watched as Matthew skilfully stitched the layers of ripped muscles together. Finally he stitched the skin together, leaving two small holes at each end to allow the wound to ooze. All four of them were covered in blood and water. The young man remained unconscious for several hours, while the four cleaned themselves and the floor. The operation had taken over two hours and Beth was surprised to find many of the commotion still sitting on the steps outside waiting for news of the young man's death. She made tea for everyone and told them that he was alive and asleep, but it would be days or weeks before they would know if he would survive.

Mustapha and Maud remained with him all night. Mustapha administered pain relief and Maud held his hand and quietly reassured him. His pulse was strong and Mustapha knew that youth was on his side. Every few hours Mustapha cleaned any seepage form the wound with boiled salt water and let it dry naturally and covered it with a new dry dressing. Matthew and Beth arrived early and Mustapha and Maud slept for a few hours in the beds in the room next door. At lunchtime the patient had his first spoonsful of warm sweet tea. The young man's mother arrived. It was Eve, the little girl unable to speak until his grandfather had restored her voice. She had come to see if her son was alive. His young wife, heavy with child, had been sobbing uncontrollably all night long and Eve was worried for both her and the baby. Mustapha asked her to wash her hands and face and remove her coat and then he took her to see her son. Arthur was pale, weak and sleepy from the ordeal and the potions but he recognised his mother. She kissed his hand and told him that she would look after Sarah until he was well again, and that she would now hurry home to tell her the good news and then she would stop crying. Mustapha provided her with a mild sedative for her daughter-in-law and Eve was putting on her coat and thanking Mustapha when the door was flung open and Sarah, unable to bear not knowing if her husband was alive or dead, rushed into the room, still sobbing.

Mustapha immediately walked her into the adjoining room where Maud was still asleep, retrieved the sedative from Eve and made Sarah sit down and be quiet and take two spoonsful. He explained, quite firmly, that her husband was alive, but not out of danger. He must be kept quiet and not upset in any way and hearing her crying would not help at all. She sniffed and gulped and wiped her nose on her sleeve. Her eyes were swollen and red and her face blotchy. She wanted to see her husband. Mustapha was adamant that she would not see him until she had calmed down, washed her face and could manage to smile. Beth gave her a cup of sweet tea and Sarah, exhausted by grief, lay down on the bed sniffing dejectedly. Eve and Mustapha sat in the office drinking tea and talking about his grandfather.

Beth peeped in and said that Sarah had fallen asleep. Maud got up and started preparing chicken broth for the patient. Peace reigned in the sick house for an hour or so and Arthur managed to swallow a small bowlful of chicken broth and dropped off to sleep. Beth took a cup of tea to Sarah and found her clutching her belly and drenched in amniotic fluid that dribbled off the side of the bed and ran in a meandering line across the wooden floor. Mustapha's keen nose detected the familiar smell. He took a potion from the shelf and turned to Eve.

'It is one of *those* days Eve. I do believe your grandchild intends to make its entrance!'

Mustapha controlled her pain and at five to midnight, Sarah gave birth to a son. It was Maud's first solo delivery, she passed the child to the delighted Eve and Arthur heard his son's first cry from the next room.

The following morning Mustapha checked Arthur's stiches. The wound was still draining, but as yet there was no sign of infection. He reduced the level of pain relief. Arthur passed urine with no problems, but Matthew would not allow him to return home until his bowels had resumed normal activity. Sarah carried in the baby to meet his father and they named him John Mustapha Matthew.

Sarah, Eve and little John left the sick house the following day. Arthur stayed for almost two weeks, watched closely by Matthew and Mustapha. After four days he was allowed solid food, braised chicken and vegetables. After a week he was allowed out of bed and on the eighth day he used the commode. Mustapha stopped the pain relief so that Arthur's healing body was aware of its limitations. By the tenth day Arthur was able to shuffle about slowly. Getting up into a standing position and sitting down again still gave him pain, but by day twelve both Mustapha and Matthew believed him to be out of danger, they removed his stitches and helped him into a cart and drove him home to complete his recovery. The villagers, particularly the ones that had witnessed Arthur's terrible injuries, believed it to be nothing less than a miracle and never tired of looking at his extensive scars that he displayed with pride. The villagers resumed their original, vigilant task of waiting for someone to present with the fatal bellyache.

Chapter 15

Sophia was making tea in the kitchen when Olivia came in and sat down at the kitchen table.

'Sophia, has Hugh asked you to marry him?' she asked nonchalantly.

'What? Good gracious no! Why do you ask?'

'You do spend a lot of time together.'

'We are friends, Olivia. I am very fond of Hugh, but as a friend not as a potential husband!' she laughed. 'Besides, his mother would not approve!'

'Oh.'

Sophia carried the tea to the table and sat down opposite Olivia, who was studying a mark on the table.

'Olivia.'

Olivia looked up and a slow blush that had begun on her cheeks took possession of her entire head and she covered her face with her hands.

'Ah.'

'Damn and blast it!' hissed Olivia.

'So, how long have you been harbouring feelings towards Hugh?' giggled Sophia.

'Be quiet, Sophia! And don't you dare tell anyone!'

'Oh Olivia, don't be silly! Do you think he is fond of you?'

'I have no idea, he hardly ever speaks to me!'

'You are not easy to speak to!'

'What?'

'Whenever he is here, you are either reading a book and ignore him or you leave the room! He probably thinks that you do not like him.'

'Oh.'

'I know he likes your eyes, he thinks they are extraordinary. He told me that the first time he looked into your eyes, he instantly forgot your name.'

Olivia went very red again.

'Just be pleasant to him Olivia, talk to the man. If you don't, I'll tell him that my cousin would like to marry him!'

'You wouldn't dare!'

'Oh yes I would! I'll give you a month!'

Olivia tossed and turned in her bed. She was angry with herself for giving her feelings away to Sophia. Sophia found it so easy to be friendly. Olivia's cool haughtiness was just a mask to hide her crippling shyness. It was effective, people were fooled by it and they kept their distance. She also knew that Sophia would keep her word and tell Hugh if she failed to make an effort to speak to him. Olivia had been one of the glut of four babies born in a month in the big house. Joey had soon become the leader of the pack and his boisterous antics soon drove Sophia to the gentler company of her brother Mustapha, old Mustapha and granny Mary. Olivia was a quiet child and as soon as she could read she chose to immerse herself in books, and she had remained there. She preferred her friends at a safe distance, in the pages of her favourite books.

Grandy and Hugh arrived in time for Sunday lunch and Sophia managed to manoeuvre the seating and force Olivia to sit beside Hugh. She sat opposite Olivia and tried to encourage her to tell Hugh about her visit to Portugal. Olivia choked and glared at Sophia who raised an eyebrow as a gentle reminder. During the afternoon Sophia tried in vain to encourage a conversation. She sent Olivia to serve Hugh's tea and she did manage to look him in the eyes and smile at him for a second before she rushed away due to a severe blush. During that same second, Hugh felt his heart miss a beat.

Sophia was amused and frustrated by the lack of development. She had watched granny Mary, who had no understanding of, or patience with hesitancy and shyness and Sophia had adopted a similar approach to life. She decided to talk to Hugh and explain that her cousin was very fond of him, but also very shy. Hugh shuffled uneasily and blushed profusely at the news and Sophia realised that progress would be slow. She was unaware that she was Hugh's first and only friend. Their relationship had developed due to her confident, warm nature and her failure to notice that his confidence was paper-thin. Despite his family's social standing, wealth and privilege, Hugh's life had not been a happy one. His memories of childhood were limited to the dark green, austere nursery inhabited by an intimidating nanny, obsessed by routine. The clock on the mantelpiece relentlessly divided the day into mealtimes, bedtimes and sitting quietly times. Nanny wore black clothes and a white apron. She was stout and smelled of soap and her sparse hair was dragged into a knot at the back of her head. She had a dark brown, raised mole on her chin that sprouted hair. She said that she had eyes in the back of her head and Hugh believed her. He would spend days without seeing anyone but nanny. Sometimes she scrubbed him and changed his clothes and took him downstairs to say goodnight to a man and woman that she said were called father and mother. His life changed abruptly when his wailing baby sister arrived in the nursery, accompanied by a wet nurse, and he was sent to his bedroom whenever she had her meals. Hugh spent hours looking out of his window at people, collectively known as servants, hanging washing on the lines and toiling in the large garden. Nanny frowned upon taking children outdoors and believed that exposure to fresh air encouraged disobedience. By the time a second sister arrived, Hugh's days were dominated by an elderly gentleman who taught him to read and write.

By the time he was twelve, nanny had taught Hugh to only speak when he was spoken to and he watched her uncompromisingly impose her iron will on his two little sisters. As soon as they learned to talk they were taught to be quiet and listen. Before he left the nursery for good, she had moulded their childish laughter and temper tantrums into silent obedience. Replaced their running and jumping about with sitting still, annihilated their curiosity and taught them to fear.

Life downstairs was not dissimilar to the nursery. Hugh spent his days with his tutor learning geography, mathematics and Latin. His mother was thinner than nanny and without the hairy mole, but in other respects she was the same. She rarely smiled and frequently reminded Hugh of his 'duty'. His father was rarely present except at the evening meal and largely ignored Hugh.

Hugh's duty, as sole heir to the Lyle fortune, had been planned long before he was born. His parents had done their duty, as had their parents before them. Social standing, wealth and land were paramount. Hugh was expected to marry a young woman of high status, with a fortune in respectable 'old money' that would further swell the coffers of the Lyle family. His mother vetted the suitable young women. Even before he had met Sophia and her family, Hugh had been an unwilling participant. Since meeting them he promised himself that he would marry someone that he loved, regardless of her wealth and social standing. He had watched his parents' miserable existence. They inhabited the same house but they shared a belligerent, antagonistic relationship. His mother spent her time browbeating his sisters and grumbling loudly at her husband. His father had avoided his wife as much as possible. With all of their wealth and status, no one in that house was happy and Hugh had assumed everyone else lived similar lives. Mustapha's family had money and land, but they shared their wealth with the entire village. Their children were free to make their own decisions. The whole family valued happiness above money and did not give a damn about status. Hugh had witnessed his father, who he had never really known, transform into Grandy. He saw him laughing for the first time in his life. Hugh wanted to have a happy life where his own children would be free to play and laugh, so he took a deep breath and went to look for Paulo to ask him if he would allow him to court his daughter.

Chapter 16

Paulo and Rose liked the quiet, unassuming young man and gladly gave him their blessing. Then Hugh, with stomach churning, wrote a note to Olivia. He told her that he had fallen in love with her the first time he met her and that he had asked her parent's permission to court her. He invited her join him for a ride in his carriage at her convenience, tucked the note into her current book that lay on the arm of the sofa and retreated to the tree house, heart thumping wildly, to await a response. An hour later, an hour that had seemed like a lifetime to Hugh, little Mustapha and Bella Mary skipped up the tree house steps.

'Aunt Olivia said that tomorrow at two will be convenient and she will bring a picnic and is it alright if we come too?'

Hugh agreed, grateful to the children who could be relied on to fill any uncomfortable silences.

The following morning Rose helped Olivia to pack the picnic basket with cheese, cold meats, pickles, fresh bread, biscuits and fruit. It was a warn spring day and they decided to drive to the sea wall, close to where Olivia's grandparents had met for the first time. Hugh helped Olivia to unpack the food and plates while the children ran up and down the slope to the estuary and found interesting strands of seaweed. Olivia sent Hugh to ask the old carriage driver to join them for the meal. Old George, taken aback by the invitation, refused, but was eventually dragged from the carriage by Bella Mary, who insisted that he sit on the blanket and eat the meal she had prepared for him. Poor George was mortified and embarrassed. Olivia apologised to him and explained that Bella Mary had thought it unfair not to share the picnic with him. He tried to relax, but was greatly relieved when Bella Mary invited him to help her and her brother to find the winkles hiding under the rocks. Hugh and Olivia listened to the shrill giggles of Bella Mary followed by an unexpected deep chuckle from George in response to little Mustapha's antics. They smiled shyly at each other and blushed crimson.

'Oh Lord!' said Olivia quietly. 'We should have a blushing competition!'

They laughed, and over the following weeks they both struggled to adjust, Olivia doggedly attempting to remove her mask and Hugh gradually becoming familiar with being deliriously happy. They continued to blush, but became less and less destroyed by embarrassment. Grandy was delighted at the prospect of a union between the families. He was even more delighted at the prospect of his wife's reaction. Olivia accepted Hugh's proposal of marriage and Hugh presented her with an engagement ring, a large amethyst to match her eyes, surrounded by diamonds and sapphires.

Hugh and his father rode home to break the news to Mrs Lyle, and Grandy wore his happy jacket for the occasion.

'Oswald! What in God's name are you wearing?'
'My happy jacket!'
'Have you lost your mind? Take it off before the servants see you!'
'No.'
'Hugh, do something!'
'Mother, we came to tell you that I am getting married!'

Mrs Lyle swayed, steadied herself against the table and her eyes narrowed menacingly.

'What did you say?'
'I am to be married!'

She sat down heavily on a chair and gripped the edge of the table. She glared at her husband and then at her son.

'To whom?'
'To Olivia Salazar, daughter of Paulo Salazar and Rose, the daughter of Aziz Shadi Rashad Salamar Badr al din.'

Mrs Lyle's face drained of colour and she remained momentarily silent. Grandy chuckled.

'Then you will leave this house without a penny!' she spat at Hugh.

'I don't think so my dear, as I wholeheartedly approve of his choice!' announced Grandy with relish.

If Mrs Lyle had been capable of getting up she would have struck her husband. She reminded him that she had spent thirty years in this house, in a marriage arranged by her parents, to an old fool who cared about nothing but his horses. She had done her duty and she had raised the children to do theirs and she refused to stand by and allow her son to bring utter disgrace on the family by marrying some foreign mongrel with no standing! They would be the laughing stock of the whole county and their unfortunate daughters would never make a decent marriage, they would be social lepers! Her voice rose to a pitch that alerted the servants who crept closer along the hallways to listen to the uproar. She begged Hugh to consider the family name, respected in the county and beyond for generations. He would not only ruin his own life but the lives of his sisters. There were dozens of suitable, respectable young women from good families he could marry, so why, in God's name would he choose to disgrace the entire family? She shrieked at her husband, ordering him to support her in denying this madness. When he refused she threatened to leave the house for good and return north to live with her parents. When neither her son nor her husband responded to her threat, she stormed from the room, colliding with the rapt huddle of servants that had collected in the corridor.

'Damn fine result son! What?' Grandy smiled triumphantly.

Mrs Lyle packed her belongings slowly, fully expecting her husband to capitulate. He had invariably obeyed her in the past. Her anger returned when she saw him riding off in his stupid jacket with her son and she marched to her daughters' rooms and demanded that they too pack their clothes as they were leaving to live with her parents as their damned brother was about to disgrace the entire family and their idiot father was refusing to stop him. The confused girls, unaware of the recent developments, remembered previous unpleasant visits to their grandparents' home. Their grandmother was a more malignant, vicious version of their mother and their grandfather frequently subjected the girls to attacks of disgraceful, lewd behaviour, exacerbated by his whisky consumption. Elizabeth, the elder of the two stood up as her mother left the room, issuing orders to be ready first thing tomorrow morning. Annie began to cry.

'I shall not go!' said Elizabeth. 'And neither will you!'

'But she will make us go!'

Elizabeth assured her sister that they were not going to their grandparents' home. She ran downstairs and out to the stables looking for George. He was polishing the carriage. Elizabeth asked him to take her and her sister to wherever it was that her brother and father frequently visited. George, having received news of the family squabble, readily agreed and

Elizabeth collected her sister and they made their escape. Elizabeth experienced some misgivings as they approached the house on the edge of woodland. It would be dreadfully rude to arrive unannounced. George, however, familiar with the family, had no such reservations and he jumped down from the carriage and tapped at the door, leaving the girls in the carriage. Sophia answered the door and ran out to the carriage to welcome the young women. By the time they entered the large bright room, extra chairs had been placed at the table and Elizabeth, Annie and George were invited to join them for the meal. The startled young women took their seats, too stunned to speak. They watched as a beautiful woman with almost white hair smiled at them and served them some food and passed the bowl to George, who helped himself! Elizabeth and Annie stared at each other in wonder. Their father was at the other end of the table wearing an extraordinary jacket, flanked by two very attractive women. Hugh sat smiling beside a woman with eyes the colour of violets. There was a man with long black curls and piercing black eyes that flashed when he spoke. The young women ate their food in mystified silence, listening to the people talking and laughing. Their father waved and smiled from the other end of the long, crowded table and they smiled wanly in return. The plates on the table were swiftly changed as the delicious puddings were served and the tall glass pots of tea arrived. People began to leave the table and Hugh sat beside his sisters and they told him that they did not want to go with their mother. Annie looked tearful and he assured her that she did not have to go anywhere against her will. Sophia introduced the young women to everyone and informed them that they would be staying the night. They would have Khalid's room that overlooked the woods at the rear of the house. Hugh and Olivia invited then to sit in the tree house with their tea, where it was quiet and they could talk. Olivia explained that her father had built the tree house for the children before she was born, but the adults used it more frequently. Hugh told his sisters not to worry, as they were welcome to live at home with him and their father and advised them to stay at the big house for a few days. Annie wanted to look into the woods, so the four of them set off into the woods. The rich, deep sea of bluebells with their heady aroma greeted them as they walked up the gentle slope. There were clumps of violets and fragile white wood anemones quivering in the gentle breeze. Tiny leaves were beginning to sprout from the tree branches and the low evening sun turned the tree trunks golden. Annie believed that it was the most beautiful place she had ever seen.

Mina and Sophia showed them to their room, dominated by the largest bed they had ever seen. The bedspread was deep red satin with silver embroidery, matching the long heavy, flowing curtains. The saffron yellow walls were decorated with wall hangings and numerous strange masks and maps and other unidentifiable objects. The floor was pale polished wood, liberally scattered with thick sheepskins. A long sofa stood against the wall under the windows, it was dark red leather strewn with silk cushions in yellow, orange and red. Mina and Sophia had piled the table with dresses and nightgowns, as the young women had no clothing with them. Olivia carried in jugs of hot water for them to wash, promising to introduce then to the bathhouse tomorrow.

Elizabeth and Annie sat in the vast bed, drinking hot chocolate delivered by their brother. They had never seen such a wonderful room and fully understood why their brother and father had been seduced by this place. Elizabeth sipped the delicious chocolate and sighed.

'I believe our lives have taken a bit of a turn Annie!'

Annie nodded in agreement and smiled broadly, her eyes sparkling.

Chapter 17

When Mrs Lyle woke up, her first thought was that she might have been unnecessarily hasty when she threatened to leave the house. This was possibly a battle that she could lose. It was early days and Hugh was not married yet. She picked up her dressing gown and headed off to tell her daughters to unpack again. Her rage boiled over when she discovered their disappearance. She searched the house and was finally reduced to interrogating the servants and learned that George had driven them away on the previous afternoon. She demanded that George be immediately brought to her. George appeared and with a stonily obstinate expression, refused to tell her where he had taken them.

'Then you will leave this employment immediately!' Mrs Lyle shouted, beside herself with frustration.

'I don't think so, it is the *Master* as pays my wages!'

Mrs Lyle stared at him, mute and impotent. George turned and left the room with a marked swagger and Mrs Lyle threw a candlestick at the mirror with such force that both shattered. Believing that she was had no alternative she packed two bags and sent her maid to summon George to take her to town. He loaded and unloaded her bags in total silence and with a detectable smirk. She had never made the long journey to her parents' home unattended and unaccompanied. It was an arduous, distressing three days. At times she was physically squashed against strangers in crowded coaches. She was reduced to arranging her own accommodation at the Inns, in filthy rooms with stained mattresses and the overpowering stench of the lower classes and their bodily emissions. She picked at the nauseating food. She regretted her decision countless times but then talked herself around to believing that she was right.

When she reached final few miles of the harrowing journey, Mrs Lyle was so relieved that it was almost over that she began to look forward to seeing her mother and father and settled for travelling by horse and cart, even though it looked like rain was imminent. Much of her anger had dissipated and she felt vulnerable and sorry for herself. Her initial reaction was that the garden was seriously overgrown and neglected. Her following reaction was that even the house looked shabby and smaller that she remembered it. Richard, the very elderly butler opened the door and failed to recognise Mrs Lyle. She pushed past him and ordered him to bring in her bags.

Richard slowly closed the door and wandered away, leaving the bags on the steps in the rain. She found her parents beside a dwindling fire. They frowned at her and she was forced to introduce herself. Her mother jumped up and flung her arms around her. Her father waved from his chair and uttered a guttural greeting. Mrs Lyle's mother assumed that she had arrived in response to the letter begging for her help that had been sent some time ago. Unable to admit she had read it and instantly obliterated it from her memory, Mrs Lyle denied receiving it. Her parents were living in reduced circumstances, largely because her father had made some unwise investments, guaranteed to pay a huge dividend, and also due to his substantial consumption of whisky. Her mother added that the surfeit of whisky had negatively influenced his decision to give a vast sum of money to a charming stranger who had promised to make him very rich. Her father nodded his head in agreement and refilled his glass. Richard shuffled in with a tray of tea and was sent back to the kitchen to bring another cup and saucer. When he failed to return, Mrs Lyle was horrified that her mother went to the kitchen for the cup. Unable to pay the servants wages, they had no choice but to let them go. Richard had nowhere to go and so he remained, although his memory appeared to be slowly disintegrating and he was prone to relieving himself in the plant pots. Mrs Lyle put her head in her hands. In less than a week she had descended from being mistress of a mansion on an estate, the largest in the county, to being the daughter of paupers! There was no one to cook, clean or light the fires! She looked around in the entrance hall for her bags and found them outside, sodden and heavy on the steps and was close to tears. She helped herself to a cup of lukewarm tea. Her father had fallen asleep and was dribbling on his shirt and her mother was staring vacantly into the fireplace at the last embers.

In stark contrast, Elizabeth and Annie had woken up to breakfast in bed, with hot bread and amber coloured jam and a pot full of piping hot tea. Sophia drew the heavy curtains. The sun streamed through the saffron voile curtains and dabbled the floor. The young women selected two dresses to wear, a deep red and a dark purple. Their mother had disapproved of such vivid colours. Then they set off into the woods and picked armfuls of bluebells and small bunches of primroses and filled all of the flower vases they could find. They were fascinated by Bill and rendered speechless by Thomas and they never wanted to go home again.

Later that afternoon the house was thrown into chaos by the return of the ship and the invasion by Sam, Khalid, Edmundo and Estavo all talking at once in a hullabaloo of adventures. Elizabeth watched Khalid, with his long black hair and amber eyes and solemn expression and thought she had never seen a more beautiful young man. He smiled at her and she blushed the Lyle shade of deep crimson. Then she realised that it was his bed she had slept in and turned an even deeper shade. The new arrivals were delighted that there would be a wedding later in the year. Khalid and the twins had brought their hammocks with them as, like Sam and Sal when they were young, after two years at sea the transition from hammock to bed took several weeks. So Grandy and Hugh remained in the twins' room and Elizabeth and Annie in Khalid's. That evening Elizabeth and Annie were introduced to the bathhouse. The wallowed in the gallons of steaming perfumed water.

'Is this all a dream?' asked Annie.

'I sincerely hope it's not!' answered Elizabeth.

Rose smiled and thought that the house really felt like home again.

Grandy, Hugh and George began planning the building of a new house to be erected on the edge of the woods between the big house and Gabriel's farm. Olivia did not want to live far away from her family and Hugh's family were reluctant to return home to the dingy, oppressive mansion. It needed to be a large house with room for Hugh and Olivia, Grandy, Elizabeth and Annie and an array of live-in servants. An encampment of stonemasons, carpenters and labourers grew at the edge of the woods and every evening someone from the family delivered a cauldron of hot stew and dozens of loaves of fresh bread. A new well was dug and two bathhouses would be attached to the rear of the building.

Meanwhile, further north, Mrs Lyle's father abruptly died in his armchair in a messy fountain of frothy blood-red vomit when the distended veins in his gullet suddenly burst. Mrs Lyle and her mother cowered in the corner of the room, clinging to each other, circumventing the indiscriminate, splattering gush. She admitted defeat then, buried her father and with her mother and old Richard, set off home, willing to beg forgiveness. They arrived four days later to find the house empty except for the servants, who had continued to cook, clean and tend the garden and waited for someone to return. She was surprised to discover that her husband and son had not visited and that they would have no idea that she had ever left. It had been the most dire, most unthinkably torturous three weeks of her life and she had learned that there was indeed a fate far worse than social disgrace.

For Elizabeth and Annie it had been the best. The outdoor life in the fresh air and sun had given their pale skin some colour, their mousy hair had lightened to a streaky golden blonde and their daily rambles in the countryside had trimmed their waists and buttocks. Grandy watched his daughters blossoming and decided that beauty and happiness were contagious.

Chapter 18

Grandy and Hugh had kept pace with developments at the Lyle residence via old George. They learned that Mrs Lyle had returned after several weeks accompanied by her mother and an elderly servant and it was believed that her father had recently died.

The butler, known as Mister Archibald by the staff and plain Archie by the family, was horrified by the smell of old Richard and his dogged attempts to answer the front door and urinate on the ferns in the entrance hall. Mrs Lyle had brought him with her, as she had no idea what else to do with him. One of the cooks took pity on him after hearing his feeble screams when Mister Archibald dragged him by the ear from the entrance hall for the umpteenth time that morning. She stripped him, washed him, cut his yellow horny nails, picked off his substantial colony of lice and bathed the puss-ridden scabs that congregated in his armpits. In clean clothes he smelled better, but he had been a butler for almost sixty years and nothing could deter the addled old man from heading to the large entrance hall where he lurked, waiting for the opportunity to answer the front door when the bell rang. Eventually, an unused room at the rear of the house was assigned to him. They attached a bolt on the outside of the door and they nailed the windows shut to prevent his escape and everyday someone informed him that it was his day off.

Grandy and Hugh were both surprised by the change in Mrs Lyle when they visited the house to collect items that Elizabeth and Annie required. She was markedly subdued and looked very tired. She even failed to react to Grandy's happy jacket. She told her husband of her father's death, but omitted the details of the family's decline to rob him of the chance to gloat.

Mrs Lyle's mother rarely left her room and spent her days staring out of the window without seeing anything. She took her meals in her room and was prone to long periods of crying. Mrs Lyle visited her each afternoon but was uncomfortable with her mother's grief, constant apologies, self-recriminations and embarrassing displays of gratitude.

The wedding date was set for August as Hugh and Olivia intended to spend their first seven to eight months of marriage sailing with the ship to North Africa and Turkey. Sophia and her team had already begun the task of designing and making the wedding outfits. She had laid claim to most of the silk brought back from the last voyage. Olivia would wear violet silk and the overall theme would be a multitude of rich purples, lavenders and soft blues. Grandy insisted that he would like a set of clothes like Mustapha wore, but in happy colours instead of white. The new house was progressing and the aim was to have it completed the following spring, in time for the return of the ship and Hugh and Olivia. Rose, Maria and Mina, given the task of producing the soft furnishings were already sewing cushion covers, sheets and curtains.

In early June Mrs Lyle's mother developed an intermittent, disabling headache accompanied by dizziness that forced her to stay in bed. Mrs Lyle sent for her physician who recommended a strong purgative that reduced the unfortunate old woman to soiling the bed and did nothing to alleviate the headache. When the intensity of the headaches increased and the physician was called again, Mrs Lyle's mother managed to find the strength to kick him in the groin. In late June she was suffering so much pain that she regularly woke Mrs Lyle with her screams that were occasionally heard as far as the servant's quarters. Mrs Lyle despaired as she watched her mother rocking in agony and pleading for death to come. So when Hugh, alerted by old George, arrived with Mustapha one morning, his mother lacked the strength to deny him access to the sick woman. Mustapha promised the exhausted, terrified old woman that this remedy would not make her sick, it would just relieve the pain, so that she would be able to sleep. She looked at his gentle face and hypnotic eyes and obediently opened her mouth and swallowed two spoonsful of the amber liquid. He held her head and gave her some sips of warm, sweet tea, held her hand and stroked her brow until her pain began to subside. Old Iris felt the vice-like, sickening pain ebbing away into the distance like a receding tide and she began to sob with utter relief. She clung to Mustapha's hand, unable to verbalise her fervent thanks.

'Now sleep.' Mustapha smiled. 'I promise you I will be right here when you wake up.'

Iris smiled though her tears and drifted into the first deep sleep for weeks. Mustapha kept his promise and took her hand as she woke several hours later. Her pain was miles away, like a rock submerged at high tide. She was able to explain the pain to Mustapha, the increasing intensity and her belief that she was slowly losing her sight. Mustapha quietly explained to her that her condition was likely to be incurable, but that he could keep her pain at bay until the end. She patted his hand.

'That is all I ask. I have no fear of death and I thank you for your honesty.'

Mustapha examined her, her heart was strong and he told her that she probably had many months before the end. He arranged to visit her every week, bringing a supply of his remedy that he would entrust to her daughter. If she needed him she must send George with a message and he would come immediately. He explained to both women that one spoonful would be enough to alleviate much of the pain, but two could be taken if necessary and when she needed to sleep. Iris's agony had been so severe that she had forgotten what it had been like to feel no pain and she was filled with a euphoria that drove her from her room and outside into the splendid gardens. She continued to experience occasional dizzy spells and needed to sit down until they passed. Iris spent her time smelling the flowers and inspecting the vegetable gardens and talking to the aged dog, retired from a life of herding sheep that had taken to following her everywhere. Mrs Lyle watched her mother through the window and struggled with conflicting thoughts. It was such a relief that her mother had stopped screaming, and she was grateful. But it was disagreeable to be grateful and beholden to a member of that family of foreigners and tradesmen that had splintered her own family. Mustapha's potions had given her husband new legs. Oswald had then become disobedient and ran off. Her only son intended to marry into the family. Mrs Lyle rued the day she had engaged the services of Sophia Badr al din, as that meeting seemed to her to be the start of all subsequent disasters. Mustapha arrived every week and was warmly welcomed by her mother, who lit up when he entered the room, and he had the audacity to refuse payment for his remedy. Mrs Lyle was disturbed by his black eyes that searched her soul and forced her to look away. The dog, named Spot by her mother, even had the audacity to wag his tail wildly when Mustapha arrived, sat beside him and rested his chin on the young man's lap and gazed adoringly into his eyes.

Mustapha's manner was impeccable. He invariably asked Mrs Lyle about her mother's progress when he handed over the bottles of remedy. The afternoon that he looked into her eyes, and with genuine concern in his own eyes, respectfully enquired after her own health, she was ravaged by the uncontrollable desire to fall at the feet of this strange young man in pyjamas and give vent to all of her troubles, fears, anger, shame and dreadful disappointments. She tried unsuccessfully to stop her eyes filling with tears and shook her head. Mustapha saw the tears and her great discomfort and he took her hand warmly and bid her good afternoon and left, closing the door quietly. Mrs Lyle was so disconcerted by her own reaction that she headed for the brandy bottle and took a stiff drink to calm her nerves. She glanced out of the window and saw the dignified young man riding down the drive and was overwhelmed by a deep melancholy that she did not understand and she slumped into an armchair and cried her heart out.

Mustapha, deep in thought on his way home, had sensed Mrs Lyle's painful internal struggle between despair and pride. He felt great sympathy for her, a lonely woman who had just lost her father, nursing her dying mother with no support from anyone. He decided to talk to both Grandy and Hugh in an attempt to elicit their help.

Grandy searched his soul and realised he also felt sympathy for his wife. She was an awkward woman but he had to admit that her current circumstances were far from enviable. He rode over to see her the following day, armed with a bottle of a tonic potion from Mustapha and a message to drink a glassful each morning to keep her strength up under the difficult circumstances. Mrs Lyle was astonished to see her husband, without his daft jacket for once, with offers of help. He gingerly mentioned Hugh's wedding and told her she was welcome to attend. She was silent for a while and then explained that it may be difficult due to her mother's illness, but she sent Hugh her best wishes for his marriage, although the sentence almost choked her. She was too tired to continue to fight. Grandy stayed for tea and patted his wife on her shoulder as he left.

Mrs Lyle drank a glass of Mustapha's tonic each morning and after a few days had to admit she did feel calmer and less tired. Mustapha arrived earlier than usual to see her mother who was somewhere in the garden with Spot. A servant was sent to find her and Mrs Lyle found herself telling him the details of the sudden death of her father. He said that it was a terrible death to witness and not uncommon amongst heavy drinkers whose throats and gullets had been damaged by alcohol. He gently explained that it would take some time to properly recover from the traumatic event and Mrs Lyle could not risk answering him due to the lump in her throat. She realised that she could cope with any amount of anger and nastiness. It was kindness and gentle concern that broke her. Mustapha told her that it was not unusual to experience nightmares, disturbed sleep and bouts of tearfulness. He explained that his grandfather had told him that when we are physically wounded we bleed, and that bleeding allows the body to heal, but when we are emotionally wounded we need to shed tears in order to heal. He passed a clean white handkerchief to Mrs Lyle and whilst she dabbed at her eyes he added.

'And my grandfather was the wisest, kindest man I have ever met and I continue to miss him very much. Both of my own parents are still alive and well, so I am unable to comprehend just how hard life must be for you at present.'

Mrs Lyle looked up, tears rolling down her face.

'Do you mind if I ask you something?' Mrs Lyle whispered.

Mustapha shook his head with a smile.

'Did you marry for love?'

'Of course, what other reason could there be to marry?'

Mrs Lyle experienced a similar revelation to her husband's, a realisation that she had long ago made a wrong turn in her life and now it was far too late and that was so very sad.

Mrs Lyle continued to take her tonic potion that Mustapha delivered along with her mother's pain relief. One afternoon he arrived with a box containing a tall glass teapot and glasses and startled the servants when he arrived in the kitchen and asked if he could make some tea. Mouth open, the cook passed him the kettle and watched in astonishment as he filled the kettle and put it on the stove. He made the tea watched by the servants and as he left with his tray he apologised for disturbing them.

He presented the tea to Mrs Lyle and her mother. It was different to their usual tea, it was more gold than brown and sweetened with honey and he said it was very good for them. The weekly delivery soon evolved into afternoon tea with biscuits and sometimes with cakes. Iris asked him about his family and Mustapha gladly told her. After he left, the two women continued to talk and Iris took her daughter's hand and said how sorry she was that she had had such a lonely childhood, that she had no brothers of sisters and that she was sorry that she had encouraged her to marry an older man, despite his fortune. She was sorry to be a burden and sorry for her husband's past behaviour. Mrs Lyle was shocked and stared at her mother. Iris went on to explain that her own life had been the same. Her parents chose her husband and it was not a happy marriage. They all did their duty and paid a high price. The women talked long into the evening and in the end Mrs Lyle thought about her own children and part of her was glad that they had possessed the courage to break the chain that had held her, her mother and probably her grandmothers. It may be too late for her, but not for her daughters!

Mrs Lyle assured her mother that she was not a burden and that she was enjoying the time they spent together, and she meant it. Meanwhile, Mustapha sat in the tree house trusting that his plan was coming to fruition.

Iris's condition failed to deteriorate as quickly as Mustapha feared that it would. Her pain rarely broke through the remedy, her dizziness dissipated and she believed that her eyesight had improved. Her appetite was good and her dark shadows around her eyes had gone. This led Mustapha to consider that she had possibly had a severe abscess in her brain, rather than a growth.

Chapter 19

Khalid grew very fond of Elizabeth and she was secretly euphoric. He was attracted by her demure, gentle nature, a contrast to most of the confident, strong and occasionally belligerent women in the household. She listened with rapt attention to his stories from his voyages and was the only one who gasped in horror at the alarming deprivations he had experienced. Elizabeth had not travelled and had no stories and with her he felt confident and exciting. He was no longer the weakest one who was convinced of his father's disappointment. She laughed with him and not at him.

Elizabeth had not had a conversation with a young man before and she had never even been alone with one. She was shocked and delighted that the family ignored the strict social rules and chaperones did not exist. As she listened to Khalid she could look into his amber-coloured eyes, with their black lashes, at his long, thick silky hair that she was dying to touch. At times she forgot to listen and at other times Khalid became so animated that he grabbed her arm, causing her to blush from her throat to the top of her head.

The summer was hot and dry and the harvest began early and Elizabeth accompanied Khalid on the horse and cart, delivering great jars of water laced with sugar and salt and flavoured with the juice of any available fruits to the hot, dusty workers in the fields. Life became hectic with preparations for the end of harvest party and the wedding of her brother and Olivia. Elizabeth, Annie and Bella Mary were to be bridesmaids. Esther has designed the dresses, using the deepest shade of violet for the sisters and lured the stubborn Bella Mary out of her happy dresses by producing a striped dress using all of the shades of purples, violets and pale lavender-blue. She made Grandy's outfit in three shades of purple and he called it his happy pyjamas. Olivia was to wear a lavender dress, heavily embroidered with violet silk thread. The entire village was bubbling with mounting excitement and a week before the harvest party the inhabitants began to arrive and help with the preparations. Joey took a break from the wood carving in the new house to build the bonfire and Harry and Big Ern built the spits for the carcasses.

Elizabeth and Annie had declined the suggestion to visit their mother, fearful that she would not allow them to return to their new life. They threw themselves into the strange festivities, where the house filled with bustling, laughing women from the village. They rescued the unimpressed Thomas from a crowd of curious children trying valiantly to release him from his rocky prison. They carried out the trays of hot potatoes and bread and helped to slice up the meat from the spits. After the meal the music started in earnest and Khalid asked Elizabeth to dance. Annie watched the arm wrestling competition and was impressed by a tall fair-haired young man, with arms like thick rope. He eventually annihilated the opposition and smiled at her as she applauded. He had the most extraordinary green eyes and a mass of sun-streaked fair, curly hair. His name was Amos and he was the blacksmith's son. Annie spent the evening dancing with him and he swung her in the air as if she were a feather. Amos invited her to go with him to the shrine and they followed the procession of people walking along the lantern-lit pathway in the woods. The clearing was bright with candles and the villagers were singing their best loved songs to the tunes of the band. Amos lifted Annie onto his shoulder for a better view and she felt so free and happy and smiled to think of her mother's reaction to the situation. She could feel the heat from Amos's shoulder through her skirt and thought she should feel dreadfully ashamed of herself, but she did not! Amos delivered her to the back door of the big house, kissed her hand and bid her goodnight with a bow and skipped off home without having any idea that he had spent the evening with the daughter of landed gentry who owned vast swathes of the county.

Annie sat in bed with a cup of hot chocolate gazing at the wall and reliving the most wonderful day of her life when she heard a commotion downstairs. Her sister Elizabeth had just accepted a proposal of marriage from Khalid Badr al din.

A week later, Hugh and Olivia awoke on the morning of their wedding. The sky was dark and threatening, accompanied by distant rolls of thunder. Mrs Lyle, staring out of her bedroom window believed it an omen but everyone else thought it was a damned nuisance. Joey and Big Ern, helped by men from the village, erected sheets of old sail canvas on poles at the front of the house to protect the spits, already loaded with carcasses. Esther arrived to supervise the dressing of the bride and bridesmaids. Mrs Lyle's mother insisted that she attend the wedding of her only grandson, Mrs Lyle reluctantly agreed following a heated debate in which her mother tearfully refused to give way. They slipped into the rear of the church, unnoticed by most people, their attire more suited to a funeral. Mrs Lyle was tempted to leave when she saw her husband dressed in gaudy purple pyjamas but her mother was entranced by the rich purples, violets, lavenders, the mass of flowers and the clusters of candles, swinging gently in purple lanterns. Hugh saw his mother and grandmother as he was leaving the church with his new wife on his arm. Olivia curtsied and Mrs Lyle, momentarily captivated by her violet eyes, had to admit that Olivia was indeed a very beautiful woman and she understood why her son loved her. Mrs Lyle's mother uncharacteristically flung her arms around her startled grandson and Mrs Lyle pulled her away to avoid a scene. The old woman stood transfixed and watched the procession of the family as it made its way from the church. Sir Oswald's face lit up when he saw his wife and her mother. He was attached to a little girl in a purple striped gown with pale ivory curls and black eyes. Mrs Lyle declined the invitation to the festivities at the house but her mother accepted. Once in their carriage, Mrs Lyle informed her distraught mother that they were going straight home. But old George had already been given strict instructions to transport them to the party and he drove with a smile on his face despite the vehemence of Mrs Lyle's threats. Sir Oswald helped his mother-in-law from the carriage, introduced her to Maria and then assisted his wife. Mrs Lyle was white with rage. She dug her nails into her husband's arm and muttered eternal vengeance. He led her into the house to join her mother, who was seated beside the window where Maria was pouring tea. She sat stiffly beside her mother who was complimenting Maria on the lovely room, bright and inviting, even on a dull day. Mrs Lyle endured the afternoon with a stoicism born of superiority. It was worse than she had ever imagined. The foreign, multi-coloured family was one thing, but the presence of the lower classes, running in and out of the house without bowing their heads and speaking to the family using Christian names, beggared belief. These foreigners had no respect for tradition, no understanding of the necessity to keep separate the distinct breeds of people. Allowing this familiarity between the breeds would result in disaster, people must know their place in life and it was the duty of her aristocratic breed, that were able to trace their lineage to royalty, to keep the lower orders in their place. It was dire enough that her only son had married below expectations, but to see her daughters rubbing shoulders with the lower classes, people with threadbare clothing and grubby hands was a step too far. She wondered if she was witnessing the end of civilisation, the very beginning of the end of the natural order of hereditary status.

Mustapha watched her from across the room. He could see her profound discomfort and pitied her, wedged uncomfortably between her jubilant mother and Bella Mary who had lugged Thomas in to meet her. Mustapha rescued her and took her upstairs to the quiet sitting room overlooking the woods. He introduced her to a tall, slim woman with long pale hair who appeared to float rather than walk. Isabella served hot sweet tea and Mrs Lyle wished it had been a very large brandy. That's another unnatural thing, thought Mrs Lyle, the married women wander about with their hair hanging loose down their backs like children. Sir Oswald entered the room in his ridiculous purple pyjamas with their eldest daughter Elizabeth and a very dark skinned man with long straight hair and eyes like a cat. The news that they were to be married in the spring was the final straw and Mrs Lyle slumped forward and surrendered to a welcome fainting fit.

Mustapha revived her with smelling salts and gave her a potion of opium and bhang to calm her nerves and alleviate her discomfort. He emptied the room and sat holding her hand whilst tears rolled slowly down her face and waited for the first smile of potion-induced oblivion. Within ten minutes she was giggling and in another ten announced to Mustapha that she wished to join the party!

The rain had stopped and the musicians were playing a lively tune and to the utter consternation of her family, Mrs Lyle dragged Mustapha outside to the crowd of dancing villagers and demanded that he dance with her. She soon threw off her hat and coat and danced with men with grubby hands. She ate spit roasted meat and hot, fresh bread. She played with the children and hugged her daughters. She stood hand in hand with her mother and watched the bonfire and despite the fine drizzle, laughed and clapped her hands at the fireworks that marked the end of the festivities. She fell asleep in the carriage on the way home and she never spoke of that evening again. Nobody knew whether or not she had any recollection of the events, so nobody ever broached the subject.

Chapter 20

Sam, in his mid-fifties, had no intention of retiring from the sea voyages. He was not interested in George's suggestion of purchasing a steam ship, a new invention that would never be becalmed. Sam pointed out the wind was free and took up no space in the hold. Khalid was relieved that his father still captained the ship and eternally grateful that Edmundo and Estavo had chosen to join him. Khalid prayed fervently for the day when they could replace him on the voyages and he could remain at home with Elizabeth and raise a family and never set foot on foreign soil again.

Most of the family went to the dock to see the ship off on a crisp, bright early autumn morning. Olivia and Hugh were as excited as the twins, who had been waiting to sail ever since they had arrived home from the previous trip. Elizabeth sobbed uncontrollably and Khalid, fearful of his own tears being seen, disappeared below deck. By the time they were in the English Channel, Hugh, who had not previously ventured from dry land, was feeling considerably queasy. Olivia and Yusuf the cook made ginger infused tea that settled his stomach but he suffered for almost a week from severe bouts of seasickness, that were much worse at night due to being below deck. So Olivia lashed up their hammocks on deck, fed him ginger tea and mopped his brow. By the time the ship had rounded the Iberian Peninsular and entered the Mediterranean, the colour had returned to Hugh's cheeks and he began to enjoy the voyage. Khalid moped in his cabin, dreaming about Elizabeth.

The ship docked in North Africa and Sam, the twins, Olivia and Hugh set off south towards Marrakech. Olivia's initial mounting of her camel was reminiscent of her grandmother's first attempt, Sam and Hugh found it hilarious but her younger brothers shook their heads and sighed. Hugh gazed around in wonder at the scenery, the snow covered Atlas mountain range and the flat desert that stretched as far as he could see, dotted with clumps of strange trees and squat, flat buildings the colour of sand. He watched his wife's heroic attempt to remain aloft, her camel tied to her uncle's mount. He had never been so happy. In the last couple of years, his life had changed so dramatically it made him dizzy. The little group, accompanied by two camel drivers and a string of camels, with varying temperaments, meandered at a leisurely pace through the landscape, camping at night under the stars, observing the tea ceremony that had fascinated Sam when he was a boy and eating goat stew. On the third day they arrived at their destination to a warm welcome from the same family that Aziz Shadi Rashad Salamar Badr al din had brought Lily over sixty years ago, and then Sam and Sal almost fifty years before. The family resemblance was so strong that several of the older inhabitants experienced moments of extreme confusion and used the wrong names. The women escorted Olivia to the bathhouse and old Sameh, who had been fourteen when Lily had visited thought Olivia was a ghost of her grandmother. She had the same violet eyes and throughout her visit Sameh continued to call her Lily.

Hugh accompanied Sam and the twins to the tannery the following day. He discovered how to assess the quality of the hides by touch and smell and even enjoyed the unpleasant smell that had turned the stomach of Khalid on his only visit. He listened to the protracted bartering carried out on a rug on the sand around a large pot of green tea, despite not understanding a word of it. He was impressed with Sam and the twin's ability to converse in other languages. His own tutor had taught him Latin, which was to prove utterly useless throughout his travels.

The men sat on rugs and cushions during the evenings, catching up on each other's news and reminiscing on the past, when Gabriel's accident prone son Henry had run off with the Bedouin tribesmen. Estavo translated the stories for Hugh. A week later they made their journey back to the ship, the camels loaded with bales of leather hides and a crate of silver and coloured glass lanterns that Olivia had fallen in love with at the souks.

The ship headed east, hugging the coast of North Africa and Hugh sat in his hammock on deck mesmerised by the view, unwilling to miss anything. Olivia arrived with two bowls of hot soup and as they sat together in the hammock he thought he would burst with sheer joy and turned his head away to hide his tears.

Winter threatened suddenly that year in the village, as early as October there were sharp frosts and downpours of icy sleet. Isabella and little Mustapha covered the garden with fresh layers of straw to protect the plants. Fortunately, the roof was on Hugh and Olivia's new house and Paulo insisted that the workmen move their camp inside the house where Joey kept the large fire alight. He had moved in and worked from sunrise to sunset on his intricate carvings. He carved the beams and the thick supports, inspired by the shape and grain of the wood. He carved patterns and creatures and in the corner of one room her rebuilt an entire tree with twisting branches and leaves that trailed across the ceiling and walls. Paulo, whose love of wood matched Joey's watched him at work, saw the rabbits emerging from the skirting boards and the brambles, complete with blackberries growing around the kitchen doorframe. Eventually, following a lengthy discussion regarding staircases, they combined their skills and produced an unbelievably elegant spiral staircase that defied gravity, with exquisite lilies growing from the bannister rails. The handrail was carved into a long thick rope with a large knot at the base and Joey even carved the frayed end to appear to be moving in a breeze. Occasionally, someone wondered if the stunning, sometimes bizarre woodwork would be to Hugh and Olivia's taste, then forgot about it again.

Mrs Lyle saw her mother through the window sitting with her back against the old oak with her beloved sheepdog. She put on her coat to go and join her in the rare afternoon sun. She briefly thought her mother had fallen asleep against the tree, but closer inspection revealed that the old Iris was dead, still smiling and with her arm still around the dog. In the same week, Reverend Knightly died peacefully, attended by his family and Mustapha, and then Bill the monkey was found dead on the hearthrug. The sick house became very busy with people suffering from severe colds that settled on their chest, causing dreadful wheezing and difficulty in breathing. Mustapha, Matthew, Maud and Beth, who was heavily pregnant with her first child, began staying the night at the sick house, too exhausted to go home. Large saucepans of water boiled on the stoves, providing steam and loosening phlegm. The old, frail and the very young suffered the most severely. Following the deaths of five of the elderly and two infants, Mustapha ordered Big Ern to take Beth, ignoring her protestations, and deliver her to the big house and remain there with her until the child was born. That evening Mustapha stocked the bathhouse with remedies and left instructions to keep the fires in the bathhouse alight and the pans filled with water. Then he studied his grandfather's recipes and with Isabella's help mixed a considerable quantity of potions for mucus thinning and reducing temperatures and returned to the sick house. The babies worried him the most, unlike adults and older children they were unable to cough and shift phlegm effectively and the tiny lungs soon filled with mucus. He decided that the only way to empty a baby's lungs needed gravity, so he began raising the baby's legs higher than the head, either on a pillow or by holding the baby facing downwards, allowing the mucus to drain from the nose and mouth. He instructed mothers to keep them in a steamy atmosphere, keep them facing downhill and gently pat the back to encourage the mucus to come out. Mother's told each other and soon the whole village adopted the new treatment for snotty babies.

Little Mustapha ran all the way to the sick house to inform his father that Beth's labour had begun. By the time he arrived home Isabella had already administered the first dose of remedy as Beth's pains began suddenly whilst walking in the woods with Big Ern. He had carried her back to the house and they were both soaked with amniotic fluid and Big Ern was beside himself and more in need of a remedy than Beth, who sat grinning on a large towel in front of the fire. She had delivered so many babies she had lost count. She knew that the waters breaking early in the labour and strong regular pains often indicated a shorter labour, and now Mustapha was with her she had no fear at all. Rose and Maria filled the bath with mounting excitement as it was a long time since the last birth, that of Bella Mary, over six years hence. Mustapha helped Beth into the deep warm water and gave her a stronger remedy to alleviate the pain he detected in her eyes. Poor Big Ern did not know what to do or where to put himself. They had waited a long time for this baby and were on the point of giving up when Beth became pregnant. Mustapha gave him a mild remedy and encouraged him to sit beside the bath and hold his wife's hand. It was not entirely successful, as Big Ern burst into tears and Beth was the one holding his hand. Rose delivered tea and biscuits and a piece of Big Ern's favourite cake, which he was unable to eat due to his distress. Beth found it funny and laughed until she cried. An hour later Beth told Mustapha that she wanted to push, throwing her husband into a renewed bout of panic. Isabella had joined them and she helped Beth into a kneeling position and Mustapha let down the rope erected by his grandfather. Everyone was expecting this stage to be hard work, due to the size of the father and the size of Beth's belly, but before Mustapha was able to give her the stamina potion and following three major pushes, the dainty little girl with chestnut hair and bright green eyes bobbed to the surface of the water, weighing no more than seven pounds. Beth fished her out, kissed her and passed her to Isabella who rolled her in a warmed towel and gave her to Big Ern, who stared at her in disbelief, Mustapha led him from the bathhouse, leaving Isabella to take care of Beth.

'Come.' Mustapha said as he led father and daughter out of the front door.

The sky was full of stars and a new moon and Mustapha asked to present the baby to the world. Everyone in the house, with the exception of Beth and Isabella, assembled at the windows to watch Mustapha hold the child aloft and thank God for the gift of life in a language Big Ern did not understand. They named her Eva Violet.

Chapter 21

Hugh was mesmerised by his first glimpse of Constantinople. The glittering city that rose from the sea was dominated by the grandeur of the numerous domed mosques and their delicate minarets. The port was busy, with countless ships moored side by side. Goods brought overland from China, India and the Ottoman Empire attracted merchants from Europe and even the Americas. Next morning, Sam, Hugh and the twins went ashore to track down silks, tea, porcelain and spices. Sam ignored the traders on the docks, preferring to search out top quality goods housed in warehouses within the city. Hugh wanted to stop and investigate everything until Sam promised him that when they had completed their purchases and everything was loaded, there would be plenty of time to explore the city with Olivia. They found the spices first, lured by the smell. Sam bartered for sacks of pepper, ginger, turmeric, chilli, mustard seed, garlic, star anise and tamarind. Hugh wandered about, dazzled by the colours of the samples of spices in wooden boxes, rich reds, vibrant oranges and the strange shapes of the produce. Sam intervened when the unsuspecting Hugh was about to eat a chilli offered to him by a grinning Turk with very few teeth. They had lunch, a local dish of lamb patties and stew containing all different kinds of beans, from large white to smaller dark brown. Hugh counted nine different varieties. They finished the meal with a delicious sweet that reminded Hugh of the first meal he had back at Olivia's home. After acquiring several chests of Assam tea the group meandered back to the ship by which time the surfeit of beans began playing havoc with their digestive systems. Sam found two sets of suitable clothing for his niece explaining to the naive Hugh that in this city, beautiful women are bought and sold, and frequently stolen, like merchandise. The following day, Sam insisted that Hugh accompany him to search for porcelain and silk, loath to leave him with Olivia in case he was tempted to take her ashore alone. The silk warehouse was a long, low building, crammed from floor to ceiling with bolts of silk in every colour of the rainbow and every shade between. There was also patterned silk that Sam initially thought was printed but on closer inspection the pattern was woven with different coloured threads. Sophia's shop used a great deal of silk, she wanted very delicate silk for nightwear and undergarments, medium weight for dresses and heavy silk for curtains, cushions and coats. Sam ordered every colour and weight and pattern, twice as much as he used to buy, hoping that he would have enough to deliver to London after Sophia had made her choice. Then he found twenty cases of the very popular blue and white porcelain from China.

The lengthy, overlapping call to prayer woke Hugh each morning at five. Olivia, and it seemed to him, everyone else stayed asleep. He rose quietly and went up on deck. By the time Sam had emerged from his prayers, Hugh had been lured down the gangplank by an excited vender offering a steaming cup of tea. He had drunk the tea and been sold, at an extravagant price, a bad-tempered, razor-toothed monkey in a gold brocade vest, complete with pus-filled eyes and fleas. Sam shook his head wearily and grasping the monkey by the scruff of the neck, marched it from the ship and flung the screeching animal at the vendor. He made no attempt to obtain a refund for Hugh, hoping he would learn a valuable lesson.

'I would be grateful if you did not tell Olivia about that.' Hugh murmured, looking distinctly sheepish.

'Not tell Olivia about what?' she said, approaching with cups of tea.

'Erm.' Muttered Hugh.

Sam snorted with laughter and wandered away to a safe distance with his tea.

'Well. What.' She demanded impatiently.

'Erm.' he repeated.

Hugh, sorely embarrassed, told her about the monkey and that Sam had thrown it back to the vendor and she laughed so much she had to put down her tea. Hugh, red in the face, went below deck for a sulk, trying to get far enough away to be unable to hear his wife and her uncle laughing.

By the time Hugh emerged later, everyone aboard knew about the monkey and finally, Hugh was able to put on a brave face and smile. The situation was exacerbated by the subsequent actions of the frantic vendor, who attempted desperately to return the filthy creature to Hugh whenever he ventured ashore. It was hilarious for a day or so, but eventually Sam, flanked by his nephews, grabbed the vendor by the throat and threatened to throw both him and his monkey in the sea.

Olivia wanted to visit the hamam, the bathhouse that her grandmother had visited when she was first married. Ever since she had heard the story as a child, she had made it one of her wishes. Sam had also heard the story from his father, about how swiftly the news of the white woman with amethyst eyes had spread around the city. He told Olivia she could go on the day before they sailed and to be on the safe side, he gave a generous donation to the Imam of a nearby mosque, in exchange for the services of his two middle-aged sisters who would escort and chaperone Olivia. The next day, the whole family, even Khalid, went ashore to go to the market. Sam bought a vast quantity of Turkish delight in various flavours, a favourite delicacy at home. Olivia found bedspreads that she simply had to have for the new house and more, lanterns. These were unlike the ones from Morocco, these were like blue and purple glass jars with metal rims and suspended on long brass chains.

Then Olivia found the jewellery section and persuaded Hugh to buy a significant quantity of bracelets and necklaces for the family at home. Inspired, Khalid purchased a sapphire necklace for Elizabeth. Sam had to hire a cart to transport the goods back to the ship after Olivia had finished at the wall-hanging section, the rug section and a further visit to the lanterns.

The following day, Sam escorted Hugh and Olivia on a journey around the mosques and palaces of the city. Hugh was enthralled by the vibrant colours of the ceramic tiles and the mosaics made from pure gold, as bright as the day they were made, which in some cases was several hundred years ago. They climbed to the top of the highest minaret for a panoramic view of the city. Olivia wanted to buy some ceramic tiles for the new house, requiring another cart to transport two crates of enormous weight back to the ship and Sam, remembering taking his sister Rose to sea, and the chaos that ensued, vowed that this would be the last time he allowed a woman on his ship.

In the morning, the Imam's sisters arrived to take Olivia to the hamam, Sam and the twins went with Hugh, as by now, nobody was willing to let him ashore alone. They sailed the following day to Sam's great relief. Hugh stood at the stern of the ship and watched Constantinople slowly disappear from sight, believing it to be the most beautiful city in the world. They stopped briefly at Crete for fresh water and supplies as they sailed westward towards home. Sam discouraged any unnecessary trips ashore, in case Olivia found anything heavy. A day and a half later, out of sight of land, Olivia felt uncharacteristically sick. They all heard a low rumbling sound and the whole vessel shuddered and several minutes later, the ship was lifted by a huge swell, followed by others, gradually reducing in size. The ship lurched and rolled and Olivia was sick over the side. Crete had suffered a violent earthquake and Olivia was carrying her first child, two facts that nobody aboard the ship was aware of.

Chapter 22

Mrs Lyle missed her mother acutely. She had not expected to, they had never been particularly close. But during the last year or so, she had been her only company, her entire family having deserted her. She had always assumed that her children would marry and bring up their families under her roof and that the nannies would present the children, clean and polite, each evening before bedtime. She had imagined taking walks in the grounds of the estate with her daughters and her daughter-in-law. She would have organised splendid weddings and christenings and be the envy of the county and beyond. Now all she had was a weekly visit from Mustapha, whom she was reluctantly fond of. He conveyed messages from her daughters inviting her to visit, which she declined.

She sent messages inviting them, but Annie was scared to go alone and Elizabeth had not seen her mother since the day of Hugh's wedding, when she had fainted after meeting Khalid. The weather had not helped the situation, some weeks the snow even deterred Mustapha from making the journey and she knew how busy the sick house kept him. So she sat in her room, drank brandy and tried to forget it all.

Grandy divided his time between supervising the progress at the new house, where he got in the way of the men who knew exactly what they were doing. The rest of his time he spent with Gabriel and the horses. Gabriel's sons, Charles and Aziz had taken on the hard work, leaving their father and Grandy to reminisce about their favourite horses. They sat for hours in the stables next to the hot stove and savoured the smell of warm horse, steamy breath, flatulence and the taste of a nip of brandy from Grandy's hip flask in their tea. That afternoon they awaited the return of the two, brown and white heavy horses, employed to transport firewood to the village green. They heard the steady thump of their hooves at least a minute before they arrived, snorting and steaming, their long feathers of hair caked with snow and ice. Gabriel and Grandy unhitched them and they plodded heavily into the warm stable, their nostrils steaming like dragons, acknowledging the other horses with a soft whinny. Their backs were dripping wet with melted snow and sweat and Gabriel rubbed them down with handfuls of dry straw until they stopped steaming, indicating that their thick hair was dry, then brushed them with a stiff brush to remove the dust and bits of straw whilst Grandy poured the hot water into their buckets of bran to make their favourite bran mash. They nuzzled at Grandy's pockets in search of a carrot or an apple. He stroked their faces as they crunched the carrots. Gabriel brushed the ice from their feathers, paying particular attention to the back of their hooves, under their thick feathers. He washed the area and dried it thoroughly and finally spread it with an oily ointment to prevent mud fever, a remedy made by old Mustapha when Gabriel was a young man. Then he brushed their and tails and slapped their shoulders.

'Good boys.'

They rumbled in reply and smacked their lips as they ate their warm mash.

Sophia's little shop remained very busy and although she continued to visit regularly, it functioned perfectly well without her, so she went upstairs to her cousin George and asked him to prepare papers for the workers, so they could run the shop as a cooperative. Esther visited George monthly with the order book and he kept a record of their purchases and sales. He had grown fond of the quiet, unassuming, intelligent young woman who was as meticulous with figures as she was at her needlework, and he was overcome by a feeling of loss and sadness. She had often presented him with a new handkerchief with his initials embroidered in the corner. She was due to visit the following week and George vowed that he would offer his future services as a bookkeeper, despite her being eminently capable of the task. Deep down, he really wanted to ask her to be his wife.

Esther arrived the following week, covered in snowflakes and shivering. George had seen her through the window and had a pot of hot tea and warm biscuits waiting for her. He had asked his mother to make the biscuits and fidgeted around in the kitchen choosing cups, filling the best sugar bowl and searching for a clean tray cloth. Rose made the biscuits and wondered what had got into him. Sophia joined them and presented Esther with the papers and announced that she and her four compatriots were now the owners of the shop. Esther burst into tears and George, alarmed gave her his handkerchief. It was one that she had made and she cried harder. Sophia assumed these were tears of utter happiness, gave her a hug, called her a silly thing and left. George poured the tea and held Esther's hand and reminded her what a wonderful opportunity this was for her and her colleagues. They would no longer draw a wage with the odd bonus. They would divide the profits between the five of them each month. Esther calmed down, wiped her eyes and blew her nose. All week long George had rehearsed his offer of remaining bookkeeper for the shop but his courage failed him and he rambled on about the weather. They ate the biscuits and finished the entire pot of tea and when Esther took her leave George was appalled to hear his own inadequate words, wishing her the best of luck.

George watched the tiny vulnerable figure of Esther as she walked across the field, head down against the wind and he grabbed his coat and ran down the stairs. He almost knocked his mother over as he ran out of the door into the snow, leaving the front door swinging open. Rose shut the door. George rarely went outside and never in this weather. She watched from the window as he ran across the field behind Esther. Rose shook her head and assumed that Esther must have left something very important behind.

'Esther!' George shouted against the wind.

She stopped and turned to see George running, his long black curls covered with snowflakes. He intended to ask to be her bookkeeper, he intended to ask if he could walk her to church on Sunday. Instead, he looked into her eyes, fell to his knees and asked her to be his wife. Esther's jaw dropped and she felt a surge of wonder as if all her dreams had come true, she felt the world spin and lost the use of her legs and slumped to her knees on the ground in front of George.

'Yes.' She whispered, praying fervently that she would not awaken in a minute and all of this be a beautiful dream.

Rose squinted through the window at the distant figures that seemed to be sitting in the snow.

'This family!' she muttered and went to prepare lunch.

Several minutes later, George and Esther appeared in the kitchen, hand in hand, snow-caked and grinning like idiots and suddenly it all made sense to Rose who shouted the news to the rest of the family. Esther stayed for lunch, pinching herself, still petrified that she would wake up. George was so proud of himself that he was unable to stop smiling and looking at Esther. Rose gave Esther a sapphire ring, surrounded with amethysts that her father Aziz

Shadi Rashad Salamar Badr al din had given to Lily, George's grandmother.

George braved the weather and walked Esther back to the shop and she was so excited to tell them she was to marry George that she forgot to tell them that they now owned the business. Esther's father had died when she was young and she lived with her widowed mother and younger brothers and sister. They walked to her home and George asked her mother's permission to marry Esther. Flustered, Esther's mother wiped her hands on her apron and curtsied, wobbled and had to sit down.

George ran home across the field, oblivious to the cold. He was so pleased with himself that he occasionally jumped into the air. He was dying to tell someone else, so he ran through the woods to Gabriel's farm, flung his arms around Ellen Lily and told her the news. Then he burst into the stables to tell Gabriel and Grandy who were still talking horses. He lifted Grandy into the air and swung him round.

'I am going to marry Esther!'

It took the family some time to adjust to the new George. Prior to this he had been a quiet man who only ventured downstairs for meals or when Rose prized him from his accounts to share in special occasions. He had spent his days surrounded by ledgers. Twice a year he went to the bank in London, to change currency and gold and make investments. He was the only person who had any idea how much money and assets the family possessed. Now he appeared at odd times, dancing about and hugging people who were least expecting it. It was as though he was making up for years of isolation amongst his books. He even borrowed a horse from Gabriel, so that he could visit Esther every day. The wedding was planned for early summer, when his twin sister and younger brothers would be home from their voyage.

Chapter 23

Sophia was at a loose end having handed the shop over to her protégées. It was early spring, most of the snow had melted and the air was crisp and fresh, so she took one of the horses and rode through the marshes to the sea wall. She rode to the 'point' where the river made a sharp turn to the right on its way from London. The shore smelled refreshingly salty and was littered with driftwood, torn fishing net and the odd boot. She discovered an interesting piece of driftwood, bleached almost white by years of floating about. Joey would make use of that. She lugged the driftwood up the sea wall. Mounting the horse with the driftwood under her arm proved impossible so she tried to tie it to the saddle with her scarf and a piece of string from the shore. She was concentrating and failed to see a man approaching from the marsh. He was a large man with thick curly hair and a bushy beard and he wore a long, thick sheepskin coat. Sophia jumped when she suddenly caught sight of him, just a few yards away.

'Need some help miss?'

'Oh, er. Yes I think I might do.'

'I'm Tom Martin, shepherd from the top farm, Miss.'

'I'm Sophia, from..'

'I know who you are miss, from the big house by the woods. My own father was born in that house over forty years hence.'

'Then we must be related!'

'Indeed we are miss, my great-grandfather William was brother to your great-grandfather John, which makes us third cousins, or something like that.'

'Please don't call me miss as we are cousins, call me Sophia.'

Tom picked up the heavy driftwood as if it were a matchstick and slung it onto his shoulder.

'That's my cottage over there, I can offer you tea if you'd like.'

'Thank you, that would be lovely Tom.'

Sophie led the horse and they walked the half-mile or so to the cottage, surrounded by bleating sheep, hopeful of a new sheaf of hay.

The cottage had an overhanging roof on three sides, two sides sheltered the sheaves of hay and the other side a stock of firewood, which kept the inside surprisingly warm. It was larger inside than Sophia had thought it would be. A large stove crackled in the centre of the room and a kettle sang on the top. Two black and white dogs lay warming their bellies. They jumped up and sniffed her feet and legs. A word from Tom sent them to sit quietly under the table. A variety of pots and cups hung on hooks from the ceiling and a large armchair stood beside the fire. There was a sturdy table and two chairs in the corner and a large bed under a mound of sheepskins. Tom explained that he lived here during most of the wintertime, but when the lambing and shearing was over, he moved to the farm to help out, as sheep didn't require much attention during the summer months. In very bad winters he moved the sheep to the higher ground beside the farm. Tom removed his coat and hung it on a nail at the back of the door and topped up the teapot with boiling water. His arms and shoulders were heavily muscled, from years of manhandling sheep, Sophia assumed. His face was ruddy from years in the fresh air and he had very dark blue eyes that smiled before he did and he smelled of the outdoors, only warmer. She suddenly realised that she was staring at him and quickly began to look around the room. The late afternoon sun shone in the two small windows, casting two beams of light across the room.

'I had best be going, it will be dark soon.'

'I'm going up the village tomorrow for some supplies, I could drop your lump of wood off if you'd like.'

'I couldn't trouble you, really.'

'It would be my pleasure Sophia and no trouble at all, I know the way. Besides, I'd like to pop in and see old Gabriel whilst I'm there.'

Tom lifted the startled Sophia onto her horse and slapped its rump.

'See you tomorrow Sophia.'

'Bye Tom.'

Sophia realised that she was slightly trembling as she trotted up the pathway, after a few minutes, she turned to look back at the cottage and Tom was still standing outside and he had seen her turn and he had waved, as though he knew that she would turn to look back. She felt her face flush and would not allow herself to look back again.

Dinner was about to be served when Sophia arrived home, so she changed her clothes and went downstairs to eat.

'Nice ride today?' asked her mother.

'Yes, very nice.' She answered. 'And, I met a relative.' She added, staring hard at her food as she felt her face redden.

'Who was that?'

'Tom the shepherd, he lives on the marsh and says his father was born in this house.'

'I remember that!' Sal added. 'That was not long after we all moved here and grandfather John thought that old Mustapha was the Lord Jesus Christ!'

'We moved in so that my father could look after him, he cried all night when they baby was born.' Said Maria.

'Why?' asked Sophia, raising her head in surprise.

'Because he believed he was in heaven and that for a baby to arrive, it had to have died on earth!'

Sal and Maria were the only ones able to remember John, Rose was too young to remember much. The rest of the meal was spent relating the more amusing stories, ending with when Grandfather John died of laughter at the kitchen table with Mary, as he was unable to remember what an egg was called.

'Anyway.' Said Sophia. 'Tom is kindly delivering a piece of driftwood I found for Joey, tomorrow at some point.'

Maria and Rose watched her cheeks redden and looked at each other.

'Spring is coming early this year!' chuckled Maria.

Sophia glared at her mother and left the table.

When she woke the following morning, she turned over and peered at the window to gauge the weather through the chink in the curtain. She stretched and relaxed, then jumped up in alarm, thinking that Tom may well be one of those men who rise at daybreak and may already be well on his way. She leapt from her bed to dress, but found it difficult to decide what to wear. She settled on a soft woollen dress in muted green, brushed her long hair till it shone, put on her boots and went downstairs for breakfast. He mother raised an eyebrow and glanced at Rose. Sophia generally appeared in a dressing gown with her hair resembling a bird's nest at this hour.

'Where on earth did you find that old dress?' asked her mother. 'I think it used to be mine!'

The remark sent Sophia back upstairs to change. This time she chose one that Esther had made last year in lavender wool with purple cuffs and hem, with a matching purple shawl.

Isabella was under the weather and failed to come down for breakfast and Mustapha made her a pot of ginger tea to settle her stomach. Mina adjourned to the sewing room with Elizabeth and Annie, she was teaching them to make cushion covers and curtains for the new house. Rose and Maria were in the kitchen preparing vegetables for the lunchtime roast, whispering and giggling. Sophia, attempting to appear nonchalant, shut the kitchen door and stationed herself on a sofa to read a book, where she had a clear view of the front meadow without turning her head. She took deep breaths, she was angry and confused by her churning stomach and her uncharacteristic blushes. She told herself that she was always the calm, confident one and to stop being so silly. Unable to read she put down her book and knelt on the sofa and scanned the meadow and beyond, but there was no sign of Tom, who had come in to the kitchen via the back door and was talking to Rose and Maria who had not seen him since he was a boy. Sophia turned as she heard the kitchen door opened and there was the smiling Tom in his sheepskin coat with a bunch of snowdrops he had gathered on route. Oblivious of her discomfort he strode across the room, handed her the snowdrops and kissed the top of her head.

'Morning Sophia, you are looking very fetching this morning I must say1'

Then he dropped his coat on the floor and sat down in the chair beside the fire and looked around the room. Sophia had not moved, she sat with her mouth open holding the snowdrops.

'Erm, er, would you like tea?' she managed eventually.

'I would indeed, my dear!'

As Sophia walked past him on the way to make tea, he laughed and slapped her firmly across the backside, sending her into the kitchen at an accelerated speed and with a very red face. She leant on the table for support and then sank into a chair, breathing heavily, the snowdrops still in her hand. Maria, stifling her laughter put the snow drops in a vase and Rose put together a tray of tea, biscuits and fruit cake. She put the little vase of snowdrops on the tray and sent her flustered niece to serve Tom's tea. He saw her reddened face.

'Sorry Sophia, I didn't mean to offend you, I just couldn't help myself!'

'That's quite alright, I am not offended in the least.' She heard herself say. 'I was just a little startled.'

'I can't think of anything I'd rather do than startle you!' he laughed, his dark blue eyes smiling into hers and she found it difficult to look away.

They drank their tea in relative silence and Tom ate all of the fruitcake, remarking it was the best he had ever tasted. Sophia returned the empty tray to the kitchen and leant against the table, her Aunt Rose put her arm around her shoulders.

'It was that way when I met your Uncle Paulo Sophia, and when my own mother met your grandfather, it's nothing to fret about, enjoy yourself my love, it's the start of a wonderful adventure!'

'Sophia!' Tom shouted from the other room, 'Where do you want me to deliver this lump of old wood?'

Maria squeezed her daughter's hand and smiled. Sophia smiled back, gathered all the strength she could muster and shouted.

'I'll show you!'

Tom retrieved the wood and slung it on his shoulder and the couple walked along the well-worn path to the new house. Tom put his arm around Sophia's shoulder and looked down into her face with a grin. A short time later she threw caution to the wind and slid her arm around his waist. They walked in silence, arm in arm to the new house, a journey which neither one wanted to reach the end of.

Joey was delighted with his wood, he propped it against the wall and studied it while Sophia showed Tom Joey's carvings. Tom was impressed and promised to keep an eye open for any decent lumps of wood washed up on the shore. Sophia invited Tom to stay for lunch, after which they could go through the woods to Gabriel's farm.

Lunch was roasted beef, roasted parsnips and potatoes, carrots and greens with a peppery gravy and fresh horseradish. Tom managed two helpings and finished the meal with a resounding belch.

'I do beg your pardon!' he said with a laugh.

Tom chased Sophia through the woods on the way to Gabriel's, caught her quickly and slung her over his shoulder and ran the rest of the way with her squealing with laughter. Gabriel was surprised to see him and even more surprised to see him carrying the flushed, unusually dishevelled Sophia.

Sophia sat with Grandy in the stables while Gabriel and Tom went to look at the horses. Ellen Lily made hot chocolate and when she saw the look exchanged between Sophia and Tom when he joined them in the kitchen, she knew another wedding was not far off.

'The sheep are about to start lambing any day now.' Tom said on the way back through the woods. 'So I'll be a trifle busy for a while, you could come and watch if you'd fancy.'

'I would love to, I could bring a pie or something to save you cooking.'

'That's settled then.' Tom kissed her hand, sending shivers up her arm and into her belly.

Sophia watched him walk home across the meadow with the rest of the fruitcake in his pocket and she wanted to run after him. She had only known this man for a day and yet it was as if she had known him forever. When he was out of sight she collapsed into the chair beside the fire, the chair he had sat on and stared into the fire.

Next morning Sophia was up early, worrying her mother and aunt to help her make a pie to take to Tom, as she was going lambing with him.

'Wear something old then, lambing is a messy job!'

Two hours later Sophia was trotting across the marshes, dressed in her brother's discarded pair of baggy trousers and long shirt, her grandmother's old coat and a pie wrapped in a blanket. Tom laughed at her attire and slapped her backside as she bent over to put the pie beside the stove to keep warm. This time she chased him outside, threatening to slap him. Two lambs had been born the day before, but so far none had arrived today. Tom showed her the signs to look out for in the ewes, indicating they were about to lamb. They became restless and often sidled off to be alone. The lamb would follow the first moving thing it saw, the ewe knew this, so she would endeavour to find a little privacy. Some ewes had only one lamb, most had two, occasionally, one had three. Three lambs were too many to care for and the third was often hand reared or disguised and given to another ewe with a stillborn or only one lamb. Sophia circumvented the large marsh, paying particular attention to the ewes standing beside the short horny hedges. She shouted to Tom when she saw what appeared to be a lamb emerging. By the time he reached her, the lamb had landed in a slippery, steaming heap on the grass. Tom cleared its face and rubbed it hard with a handful of grass, it raised its head and he pushed it under the ewe's nose, who startled to sniff and lick it dry. A few minutes later, another lamb slid to the ground with a plopping sound, but failed to raise its head and Tom lifted it by the back feet and swung it to and fro like a pendulum until he felt the life in it and then he laid it at the ewes feet for her to clean. Sophia watched him work and was impressed. There were no more lambs that afternoon and Tom had the feeling that tomorrow the ewes would make up for the lull by all giving birth at once, which was the usual contrary way of sheep.

Tom and Sophia sat together on the doorstep, shoulder to shoulder and watched the sheep whilst they ate a slice of pie and drank their tea.

'I don't suppose a beautiful rich woman, such as yourself, would ever consider marrying such person as a shepherd?'

'Ah, don't you be so sure Tom, I think she may jump at the chance!'

Tom put his arm around Sophia and hugged her, kissing the top of her head. She could feel his heart thudding as she leant against his chest and knew she had come home. He kissed her for the first time when she was about to leave, she was intoxicated by his warm, earthy smell, her legs turned to jelly and she felt herself blissfully dissolve. That evening, she looked back countless times, he was always still there, waving to her or dancing around wildly, scattering the sheep.

Chapter 24

The normally smooth, relaxed routine at the big house abruptly descended in chaos interrupted by periods of sheer calamity. Carts carrying sofas, previously ordered by Olivia for the new house arrived at unexpected intervals, coinciding with Big Ern and Harry delivering tables, chests, cupboards and chairs, made in the workshop. Joey was disturbed from his carving by Mina who was trying desperately to put up curtains with the assistance of Elizabeth and Annie, neither one famous for their practical skills. Sophia had taken to rising early, rushing out before breakfast, leaving the kitchen in various degrees of messy disarray, dependent on how successful her efforts had been. Isabella was expecting her third child and suffering from severe sickness, resulting in Mustapha dashing to and from the sick house, which was short of staff following the birth of Eva Violet. The chaos drove Big Ern, Beth and the baby back to his mother's for some peace. Little Mustapha and Bella Mary were relieved to go to school. Rose and Maria divided their time between the houses, cleaning and cooking, making up the numerous beds in the new house, tacking yards of brightly coloured silks and natural calico to the bare walls, sweeping up behind Joey who left a trail of wood chippings and sawdust wherever he went. Sal was tasked with keeping the bathhouse fires alight, so that Sophia, who arrived home each night, dead tired and plastered with sheep debris could collapse into a hot bath. Paulo busied himself at the new house giving the final polish to the new furniture. Then, as evening arrived, Rose and Maria would serve the meal to the distracted family, who ate whilst making mental lists of what needed to be done tomorrow. Grandy, who had kept out of the way at Gabriel's during the day valiantly tackled the vast piles of washing up. Bella Mary helped him dry it and put it away, whilst the exhausted Rose and Maria dozed beside the fire.

By the time the ewes had all given birth, Sophia had learned to swing a lamb, help pull out the stubborn ones, skin the dead ones and stretch the tiny, bloody fleeces on to the orphans. On the first Sunday after the lambing, Tom arrived unexpectedly, squeezed uncomfortably into his only formal clothes, his curly hair washed and brushed and his beard neatly trimmed. Sophia hardly recognised him. He had come to ask Paulo for her hand in marriage, although, if the truth was known, he had already laid claim to rather more of Sophia than her hand, and rather more than her father would have approved of.

A week later, the new house was almost ready for the return of Olivia and Hugh. Grandy and his daughters moved in and three young village girls were hired as live in help and a more mature woman given the job of cook. The girls set about lighting fires and airing the house, opening the doors to dilute the overpowering smell of Paulo's polish. Mina fiddled about with cushions and rugs until she was satisfied with the colour combinations. The main sitting room was purple with vibrant cerise and Hugh and Olivia's bedroom was purple and shades of soft pink. Grandy's room was deep red. Elizabeth let Annie choose the colour of their room, as she would be moving back to the big house after her marriage to Khalid. Annie settled on a soft shade of lavender blue and a dark blue. The dramatic tree room, Joey's greatest achievement, was to be the dining room. The walls were natural calico and the curtains a pale sage green and one wall was covered with a large wall hanging in numerous shades of green that had been in the attic at the big house for years, due to nobody ever having found a suitable place for it.

After the frantic rushing to get the house finished, a prolonged anti-climax enveloped the family, interrupted by periods of excruciating impatience and in Elizabeth's case, a dread that the ship had sank. Apart from rough seas slowing their journey when they left the Mediterranean, their trip home was uneventful. By the time they sailed into the estuary on a bright, early April morning, it had dawned on Olivia that she was expecting a child. Sophia noticed the familiar masts moving slowly up the river as she approached Tom's cottage and together they walked around the sea wall to see the ship dock at the jetty. Khalid was off the ship first and he confiscated Sophia's horse without even introducing himself to Tom was and rode off at a gallop to find Elizabeth. Olivia was puzzled to see her cousin in the arms of a large man draped in sheepskin with straw in his hair. She pushed Hugh to speed his progress down the gangplank in her rush to find out who on earth he was and to tell her cousin her own news.

'This is Tom.' Shouted Sophia anticipating her question. 'He is my future husband!' Olivia valiantly tried to compose her face.

'How do you do?' she held out her hand.

'Much better than I used to, I must say!' Tom answered with a broad smile, squeezing Sophia and kissing the hand of Olivia, who was so busy figuring out where Sophia could possibly have found him, she almost forgot her news.

Feeling embarrassed, Olivia tried to whisper her news to Sophia, but Tom heard.

'Well, congratulations ma'am, you didn't waste any time!'

Olivia's face reddened.

'Please, call me Olivia.'

Hugh arrived. He looked well, his pale face had tanned from the sun and wind and his fair hair had lightened, he looked happy and relaxed and greeted both Sophia and Tom with a recently acquired uninhibited warmth.

Khalid's unforeseen arrival in the big house kitchen, causing Elizabeth to drop her biscuit into her teacup, alerted the rest of the family to the imminent arrival of the rest of the family. Mass excitement, anticipation and a small amount of trepidation spread throughout the entire family. Grandy, Annie, Rose and George rushed to the new house to arrange the welcoming committee. Rose swept up the wood shavings from around Joey's feet and confiscated his hammer and chisel. Then they waited, fidgeting with excitement for the cart to arrive. Olivia had insisted of having most of her purchases loaded on to the cart, so it took some time, by which time the family and new help had got bored and made a large pot of tea and were sitting on the grass outside of the new house, listening to Rose argue with Joey concerning the current whereabouts of his hammer and chisel when the cart finally arrived.

Once the initial greetings and hugs, and the news of expected babies and this year's surprise marriages were done with, it was decided that Joey should show the couple around the new house as he was responsible for the most unusual aspects. The rest of the family followed at a safe distance, trepidation levels high. The large spiral staircase dominated the entrance hall and took the couples breath away, so Joey escorted them up the stairs, pointing out the lilies and the ropes. The family remained in the hallway whilst they wandered through bedrooms, cherub faces peered down from the beams and small animals poked their heads out of the skirting boards. Joey was so busy pointing things out, and even more keen to get the couple back downstairs, he failed to notice their stunned silence.

Joey ran down the stairs, followed slowly by Hugh and Olivia. The family jostled out of the way as he escorted them to the purple and cerise living room with flowers and vines entwining the fireplace and beams. Joey saved his proudest accomplishment for last, the tree room. He flung open the door and ushered them in. His impressive tree with its gnarled branches supporting the ceiling stopped them both in their tracks. The two windows contained a mixture of clear glass and blue glass squares, which gave the impression of a blue sky in all weathers. Joey flung open the heavy double doors, dotted with panes of pale blue glass, that opened on to the gardens, to reveal the woods with its timely seasonal majesty…. a carpet of bluebells.

Olivia threw her arms around Joey and burst into tears.

'Don't you like it?' he cried in disbelief.

'Joey, I absolutely love it, it will be like living inside a fairy tale!'

'Good, because Aunt Rose has hidden my hammer and chisel because I keep making a mess and I don't know where they are! And, I was halfway through a horse on the upstairs landing!'

'Mother!' shouted Olivia. 'Give this extraordinary, gifted man his tools back!'

Rose scuttled off and returned with the hammer and chisel.

'Make as much mess as you like Joey and thank you for a wonderful house!'

Joey skipped up the stairs to continue with his horse, and Mina, who had been there for the last few minutes almost burst with pride.

That evening, the entire family gathered at the long table in the tree room, made by Harry, Big Ern and their chippies. The table seated twenty-six, and by the time Nellie the cook and the three village girls, Daisy, Ellen and Vera joined them for lamb stew, dumplings and hot, fresh bread, there was only one vacant seat. Olivia made a mental note to order six more chairs from Richards Brothers.

Chapter 25

Everyone decided that a triple wedding, in early June deemed be the best idea. Both George and Sophia would have preferred quiet weddings with no fuss, but that was not possible in this village. Nobody in the village was at all surprised that the glamorous Sophia was marrying a shepherd, or that George was marrying a seamstress, or that Khalid was marrying an heiress from the richest family in the county. The villagers were accustomed to the colourful, generous family who flouted convention. They just looked forward to the celebrations.

The new owners of the shop voted to keep the name above the door in honour of their benefactor. They were busy making wedding dresses. Frank and Jack measured Tom and set about designing and making him an outfit that was both smart and comfortable. Tom didn't care what colour it would be and left it up to the tailors. Frank decided on pale greyish-brown tweed for the jacket, with a slightly darker waistcoat and an ivory silk shirt. Sophia chose ivory stain for her dress. Esther opted for pale blue silk and Elizabeth chose a deep violet blue silk, to match the necklace Khalid had brought her from Constantinople.

The big house was crowded and it was decided that following the weddings, Khalid and Elizabeth would live at the new house, due to there being spare rooms there. George hired two village girls to help Rose and Maria with the mammoth task of providing meals for everyone. The girls, Helen and Amy moved into the room overlooking the stables, occupied by Gabriel when he was a young man.

Sophia had been one of the glut of four babies all born within days of each other. As a tiny girl, as soon as she could toddle, she had voted with her feet and escaped from the mayhem, preferring the company of her quiet older brother. She would follow him and watch him carefully tending to the poppies in the garden and sit with him and granddaddy Mustapha in the tree house. During the pandemonium of family celebrations, when the gang of small children became riotous, Sophia and Mustapha would creep upstairs to the tranquillity of granddaddy and Mary's sitting room, where they quietly squeezed themselves into the two armchairs beside Mary and Mustapha in front of the little fire. Sophia had never felt so safe and happy as when she was curled up beside either one of them. They both smelled the same, like warm herbs, although Mary was a great deal softer. Sophia experienced that same, safe, peaceful sensation when she sat close to Tom, on the doorstep of his little cottage, watching the sheep. Her eyes filled with tears as she remembered just how much she loved that old couple and how much she still missed them. Instinctively, Tom tightened his hold on her and kissed the top of her head, just as Mary would have done when she was a child.

Maria was horrified when Sophia told her not to bother to prepare her room for her wedding night. She intended to spend it in Tom's cottage on the marshes. Maria sought the support of Rose to persuade Sophia, but Rose, remembering how she felt when she had fallen in love with Paulo, sided with Sophia and it was settled.

The day of the wedding dawned sunny and warm. The big house was buzzing with excitement. Emily and Sally delivered the wedding dresses to Sophia and Elizabeth and then took Esther's dress to her home and stayed to help her dress. Frank delivered Tom's new clothes and found him sweeping, beating rugs, arranging flowers in old cups and generally tidying his cottage. Frank waited until he was finished and then helped him to dress. Tom was impressed with his outfit, as comfortable as his old work-clothes but a great deal more stylish.

The entire village, dressed in their best, had assembled itself outside the church for the weddings.

Khalid and George had arrived first and were waiting in the front pew. Tom grinned and nodded to the congregation who stared at him as he walked up the aisle. Khalid and Elizabeth were to be married first and she arrived, blushing, her hair piled up and decorated with blue silk flowers and she carried a bunch of purple poppies and forget-me-nots. Her mother did not attend the wedding but she sent her apologies, her best wishes and a large parcel of beautiful bed linen. The next to arrive was the dainty little Esther in her pale blue silk, her fair hair brushed loose and reaching her slim waist, trying not to show how terrified she was. She carried a bunch of white poppies and Rose had woven a simple crown of white poppies and forget-me-nots for her head. She took George's breath away as she walked towards him, looking so fragile and delicate he wanted to protect her for the rest of their lives. The two newly married couples sat side by side holding hands, and Tom took his place to wait for Sophia's entrance. She thought he looked like a country gentleman in his new clothes, his unruly rust-brown curls brushed and shining, as she entered the church. He turned to see her as she approached up the aisle. She wore a simple, elegant ivory satin dress that accentuated her creamy skin and her virtually black eyes, eyebrows and long ringlets that hung loose over her shoulders and down her back. She carried no flowers and her only adornment was a solitary white poppy pinned behind her ear. Tom was mesmerised. She smiled broadly and he returned her smile. Tom winked at her when they were pronounced man and wife, not a moment too soon, as she was already carrying his child.

The couples left the church, met by the cheers of the villagers unable to get inside the crowded church and the long, disorganised procession meandered its way to the big house meadow, on carts, horseback and on foot. The spits had been alight since daybreak and the smell of slowly roasted lamb and beef welcomed the hungry guests. The mounds of bread dough rising under the damp cloths went into the large ovens, along with trays of potatoes. The musicians chose their spot at the edge of the meadow and began to play.

Sophia took Tom up into the tree house with a pot of tea and they watched as little Esther was inundated with gifts and hugs from the village women as she strolled around the meadow with her new husband, finally beginning to accept that this was not all just a wonderful dream. Rose delivered two large platefuls of meat, hot bread, crispy potatoes and a jug of peppery gravy to Sophia and Tom when she noticed they were up in the tree house. She kissed them both and told them she had packed two bags of necessities and put them on a cart beside the stables, ready for when they wanted to leave.

'Thank you so much Aunt Rose.' Sophia whispered, and hugged her warmly, grateful for her sensitivity and uncanny insight.

Tom consumed everything that Sophia left on her plate, too full to eat anymore, and long before the bonfire and fireworks began, they had hitched a horse to the cart and driven off to the cottage on the marshes, Sophia still wearing her wedding dress. Tom made her wait outside the cottage for a minute or two and then lifted her and carried her inside. She was touched by the effort he had made. The flowers in the old cups, the dozens of lit candles and the strong aroma of jasmine, secretly given to him by Aunt Rose to ward off the smell of warm dog.

The couple went for a walk along the seawall to watch the sunset and they discussed the house they would build, nearer to the village, just beyond where the worst floods had ever reached. It would have a big fireplace, an upper floor and a bathhouse and enough room for a big brood of children.

Rose had packed one bag with cold meat, cheese, bread, pickles, jams, biscuits and fruitcake. In the other bag she had packed three dresses, a coat, hairbrush, soap, towels and two beautiful nightgowns that she had made for Sophia. One was in a fine cream silk with white embroidery and the other one was deep violet, embroidered with a solitary white poppy. Sophia made Tom look away as she changed into the cream nightgown. When he turned to look his hands began to tremble and he took her in his arms and they remained in the cottage for over a week, rarely emerging and never venturing further than the seawall.

Chapter 26

Olivia commandeered the services of Joey, who had a good eye for design, to help her position her new wall hangings and dozens of coloured lanterns around the house. Elizabeth thought she should choose a room suitable for a nursery, but Olivia curtly remarked that a baby's place was in bed with its mother or in a cradle next to her bed! This proved to be an early indication that the relationship between Olivia and Elizabeth would not run smoothly.

Isabella sickness had passed and the family began to look forward to the two new additions, calculated to arrive during August and September.

Hunger finally forced Sophia and Tom out of the cottage and up to the big house for a decent meal and to return the disgruntled horse subjected to a surfeit of curious sheep and hyperactive lambs. Rose watched the two very different couples at dinner. George and Esther's relationship still retained an awkward timidity, in stark constant to the easy, unrestrained, immodest display of affection between Tom and Sophia. Rose considered the strange phenomenon that is love. For some couples, like her son George and his wife, they had gradually developed a regard for the other. A quiet, unspoken affection grew gently, without either of them speaking of it. They chose caution and neither dared to disclose their feelings. Rose smiled, were it not for Sophia giving the shop away, thereby ending the need for them to meet, they would have continued to meet monthly and dream quietly, possibly for years! Sometimes, love is a sudden seismic explosion, a passion that disregards all circumstances and dissolves good sense! That had been the way for her when she met Paulo. She would have given up everything to be with him and she loved him as much today as she did then. Her mother Lily had experienced both. With Aziz Shadi Rashad Salamar Badr al din it had been an all-consuming passion and in later life, the gentler variety of love with her cousin Joseph. Watching Sophia and Tom, she was reminded of the way her own parents were when she was a child.

After the meal Sophia brought up the subject of the house they wanted to build and Sam offered the services of the carpenters on the ship. George explained that the family owned the swathe of land between the bottom of Pond Hill, containing the upper marshes and Tom's family owned the marshes from there to the seawall, so they were free to choose their spot. He offered to send word to the stonemasons, so that they could begin the foundations, chimney and bathhouse. Joey got very excited when Sophia asked him to help with the design as he had exhausted the patience of even Olivia with his wood chippings. Tom wanted some driftwood in the house, as it had been a piece of old driftwood that had been responsible for bringing him and Sophia together.

 The following morning Sophia and Tom were on the marshes walking to and fro deciding where they wanted the house and Joey was on the shore dragging promising lengths of salt water preserved timber and stacking it on the seawall. Tom and Sophia settled on a nice even patch of grass beside a thicket, not a hundred feet from the ditch where the newly born Isabella would been buried alive, had it not been for the kindness of a young man named Joshua. Tom marked out the foundations with sticks and string and the couple stood together in what would become their living room and tried to imagine what it would be like. During the next few weeks, carts arrived laden with rocks, sacks of mortar, bricks, slates and slabs of stone. Labourers dug foundations and a well. By July, the foundations and well were completed and the large central chimney was growing taller. Joey was in the woods making wattle and daub panels to insulate the building that would be brick built on the ground floor and timber built above. Sophia was so impressed by Joey's ability to understand and interpret what she wanted and even more impressed by his own ideas, far superior to hers, and it must be said she had become slightly bored with the whole process of house building, that she told him to do what he thought best and returned to spend her days with Tom and the sheep. Tom cooked delicious lamb stews on the stove. In July she felt the baby move.

Joey had been a strange child, a constant source of frustration for his father and a constant heartache for his mother. Mina loved him so much and it had pained her to see his restless discomfort, his constant failures and the teasing that he suffered. He had at last found his place and was in demand and a calmer, smiling Joey emerged. He spent his time carefully explaining plans to the builders, searching Harry and Big Ern's workshop for just the right piece of wood for carving. Some nights he failed to go home, working by candlelight until hunger and fatigue overtook him and he arrived in the kitchen of the big house, covered in sawdust, in search of food and fell asleep at the table. Mina fussed around him, preparing food and a hot bath. Left to his own devices, Joey's imagination held no bounds. He designed a large fire grate, festooned with horse-chestnut leaves, to stand below the stone chimney and took it to the forge, where Amos and his father's considerable skills were not found wanting and they relished the challenge. So Joey asked them to make an elegant circular chandelier to hold ten candles, which would hang from the ceiling. He had then make a number of hooks to attach to the ceiling so the chandelier could be moved around. Joey, impressed by their workmanship, ordered two more chandeliers to save the bother of moving them. The cooking range was placed along the far right wall of the building in the large ground floor room. At the other end, a staircase led up to a mezzanine floor, supported by carved trees with carved ivy growing up and twisting around the balustrade that ran the length of the room. The bed was housed up there, warmed by the stone chimney. The large four-poster bed, with its supporting poles carved like ropes was hung with heavy, natural coloured wool curtains, decorated with large appliqued poppies in black and purple, the work of Esther. The bed was covered with a bedspread made of eight sheepskins, a patchwork of all the shades of sheep, from cream to dark brown. The interior walls were covered with natural calico. The floors were of limed oak. A table and six chairs stood below the mezzanine floor in the far right corner. Sophia had ordered two large sofas and two armchairs in brown leather and she and Tom arrived to see them, but Joey refused to let them in to look, insisting that it was almost complete and he wanted it to be a surprise. Sophia hugged Joey, and she and Tom made their way home, wondering what he had done. The bathhouse was built at the rear of the house, accessed by a door in the far left corner, where Joey put the sofas and he stood the two armchairs beside the fire. Harry and Big Ern carried the big front door, complete with impressive hinges that swirled across the width of the door and would not have been out of place on a cathedral, made by Amos. They hung the door and fitted the latch while Joey hopped about with unconcealed excitement. For the final touches, Joey elicited the help of his mother and Esther. They raided the attic at the big house, unearthing the carved wooden chests of various sizes that Sophia's grandfather had brought back from his voyages that would provide good storage space. They found a very large rug with black and blue stripes. They raided the kitchen, looking for redundant pots and pans and Rose gave them a crate of Chinese porcelain. They collected the all the purple and blue cushions from Sophia's old room, folded most of her remaining clothes and put them in the trunks. They lugged her black lacquered dressing table down the stairs. Then they went to the new house and pleaded with Olivia for half a dozen coloured glass lanterns. Mina, Esther and Joey piled the goods onto the cart and set off to the house. The leaded glass panels had arrived and Joey fitted them into the window frames whilst Esther and his mother unloaded the cart and arranged to pots and pans and crockery on the shelves, long planks of wood supported by randomly shaped pieces of driftwood. Joey hung the coloured lantern from the large wooden starfish, carved from bleached driftwood attached to the ceiling above the table. Esther helped him carry the dressing table upstairs and Mina busied herself arranging cushions and unrolled the large rug that ended up under the two armchairs beside the fire.

Joey was finally satisfied, Mina was so very proud and Esther, who loved Sophia dearly, was glad she could help. Unable to contain their shared excitement, Joey set off with the cart to collect Sophia and Tom, leaving his mother and Esther to light the numerous candles for maximum effect.

Mina and Esther stood outside on the two steps that led up to the front door, a safety measure insisted upon by Joey in case a flood ever reached as far as the house, and watched impatiently for the cart. Joey had found the couple walking the seawall and shouted that their house was ready for their inspection. Mina had lit the fire and put the kettle on to boil. Sophia was off the cart before it had stopped and she ran into the house, followed by the dogs, then out again like a whirlwind to grab Tom and push him inside. Joey stood outside and waited for a response. Sophia jumped down the steps and grabbed Joey and kissed him and hugged him.

'Joey!' She said breathlessly. 'It is so perfect!' and ran back inside, then out again and invited him and his mother and Esther inside.

Tom stood with his hands on his hips and looked around his new home and was lost for words. He flung his arms around the startled Joey and almost squeezed the life out of him and Joey assumed he liked it. Mina made the tea and carried it to the table. Sophia was upstairs admiring the poppies on the bed drapes that she recognised as the work of Esther. Mina called her for tea. She joined them eventually, dragging herself away from so many wonderful things to look at, her eyes shining and brimming with tears.

Chapter 27

The August harvest, gathered intermittently, due to the unstable weather, was almost complete when the major storm threatened. The towering black clouds built above the dark estuary and the farm labourers hurried their sweating horses, pulling heavily loaded carts with the last of the crops into the shelter of the barns. Gabriel called his horses into their stables. The village women called their children indoors. The air was hot and humid and Olivia was particularly grumpy. She had had enough of her pregnancy, her legs were swollen and she was constantly tired, but unable to sleep well due to the sticky heat and her back had been aching for days. She was impatient with Hugh, who was accustomed to this from own mother and so, like his father before him, gave Olivia a wide berth, which made matters worse. Annie, the placid one, coped with the situation by giving in to Olivia, but Elizabeth was fed up with it. She complained to Khalid, expecting him to have words with his cousin. Khalid, horrified by the very thought of tackling the presently dangerously volatile Olivia, failed to do so, causing friction between him and Elizabeth. Grandy escaped from the tense atmosphere and spent his time with the peaceful Gabriel. Consequently, when Olivia's pains began with a vengeance, coinciding with the first clap of thunder and torrential downpour, nobody heard her shouting for assistance. Scared and tearful, Olivia slowly made her way, between pains, along the landing, down the spiral staircase and out to the kitchen at the back of the house. The three village girls were under the kitchen table and Nellie the cook jumped up as Olivia struggled into the room, sobbing and shaking. Nelly sent one of the reluctant wide-eyed girls to find Hugh. She returned with Khalid, as Hugh was nowhere to be found. The bathhouse fires were unlit and there was no wood ready to light them with, due to the lack of foresight of the inhabitants of the new house. Nellie sent Khalid to the big house for help. He arrived like a drowned rat at the back door and dripped into the kitchen. Mustapha was at the sick house and unlikely to return until the storm had passed. When Rose discovered that the fires were unlit and nothing was ready for the birth, her initial thought was to bring her daughter home, but in this storm it would be a nightmare journey. She sent Paulo for dry wood from the stables and he ran ahead to light the bathhouse fires. Isabella gave Rose the remedies and explained which ones to administer and how to measure the amounts and said she would send Mustapha as soon as he arrived. Rose and Maria, who had assisted at several births set off to the new house, clutching each other when the thunder clapped above them, convinced they would be struck by the lightening before they reached the new house. Olivia was in a state of frantic panic by the time they arrived. Nellie had had the foresight to make tea and Rose immediately gave Olivia the first remedy and a cup of hot tea. Olivia continued to thrash around on the chair, shouting for Hugh. Her panic gradually subsided as the remedy took effect and then she just cried. Rose moved her to a sofa in the sitting room and Annie sat with her whilst Rose and Maria stood in puddles of water in the kitchen and drank a welcome cup of tea.

Paulo had the fires well alight and the two largest pans on to boil. Nellie dragged out the largest pans she could find and put them on the range to heat up. The storm raged overhead, eliciting squeals of terror from the village girls who resorted to the shelter of the table, ignoring threats from Nellie. It was not long before Olivia began screaming again as the strong pains broke through the remedy and Rose gave her the stronger dose and prayed that Mustapha would be here soon. Olivia cried for Hugh, who was blissfully oblivious of the drama, sitting in the stables with Grandy and Gabriel, drinking tea laced with brandy and shouting above the deafening clamour of the heavy rain on the roof.

Maria suggested that it might help to put Olivia in the bath as the warm water soothed the pain. The robust Nellie lugged the large pots and helped Maria fill the bath, astonished that they were going to put Olivia in the water when she was just about to have a baby. When Olivia's pains had subsided Rose and Nellie helped her to the bathhouse. She struggled wearily through the kitchen leaving a river of amniotic fluid on the floor.

'She has wet herself!' Shrieked Annie, slipping on the wet floor.

'No dear, it's her waters.' Explained Nellie.

Annie, with no experience of the birthing process was none the wiser. Olivia, once in the warm water, promptly fell asleep. Annie thought she had died and Rose feared that she had been too generous with the last remedy. They took it in turns to support Olivia so she did not sink under the water and waited. Undecided whether or not to remove Olivia from the water, Rose and Maria were worried. Nellie, who thought putting her there in the first place was an outrageous mistake, was all for fishing her out again.

'Olivia!', shouted Rose, gently shaking her daughter in an attempt to awaken her. Olivia flopped about, unresponsive.

Gravely concerned, Rose and Maria took Nellie's advice. Getting the sleeping Olivia out of the water proved much trickier that getting her in. The bath was deep, the sides high and Olivia was heavy, floppy and slippery. They heard the backdoor slam and a moment later a very wet Mustapha splattered into the bathhouse. Rose and Maria were so thankful and relieved they both let go of Olivia. Nellie grabbed her hair and stopped her head from submerging. Rose told Mustapha everything that had happened. He grasped Olivia's head and opened each of her eyes in turn. He demanded hot, very sweet tea and the stamina remedy. He felt for her pulse. When the tea and remedy were beside him he slapped her face sharply, ducked her under the water and slapped her again.

'For the love of God!' bellowed Nellie, but a flash of Mustapha's black, serious eyes in her direction silenced her.

Olivia opened her eyes and before she could gather her senses, Mustapha gave her the remedy, washed down with hot sweet tea. He asked his mother to get in the bath behind her and lift her shoulders free of the water. He rolled up his sleeves and leant into the water, he could feel the baby's head close to crowning and he needed Olivia to push. Nellie had to avert her eyes, she had heard he delivered babies, but the sight of a man doing that to a woman was unthinkable. He splashed her face with cold water and poured some down her back. This made her jump and she opened her eyes, confused and disorientated.

'Olivia!' He spoke quietly and firmly. 'Listen to me, your baby needs to come out and I need you to push!'

She stared at him. He held her head and looked deep into her eyes.

'Olivia, it is time for the baby to come. I need you to listen and do as I say.'

'Mustapha!' Olivia whispered. 'You are here!'

'Yes Olivia, now I need you to kneel at this end of the bath and listen to me, the baby is coming. Your body knows exactly what to do, there is no need to fear. Come.'

Olivia knelt, her arms hanging over the side of the bath. Mustapha held her hands. The stamina remedy gradually counteracted the strong pain remedy and she could feel the urgent need to push and her eyes widened in alarm. Mustapha reassured her and encouraged her to push long and hard. His eyes never left her face for the half hour of pushing and she drew strength from his constant reassurance. Nellie watched and listened to his calm, quiet voice and saw its effect upon Olivia and felt ashamed that she had shouted at him. Rose caught the baby as it floated to the surface, a little girl with a head the shape of an elongated egg. Mustapha explained that the shape of the head was due to her being stuck low in the birth canal for far too long. It would right itself in a few days, so, put a nice bonnet on her and forget about it.

The storm had passed, although nobody in the bathhouse had noticed when. Mustapha rolled the baby in a towel and took her outside and presented her to the clearing sky. Rose and Maria cleaned Olivia up and dressed her in a clean nightdress and found clothes for the baby, including a nice bonnet. By the time Hugh and Grandy arrived she was on the sofa with her daughter. Hugh kept apologising until Olivia pointed out that he would have been of no use at all, and it was Mustapha she had needed.

Nellie made Mustapha a fresh cup of tea and presented it to him with a piece of her best cake.

'I believe Sir, that you saved that little baby's life today and probably the mistress's as well, Sir.' She whispered.

'I am not Sir, Nellie. I am only Mustapha.' He smiled and kissed Nellie on the cheek and she blushed and harboured a 'soft spot' for Mustapha for the rest of her life.

Annie, who had been forgotten about in the corner of the bathhouse, took days to recover from the whole harrowing experience.

Later, Olivia discovered that her brother Estavo had run through the worst of the storm to get Mustapha, and that her days of back pain had been actual labour, hence the shape of little Victoria Jane's head, moulded by her prolonged struggle to get out, which righted itself within a week.

Two days after the arrival of Victoria Jane, the family at the big house went to bed and when they rose in the morning discovered that Mustapha had delivered Isabella of a son at four in the morning. It had been a quiet, peaceful, intimate birth and they had named him Aziz Salamar after his great-grandfather.

Chapter 28

The first few weeks in their new house was full of surprises for Sophia and Tom and they regularly discovered items and carvings that they had failed to discover on first inspection. The ivory cotton sheets, embroidered with a line of sheep along the top edge, the carved mice running along the skirting board, the broom handle of entwined serpents and the handles on the poker and shovel that were metal bulrushes.

Tom spent the autumn building fences and digging an area ready for a vegetable garden. He was initially suspicious of the bathhouse, but after a hard day's digging, submerging his aching body in hot water, surrounded by candles, a hot cup of tea and a warm towel, he deemed the bathhouse a damn good invention. Joey delivered a cartload of wood for the winter and a cradle, made by Paulo and carved by him with stars, a moon and a sun with a smiling face.

Sophia explained to her mother and Aunt Rose that as this was to be her and Tom's first Christmas, and due to the baby, the last one they could spent alone together, so they would not be visiting on Christmas day. She visited her brother at the sick house and when he told her she may be having twins, due to the size of her belly, she admitted to him that the baby was not due in March as everyone had assumed, but more likely to be January. He gave her three bottles of remedy, clearly marked with directions and to be used in emergency situations such as heavy snow. Mustapha knew he could not persuade her to stay at the big house and made her promise to send for him when her labour began.

Rose and Maria sent a hamper of food to Sophia and Tom on Christmas Eve, and they spent two days in bed, punctuated by brief periods of making tea, preparing plates of food and throwing logs on the fire. Christmas dinner was available at both the big house and the new house and, the weather being pleasant, the family wandered between to two.

It began to snow the day after Boxing Day, and Mustapha regularly watched the skies.

'It won't be very thick snow this year, there is no need for the sheep to be moved!' announced little Mustapha, sensing his father's concern.

Mustapha smiled at him and asked him what he saw in the skies. His weather prophecies were invariably uncannily accurate.

'I don't see it, I feel it somewhere inside of me'

Little Mustapha was in his twelfth year and very like his father.

'The ability will be very useful when I become a sea captain!'

Little Mustapha had not grown out of the idea of going to sea and was already worrying at his great uncle Sam to take him on the nest voyage, due in the spring and bound for the Indian Ocean.

Mustapha rode from the sick house each day to check on his sister. In mid-January, Mustapha woke with Sophia on his mind and unable to settle, rode to her house. He found Sophia drinking tea beside the fire. She pointed triumphantly to the cradle, containing a tiny baby rolled in a towel.

'Meet Tommy!' she said with a laugh.

Mustapha picked him up and sat beside the fire. He unrolled the towel to inspect him. He was a healthy individual with dark hair and black eyes.

'Where's Tom?'

'Cleaning the bath and disposing of the afterbirth. Help yourself to tea, it's fresh.'

'Tell me what happened, why didn't you send for me?'

'Well, I had a backache yesterday, so I went to bed early, but my back kept me awake so I took a small dose of remedy and asked Tom to heat the water as I thought a nice hot bath would relieve it. Then I woke up and knew that the baby was on the way. I wouldn't let Tom leave, fearful of being alone.

So I took another dose and got in the bath and Tom delivered him about a half hour ago!'

Mustapha put Tommy in the cradle and was pouring his tea when Tom came in from the bathhouse, his face red and smiling.

'Congratulations Tom! You did very well!'

'Oh! Not a lot different to lambing if you ask me.' Answered Tom. 'And she was a deal more cooperative than some ewes!'

He poured a cup of tea and sat on the rug beside the cradle.

'He's a beauty!' he said and reached up to squeeze Sophia's hand. 'Do you think people will believe he's a seven month child?'

'No.' said Mustapha with a grin.

Sophia giggled.

'Didn't think so!' laughed Tom.

Mustapha carried little Tommy outside and, to Tom's astonishment, loudly presented him to the heavens.

'It's what he always does.' Explained Sophia.

Mustapha checked that all was well at the sick house and rode home to tell his mother and Aunt Rose, they were in the kitchen preparing lunch.

'Sophia has a son.'

'What?' shouted his mother, dropping a knife, and Rose just smiled.

'They've named his Tommy and he is beautiful, with dark hair and black eyes.'

'Thank God you went there this morning!' sighed Maria.

'I wasn't there, Tom delivered him and he said it was like lambing.'

'How is the poor mite?' asked Maria. 'He is so very early to be born.'

Mustapha and Rose glanced at each other.

'No it's not.' Rose said quietly and took Maria's hand.

Maria frowned with confusion, then her eyes widened.

'You mean….the girl was with child…..before..'

'Yes.' Said Mustapha and Rose together.

'And you two knew?'

'Mmm.'

Maria sat down at the table with a sigh.

'When can I see my grandson?' she smiled.

'I'll take you both tomorrow morning and I'll tell the rest of the family they are not ready for visitors yet.'

'My goodness!' exclaimed Maria as she held Tommy for the first time. 'He looks so much like Mustapha when he was born!'

Rose agreed he had the penetrating eyes of the generations of Mustapha's.

'Then I think it's only right that he be christened Thomas Mustapha!' suggested Tom.

Rose gave Sophia a parcel of baby clothes that she and Maria had been making for the last few months. Maria handed Tommy to Rose, burst into tears and to everyone's surprise flung her arms around the unsuspecting Tom. He hugged her warmly, kissed the top of her head, picked her up and swung her round until she began to laugh.

The following day Sal visited, bringing Sophia a bunch of snowdrops. Tom was outside chopping a pile of firewood and the dogs ran around sniffing Sal's legs. Sal helped Tom bring in the wood and sat holding Tommy while Tom made the tea. It didn't seem so long ago that he held his own babies and he had missed much of their childhoods. His daughter looked so happy and he was glad that she had married a man who did not go away on voyages for long periods of time.

Chapter 29

George, the only one with the slightest interest in new technology, purchased two seed drills. The contraptions were pulled by a horse and distributed seeds into furrows made by blades on the base of the machine. A further blade pushed the soil back over the seeds. A man sat on a seat at the rear of the machine, keeping the hopper at the top full of seeds. Some of the men and all of the horses were very suspicious of the clanking, ungainly contrivances. Eventually, Gabriel's sons Charles and Aziz accepted the challenge. It took considerably longer to acclimatise the horses than to familiarise the men.

Finally, with a great deal of patience, encouragement and rewards of carrots, the faithful old horse Prince became the first horse to successfully pull the seed drill, at a reasonable speed, in a straight line, without bolting or unseating the man at the rear of the device.

Apart from an early setback, caused by one of the men at the rear attempting to unblock a congested seed pipe with his finger, rather than a stick, whilst the machine was in motion, almost severing his finger, resulting in the older more resistant men exchanging 'I told you so' looks, it was not long before the seed drills became an essential aspect of planting. Doctor Matthew stitched the finger back together. The man lost sensation in the tip of his finger, a constant reminder to be more careful in future.

The ship was due to sail to East Africa for wood and India for spices, tea, silk and gemstones. Hugh wanted to go with them but Olivia silenced him with a withering stare. Khalid did not want to go, backed by Elizabeth, who refused to be left behind to cope with Olivia alone. Edmundo and Estavo could not wait to get away and little Mustapha drove everyone to distraction with his constant pleading. After days of squabbling and the occasional raised voices, Sam left Khalid behind and agreed to take little Mustapha along with the twins.

Peace finally settled in the big house after the ship sailed. It was not quite so peaceful at the new house. Victoria had begun to crawl and avidly explore her environment. She was a happy confident child and Olivia allowed her free run of the house. Elizabeth was sick of being dribbled on as soon as she sat down, sick of finding her needlework scattered, her cottons and silks unravelled and chewed. Sick to death of the red-faced, snotty, piercing squeals from the child each time she attempted to retrieve her book and frustrated by everyone else's tolerance. Hugh loved his daughter and wanted her to have a childhood different to his own. He did not mind being dribbled on, urinated on or having his hair pulled and disagreed vehemently when Elizabeth suggested it was time to get a nanny. Olivia reminded Elizabeth that this was her house and her child and to mind her own business. Elizabeth complained to Khalid and pleaded that they return to live at the big house, as she could no longer cope with the situation. Khalid began to regret his decision not to go with the ship and told her not to be hasty. Elizabeth walked to the big house to see Mina and explain her problems and was met with Aziz, who climbed up the sofa and tried to share his half chewed biscuit with her. Isabella laughed and returned him to the floor. A few minutes later he returned with a huge smile and handed her a dead spider. Elizabeth jumped up in horror, causing the family to cry with laughter. In despair, she marched furiously up the path to the new house, her eyes stinging with tears. She never wanted a baby, and should she be unfortunate enough to produce one then she would most certainly give it straight to a nanny. She could find no support. Her sister Annie, present at the birth, loved little Victoria and Grandy was delighted that she was surrounded by love and not subjected to a fierce nanny who discouraged contact with the rest of the family. Elizabeth failed to understand how the whole family found the tiny, sticky tyrant a fascinating creature! She was so angry that she even considered moving to live with her mother. Khalid stated he had no intention of spending his days under the roof of a woman who glared at him as if he were a cockroach. Desperate, she took a horse and rode to visit Sophia, who she was very fond of. Elizabeth found Sophia outside on the marsh, helping her husband with lambing, little Tommy tied to her back. Elizabeth pretended that she was just out for a ride and took her leave, wondering for the first time if she had made a dreadful mistake marrying into this unconventional family.

Little Mustapha spent several hours a day with his Uncle Sam, his globe and the navigational charts. Sam was impressed by his knowledge of the world and his enthusiasm for new information. He never stopped asking questions and was frequently discovered sitting on deck at night with the sailor on watch, learning about the stars. His prophecy of a storm coming in the Atlantic materialised, he remained on deck throughout, roped to the mast, lashed by rain and watched how the crew furled the sails, tied down any moveable objects, fought to control the wheel and ride out the heavy seas. He watched as the distant coast of Africa slipped slowly in and out of view. The temperature increased as they sailed south and a few days after his uncle pointed out the slave ships on the horizon, they were nearing the equator. Little Mustapha hopped about at the idea of entering the Southern Hemisphere for the first time. Sam, aware of the sense of anti-climax he and his twin Sal had experienced on their first voyage when absolutely nothing had happened when they crossed the equator, decided to make it more memorable for the boy. Little Mustapha had calculated that they would cross at approximately two-thirty six in the morning by the light of the stars and a full moon. As they crossed, Sam let off a distress flare that burst in the night sky, made little Mustapha jump and celebrated his first of many visits to the southern hemisphere. A few days later they were becalmed and the crew began fishing with baited hooks. They caught a variety of fish and they threw back very ugly ones they had never seen before. They kept the two large, barrel shaped fish with skin like sheets of silver and flesh of a bright, orangey-pink that fed the entire crew that evening.

Several weeks later, following days where there was not a breath of wind, and other days where the breeze filled the sails and blew the ship south at a fast pace, they finally rounded the Cape of Good Hope and set a course northwards, up the East side of Africa in search of timber. Little Mustapha watched as the vast shoals of herring were pursued by pods of dolphins, sharks and immense whales that surfaced at intervals blowing spouts of water. After two days of going north, little Mustapha begged his uncle to turn back, there was a terrible storm coming from the east, heading in a north westerly direction and if they continued on their course they would sail into its centre. Sam could see no sign of a storm in any direction, but little Mustapha pleaded that he just stop and watch the eastern skies. In less than an hour, the eastern sky began to darken ominously and the wind picked up considerably and he finally convinced Sam to turn south again. An hour later the sky behind them was dark greyish blue and the clouds were swirling fast and the wind continued to increase. Sam steered the buffeted ship into a welcome inlet between a strip of land and the mainland and continued south. The sky to the north turned black and the wind raged accompanied by torrential, driving rains. The storm raged all afternoon and into the night. The ship hid in the shelter of the inlet. At dawn the skies were clear again and the sea calm. Little Mustapha announced that it was now safe to resume the journey north. The storm had been a tropical typhoon and as they headed north they witnessed scenes of appalling devastation. Trees, bodies and all manner of undulating debris floated in great forlorn patches in the sea and on the distant shore they could detect the remains of swamped villages, smashed to the ground by the force of the wind and rain. This was the area the ship would have reached if little Mustapha had not made such a fuss and stopped them.

'I have no idea how you do it son, but I will never doubt you again!' Sam shook little Mustapha by the shoulder, recalling that his father had told him that old Mustapha had saved the ship on many occasions in the past with his forewarnings.

The crew renamed him 'the seer'.

It was several days sailing before the desolate coastline showed any sign of improvement, and weeks before they docked at a large, bustling port where they took on provisions and found a source of ebony, blackwood, satinwood and a striped wood called zebrano.

Little Mustapha walked down the white sand, so hot it burnt the soles of his feet and paddled in the pale green, clear, warm water. He discovered a large, black sea cucumber hidden in the dark green sea grass, but he had no idea what it was. Little fish swam around his feet. Noisy little green birds were busy weaving small baskets that dangled from the tree branches. Tall, very dark, thin men with startling white smiles climbed to the tops of the tall thin trees and cut down the fruits, named cocoanuts. They chopped the top off and Sam told him to drink the milk. That night, Sam, the twins and little Mustapha hung their hammocks on land in a house on stilts built of wooden poles, bamboo and gigantic leaves and after a meal of spicy stew and flat bread, they lay and listened to the unfamiliar screeching of wild creatures. Next day, little Mustapha embarked on writing a detailed journal of his experiences to read to his parents and Bella Mary when he returned home.

Chapter 30

The villagers had long forgotten the race to be the first one to present Mustapha and Doctor Matthew with the particular bellyache they had been waiting for. When twelve-year old Joe, not one to make a fuss, complained he felt hot and his belly hurt, it was his grandmother who remembered the symptoms, high temperature, bellyache and sometimes sickness and diarrhoea. Joe said he had already been sick. His mother wanted to give him mustard water to purge him, but his grandmother put her foot down and insisted they take him to the sick house. Mustapha gave him some pain relief and Maud boiled water to wash him. Mustapha ran to the workshop and asked Harry to ride to the vicarage and collect Matthew, telling him it was a suspected appendicitis. Harry forgot the word on the way, but Matthew knew what he meant. By the time Matthew reached the sick house, the boy was washed and lying on the bed in the clean room and Maud was fishing instruments from the boiling water. He examined Joe and as he pressed gently on the taught abdomen he noticed the child wince with pain when he removed his hand, a reliable indication of appendicitis. Mustapha had prepared the sleeping draught, a mixture of sedative and pain relief, and within a few minutes Joe was asleep. Mustapha and Matthew scrubbed their hands in the bowls of hot soapy water prepared by Maud. Then Matthew made an incision in Joe's abdomen to the right of centre. He had watched the operation many times and assisted on two occasions, but never attempted it alone. Mustapha watched as he cut through the muscle layer to reveal the intestines and bowel. Maud held her breath. Matthew delved his hand into the boy's abdomen searching for the lower bowel. He located it quickly and pulled it up through the incision. The appendix was swollen and deep red, but to Matthew's immense relief, it had not yet ruptured. He cut off the appendix and gave it to Maud and carefully stitched the small hole. The rest of the bowel appeared healthy, so he gently replaced it, stitched together the muscle layer and the skin. Mustapha was surprised how simple the operation was and believed he could do it himself if he had to. Matthew pointed out that it was much easier with a sleeping patient. No matter how many people attempted to restrain the screaming, terrified patient, unimaginable agony drove them to writhe and wriggle, hampering the doctors and accidental damage to surrounding tissue was all too common.

Matthew and Mustapha explained to Joe's grandmother that she had been right to bring him and that the appendix had not burst and released any poison into his belly and that he owed his life to her good judgement. She wanted to see what they had cut out and Maud showed her.

Joe slept for several hours. His temperature subsided and apart from when he tried to sit up was relatively pain free. Mustapha gave him mild pain relief for a couple of days and Joe learnt to avoid laughing, coughing and to hold his nose to prevent a sneeze. A week later he was sent home. Curious neighbours arrived to see the scar and study the shrivelled appendix that he insisted on keeping.

Bella Mary asked her father to explain the operation in detail. She was fascinated by the workings of the body. She had read many of the old medical papers, given to old Mustapha by Matthew when he was studying at the London Hospital. Old Mustapha had left many old journals crammed with tiny writing and diagrams, but the earlier ones were written in Arabic. Frustrated, Bella Mary sought the help of her grandfather Sal who had learned the language from both his father and old Mustapha. They spent many hours together in the microscope room and after several months of study Bella Mary was able to begin to decipher the old journals. They contained recipes for potions and remedies he had learned and developed throughout his years at sea, and detailed descriptions of injuries, diseases and treatments. The notes that interested her most were about anatomy and the actual workings of the body. She had seen the detailed drawing by Leonardo Da Vinci, provided by Matthew that had fascinated old Mustapha, and she compared them to very early drawings by her great-grandfather. He had not possessed the artistic skills of Da Vinci, but many of the sketches, completed years before he had seen the Da Vinci drawings, were remarkably similar. Bella Mary had read about a seventeenth century physician called William Harvey, attributed to be the first to discover the system of blood circulation, so, she was amazed to find in old Mustapha's notes, an Arab physician who had already discovered the same information five hundred years earlier, and he had the longest name she had ever seen. He was called Ala-al-din abu Ali ibn Abi-Hasm al-Qarshi al Dimashqi, fortunately, he was known as Ibn al-Nafis.

Old Mustapha had written extensively on the subject of cleanliness. He wrote about his elderly mentor, Jian Ou Yang, who was obsessed by cleanliness, believing it to be essential to a healthy life. The venerable old man had travelled extensively in his youth and told Mustapha that he was able to smell a European Christian at thirty paces. Their Church had advocated that bathing was a sinful act and would let all kinds of diseases enter the body and that filthiness protected against disease and was a sign of holiness. Jian Ou Yang believed that this was a strong contributory factor in the prevalence of plagues in Europe. It was from this elderly man the old Mustapha had learnt to boil surgical tools and scrub his hands with soap and water, both before and after touching a wound or a sick person.

Old Mustapha had also written about different diseases and how some of them spread from person to person, whilst other sicknesses did not spread at all. He believed that colds spread from one to another by breath containing small particles. Others sicknesses were spread by touch. Bella Mary spent weeks poring over the old papers and relating her discoveries to her father. She studied objects under the microscope, before and after being boiled and could see no difference. She assumed whatever she was looking for was either invisible or too small even for the microscope. She was extremely displeased when her father informed her that women were not allowed to enter medical school and become doctors.

Chapter 31

Elizabeth was miserable and descended into a permanent bad humour, fuelled by Khalid's daily visits to his mother and the noisy, irksome babies that, despite leaking from most of their orifices, provided a constant source of amusement to everyone else. She resented the familiarity of the 'help', treated more like members of the family, rather than servants. Her sister Annie was out of control and regularly disappeared in the evenings and nobody seemed to notice or care about where she was going. Her father was no help at all.

'As long as she is happy.' Was all he said and he continued to chase the shrieking Victoria around the house. Elizabeth considered that perhaps her mother had been right all along and her father was a useless old fool.

Annie was happy. Elizabeth demanded to know where she went in the evenings and Annie, red in the face, said she went walking and declined the offer of her sister's company on her walks.

Then, at dinner, Hugh and Olivia proudly announced that they were expecting another child. Elizabeth had tried to smile as she felt her heart sink lower.

In despair, Elizabeth went to visit her mother, who was startled to see her and even more startled when she broke down and cried about the disgusting behaviour of babies allowed to run loose and terrify her with spiders, who destroyed her needlework, dribbled on her clothes, urinated on the furniture, made her books sticky and were never disciplined! Servants who called her Elizabeth, who sat next to her at the table and along with everyone else, laughed at her discomfort! Then there was Annie, who was allowed out alone and nobody bothered to find out what she was up to! Father didn't care one bit and was too busy with horses to worry about what Annie was doing.

Mrs Lyle listened, valiantly trying to disguise her triumph.

'And now.' Sobbed Elizabeth. 'Olivia is having another brat and I can't go back to the big house as there's a child with black eyes who can see my fears and brings me spiders, and Sophia walks around with her child tied to her back while she tends sheep!

These people have money, so why do they live like that?'

'Why do you not come here for a time?' asked Mrs Lyle.

'Khalid won't come. I have already asked him.'

'You need a break my dear, you could come alone.' Suggested Mrs Lyle, greatly relieved.

Elizabeth sniffed miserably and wiped her red eyes with her handkerchief.

'Perhaps your sister would come with you?'

'No, she won't, she loves it there! She watched that little tyrant being born and thinks she is wonderful! She treats Nellie the cook like a mother. She does exactly what she wants, going out alone in the evenings, coming home with muddy boots and grass on her clothing!'

Mrs Lyle poured two generous glasses of brandy for herself and Elizabeth and kept her thoughts to herself. She suggested that Elizabeth return home, speak to her husband and sister and return in a couple of days for a nice rest. She was welcome to stay for as long as she liked.

Khalid believed Elizabeth when she said she was going to stay with her mother for a few weeks as her mother was dreadfully lonely and had nobody to talk to. She was not greatly missed when she left and Olivia was frankly glad to see the back of her and the dark cloud that pursued her from room to room. Grandy was saddened by her inability to adjust to the unorthodox way of life.

Elizabeth initially revelled in the peace and quiet, the absence of marauding toddlers and a plethora of servants that 'knew their place!' Her mother was victorious, smug and often inebriated. Within a short time her jubilance became more apparent, particularly after several glasses of brandy, and she began to remind Elizabeth that her situation was her own fault and that she had shown an appalling lack of good judgement. Elizabeth tried to defend herself but she was no match for her mother who had a lifetime's experience of stridently browbeating and haranguing lesser beings. Some mornings her mother was agreeable and they strolled in the grounds with Spot, but after lunch the brandy would appear and her mother would gradually evolve into a variety of people. Some days she became morose and tearful, she begged forgiveness and even tried to hug Elizabeth. On other days she became critical and cruel and on the good days she fell asleep in her chair. Elizabeth was at a loss, she had been unhappy at the new house, fed up with living under Olivia's roof and coping with unpredictable babies. Yet she had been so happy there when she and her sister first shared Khalid's room at the big house. She was so ecstatic when she married him and yet she had been miserable soon after she moved to the new house. She missed Khalid, she missed the bathhouse and the food.

Elizabeth watched her sleeping mother, slumped in her armchair, mouth agape, snoring and dribbling. Her forehead was heavily wrinkled from years of frowning her disapproval and her nose had grown longer and sharper. Her clothing was stained and Elizabeth was convinced that she frequently slept fully dressed in her bed. She smelt of stale brandy with a hint of urine and mothballs. With tears in her eyes, Elizabeth collected her belongings and with one last look at her mother, she quietly left and asked old George to take her to the big house.

Mina was surprised and delighted to see her and startled when she broke down and cried. She told Mina about her mother, her drinking, her raging moods and her cruel remarks, she told her how happy she had been in the big house and how miserable she had become in the new house, she told her that Olivia didn't like her and that the babies were uncontrollable and that she did not know where she belonged or what to do. Mina hugged her, stroked her hair and told her not to worry. She told her how lonely she had felt when she first arrived in the family, particularly when her husband had returned to sea. Her saviour had been old Mustapha, who could speak her language and knew her country. Gradually he had helped her to find her place and once she had her beloved children all was well with her. Elizabeth explained that she did not like children and never wanted any and Mina assured her that it would be very different when she had her own children, that she would love them immediately and totally. Elizabeth was not convinced.

Mina took control of the situation. She sent for Khalid and told him that he was moving back to the big house and that he and Elizabeth would live at the west end of the house with her and Joey. She moved Joey into a smaller room and converted his old room into a sitting room for Khalid and Elizabeth. The following morning Elizabeth woke feeling better for the first time in months, the sun shone through the curtains and lit up the room she had slept in with her sister when she first arrived. Mina tapped lightly on the door and delivered breakfast in bed. She was dressed in a sky blue sari, her hair was plaited in a thick braid that reached her thighs, her smile was as bright as her dozens of gold bangles that jingled on her slim arms and she smelled of jasmine. Elizabeth watched her slight, graceful figure leaving the room and was moved. She jumped out of bed and ran after Mina and hugged her.

'Thank you!' she whispered.

'I have waited so long for a daughter my dear, it is my pleasure.'

Chapter 32

Isabella's time was limited by the boisterous antics of Aziz, Mustapha was busy at the sick house and little Mustapha was in the Indian Ocean, so much of the gardening fell to Bella Mary. She had been studying her great-grandfather's recipes for ointments and balms that aided healing and avoided deadly infections. He had written of the properties of garlic, hops and lavender, all of which he believed were very powerful aids to healing. Bella Mary decided that she was going to make some ointments of her own and test them on minor wounds initially. Elizabeth watched from the tree house as Bella Mary was struggling to dig an area of grass beside the garden. She took her a drink and asked what she was doing and Bella Mary explained that she was enlarging the garden to grow a number of plants for her new ointments. Elizabeth enlisted the help of her husband and by the end of the day the three of them had succeeded in digging a substantial area. They cleared the weeds and the large stones and Paulo offered to build the fencing to prevent Thomas from eating whatever she planted.

Bella Mary showed Elizabeth how to harvest the poppies and the lavender. They spent days together wandering in the woods and along the hedgerows searching for wild garlic and hops that Bella Mary dug up and transplanted into her new patch of soil. The girl's enthusiasm inspired Elizabeth. They dried hops and lavender in the sun and crushed them to powder in old Mustapha's pestle and mortar. They mashed cloves of garlic into paste and mixed the ointments. Bella Mary numbered the jars to indicate the ingredients of each one and laid in wait for someone to suffer a minor wound. Joey was first to oblige with a deep scratch caused by a thorn bush. Bella Mary cleaned the scratch and administered ointment number one that contained just mashed garlic. The wound healed quickly, but her father reminded her that it may have healed without any intervention and she needed to wait for signs of an infection, like a reddening of the skin, local discomfort and pus. Then she would know for certain whether or not her ointment was a success. She gave her father a little jar of ointment one to take to the sick house in case anyone arrived with an infected cut. The first real test of her ointment was on Grandy's horsefly bite that had been well scratched with dirty nails. By the time Bella Mary discovered the bite a scab had formed and the surrounding area was hot, red and painful to touch. Delighted, she subjected Grandy, who sat gritting his teeth in pain, to a thorough washing of the area, scab removal, pus squeezing, ointment smearing and clean dressing application. She found him with alarming regularity during the next few days and inspected his wound, poked at it, measured the area of redness and applied more ointment and new dressings. After three days there was a definite sign of improvement and she insisted that he show her father. Bella Mary, with an air of authority marched Grandy to see Mustapha, removed the dressing and read from her notes the progress of the redness and gradual reduction of pus. Mustapha was impressed and Grandy was prematurely relieved. Bella Mary continued to pursue him for another week, fiddling about with his horsefly bite until the wound was no more than a small, discoloured patch of skin. Bella Mary, whose ointment making resulted in her constantly reeking of garlic, noticed than even of the warm, damp humid nights when mosquitoes flew up from the marshes, they gave her a very wide berth. Intrigued, she visited the marshes to the north east of the village. Here the marshes were soggy and water logged, and generally avoided by the shepherds. She was delighted to discover that the clouds of mosquitoes retreated when she approached. The following day she collected strings of garlic and several pots of ointment and took them to Sophia, with instructions to apply the ointment to her boy during damp, dull weather.

 Maria answered a knock at the back door on Sunday afternoon and was astounded to discover Levi

Hoare the blacksmith, nervously fiddling with his cap on the doorstep, asking to see the master and his lordship. She invited him inside and asked him to sit while she put on the kettle for tea and summoned her husband. When Sal arrived in the kitchen, Levi rose awkwardly, dropping his cap.

'Good afternoon Levi, what can I do for you?' Asked Sal with a smile.

'Sorry Sir,' stuttered Levi. 'It's you and his lordship I need to be seeing on a private matter.'

'Levi, my name is Sal and I suppose you mean old Grandy?' laughed Sal. 'Please sit down and have some tea and I'll send for him.'

'Thank you Sir, er, Mister Sal Sir.' Levi lowered his powerful body, built by years of beating metal into submission, back into the chair.

Maria poured the tea, put a plate of biscuits and fruitcake on the table and sat down with her husband and Levi. Khalid went to fetch Grandy.

'Sorry for the trouble Mam.'

'Don't be silly Levi, have a piece of cake with your tea. Grandy won't be long.' Maria tried to make the poor man feel welcome. 'It's been a lovely summer, has it not?'

'It has that Mam.' Answered Levi staring into his tea, fidgeting with discomfort.

'I've seen that beautiful fire grate that you made for my daughters house Levi, and those wonderful chandeliers, you must be proud of them!'

Levi's stoic face transformed with a broad smile.

'Meself and the boy made em Mam, never done the like of it before! Did you see the bulrush poker?'

'No I didn't but I'll make sure to look next time I'm there. You also made those incredible door hinges I suppose?'

'Yes Mam, that young Mister Joey give us some headaches, but we was paid handsome and we did a deal of learning, me and the boy.' Levi settled more comfortably into the chair and helped himself to another piece of fruitcake.

'Yes mam, we learned a lot, me and the lad.' He grinned. 'Nice bit of cake Mam, I must say!'

Grandy arrived, wondering why the blacksmith wanted to see him instead of Gabriel. His appearance in the kitchen threw Levi into a panic of trying to rise from his chair and finish chewing a mouthful of fruitcake.

'Your Lordship.' He choked, bowed his head and resumed fiddling with his cap. 'Tis a delicate matter I need to speak of, your Lordship, Sir!'

'Sit down Levi.' Whispered Maria, she placed her hand on his arm and smiled. 'We all call him Grandy.'

Grandy sat down and picked up his tea.

'What's this delicate matter that I can help you with?'

Levi's face reddened, he took a deep breath, looked at Maria and then at Grandy.

'Your Lordship Sir, it concerns my boy Amos and your girl Annie, I mean Miss Annie, Sir.'

All eyes turned to Levi, frozen stiff in the deafening silence.

'Come on Levi.' Maria took his hand. 'Just tell us.'

'I don't know if you know, but young Miss Annie visits with us and the boy is grown too fond of the girl, I don't want the boy to be hurt Sir, nor her either, as she seems fond of him too. I know its not right that he is walking out with a lady such as your daughter and I need your help to put a stop to it afore its too late, if you get me drift, Sir. Sorry Sir.'

Levi took a breath.

'I've tried to keep an eye on em Sir. It's just me and Amos see, as the wife died when he was young. But they go out for walks alone. I've told the boy time and again I'll kill him if he ever tries anything improper with the young lady. I told him there's no future in it, that she is a real lady and not for the likes of him, but he damn well says he loves her and that she do love him too! I'm at my wits end, that I am Sir. I can't sleep for the worrying!'

'Well, well.' Said Grandy with a smile. 'That explains where she goes every evening and why she has a spring in her step!'

Levi, who had not known what to expect, was staggered by the reaction from Annie's father.

'What shall we do Sir?' pleaded Levi. 'I've tried talking to him. Maybe you could talk to Miss Annie and stop her coming to see the boy?'

Grandy shook his head. 'I just want her to be happy!'

Levi stared at him in disbelief.

'Are we talking about the young man who wins the arm wrestling every year?' asked Grandy.

'We are Sir.'

'The same one who dances all evening with my daughter?'

'Yes Sir, when he first met her, she never said who she were and he thought she was one of the serving girls from the village. He didn't know who she were till he saw her all dressed up at your Miss Elizabeth's wedding in the spring of last year! I warned him to stop seeing her, but your Miss Sophia had gone and married a shepherd and it gave the silly young fool new hope!'

'So.' Said Grandy. 'Does your son want to marry my daughter?'

'He does that Sir, I've told him he's got to stop this nonsense and find a nice young village woman and not go around disgracing ladies!'

'And does my daughter want to marry your son?'

'I don't know Sir, he says she does, but I think she must know it can't happen and that she will marry a rich man someday and it will break my boy's heart, that's why we got to put a stop to it!'

'Levi, do you mind me asking.' said Grandy. 'Did you love your wife?'

Levi's face softened as he smiled.

'I did that Sir. I loved her from when we were children together. She was never strong and she died when the boy was six, but I still talk to her every day and love her as much as ever.'

'I married a woman I did not love and spent thirty miserable years with her. Our families arranged the marriage and we both accepted it and did our duty. I would never subject my children to that hell. I vowed several years ago that my children should only marry for love. If your son is serious about marrying my daughter then tell him I expect him to come and ask for her hand and if she is agreeable I will give them my blessing.'

Levi was struck dumb. In the weeks leading up to this meeting, he had played out numerous scenarios in his mind. He had never even considered this possibility!

Maria made fresh tea and Grandy shook hands with Levi and poured a drop of brandy from his flask into each of their cups. Levi wiped his eyes with his cap.

Annie went very red in the face when Grandy told her that Levi the blacksmith had visited him.

'I hear young Amos wants to marry you.'

Annie's eyes opened wide and her bottom lip quivered.

'Do you love the young man my dear?'

She nodded her head and the tears rolled down her cheeks.

'Then why are you crying my dear child?'

She shook her head and flung her arms around her father's neck.

'I am expecting him to come and ask me for your hand Annie, so I need to know if you wish me to agree.'

There was a prolonged period of heartrending sobbing before Annie managed to answer.

Chapter 33

Sam sailed the ship north-east, in a more northerly direction than usual as he wanted to show little Mustapha the coastline of Southern Iran, where his great-grandfather Mustapha and his great-great-grandfather Salamar had seen the sea for the first time. Where Salamar had ran away to sea and Mustapha had reluctantly followed him and where, some twenty years later Mustapha had taken the young Aziz Shadi Rashad Salamar Badr al din, Salamar's orphaned son, to begin a life at sea. Little Mustapha was grateful, he stood on the deck and felt very close to his great-grandfather. He saw a tall man and a young boy about the same age as him standing in the sand on the distant shore and he waved. They waved back. It was one hundred years since Mustapha and Aziz Shadi Rashad Salamar Badr al din had stood there.

Tiny boats rowed out to the ship with fresh fish and fruits. Sam paid two boats to take him, the twins and little Mustapha to stand for a while on the warm sands of the home of their ancestors.

Little Mustapha wrote it all down in his journal and realised how keenly he missed his mother and father. He wrote about the extraordinary colours of the ocean, the bright blue, turquoise and deep emerald. He described the pale gold sand and tiny islands topped with palm trees. He tried to record everything in fine detail, so that his father would know exactly what it was like. He collected shells and drew the shapes and colours of the peculiar fish. He sat with his head hanging over the prow of the ship and stared into the eyes of the leaping, squeaking dolphins and twice he saw a vast whale dive below the surface, its tail fin as big as a mainsail, that splashed so hard he felt the droplets of water on his face as they sailed east-south-east, heading for the west coast of India.

Edmundo and Estavo took turns in the crow's nest searching for the first glimpse of India, Aunt Mina's country that they fell in love with on their first visit. Their excitement was contagious and by the time they docked Yusuf the cook pleaded to go inland with Sam, the twins and little Mustapha, who took his journal with him, convinced that he would forget the details of his experiences if he left it behind. He smelt India before he went ashore. Odd wafts and unusual aromas from the busy dock reached him on deck, whetting his appetite for the journey ahead.

Sam hired a large cart and two horses. The countryside was lush and green, thanks to a good monsoon. The track was dry and dusty, but heavily rutted from the vehicles that had passed when the track was soft mud. It was a bumpy ride. The little village exploded into uproar when the inhabitants recognised Sam and the twins, whose antics involving tree climbing and water carrying still entertained them during the long warm evenings. The women made a great fuss of little Mustapha and his searching black eyes that could see into their souls as far as their previous lives. They sat him in a hammock and decorated his hands and feet with henna tattoos and declared him a guru after hearing that he had saved the ship, and the lives of everyone aboard, from a deadly storm that would have reduced the ship to kindling. In the evening, the rapt women and a couple of the men watched the sky as little Mustapha told them the names of the stars and constellations. He wished that he had brought his globe, so that he could show them where he lived. He tasted his first mango.

Next day the men set off to collect spices from other villages, accepting the offer of help from Yusuf who wanted to see as much of the country as he could. The twins were busy discovering whether they could still climb palm trees. The women were busy preparing food, carrying water and washing clothes and little Mustapha was busy drawing and writing in his journal.

Yusuf proved very useful. A week after their arrival, a young woman, startled by a snake had tripped with her water jar. It landed heavily on her arm. The women ran in the direction of the screams and helped her back to the huts. Yusuf took control of the situation as it was obvious she had broken her arm. He gave her a potion for the pain before attempting to examine her arm. The skin was not broken but both of the bones in the forearm were. Yusuf enlisted the help of her husband and two of the women. He instructed the women to hold her tightly from behind and told her husband to pull and stretch the injured arm whilst he felt along the bones and realigned them as best he could. He bandaged the arm and added the thin strong splints made from ebony and then more bandages, regularly checking that the bones remained in place. Throughout the treatment the young woman felt no pain, she hummed quietly and occasionally laughed. He put the arm in a sling and explained that she must not use the arm for six weeks, by which time the bones would have knitted together again. The villagers had seen broken bones before, but they had never witnessed such a quiet treatment, usually it was accompanied by a great deal of squealing and groaning, despite a large drink of bhang and yoghurt, even from the men.

They stayed at the village for almost a month. Yusuf left a bottle of remedy with the woman who delivered the babies, with instructions to remove Shanti's splint after three more weeks and be careful with the arm for the first month or so. The twins helped to repair and re-thatch the roofs on some of the huts. Sam spent his time snoozing in a hammock under the trees. The women showered the group with little gifts on their departure and tried to persuade Sam to leave little Mustapha behind. Little Mustapha sat on top of the sacks of spices and waved until the village was out of sight, his journal beside him, containing all of his precious memories. At such times, he wished that he could be two people, so that he could leave one of him here and take the other one with him. The journey back to the ship was a silent affair, each person struggling to let go of the people they had come to love in a very short time, striving to remember who they were a month ago and get on with what they were supposed to be doing!

The following day they set off through the market in search of silks and tea. Sam told little Mustapha he could get gifts for the family. He chose a length of ivory silk embroidered in silver thread for his mother, a new set of clothes in powder blue for his father and when he was buying bangles for Bella Mary he suddenly remembered that he must have another brother or sister! He bought a carved wooden horse with a mane and tail made from strands of silk. The twins found a wall hanging festooned with fluffy sheep for Sophia's new house and a dark blue bedspread embroidered with tiny mirrors for George and Esther. Sam bought a large quantity of long, soft, woollen scarves in a myriad of colours for the women. Then he found a wooden box, covered with intricate carvings, with brass hinges and a lock and key. He gave the box to little Mustapha as it was just the right size to lock his treasured journal in.

Sam felt tired and on occasions he experienced feelings of wistfulness and deep nostalgia. He watched the small islands in his favourite ocean pass slowly by and sensed he was saying goodbye to them. That this was to be his final voyage. The haunting, melancholy songs of the whales at night reminded him of his first voyage, when he and Sal were mere children and he was filled with sadness. Little Mustapha came and sat beside him and they listened to the whales together.

'I was your age when I first heard the whales.'

'Uncle Sam, do you ever miss your family when you are at sea?'

'Yes, but not as much as I miss the sea when I am at home.'

They sat in silence for a time.

'So you have been going to sea for almost fifty years! How lucky you are Uncle Sam. You have friends in so many countries and so many wonderful memories.'

'Yes.' Smiled Sam.

'I think people's lives come in different sizes. Yours has been a very *big* life indeed!'

Little Mustapha retired to his hammock and Sam smiled at the stars, his heart a great deal lighter.

Chapter 34

Mrs Lyle's consumption of brandy increased after she realised that Elizabeth had deserted her again. Sometimes she admitted to herself that she missed her daughter and that she had driven her away with her cruel tongue, yet again. At other times she hated the ungrateful, stupid little bitch. The servants were sick to death of her raging demands at all hours and the ghastly state of the bed linen they were expected to wash. As she had little idea of what went on in the house, the housekeeper took to ordering new sheets on a regular basis and burning the ones that made the poor girls retch.

When her husband told her that Annie was marrying a blacksmith it was the final straw. Mrs Lyle believed that her life had been a shameful waste of effort and dedication. She had devoted it to her three children, raising them to be respectable, responsible and above reproach. Every single one of them had let her down, disgraced themselves and the name of her family. A matter of weeks later her distraught maid found her dead in her bed, plastered in orange vomit. She was buried in the family vault, attended by her husband and son and a straggle of anxious servants fretting about their futures.

Olivia accompanied Hugh to the estate as he needed to speak to the servants, and against all expectations, fell in love with the dusty, drab, rambling old mansion! She ran from room to room shrieking about how she would transform the place, bring it to life and restore its former glory! She summoned the apprehensive servants and informed them of her plans. They were to give away, or throw away, the dusty, faded curtains and furniture, they were to lock the door on Mrs Lyle's old room and discard the key. They were to remove the gloomy portraits and store them in the attic, rip off the disgusting wall coverings, throw away the rugs and make ready for the transformation that would begin in the spring after she had given birth. She instructed Archie the butler to employ some workmen to scrape the years of grime from the wooden floors and panelling and sand and polish them and find someone to measure the windows and make a list. Hugh watched her with a smile on his face, his beautiful wife, a woman who knew exactly what she wanted and one who had no comprehension of not getting it! The servants stood reeling with shock, unsure of whether to be relieved or traumatised.

Grandy was delighted that someone had the courage and the energy to transform the miserable old place and he hoped he would live long enough to see the results.

Amos and Annie's forthcoming marriage was announced at the harvest party, three years from the day they first met. They were to be married in spring. Annie insisted that she wanted to live at the forge and look after Amos and his father. She had already transformed their tiny living room and was learning to cook. George arranged for the building of a larger house attached to the rear of the forge, which stood only a few hundred yards from the church.

On a cold November morning, Olivia, with the help of Mustapha, who had watched her like a hawk in the final weeks, and with her husband Hugh holding her hand, gave birth with relative ease to twin boys with nicely rounded heads! Mustapha took Hugh and the babies outside and presented the firstborn to the dawn, and then the second one. Hugh watched with tears in his eyes, the strange ceremony he had missed when his daughter was born. Grandy was overcome with glee. Rose had not seen anyone jump about like that since old Mustapha had become a grandfather! She did the same as Mary had done, sat him down firmly, threatened to lash him to the chair and gave him a cup of hot sweet tea. After days of heated discussions, the babies were eventually named, Henry George and Edgar William. By Christmas, Sophia, Esther and even Elizabeth were with child and Bella Mary asked her father if she could learn how to deliver a baby.

The winter was a mild damp one and the spring came early. Olivia, keen to transform the old mansion, enlisted the help of Joey for his design skills, and Daisy to help her manage the babies and Victoria. Archie liked Olivia, who refused to be called Madam, and trusted him to manage his brigade of servants and workmen with little interference. She regularly rushed into the building bringing the smell of spring flowers and a surfeit of enthusiasm, congratulating him of the progress he had made. She threw open the windows, ordered all the fires to be lit to air the place and skidded along the newly polished floors laughing like a child. She asked for the cobwebby, dull chandeliers to be taken down and washed. She ordered the completion of two separate bathhouses, both with four large baths. She visited the servant's quarters at the far end and insisted that they be redecorated as well.

Impatient to move in, Olivia prioritised the completion of several bedrooms, the dining room and the large sitting room.

Amos and Annie were married in May, she was dressed in blue and carried a bouquet of the last of the bluebells. Levi stood proudly in the suit of clothes he had not worn since the funeral of his wife, his belly straining uncomfortably against the buttons of his waistcoat.

In June the ship returned from sea, its unnoticed arrival heralded by the dramatic whirlwind that was little Mustapha as he rushed into the sick house, dropped his journal box on the desk and flung his arms around Mustapha's neck.

'Oh, Daddy, you have no idea how much I have missed you!'

Maud, moved to tears, left the room to make tea.

'I have a present for you!' gasped little Mustapha, opening his box. 'It is a journal I wrote so that you and mother can know where I went and what it was like!'

'Thank you son, what a wonderful gift, I can't wait to see it. I too have a surprise for you, you have a little brother Aziz.'

The two resumed their hugging.

Maud returned with the tea and little Mustapha hugged her, causing her to burst into tears.

Mustapha was taken aback by how much his son had changed. He had grown taller and his voice had deepened.

The three sat at the desk and began looking at the journal. The door burst open and Bella Mary jumped into the arms of her brother.

'I just knew you were here!'

Isabella was shocked to sees the size of her son. He had left as a child and returned as a young man and he looked so much like Mustapha had at that age. Mina was shocked by the change to Sam. He was thinner and quieter and she noticed him wince in pain first thing in the morning, when he got out of bed. His greying hair had turned white at the temples. He was gentler and more affectionate that she remembered. Mina told Mustapha. Using the journal as an excuse Mustapha took it to Sam and they looked through it together. Sam had not seen it and he was impressed with the lad's attention to detail, with his intricate drawings and the entire conversations he had recorded. Sam was overwhelmed when he found the conversation between himself and little Mustapha at the beginning of the long journey home. He had included the conversation word for word and then he had written.

'Tonight poor Uncle Sam is very sad and he should not be unhappy. He has had a wonderful life. He is a very brave man and dearly loved by his friends everywhere we go. He is sad because he is getting old and his joints ache and he believes his lifetime as a sea captain is coming to an end. But he will forever carry the sea within him, wherever he is. He will always be a great sea captain, even at home with everyone that loves him. I hope and pray he will feel better soon.'

Sam's eyes filled with tears and he wiped them on his sleeve.

'Damned cheeky young devil!' he said with a disgruntled sniff.

'Observant!' Mustapha added with a smile and passed him a bottle of the same remedy as he gave Grandy several years ago and a pot of ointment for his knees.

Two days later Sophia gave birth to another son whom they named Daniel John. This time Mustapha and Bella Mary delivered him and Tom was relegated to handholding and tea making.

Little Esther suffered a prolonged, arduous labour and lay in the bath most of the night. George, worried sick, never left her side. At one point, even

Mustapha feared the worst, but following two doses of the stamina remedy, she rallied and at daybreak she gave birth to a dainty little girl with dark eyes. Bella Mary was almost asleep on her feet and flabbergasted. The two births she had witnessed were so different and she had not realised that her father was such an outstandingly skilful man. Mustapha took Emily Rose outside to the morning sun and offered very fervent thanks for her safe arrival.

Chapter 35

Olivia, impatient to speed up the progress at Hugh's ancestral home, moved her husband, her three children, Daisy and Joey into the rooms nearing completion. This had a domino effect upon the remaining family. Elizabeth, Khalid, Mina and Sam moved to the new house with Grandy, allowing George, Esther and Emily Rose to take over the rooms on the west side of the big house. Bella Mary visited Elizabeth several times a day, watching for signs of the onset of her labour.

It did not take Olivia long to notice the very limited menu options produced by the cooks in the extensive kitchens at the Lyle residence. After a week of tasteless stews, overcooked vegetables and stodgy suet puddings, she sent old George with two flustered indignant cooks, Elsie and Florence to the big house, with orders to return home only when they had mastered her favourite dishes. Rose and Maria welcomed them into the kitchen, made them a pot of tea and showed them the room they would share during their stay. It took days for them to get used to not calling Rose and Maria 'Madam.' It took several weeks for them to master all of the spicy sauces, succulent casseroles and sweet puddings, to stop jumping to attention when they were spoken to and be able to laugh out loud when things went wrong. They gradually became accustomed to eating with the family and using the bathhouse. Eventually, deemed eminently capable by Rose and Maria, they reluctantly packed their bags and prepared to return to the Lyle residence, armed with bags and boxes of necessary ingredients. They were sad to leave and they both shed a few private tears on the way home and they entertained the rest of the servants with their adventures at the big house for months. Mister Archibald was not entertained. He believed this unnatural familiarity between ranks would lead to insubordination and unrest within the servants, occasioning disaster. He had always run a 'tight ship', with a rigid hierarchy and stern discipline. He had grown fond of Olivia, but he had sleepless nights worrying that her relaxed attitude with the servants was misguided. One day he had actually discovered her sitting on the kitchen table, surrounded by rapt servants, relating the more amusing stories from her sea voyage! The story of the Master and the flea-ridden monkey reduced them to hysteria and it was days before they settled down!

Archie spoke to Hugh, respectfully requesting that he talk to his wife. Hugh, stifling his laughter, agreed to have a word with her. Archie's plan backfired with disastrous consequences, when, the next morning Olivia interrupted his morning meeting with the servants, tweaked his moustache in front of everyone and said.

'Oh Archie, you are such a silly old sausage!'

The group descended into stifled giggles and snorts as they tried to keep their tear-stained faces straight. The footman's supreme effort to suppress his laughter resulted in an untimely, rhythmic, squeaking fart and Archie, red in the face, abruptly left the kitchen and retired to his room, followed closely by waves of raucous laughter.

Elizabeth woke at two o'clock in the morning, her belly as tight as a drum and a sensation of cramp. Not wishing to alert anyone, in case this was yet another irritating false alarm, she got up quietly and went downstairs to make a cup of tea. Mina arrived in the kitchen a few minutes later. An hour later, Mina woke Khalid and sent him to fetch Mustapha. By the time they returned, Nellie was making fresh tea and slicing cake. She had lit the fires and put on the water. Elizabeth had retired to the sofa in the sitting room with Mina. Mustapha gave her a mild remedy and left her to rest. Nellie poured his tea and blushed when he complimented her cake. She greatly admired him, the quiet man whose gentle presence softened the entire room. Nellie had never suffered a day of ill health in her life. At times she had thought she would not mind being ill if Mustapha was there to look after her!

By six o'clock Elizabeth's pains had increased and Mustapha placed her in the bath and gave her a stronger remedy. Bella Mary arrived having read the note her father had left on the kitchen table. Mustapha had put up a rope above the bath prior to Olivia having the twins and he told Elizabeth to pull on the rope when she felt the need to push. She wanted Mina to come in and wanted the somewhat disinclined, wide-eyed Khalid to sit beside the bath. Grandy asked if he could come in, as he had never witnessed the birth of a child. Nellie gained entrance by delivering a tray of hot tea. Elizabeth, dizzy with remedy, smiled at everyone that she loved most in the world. Fortified with the stamina potion, she gave birth to a dark haired daughter amidst the cheers and applause of the crowd. Mustapha lifted the baby from the water and passed her to her mother. Elizabeth watched as the tiny creature blinked and the opened her eyes and she knew that Mina's prediction had been right. This tiny girl was the most precious thing in the world. She looked at Mina who had tears rolling down her cheeks.

'I want you to name her.'

'If I had been blessed with a daughter I would have named her Aida, meaning Peace.'

'Then she will be Aida Mina!'

Mustapha rolled Aida Mina in a warm towel and the entire crowd filed out of the bathhouse, leaving Bella Mary with Elizabeth. It was a bright sunny morning and Mustapha stood at the edge of the woodland in the flickering rays of sun and when the audience became silent he held her aloft for the blessing. Sam joined them and put his arm around Mina's shoulder and she thought that she would burst with happiness. Khalid carried his little daughter inside, followed by the proud grandparents. Mustapha put his arm around Nellie.

'I'll just help Bella Mary clean up, then how about we cook some breakfast Nellie?'

Grandy, accompanied by Gabriel rode over to his ancestral home to deliver the news to Hugh that his sister had given birth and to see the progress of Olivia's refurbishment. He was astonished at the change. The old place was bright and fresh, the new colours were vibrant and there was a complete absence of the eternal dusty old furniture that had met its end on a large bonfire in the rear garden. The servants, with the exception of Archie, had smiles on their faces. Hugh asked his father if he would return to live with them but Grandy, still able to sense a penetrating disapproval from the piles of ancestors relegated to the attics, declined.

Chapter 36

The village, standing on a peninsular in the Thames estuary, was generally oblivious to the changes in the rest of the country. Very few read a newspaper, with the exception of George who had an assortment sent to him on a monthly basis. The famers and shepherds in the village cared little for events that were irrelevant to them. Their only concerns being the weather, the price of wool, corn and other crops and whether or not the harvest would be gathered before the rain set in. Most villagers had never been to London and few had been as far as Rochester. Few were even aware they had been at war with France and the United States for years. It was months before anyone in the village knew that the Duke of Wellington had beaten Napoleon at the battle of Waterloo. Some wondered who they were and very few gave it another thought. They were even ignorant that the Corn Laws had been introduced, protecting the farmers from cheaper foreign imports. Most knew that King George was on the throne, although, due to the recent heavy turnover of Kings and Regents, they did not know which one.

There were no cotton mills, coalmines or smelting works to disturb the inhabitants and poison the air and it was many years before the temperamental old seed drill was superseded as the most advanced piece of machinery. George gave up sharing his newspapers with Esther, who was mortified to discover that young children were forced to work in factories and that many died very young. Grandy died so peacefully that Gabriel, who was in the stables with him, thought he had dropped off to sleep. He had left instructions that he did not want to be buried in the family vault, but in the village churchyard and that he wanted everyone to celebrate the final, very happy years of his life. He left the estate to Hugh and a substantial income to both of his daughters and a pile of letters to various members of the family, thanking them for their companionship and love.

Gabriel, who had spent his days with Grandy, felt the loss deeply. He had loved the old man like a father. Sitting in the stables with his beloved horses lost its allure. He was convinced that the horses also mourned the old man with the pockets full of carrots and apples. Ellen Lily tried to cheer him but Gabriel began to waste away and despite Mustapha's best efforts he was dead within six months. Ellen Lily, devastated by insurmountable grief, despite being surrounded by her family, sat in her armchair and waited to join Gabriel. They had been married over forty years and she would rather have lost her legs, or her eyes or her own life. The family prepared itself, believing she would not last the winter. But it was the unforeseen death of Maria that shook the family to its foundations. She had collapsed in the kitchen and when she finally regained consciousness she had lost all use of the left side of her body, lost the power of speech and lay in her bed with terrified, pleading eyes, locked in the prison of her own body. Mustapha and Matthew were summoned and Sal paced the bedroom in despair. Matthew had experience of the disorder and said the first forty-eight hours were critical. Sometimes patients improved over time, more frequently they died. Maria, her beautiful face lopsided, dribbled constantly as she was unable to swallow. Rose and Mustapha supported her and managed to massage teaspoons of warm sweet tea down her throat. Two nights later, with no signs of improvement, no urine output and Maria's chest heaving in a desperate effort to draw a rasping breath, Mustapha, who had not slept for three days, managed to massage enough of his strongest sedative down her throat to ensure that she would never wake again. When she was asleep he invited his father to sit with her and left them alone. Sal lay on the bed and held Maria until the laboured breathing ceased whilst Mustapha withdrew into the woods. Isabella found him at daybreak and told him that his mother had died. Mustapha was exhausted. He struggled with his conscience, unsure of whether he had done the right thing. He was unable to tell anyone what he had done to hasten his mother's death. Isabella made him hot sweet tea and he took it to the tree house, declining company, where he sat and stared blankly across the fields. When Nellie heard that Mustapha's mother had died, she dropped her tea towel and ran as fast as her considerable weight would allow towards the big house. Red in the face, she puffed up the steps of the tree house and enveloped him in a hug reminiscent of old Mary's embraces, the silent ones reserved for only the most heartrending occasions. She felt his body go limp in her arms as he began to sob. She stroked his hair and rocked his slim frame. He put his arms around her waist and hung on like a drowning man and she thought her heart would break. Isabella brought fresh tea but when she saw Nellie with her husband, she quietly placed the tray on the steps and left them alone. Nellie wiped Mustapha's face with her apron and noticed such pain in his black eyes. He buried his face in her ample chest and heaved a great sigh.

'Oh Nellie, I did a terrible thing!' he whispered.

She continued to rock him gently as he told her, with agonising sobs, what he had done.

'You always say that the remedies are a gift from God, and I know that you and God gave your mother the greatest gift of all, a peaceful, painless death.'

Mustapha looked into Nellie's eyes.

'You are the kindest, bravest man I have ever known and I just know that your mother knew that you would not let her suffer. She is at peace now.'

Nellie noticed the tray of tea and struggled down the steps and retrieved it. It was still warm, thanks to the towel wrapped around the pot. They sat in silence and drank their tea. Mustapha reached over and took hold of Nellie's hand, reddened and chapped by a lifetime of hard work, and squeezed it hard.

'Thank you Nellie.'

The ship sailed a month later. Sal, unable to bear the house without Maria, sailed with it. For the first time in years, Sam and Sal sailed together again. They were old men and they knew this was likely to be their last voyage. Edmundo and Estavo navigated and little Mustapha watched the weather. The elderly twins lay in their hammocks on deck, as they had done since they were twelve. Being at sea helped Sal cope with his loss, as he was able to convince himself that Maria was still in the kitchen with Rose. Sal had already made his final plans. He intended to slip quietly over the side of the ship during the night on their return journey, leaving a note of explanation for his brother.

Back at the big house it was Emily Rose and Aziz that helped to ease the pain and fill the great chasm that Maria's death had left and Rose found unexpected support from Esther. Sophia was with child again and hoping this time for a daughter that she would name Maria. Ellen Lily had failed miserably in her attempt to die, instead she returned to the big house to be with Rose and the children. Little Aida Mina brought great joy to the new house. She was a cheerful baby with the amber eyes of her father and dark hair. Elizabeth did not relegate the baby to a nursery and hire a nanny. She was not the most confident of mothers and prone to worry, but Mina was always there to support and encourage her, and Aida Mina was soon crawling around dribbling on books and needlework. Mustapha became a regular visitor to Nellie's kitchen and she always made sure there was a fresh cake in the tin.

Chapter 37

During the first few weeks at sea, Sam frequently poked his nose into the activities of Edmundo and Estavo, despite them having become eminently capable. Sal spent time with little Mustapha. This was how he had imagined he would have spent time with his son. But, as soon as he could crawl, he had chosen the company of his granddaddy, Maria's father Mustapha and Mary. He spent his summers in the garden with them and his winters in their little sitting room. When Sophia was born, she followed her brother's example and adopted the company of the old couple. Young Mustapha had no interest in the sea and developed a fascination with the microscope room and his granddaddy's potions. Over the years, Sal had watched his son become more like his grandfather. He had watched him develop remarkable skills and he was very proud of him. The love of the sea had skipped a generation and settled firmly in the heart of little Mustapha.

'Your father was never interested in a life at sea.' Remarked Sal to his grandson on a bright afternoon in the Mediterranean.

'Daddy didn't like the sea as it took you away from him so much.'

'What?' Sal gasped.

'He missed you so very much and has always believed that he let you down and that you were disappointed in him.'

'No! I am very proud of him, very, very proud!'

'Oh.'

'I have always loved him dearly!'

'Oh.'

Little Mustapha resumed his writing in the new journal oblivious of the bombshell he had dropped. Sal frowned at the horizon besieged by conflicting thoughts. He had felt redundant as a father when his children seemed happier with their grandfather and he had largely ignored them. He was horrified by the realisation that his son had needed him and that he believed he was a disappointment. Troubled, Sal tried to find something, anything to occupy his time. He searched for some lengths of rope and taught little Mustapha to splice. That night Sal lay awake in his hammock and thought back to his son's childhood. He had been a slight, quiet, serious little individual not given to displays of emotion like the other children. Then Sal remembered vividly when the little boy had stood silently beside the sofa watching him when he had just returned from a long voyage. He had assumed the child was waiting for one of the gifts being handed out. Now, some thirty years later he was profoundly ashamed and passionately wished that he had scooped the little boy up and hugged him to within an inch of his life!

In Constantinople the ship was loaded with silks and porcelain, tea and spices. Little Mustapha worked on his journal, filling the pages with sketches of the elegant mosques rising into the skies and the tall columns supporting the roofs of the extensive cisterns underneath the city. Sal asked if he could look at the journal and little Mustapha handed it over. As well as the drawings and the log of their journey, little Mustapha included personal messages to his father, mother and sister.

'Daddy, I love and miss you very much. Grandfather has taught me to splice ropes. He is still sad, but not quite so much as the days pass. He and Uncle Sam continue to get in the way of the crew, who know what they are doing. The Mediterranean is pleasant but not as beautiful as the Indian Ocean. Constantinople is very beautiful. There are great cisterns underneath the city, filled with clear water that comes from the mountains. We are bringing a crateful of Turkish Delight. Grandfather has told me that he is very proud of you and loves you very much, as I do.'

'May I write something?' asked Sal.

Little Mustapha smiled and passed him a pencil.

'Mustapha, I am so sorry that I did not hug you more often! Your loving father.'

Little Mustapha closed the journal. Sal asked him why he started the journals.

'Because when I write to my father and mother, I feel much closer to them and when they read it, they feel much closer to me! It is a way of always being together.'

'I wish I had thought of it years ago, but when Sam and I were your age, we almost forgot about the family and the village after a week or so, only remembering them when we were almost home.'

'That is because you are identical twins and always close to each other and have not experienced being alone and so you have less need of others. Edmundo and Estavo are the same.'

'Mustapha, how do you know all this?'

'Great-granddaddy taught me.'

'Oh.'

From then on little Mustapha allowed his grandfather to write in the journal whenever he wanted to. Sal found it comforting to write down his regrets and apologies when he realised that his small son had not rejected him in favour of his granddaddy, but that he had failed to nurture their relationship as a father should have done. Sal began to feel better and was able to think about Maria, accept that she had gone and accept that he would always love her.

He wrote in the journal.

'I can never thank you enough for taking care of your mother, my beloved son. I love you.'

Sal felt so improved that he forgot about his plan to drown himself and only remembered it when he realised that he was looking forward to going home!

The weather was favourable and the wind brisk. The ship was home in record time, sooner than expected in early spring.

Sal watched, and envied, the uninhibited display of emotion when little Mustapha leapt on his joyful father. Two nights later Mustapha read the journal with the messages from his father and was greatly moved. He picked up the journal and made his way to his father's room. Isabella found them in the morning, fast asleep in the same bed, two trays with empty teapots and plates balanced at the foot of the bed.

As little Mustapha was now as tall as his father, the family unanimously decided he was now to be referred to as young Mustapha.

Chapter 38

Sophia, almost as consistent as Tom's ewes, gave birth to another son. They named him Edward Salamar and called him Teddy. Tom carved little wooden animals for the children to play with, just as his great-great-grandfather had done for his children. His clumsy efforts were put to shame when Joey arrived with a rocking horse he had made. The majestic horse had wild eyes and big teeth. The mane and tail were real horsehair. Tommy loved it but Danny hid in Sophia's skirts, wide-eyed and terrified of the ferocious looking beast. He preferred his father's tiny animals and Tom felt better. Tommy named his horse Rocky and it was weeks before little

Danny was able to stop circumnavigating the entire room in order to avoid the petrifying vicinity of Rocky.

The temperature rose unusually high in the spring. The trees and flowers burst into life during four days of hot weather and were then battered and broken by the first of the storms. The storm passed quickly, followed by more fine warm days and a further storm, bringing torrential rain that ran in rivers down the main street. Then the hot sun returned and the entire village steamed like wet washing in front of the fire. The mud dried into uneven ruts until the next storm reduced them to slippery mud again. It became known as the 'summer of storms.' Apart from the tall, lone elm, a landmark in the village for as long as anyone could recall, and one barn, the storms did little structural damage and the lightening failed to strike anyone down. Some of the storms passed mercifully quickly, others rolled around for hours. It was the crops that suffered brutally. Tiny plants were washed out of the soil, to be swiftly shrivelled by the scorching sun. By June, the days were blisteringly hot and sunburn and sunstroke took its toll. The men working in the fields developed sore, stinking feet, a consequence of being permanently damp. In the worst cases, layers of skin stuck to the insides of their boots leaving the soles of their feet stripped and red raw. Everyone prayed for the end of the storms and for a few days they were hopeful of a drought, as the sun shone and there were no clouds in the sky. The next storm sneaked up under the cover of darkness and the villagers woke to a saturated village once again. Slugs and snails capitalised on the warm, wet conditions and multiplied, eating any plants not killed by the storms. Bella Mary surrounded her garden with crushed eggshells and transferred the chickens into the fenced garden to eat any slugs and snails undeterred by the eggshells. Her garden, sheltered by the woodland and on well-drained soil, suffered less damage than most and the poppies flourished. The mosquitoes also thrived in the damp hot summer and the incidences of malarial fevers rose at an alarming rate. Bella Mary, reeking of garlic, distributed strings of garlic around the village. The crops not washed away rotted in the fields. The potatoes suffered blight and the corn turned black and mouldy in the flattened fields. Everything was damp. The walls developed a black mildew, the curtains went mouldy, cooking pots rusted on the shelves and fungus invaded the backs of cupboards. The horses suffered from mud fever, the sheep from maggots and frogs invaded the homes of the beleaguered inhabitants. Salt solidified, milk spoiled and bugs proliferated in the flour bins. The hot, sticky villagers were too exhausted to even vent their frustration by shouting at each other. They would have dearly loved to shout, to wallop someone or kick a passing dog, but they were destroyed by an all-consuming apathy. More than a dozen older inhabitants died that summer. They had become so dispirited and lethargic that they gave up breathing. Graves were dug and the following day the holes were half full of water and the distressed relatives watched in horror as their loved ones coffins bobbed about on the water's surface, then sank slowly and unevenly, emitting bubbles of air, undignified gurgles and clonks. The gravediggers were reduced to dropping great lumps of broken gravestones on top of the coffins that threatened to rise up in the watery mud as they tried to fill the grave. The gravestones broke open one of the coffins and the Reverend ushered the mourners away from the graveside so they would not see the corpse of their loved one undulating listlessly in the muddy water. Some women became hysterical and one refused to commit her mother's body to a watery nightmare and demanded that she be left on the surface until the grave was dry. The coffin was flimsy and when her husband returned to see if the water had subsided, he discovered the coffin broken open and his unfortunate mother-in-law half eaten by foxes or dogs. He shoved the coffin into the watery hole, threw in the bits strewn around by the animals, searched unsuccessfully for a missing foot and filled in the grave with the surrounding mud. He lied to his wife and told her the hole was nice and dry and prayed that the absent foot would not be found. Two small boys found it, greenish and maggoty, behind a gravestone beside the church wall. They picked it up and took it to the sick house. Maud squealed and Mustapha quickly wrapped the foot and buried it in the earth behind the sick house and made the boys wash themselves thoroughly with hot water and soap. He told the boys that it had been a piece of an animal and that was the end of that.

It was not until August that the storms abated and well into August before anyone dared breathe a sigh of relief. There was no harvest to gather and what remained of the spoiled crops was ploughed back into the soil. George was busy ordering in vast stocks of flour and vegetables to replenish the empty barns and ensure the village had enough provisions for the winter. At the end of August the big house threw a massive party, with a surfeit of food and fireworks. The main attraction was the piles of new boots to replace the hard, shrunken, foul-smelling footwear currently limping around on blistered feet. There were two crates of woollen socks and one by one the excited guests donned a new pair of socks and boots and when the bonfire was lit, they lined up to incinerate their old ones. The houses eventually dried out and the musty smell disappeared and the toadstools in the cupboards shrivelled up and turned to dust. It had been a good summer for grass and the animals grew fat and in September the hay harvest filled the barns.

October was dry and cold and by the middle of the month, the night sky was clear and full of stars and the frost grew like grass. It was so cold that Charles and Aziz began shifting dead trees to the village green. In November, gale-force, icy winds whipped the village. Tom built high fences at the rear of his house and moved his chilly sheep in from the far marshes to the relative shelter of his backyard. The wind broke large branches from the trees and would have uprooted the trees were their roots not so firmly frozen into the earth. The wind blew the protective straw from Bella Mary's garden as fast as she could replace it. Eventually she covered the thick layer of straw with old sheets and sails, anchoring them with sharpened wooden stakes hammered into the hard ground. When they had fed their animals and gathered the wood, people huddled around their fires, thawing frozen fingers and scratching chilblains. It was too cold for snow and weeks passed without the icicles melting. Animals were provided with extra bedding and dogs that usually lived in their kennels were dragged indoors. Cows were pushed into the barns that warmed up quickly, thanks to the heat given off by the puffing, grunting cattle. The chickens moved in with the cows. Joey delivered a cartload of wood to Tom and Sophia and stacked it against the exposed side of the house. Big Ern and Beth opened the school just before Christmas and lit all the fires and the coldest families moved in. Joey brought a cartload of meat and vegetables and thirty-five villagers had a warm, joyful Christmas.

Chapter 39

Sam and Sal decided that would make one last voyage, to their favoured Indian Ocean and India, a country that they both loved. They would leave in the spring and return the following summer. Mustapha gave Yusuf a large supply of the remedy and ointment now used by both Sam and Sal for the aches in their knees and their backs. After the year of freak weather, they were all looking forward to warm sun and gentle winds. Young Mustapha dreamed of arriving in his favourite village once again where there was no ice or freezing wind and where even the rain was pleasantly warm.

Maud spent February at the sick house, nursing a man named Jack. He had a badly broken leg resulting in a heavy fall on the ice and Matthew and Mustapha wanted him to avoid any weight on the limb for at least six weeks. Maud moved into the sick house, fed him, washed him and made sure he remained in bed. By the time his leg had healed, he had proposed to Maud and she had accepted. Maud was in her thirties and had long accepted her fate as a spinster. To the great delight of everyone who loved Maud, the couple were to be married in early summer. Jack was an animal doctor, specialising in cattle and dogs. He had been visiting a sick cow when he slipped and broke his leg. His parents had died and he lived with his sister and her family in a village some ten miles away. Jack never returned to his sister's. He was fascinated to learn of the remedies and potions available at the sick house and even more fascinated to discover that they had remedies for animals. Jack Filmer had a magical way with animals akin to old Mustapha's way with people. The most cantankerous animal was cooperative and trusting in his hands. Jack rented a small property not fifty yards from the sick house, where he and Maud would live after their marriage. Isabella and Beth helped Maud and Jack to furnish the little house, providing them with everything they would need. Maud was not skilled in cooking, apart from chicken soup, so Mustapha arranged for her to visit the new house one day each week to learn to cook with Nellie. Jack explored the marshes and found Tom and Sophia up to their knees in lambs and toddlers. The sheep had unanimously decided that today would be a good day to produce lambs. Jack rolled up his sleeves and helped and Sophia rescued a newly born lamb from the unwelcome attention of Teddy and returned it to its fraught mother. She gathered the boys and sat them on the bathhouse steps, with orders to remain there or risk being shut indoors. Tommy and Danny sat obediently on the step but Teddy crawled off to retrieve his lamb. Sophia stopped him, causing an instant, furious squealing fit. She grabbed him by the scruff of the neck and lifted him up, his tiny legs flailing wildly. She held him at arm's length, ignoring his piercing screams and marched him indoors. Eventually, the sheep, who had decided that today was a good day to lamb had finished giving birth and relative piece settled on the flock that had almost trebled its size in one day. Tommy and Danny remained on the step until their father allowed them to come closer and stroke some lambs. Jack stayed for stew, dumplings and hot, fresh bread, butter and cheese. Teddy had recovered his composure and all that remained of his outburst were his red, puffy eyes. Tom and Jack became good friends and Jack became a regular visitor, occasionally accompanied by Maud.

The ship sailed off on a warm spring day. Mina went to watch for the first time, fearing that she may never see her husband again. She felt sad on the journey home but her spirits were rapidly lifted by little Aida Mina's enthusiastic welcome.

Olivia, heavily pregnant with her fourth child, had completed her refurbishment of the mansion. Henry and Edgar ran about all day, chased by the intrepid Daisy. Victoria, now five, was becoming excellent company. Olivia hired a governess, a young, shy woman named Helen, to teach Victoria as the journey to the school was much too far to travel twice a day. Olivia had seen several governesses before choosing Helen. She had a nice smile and was the only one not to frighten Victoria. Intimidated by the stiff posture and unwavering, withering glances and frowns of the other four candidates, Victoria had hidden behind her mother's chair and tugged at her dress, shaking her head to convey the message, 'No!'

Olivia awoke with a familiar backache. She had learned during previous deliveries, to be suspicious of backaches, so she sent Hugh to collect Mustapha. Daisy took the twins out for their morning exercise, leaving Victoria with her mother. Olivia felt the warm, uncontrollable gush of her waters and knew from experience that the birth was imminent.

'Victoria, could you please go and find someone to help Mummy.'

'Who?'

'Anyone Victoria, the first person you can find, quickly!'

Fighting to ignore the urge to push, Olivia hung onto the arms of the chair. Victoria ran into the room, closely followed by Archie.

'Victoria, get Mummy some clean towels dear!'

Archie's general calm exterior shattered abruptly when Olivia announced.

'This baby is coming and I need your help Archie.'

He made for the door.

'Archie, there is no time, please help me!'

'What?'

Victoria returned with a pile of towels and Olivia sent her to the kitchen to ask for hot water. She instructed Archie to put a towel at her feet and find the scissors to cut the cord. Archie, trembling and with a face drained of all colour did as he was told. He helped Olivia off the chair and into a kneeling position above the towel. He tried not to look when she asked him to push her skirts out of the way.

'Sit behind me Archie and make sure you catch the baby before it falls!'

Poor Archie was forced to look. He watched as Olivia arched her back and pushed. To his horror, and if he were honest, revulsion, an object resembling a turnip loomed briefly from the rear of his mistress and then partially disappeared again. He felt hot and slightly giddy as the turnip emerged further and then stopped.

'Archie, get ready!'

Archie unfolded the towel and held it, then dropped it as Olivia's body suddenly extruded a steaming, purplish, slippery object. Archie caught it successfully and briefly thought it to be very like a Labrador pup. As the laid the spluttering child on the towel he was horrified to see that it was still attached to his mistress by a slimy, twisted rope. Olivia told him to tie the cord with cotton in two places and cut in between. With shaking sticky hands, Archie did his best. He rolled the child in a clean towel and struggled to his feet.

'What is it Archie?'

'Beg Pardon?' stuttered Archie.

'The baby, what is it?' Olivia begged as she sat down on the towel with a profound sigh.

'It's here.' Answered the dismayed, dumbfounded, overwhelmed butler. He proffered the child to Olivia.

'Archie, for Goodness sake! Is it a boy or a girl?'

'Erm....'

Olivia was hit by an attack of the giggles. Elsie the cook, alerted by Victoria's request for hot water burst into the room to find an ashen-faced Archie, awkwardly rocking a squalling baby, whilst its mother sat on the floor, crying with laughter.

Archie was far more in need of hot sweet tea than Olivia. He sagged into an armchair, still holding the now quiet baby that gazed around the room, blinking its eyes. Archie touched the tiny red palm of its hand and the little fingers closed tightly around his finger and Archie had to blink a number of times to stop the tears from running down his cheeks, overcome by unanticipated love.

Mustapha and Hugh arrived. Mustapha checked on Olivia, who was still laughing and then checked the baby.

'Come on Mustapha, tell us what it is!' Chuckled Olivia. 'Archie has failed to find out!'

'It is a beautiful healthy boy.'

Archie beamed with pride, drank his tea and then went outside for a welcome smoke on his pipe.

The boy was named Richard Archibald. Archie loved the child and always called him Turnip.

Chapter 40

A kitchen crisis gradually developed at the big house. Isabella's lack of ability made her a hindrance rather than any help. Esther was too busy with the shop and Emily. Ellen Lily was becoming dafter as the weeks went on and could no longer be trusted and Rose was old and tired. The two village girls, Helen and Amy were hardworking but lacked the skills of a good cook. Nellie helped out when she could, but was too busy at the new house to spare very much of her time. Mustapha, worried about Rose, pleaded with Olivia to send one of the cooks that she and Maria had trained. Florence jumped at the chance of returning to the big house and packed her meagre belongings and hopped about on the front steps waiting for old George to bring the carriage.

Florence's energy transformed the place. She was up at dawn, delighted to be in charge of a kitchen of her own, a dream rarely realised until middle age in her profession. She livened up Helen and Amy, taught Helen to make the sauces and Amy the puddings. She shooed Ellen Lily and Rose to the sitting room and presented them with warm biscuits and an even warmer smile with their tea. She found a bell in the bathhouse that she rang ten minutes before a meal was to be served. She sang and laughed and clattered about and reminded Rose of when she was a child and Mary had managed the kitchen. Florence produced food that old Mustapha would have been proud of, excelling at his favourite spicy chicken dishes. A cheer erupted around the table when Florence served the peppery sauce with the beef, a recipe that had been lost since the sudden death of Maria. The mood in the whole house improved and even Paulo, who had been ailing for some time, regained his appetite.

Maud and Jack married in June. Maud wore a pale blue dress, designed by Esther and embroidered with a white daisy chain that circled the bottom of the skirt and ran up the front of the dress, over the shoulder and down the left arm. Rose made her a crown of the first white poppies and forget-me-nots. Maud, with her long hair brushed loose was unrecognisable, even to herself. The whole village, still recovering from a year of uncomfortably hazardous weather, turned out for the wedding. Florence received a great many compliments in respect of her cauldron of peppery sauce. She watched the fireworks from the kitchen window with a proud smile and made herself a pot of tea and sat down heavily at the table. She had been on her feet for almost twenty hours and her ankles ached, but she was happier than at any other time in her life. Ellen Lily wafted vaguely into the kitchen with a silly smile and an outrageous hat, followed by Rose, who had spent the last half hour searching for her. She had found her at the bottom of the meadow, sitting in a wheelbarrow, being pushed at high speed by several highly amused village lads. Rose asked the disappointed boys to push her to the front door and she brought her inside. They sat down with Florence and Rose insisted on topping up the teapot and bringing extra cups. Florence laughed until she cried when Rose told her where she had found Ellen Lily, who listened attentively, wondering briefly who on earth Rose was talking about. The three women sat and listened to the last of the music in the meadow. Rose asked about Florence's family and they were flabbergasted to discover that Florence's great-grandfather Roland was, in fact, the older brother of old Mary. It made sense to Rose as Florence had always reminded her of Mary, the same cheerful disposition, boundless energy and unruly chestnut hair. Rose thought she could feel Mary's presence in the kitchen and imagined her standing smiling, glad that her kitchen was in good hands. Ellen Lily abruptly leapt to her feet and began singing and waltzing slowly around the kitchen with an invisible partner. Rose shook her head and Florence snorted with supressed laughter.

Mustapha was at a loss, as his grandfather had been when trying to treat John many years ago, of what to do with Ellen Lily. She was happy enough and could be relied upon to make everyone laugh at least once a day, so he left her alone. When her random nightly adventures became problematic, he gave her a sedative before she retired to bed, making it more likely that she could be found next morning. However, the day Rose realised that Ellen Lily, sitting in the tree house stripped to the waist, was trying to breast feed a tiny baby, she knew things would have to change. Ellen Lily just grinned absently when asked where she had found the baby. Were it not for the tumultuous hullaballoo emanating from Lily Lane, nobody would have known where the poor child came from. Mustapha hired the services of a widow from the village, Mrs May, to act as chaperone to Ellen Lily. The family was shaken and upset by the incident, aware that Ellen Lily could have left the baby anywhere and immediately forgotten about it. The possible disastrous consequences did not bear thinking about, but Florence chuckled quietly for weeks, attributing her watering eyes to the onions.

Annie gave birth to a son in her own new bathhouse, assisted by Mustapha and Bella Mary, several remedies and with her husband Amos at her side. They named him Benjamin Levi. Levi was so delighted that he ran across the road to the Inn and purchased a drink for everyone in there. Sophia, out of sync with the ewes that year, gave birth to yet another son in July, delivered by Tom on the hearthrug before he had time to fill the bath. He was named William and referred to as Billy. Sophia despaired of ever having a daughter.

That summer was mild and tranquil, as though the weather had exhausted itself during the previous year. Apart from the weeks of harvesting it was a peaceful year with gentle sun and soft rains. Bella Mary's garden proliferated. Plants grew through the fences and invaded the meadow. She divided her time between the garden, the sick house and the microscope room where she and her father constantly replenished the stock of potions. She had grown into an extraordinary beauty, as old Mustapha had predicted. She was tall like her father and willowy like her mother, her skin tanned easily in the sun and her long pale ringlets bleached almost white. Her eyes were as black as her father's and her stare unnerving. She was skilled in harvesting plants, making remedies and even inventing new ones, but her 'bedside manner', or the profound lack of it, worried her father. Bella Mary, fascinated by the machinery of a body, largely ignored the person inhabiting it. She examined and investigated, noting every detail, every response to a potion, but the ability to offer reassurance, encouragement and kindness was sadly absent. She firmly believed that it was the efficiency of the remedy that mattered most and that kind words never saved anybody. Mustapha assured her that they were just as important, but she remained unconvinced. He had to admit that her diagnoses were accurate and she was totally unflappable in a crisis, fearless and astute. She had already begun to collect pus from cattle infected with cowpox and visit the families all over the village asking to treat their children and prevent them from catching smallpox. Their parents, who had heard from their parents of the dreadful, slow, agonising, disfiguring, killer disease that had regularly devastated the village in the past and continued to be rife in the nearby towns, happily overpowered and held captive their squealing, wide-eyed offspring and allowed Bella Mary to scrape the child's skin until she drew blood, rub in the stinking pus and bandage the area. Mustapha hoped that 'bedside manner' was a quality that his daughter would gradually master as she got older.

Both Elizabeth and Esther announced they were with child in late August and Bella Mary hounded them, measuring their bellies on a weekly basis, weighing them and counting their pulse rate. She wanted to know the exact day of their last bleed. Esther remembered that hers was the last day of June and Bella Mary estimated the child's birth to be mid-April. Elizabeth had no idea when her last bleed was and Bella Mary looked down her nose at her and sighed and wrote a question mark in her book. She kept the findings for 'research purposes.'

Mustapha accepted that he had spawned an alchemist or a scientist, not a healer.

Chapter 41

The voyage down the west side of Africa was unusually uneventful. The notorious Atlantic spared them from its recurrent fury and a brisk wind carried the little ship round the Cape of Good Hope in time for summer in the Indian Ocean. Young Mustapha refused to allow his grandfather Sal up into the crow's nest without the security of a safety rope. Sam smiled and remembered when he had been the one to attach safety ropes to the young ones. It was the turn of the children to take on the role of parent, relegating the old ones to the restrictions of childhood. Sal stood in the crow's nest, attached by a rope, Mustapha and Edmundo held the other end, ready to take the weight if Sal wobbled off his perch. He remained aloft for so long that they tied the rope securely and left him there with orders to shout when he was ready to descend. The ocean was even more beautiful than the images in Sal's memory. The intensity of the greens and blues were brighter and the water more transparent. He watched the immeasurable shoals of tiny fish, flashing silver in the bright sunlight. He saw the dolphins ploughing through the shoals, snapping up the fish, whilst the great swirling, spinning shoal reformed, undulating like some kind of vast creature.

Sal, who had scoffed at the safety rope and only surrendered to the idea as young Mustapha and the twins would not have allowed him up there otherwise, had to admit they had been right. He lost his footing a third of the way down. The young men took his weight and Sal twisted and swung like a pendulum and Sam laughed himself into a coughing fit. They lowered Sal as fast as they could to avoid him slamming into the mast, then gently for the last yard. He regularly returned to the crow's nest, so Yusuf made a rudimentary harness that proved more comfortable than a rope around the belly, particularly when Sal lost his footing, which was fairly regularly. In the end, frustrated by Sal's sluggish, unsteady, creaking ascent to the crow's nest, young Mustapha and the twins took to hauling him aloft with one long, steady pull on the rope.

The ship dawdled though the islands and young Mustapha pointed out the place they had sheltered from the terrible storm to his grandfather. They docked twice in East Africa to fulfil Harry and Big Ern's request for ebony. Yusuf bought fresh fish from the local fishermen and leant that many of the ugly fish he had rejected in the past, were in fact considered a delicacy. Then they sailed east towards India, Sal waving from the crow's nest to the sailors in their heavy little ships known as dhow, meaning 'mule', that criss-crossed the massive ocean, trading from east Africa to Arabia and the Red Sea in the north and to the east, the Arabian Sea and the west coast of India. By the time they reached the Arabian Sea they were habitually soaked by the tail end of the warm monsoon rains and Sal stationed himself in the crow's nest for his first glimpse of India for many years, excited as he had been at the age of twelve.

Mustapha wrapped his precious globe in hessian sacks and wedged it into a tea chest. He had not forgotten his promise to take it to the spice village. The crew were particularly fond of this part of the voyage, where they were left to themselves for weeks, to lie around in hammocks and rest. Where beautiful women, resembling exotic birds, would glide up the gangplank wearing unbelievable smiles, and vivid, shimmering silk saris carrying bowls of deliciously aromatic curries, saffron rice, baskets of hot chapattis and balls of vegetables in crispy batter. The two sets of twins, Yusuf, Mustapha and the globe set off for the village the next morning. The ground was soft from the monsoon and the cart made slow progress, the unfortunate donkeys slipped and slithered in a supreme effort to keep moving. They stopped every hour or so to give the poor creatures a drink and a rest. The going became easier in the countryside where the tough grasses growing in the tracks gave purchase to the donkey's hooves. They arrived at nightfall and startled the unsuspecting villagers during their evening meal, the aroma of which had tantalised the cartload of men for the last half hour. The women swung into action, stoked the dwindling fires, and within an hour provided the hungry visitors with a very welcome meal, rendered even more exquisitely delicious due to the period of delay, whilst they drank green tea, bhang and yoghurt and salivated. The women found it hard to believe that the little Mustapha they loved was now a very tall man. That night the visitors slung their hammocks between the coconut trees and slept until the women woke them with hot tea and spicy porathas. Young Mustapha failed to recognise the vision in a purple and cerise striped sari that approached with bowls of fresh mangoes. On their last visit she had been a shy child that he only vaguely recalled. She had grown into the most beautiful women he had ever seen. Her smile devastated him and her huge dark eyes rendered him speechless. He watched her as she walked away with a tray of dishes, her long thick braid of hair swinging almost to her knees. Sam kicked his brother's hammock and nodded towards young Mustapha, who sat mesmerised watching the young woman bending to wash the dishes. The old twins smiled at each other and Sal shook his head. Sabia, aptly meaning beautiful woman, did remember Mustapha. She had idolised him from a distance during their last visit and was more than pleased with the man he had become. Today she had worn her next best sari, keeping her very best white and silver one in reserve.

After breakfast young Mustapha struggled to regain his composure and unpacked his globe from the tea chest. He explained to the curious villagers that it was a model of the whole of the earth, that the blue areas were the sea and the green and brown areas the land. Many in the audience remained sceptical, some were absorbed and a couple of old ones were scandalised. Young Mustapha showed them the journey they had made to reach India. The audience wondered how they could possibly find their way, and his explanation of navigating by the stars was an idea too far for many to grasp. When he pointed out Britain, where the great almighty ruler King George lived and the very important governor General Lord William came from, sheer disbelief set in. The most powerful country in the world could not be that tiny! People would be forever bumping into each other or be pushed off the edges! The villagers descended into laughter, believing it to be a good joke and young Mustapha gave up.

Sam and Sal relaxed in their hammocks, Yusuf and the twins, who had outgrown the need to climb the coconut trees, went with the men to collect the spices from other villages. Young Mustapha, feeling very unsure of what to do, wrote in his journal. The cool, fragrant wafts of Sabia as she silently delivered refreshments upset his concentration and his equilibrium. He put down his journal and realised that his grandfather and great uncle were both rocking, convulsed with silent laughter. Mustapha left his hammock and red in the face walked off between the trees, the now far from silent laughter snapping at his heels.

'Poor young devil!' Sam stated, when he had finished chuckling. It was history repeating itself and he could still remember his own trauma when he met

Mina so very long ago. He struggled up from his hammock and went in search of young Mustapha. He found him sitting beside a small stream, his feet in the cool water, dejectedly poking at the stones with a stick. Sam sat down beside him.

'It happened to me, and not too many miles north of here, when I met your Aunt Mina.'

Young Mustapha glared at him ruefully.

'It is life lad. If at the end of our stay, she feels the same way that you do, you will have to make a choice.'

Young Mustapha resumed poking stones.

'You can either stay here with her, or take her home with you. But you do need to start speaking to her soon!'

Sam rose painfully to his feet, leaning on young Mustapha's shoulder.

'Don't you worry son, it will all work out, trust me.'

Young Mustapha watched his great uncle walk slowly away, slightly bent over and favouring his right leg. Young Mustapha thought about Aunt Mina, about how she still blushed when Sam put his arm around her. She had watched him sail away in the spring, her eyes full of love and fear. They had been together for almost forty years. Young Mustapha made his way back slowly, endeavouring to rally his flagging reserves of courage.

Chapter 42

It was late summer. Isabella and Mustapha sat in the tree house drinking tea before he left to go to the sick house. Aziz was leading Emily Rose around the meadow on Moonshine, the pony outgrown by his sister. Bella Mary led the horses from the stables and waited for her father at the base of the tree house. Mustapha kissed Isabella and rode off with his daughter. Isabella watched them trot across the meadow, causing Moonshine to break into a run, and depositing the giggling Emily Rose in a heap on the grass. Below her, Bella Mary's garden was a blaze of flamboyant colour. The poppies ranged from dazzling white, through pinks and lavenders to deep reds, cerise and deep purples that verged on black. The foxgloves towered above them. The large bushes of lavender attracted a great variety of bees. The dark green rosemary had burst through the fence. Isabella watched her husband and daughter disappear into the distance and she thought about young Mustapha, wondered where he was and prayed for his safety. The distant laughter of Florence mingled with the birdsong and Isabella smiled, assuming that she was laughing at Ellen Lily again.

Ellen Lily had begun to ask where Gabriel was. At first, they explained that he was dead, which caused her great distress for the length of time it took for her to forget again. Florence decided that it was inhumane to keep telling the poor old woman that she was a widow. Some days she was widowed countless times, depending on how quickly she forgot. So Florence told her he was in the stables and would return soon. This explanation satisfied Ellen Lily.

'That man should have married a horse!' was her usual cheerful response.

She spent a lot of time with Florence, who gave her the vegetables to peel. Bella Mary believed that parts of the old woman's brain were dying. She remembered virtually nothing from the last few years, but she remembered stories from her childhood, remembered the words of songs and hymns. She could still wash and dress herself, still peel vegetables, make very good apple pies, darn socks and teach Emily Rose her letters and numbers.

'Where's Gabriel?'

'In the stables.'

'That man should have married a horse!' she cackled, not for the first, or the last time that day!

Isabella, still in the tree house, watched Harry arrive with a pile of new oak planks and poles and drop them at the base of the tree. He had come to repair the aging tree house before winter set in. He investigated the strength of the old planks by jumping on them and if they sagged or creaked, he chiselled them out and replaced them. Florence served fresh tea for Harry and Isabella, who was passing the new wood up to Harry and Aziz had put himself in charge of the nails. In Florence's wake came Ellen Lily, skipping along to her own enthusiastic singing. Mrs May brought up the rear. Ellen Lily sat on the grass and watched whilst Harry replaced a number of fence poles at the top of the tree house and three of the steps leading to the ground.

'Where's Gabriel?'

Harry looked up at Isabella and she shook her head as Mrs May quietly assured her he was in the stables.

'Ooh! That man should have married a horse!'

Florence returned to the kitchen for more tea and a slab of fruitcake and the group all sat down on the grass for a rest.

'I think I'll take a cup of tea and cake to Gabriel.'

'No need.' Answered Florence. 'I already did.'

'Thank you Florence, I always think that man should have married a horse!'

By the end of the afternoon the tree house was an eye-catching patchwork of different coloured wood. Paulo, who had built the structure some thirty years before, came to inspect Harry's repairs. Rose arrived with fresh tea and Florence disappeared into the kitchen and half an hour later the enticing smell of spicy chicken wafted out to the group sitting around the tree house. Emily Rose saw her mother in the distance and ran down the meadow to meet her. Aziz took Moonshine back to the stables. Isabella picked a bowlful of ripe, fat blackberries from the edge of the woods. Ellen Lily spent an innocent half an hour in Bella Mary's garden, singing hymns and sniffing the flowers, under the watchful eye of Mrs May. Mustapha and Bella Mary arrived home. Florence rang the bell for dinner and by the time Helen and Amy had carried the steaming dishes of food to the table, the family, plus Harry were seated.

'Where's Gabriel?'

'He's seeing to the horses and will be in shortly.'

'I don't know why that man didn't marry a horse!'

Dinner consisted of spicy chicken, spicy potatoes cooked with onions and garlic, flat, hot bread, lettuces, tomatoes and beetroot. Followed by cold apple pie and fresh blackberries, cheese and fresh warm bread.

'That was a very nice pie Florence!' Ellen Lily declared.

'You made it.' Florence responded.

'Did I?'

During tea, Bella Mary entertained everyone with news of the day at the sick house. They had lanced a boil, bandaged a badly sprained ankle, extracted a tooth and retrieved a dried bean from the nose of a three-year-old child. Maud had vomited twice and Bella Mary suspected that she was with child. Ellen Lily said that it sounded like a day in the life of her accident-prone son Henry, who had magically turned himself, years ago, into a large bronze horse.

Florence, whose status within the family had improved due to her pepper sauce knowledge, was further elevated when everyone discovered that she was the great-niece of the distinguished Mary. On her afternoon off, Florence walked into the village, picked a bunch of wild flowers along the way and deposited them lovingly on the grave of old Mary. Then she went to look at the sick house. Mustapha was surprised to see her and made her a cup of tea and showed her around. She mentioned that she had put flowers on her great-aunts grave. After she left, Mustapha ran up into the churchyard and moved the flowers to the adjacent grave, where both Mary and old Mustapha lay.

Chapter 43

The whole village, and by then even Sam, Sal and Yusuf, knew that Sabia had been waiting years for the return of young Mustapha. She had refused all offers of marriage, insisting that she was waiting only for him to return, no matter how long she had to wait. Initially, her father Sachin had been outraged. He called her stupid, ungrateful, deranged and numerous other insults, as and when he thought of them. Her mother understood her feelings and in due course, managed to persuade her irate husband to grant Sabia a limited period of years to wait. He granted her another five years before he would marry her off to any man willing to take her. Young Mustapha had arrived in year three, a total of seven years from his last visit. On the fourth day of their visit, Sachin, agitated by the lack of any advancement towards a marriage proposal, approached young Mustapha in his hammock. Sachin was a man of few words.

'Do you wish to marry my Sabia or not?'

Young Mustapha momentarily stunned, tried to stand up and overbalanced, his foot caught in the hammock.

'Well?' demanded Sachin when Mustapha stood up. 'She has, against my biddings and commands, waited for you for these last too many years. I am fed up with the waiting and waiting and she is costing me money. She has refused many suitable offers, some from very wealthy suitors. If you don't want her, I want to know and then I can marry her to another husband! Before she is too old and ugly for anyone to want!'

Young Mustapha looked down into the beady eyes of the determined, wrinkly little man and struggled to make an appropriate response. Sam took the initiative.

'My great-nephew would be delighted to marry your daughter, Sachin!'

The old men shook hands and hugged each other with great enthusiasm. It was settled, and young Mustapha collapsed into his hammock, reeling with relief and utter terror. Young Mustapha found himself paralysed by a debilitating shyness. Sabia, on the other hand, aware that her future was settled, took the initiative. Clad in her best shimmering white and silver sari, she invited young Mustapha to walk with her and by the time they returned, hand in hand, young Mustapha was smiling and had largely regained his composure. The couple married at the village in a ceremony lasting three days. Sabia was dressed in gold and red, her hands, arms and feet decorated with elaborate henna designs. On her wrists she wore dozens of tinkling gold bangles, part of her dowry. There was no uncertainly about where they would live. Sabia had for years looked forward to her journey to a faraway foreign land. Sam realised he would have to suspend his ban and allow yet another woman aboard his ship. Young Mustapha and Sabia, with her battered tin trunk containing all of her worldly goods, rode back to the coast wobbling about on the top of the sacks of spices. Sabia had never seen the sea and she clung to young Mustapha's hand as they walked up the long gangplank onto the ship. She put her hands together as if in prayer and bowed her head as she was introduced to the crew. To young Mustapha's surprise the men returned her gesture, a greeting that had become second nature to them, due to having been moored there for six weeks. Sam suggested to Sabia that she would be more comfortable in the baggy trousers and long shirts that his own mother Lily had worn during her time at sea. Sabia raised an astonished eyebrow, blushed profusely and insisted on wearing her usual attire. She accompanied the men the next day when they searched the markets for tea, silks and presents for the family. Young Mustapha asked her to choose a number of saris to take home, reminding her that home would be much colder than she was used to. Sabia had never chosen more than one sari at a time and flitted around the shop, beside herself with excitement. She chose eight, half in a heavyweight silk. Young Mustapha watched proudly, thoroughly enjoying being a husband and providing for his wife for the first time. Sabia then sorely embarrassed her husband by bartering with the shopkeeper with such sovereign skill that included twice leaving the shop and being coaxed back by the poor man with an even lower price.

'Sabia, I would have happily paid the man what he asked.'

'Then he would think you a fool and laugh with his friends! I do not wish him to believe that I am married to a fool!'

To everyone's surprise, Sabia suffered no seasickness and she spent her days on deck, transfixed by the beauty of the ocean with tiny white islands surrounded by turquoise water. She scaled the rigging, complete with sari and joined Sal in the crow's next, flapping gaily like a gaudy flag. Mustapha traced their journey on the globe as they headed west across the expanse of blue that was the Indian Ocean. She was astonished that weeks of sailing covered such a small distance on the globe and began to grasp how large the earth really was. The ship docked in east Africa for fresh supplies and Sabia was astounded by the tall, thin men with blue-black skin and fuzzy hair, who ran around naked except for a tiny loin cloth. Young Mustapha took her ashore to walk on the beach. She paddled around in the shallow water looking at the little fish, the shells and the dark green patches of thick sea-grass that swayed with the movement of the water, like grass in the breeze. She found a large, black sea cucumber that caused her to retreat up the beach. She picked up a striped, spiral shell intending to take it with her and placed it beside her feet whilst they drank fresh mango juice and watched the sea. She jumped in alarm as the shell sprouted a long thin claw and made its way back to the water. Harassed by a sudden horde of monkeys, Mustapha and Sabia made their way back on board ship, ferried in a canoe by the smiling tall, dark men. The ship meandered slowly down the east side of Africa, dropping anchor several times, waiting for spring and calmer weather in the Atlantic. Sabia watched the dolphins and the gigantic whales from the crow's nest with Sal. Occasionally the vast creatures came so close to the ship that the spray from their breathing holes sent a mist across the deck and when they dived, slapping their enormous tails, the little ship shuddered. In the less eventful hours in the crow's nest, Sal told Sabia about his wife Maria who had died, about his son, also named Mustapha that was a gifted healer and his daughter Sophia who was married to a shepherd. By the time they rounded the Cape of Good Hope and entered cooler waters, reducing the time in the crow's nest, Sabia's knowledge of the family she would soon join was extensive, as was her command of the English language. The great bluish, grey waves of the volatile Atlantic and the strong winds that made her eyes water, finally persuaded Sabia to wear a rope around her waist tied to the mast in case she blew over the side. Clad in a thick coat donated by Yusuf, she sat in a rocking hammock and watched the crew furling sails and struggling with the wheel. The weather improved as the ship sailed north and by the time they crossed the equator they had some warm days where they were becalmed. Young Mustapha pointed out the slave ships that ferried men and women in disgusting conditions, stolen from their own land and sold like animals to the highest bidder on the other side of the ocean. Sabia was horrified.

They encountered two storms, warned of in advance by young Mustapha, but with nowhere to hide, they had no choice but to furl the sails, ensure the cargo was secure, and ride them out. Sam and Sal, unsteady on their legs at the best of times, were relegated to their hammocks below deck and the intrepid Sabia impressed everyone. She was not fearful and struggled to and from the galley, helping Yusuf and bringing large mugs of tea half full by the time she arrived, to Sam and Sal. She staggered away again laughing and returned with a bag of bread and cheese slung around her neck and clambered up into a swinging hammock and shared out the food. The ship creaked and groaned as the waves crashed over the bow and the noise was deafening. Sabia continued to laugh and smile as the ship lurched and tipped violently. Sam had to admit that her presence aboard ship was less of a trial than he had expected, based on his previous experiences. His own wife Mina had screamed for the majority of the journey, convinced she was about to die, and refused to set foot on a ship again. Sabia, on the other hand, had complete and utter faith in the crew and the vessel and knew that everything was fine. She had become accustomed to the ship returning and had no idea that sometimes ships sink.

Blown off course by the storms, she watched and listened to Edmundo, Estavo and her husband as they studied the stars and set a new course for home.

It was a sunny afternoon in June when the little ship sailed into the estuary, with its grey muddy shores littered with grey rocks and black seaweed. Sabia went below and changed into her lucky white and silver sari, ready to meet her new family.

Chapter 44

Bella Mary had been accurate when calculating the birth of Esther's child. She gave birth to a son, George Paulo in the bathhouse, attended by Mustapha and Bella Mary, with George at her side, in the middle of April. Her second birth was much easier that her first, to the great relief of Mustapha. A week later, Elizabeth was delivered of another daughter, the first delivery that Bella Mary attempted with just the help of Mina and Nellie. They called her Ellen Elizabeth and Nellie burst into floods of joyful tears.

The unsuspecting family were making their way to the dining table in response to Florence's bell, when the cart pulled up at the kitchen door. Florence watched as her kitchen rapidly filled with strangers. Many of them bore a family resemblance, but she had not seen them before. She shut the oven door again and replaced lids, sensing a delay in proceedings. Sam and Sal entered the dining room first. They had grown identical during the voyage, their skins had darkened and their hair was almost white, one made a fuss of Mustapha and the other left by the front door to hobble to the new house and find his wife. The next to appear were Rose and Paulo's twins causing Rose to dissolve into tears of joy. All eyes were on the kitchen door, waiting for young Mustapha. All eyes opened wider as he walked through the door, his arm around the shoulder of a stunning, glittering young woman with a captivating smile and huge dark eyes.

'This is my wife, Sabia.'

Mouths hung open and the silence was deafening. It was Mustapha who rose from the table first. Sabia pressed her hands together and bowed her head as he approached her and he smiled warmly at his son, took Sabia's hands and kissed her on the forehead.

'Welcome home, my dear.'

There followed a frantic moving and shuffling of chairs to make room for the new arrivals. The twins sat either side of their parents, Sal sat beside Isabella, young Mustapha in between his parents and Sabia between Mustapha and Bella Mary. Florence and the girls served the meal. Chaos would best describe the hubbub of questions, everyone shouting over each other. It was Sal who stood up and begged some hush, so as not to terrify young Mustapha's new wife, there would be plenty of time for questions later, but now, let us just share a peaceful meal. The relative peace did not to last long as halfway through the apple pie Sam arrived with an over-excited Mina, desperate to meet Sabia.

Isabella and Esther escaped and put fresh sheets on young Mustapha's bed. They sprinkled jasmine oil and placed vases of fresh flowers on the windowsills.

During the next few days Sabia was ferried around to meet the extended family, she never tired, her smile never faded and she thoroughly enjoyed herself. She particularly loved Sophia and Tom's little house, crammed with Joey's imaginative carvings and a crowd of small boys with the black eyes of her husband and his family.

Due to the steady increase in the size of Tom's family, an extension to the house was underway. A two-story construction, accessed via the dining area downstairs and via the current boys bedroom end of the mezzanine floor upstairs, was well underway and Joey was busy carving. The top floor would provide a large bedroom for the boys and downstairs would become the new dining room. Due to its size, Harry and Big Ern built the new table inside the new dining room.

Sam and Sal, who started life identical and in the first few months of life Sam wore a bracelet made by old Mustapha until the family were sure they could tell who was who. During their youth and adulthood if became easier to distinguish between them. Sam grew slightly heavier and was a great deal noisier whereas Sal was calm and quiet. Now, in their old age, they had become identical again and even Mina, her eyesight less keen, was no longer sure which one was her husband. They were both thinner and their faces were brown and wrinkled from their voyage and their long hair bleached white. Rose thought that they had begun to resemble Bill the monkey. One afternoon Mina began grumbling at Sam who answered.

'Sorry Mina, I'm Sal!'

Mina apologised and laughed, but later she was beset by doubts, realising the Sam could have said he was Sal, just to stop her grumbling.

The twins died within weeks of each other, not from illness, just from old age. Mina woke up to find Sam had died peacefully in his sleep and three weeks later Sal died with Mustapha at his side. Paulo, who had been unwell for some time, had difficulty swallowing. Mustapha controlled his pain and he died soon after Sal. Rose was bereft. She had lost her brothers and her husband in a month and began to wish, that like Ellen Lily, she could lose her reason. Mina coped better as she had spent the majority of her marriage alone. She was thankful that her husband had died at her side on not on foreign shores, and her little granddaughters were a great comfort. Due to Ellen Lily's meagre grasp of reality, Rose found her more of a mildly amusing chore than good company. George assumed the position as head of the household, a role he had essentially fulfilled since the age of twelve. He foresaw a changeable period of time, both for the village and for the country. A canal, the first in the area, was undergoing construction a few miles away, bringing an influx of nomadic workers looking for lodgings and spending the bulk of their earnings at the Inns. Local residents resented finding strangers on their favourite stools, they were discomfited by the rowdy, boisterous familiarity of the newcomers and begrudged the pennies they lost during the gambling games. Beer stocks ran low, tempers flared and fights broke out. Men with cuts, broken noses, bitten ears and broken fingers began arriving with such alarming regularity at the sick house that Matthew insisted on charging them a fee. Drunks tried to get in and sleep in the beds and Bella Mary ejected them with a withering stare and a string of threats. In her absence, Harry and Big Ern were frequently summoned to fling them out. Disorder broke out. Painted women arrived on a cart on Saturday evenings and flounced around the village in clothes that scandalised the village women. The Inns refused them rooms, so they took their patrons to the churchyard. Boys climbed out of windows to catch a glimpse of the goings on and mothers boxed their ears on their return.

The King Georges had all died and William IV became King at the age of sixty-four as his older brothers had left no heir. During his brief reign the poor law was updated, child labour restricted and slavery virtually abolished in the Empire. William had ten illegitimate children, but no legitimate heir to the throne and there was talk that an eighteen year-old female niece would succeed him. The smattering of villagers that gave a damn about what happened beyond the realm of the village shook their heads in despair. George followed his gut feeling and invested a substantial sum of money in the railways.

Chapter 45

The accession to the throne by an elderly Edward had a negligible impact upon village life. Few knew and even less cared, due to the mayhem triggered by the workmen digging the canal and tunnel. Profits made by the Inns were outweighed by the damage caused and one Inn, nearest to the church, refused the workers entry. The irate workers stormed the place, broke up furniture and injured the landlord. It was not unusual on a Sunday to see ragged desperate women with emaciated children scouring the village in search of husbands who had failed to return home with wages. Not all of the workers were drunkards. Some of the men lived quietly in their lodgings and visited their families on Sundays. The villagers failed to discriminate. The disturbing sights that awaited them in the churchyard on a Sunday morning when they walked to church with their children sickened them. Discarded clothing strewn around the gravestones, puddles of vomit decorating the pathway and, not infrequently, scantily clad painted women and men with bare arses asleep on the graves of their loved ones. The strongest young men in the village armed themselves with stout sticks, ready to hit any man not behaving himself. This resulted in an escalation of the violence as many of the workers, accustomed to being unpopular, carried knives. So the villagers brought out the guns, generally used for shooting foxes and rabbits and the occasional nuisance dog. They aimed above the heads of the workers and when that failed to stop them they aimed for their backsides. The disgruntled workers retaliated by setting fire to a barn full of hay, which attracted the attention of the farmers and landowners who had newer, more powerful guns and did not restrict their target to backsides. Several workers died. The meeting of the Parish Council deemed they had brought about their own demise.

In a couple of months, the generally peaceful village had descended into turmoil. Arguments about how to solve the problems caused rifts between neighbours and families. It was the advent of cold autumn weather that alleviated the worst. Following the death of a near naked, inebriated woman who froze to death in the churchyard the painted women failed to return to the village again. Each Inn employed the services of three or four young local men, hoping to modify the workers antics. Sometimes it was successful, but more often than not, towards the end of an evening, fights broke out. The locals occasionally managed to shove the flailing, inebriated disturbances into the street and barricade the doors and listen to the irate feet kicking the rattling doors and the stones bouncing off the shutters. The village had always had its share of heavy drinkers, but by and large they were an affable bunch, more likely to fall over than initiate a fight.

Annie and Amos, who lived near the churchyard, were wakened by blood-curdling screams. Amos and Levi went out to investigate and found a man, one of the workers, impaled on the railings of the church gate, kept locked on Saturday nights due to the unwanted visitors. Levi rode to the big house a fetched Mustapha who climbed the gate and forced a strong remedy down the unfortunate man's throat, and when he was virtually unconscious, the suddenly sober workers helped to lift him off the spikes of the gate and carry him to the sick house. He was dead within half an hour, likely due to the effects of a strong sedative mixed with a surfeit of alcohol, but everyone put it down to his injuries. The Parish Council ordered the construction of new stocks, to be placed outside of the Inn nearest to the church, for the punishment of disorderly behaviour. Harry, Levi and Amos built four. One of the first two victims died of cold overnight, so the use of the stocks was limited to daylight hours. The heavy snow at the beginning of winter finally solved the problem, the route from the canal to the village became impassable to all but the most valiant, intrepid drinkers, who froze to death in a snowdrift on their way back and were not found for two months. Their workmates assumed that they had been shot dead in the village and found somewhere else to disrupt. The village gained the reputation of intolerance towards strangers and a dangerous place to drink. The remaining law-abiding workers who lodged in the village continued to be treated with distrust for some considerable time.

The end of the 'troubles' left the villagers wondering what they had found to talk about before they started. Families sat around in the evenings, reminiscing. Stories became wildly exaggerated. Incidents that had angered and vexed the villagers took on amusing twists and made everyone laugh heartily. George tried to get the Parish Council to remove the stocks but was outvoted. They were never used again, other than as a threat from a distraught parent to a particularly bothersome child.

Maud's labour began during the night. The snow was deep and although Mustapha had given her two bottles of remedy, she was fearful of giving birth at home with Jack. She would not hear of him trying to get to Mustapha, the big house being over a mile away, so Jack dragged her on a hastily improvised sledge to Tom and Sophia's house. Tom lit the bathhouse fire while Sophia gave Maud a remedy and made tea. Richard John was born next morning, delivered by Tom and Sophia, while Jack read stories to the four little boys.

Rose, Isabella, Esther, Ellen Lily, Sabia and Florence sat around the kitchen table drinking tea, chatting about the arrival of Richard John and the imminent birth of Sophia's fifth child, expected at lambing time again.

'They found her, you know.' Ellen Lily told Esther, pointing to Isabella. 'On the steps of the sick house!'

'I know, George told me.'

'Well, who do you think left her there?'

'I don't know.'

'Somebody must know!' said Ellen Lily impatiently.

'Perhaps nobody knows now, it was over fifty years ago and whoever put her there could be dead!' Rose pointed out.

Florence topped up the teapot with hot water.

Where's Gabriel?'

'In the stables.'

'I hope Sophia finally has her daughter this year.' Esther said.

'Oh, so do I!' replied Rose. 'But Isabel, Mary's mother-in-law had seven sons and never managed a daughter.'

'I had a son that turned into a horse!'

'There does appear to be a predominance of boys in this family.' Isabella added.

'Yes.' Rose said. 'I had three.'

'And I had two.' Said Isabella.

'I don't know how many I had but one of them turned into a horse!'

'You had three sons and two daughters.' Rose informed her. 'Olivia has three sons as well. Most of the women in this family have just the one daughter.'

'They found her on the steps of the sick house!' Ellen Lily told Florence. When Ellen Lily accessed a memory it could persist for days.

Chapter 46

Ellen Lily's recent habit of informing everyone, several times a day, that Isabella had been found on the sick house steps, brought back her memories of Ivy. Isabella had loved her so much. Ivy had died over forty years ago and yet Isabella continued to feel the loss keenly. She wished she could have lived to see her marry Mustapha and wished she could have met her children.

Isabella's hair did not turn grey it slowly changed from very pale blonde to pure white. She was still slim and able to move silently, giving the impression that she floated rather than walked. She looked at Rose and Ellen Lily and realised that she would be the oldest woman in the house after their deaths. Ellen Lily was in her eight decade and Rose was not far behind. They had shrunk with age and Rose had become very thin and frail, whereas Ellen Lily retained her physical strength. Rose had adopted the same habit of old Mustapha, setting herself a goal to live long enough to experience. Her latest one was the birth of Sophia's baby. Ellen Lily was incapable of that ploy, but she continued to live, in a world of constant astonishments, bewilderments and brief haphazard memories. Some mornings she would wake up in the grip of fifty-year-old memories, shout goodbye to everyone and set off for the school to teach the village children to read, although by the time she reached the edge of the field, she would forget and return to the kitchen for tea.

'Today I saw a rock with a head!'
'That's Thomas.'
'Who is Thomas?'
'The rock with a head.'
'That's what I said!'

The patchy remains of the winter snow survived into lambing. Tom had his sheep corralled in the shelter of his newly extended house. Sophia, keen to discover if she would have a daughter named Maria Rose, waddled outside to help her husband with the sheep, believing the exertion would hurry the onset of labour. Mustapha visited her every day and when he found her in the yard valiantly struggling with an uncooperative ewe, he made a pot of tea and insisted she come inside. He could tell by his sister's gait and the lowness of her belly than the birth was imminent. That evening Sophia gave birth to her fifth son Robert John and resigned herself to never having a daughter.

Tom was proud. To be father to five sons earned him a certain status in the village.

A few weeks later, Sophia, with Bobby tied to her back, rode over to the big house to show Aunt Rose, who found riding in the cart nowadays shook her bones to pieces. He was a lovely baby with black eyes, olive skin and wispy dark curls. Florence was besotted and carried him around the kitchen table singing to him and he watched her closely with his penetrating eyes. Sabia said she thought that she might be carrying a baby, and now that she had met beautiful Bobby she really hoped that she was. Esther gathered the clothes outgrown by little George and parcelled them up for Sophia. Ellen Lily, unsettled by the excitement, got lost somewhere between fantasy and a vacuum and rambled on about rocks with heads and chicken stew. Sophia left Bobby with Florence and spent a quiet hour alone in the woods picking snowdrops and the first of the primroses. The earth was obscured with the bright green, pointed shoots of the impending carpet of bluebells, and the thicker, spotted sprigs of future orchids pushing through last year's brown crunchy leaves. The trees were in still in bud, allowing the sun to encourage everything to grow quickly, before the canopy obscured its warmth. Sophia sat down on a log, listening to the tiny sounds made by insects and the whistles, squawks and flapping of the birds, smelling the rich, musty fertility of the woodland. She loved her marshes and had forgotten how much she loved, and missed, the woods.

Sophia slowly made her way down the gentle slope of the woodland towards the big house. When she detected the small distant cry of Bobby she quickened her step as she felt her breasts leaking milk, initiated by the baby's wail. When she finally arrived home in early evening, it was to the inviting smell of roast mutton and potatoes and a row of shining, smiling washed little boys waiting for their dinner. New lambs bleated outside of the window. Tom put her flowers into an old cup and placed them on the windowsill, catching the last rays of the setting sun. He carried the tray of sizzling roast meat and potatoes to the table and shared out the plates. The row of small boys jiggled with excitement as he carved the meat, shared out the crisp, golden potatoes and poured the rich, steaming gravy. Sophia watched him and he smiled at her and she realised that this was one of the happiest days of her life. She came to the conclusion that it no longer mattered if she never had a daughter as she already had more than she had ever dreamt of. Unbeknown to Sophia, that night she finally conceived her daughter.

Chapter 47

Mustapha confirmed that Sabia was indeed with child and Bella Mary calculated its arrival in October. The ship was due to sail, a short trip to North Africa as young Mustapha desperately wanted to be home for the birth of his first child.

Olivia visited her mother every month and invited her to move to the estate, but Rose could not leave the only house she ever remembered living in. Little Richard Archibald was walking and followed old Archie the butler everywhere. The close relationship between the two of them was a great comfort to Archie and he loosened the reigns on his staff, and they did not run amok of take advantage of his newly found tolerance. In fact they worked harder and complained less. He spent his afternoons exploring the estate with Turnip, as he called him, teaching him the names of the animals, trees and plants, as his own father had done when he was a child. Old Archie saw the world anew, through the eyes of little Turnip. They knelt together on the grass and studied fir cones, rabbit droppings, earwigs, snails, slugs, pea bugs and bright green moss. Turnip invariably suffered from aching legs by the end of the excursion and rode home on Archie's shoulders. Archie could not have loved the child more, even if he had been his own son and the child loved Archie. He had his own personal grown-up and did not have to share him with his brothers and sister, as he had to share his parents.

Sophia was unaware of her unborn child for months. Her last normal bleed had been before she had Bobby and she had been waiting for her first bleed. The first movements of the child were attributed to wind and her thickening waist to Tom's delicious stews. The hefty kicks eventually alerted her to the presence of a baby and Mustapha examined her and thought she was about halfway through the pregnancy. Bella Mary measured and poked and believed the baby would come as soon as Christmas.

Joey, the nomad of the family, lived between the big house, the new house and his camp in the woods, depending on what he was doing. Old Rose, struggling to stay alive for the birth of Sophia's sixth child, noticed that he had begun to spend considerable time in the kitchen. One morning he arrived with a large wooden bread bin, carved with ears of corn. A week later it was a new elm chopping board, as smooth as silk. Next came a heavy knife block decorated with primroses, big enough to hold a dozen sharp knives. Rose assumed he was at a loose end. Joey was in his early forties, as was Rose's first twins and Sophia. He had always been a strange child and Mina had worried about him until he discovered his talent for woodcarving and became popular and genuinely venerated for the first time in his life.

Rose, Ellen Lily and Florence were sitting in the kitchen drinking tea after breakfast, when Joey stalked purposefully into the kitchen with a bunch of flowers. Florence blushed profusely as he handed her a bunch of field scabious, ox eye daisies and wild roses. He found himself a cup and poured his tea and sat down at the table. Rose was stunned and Ellen Lily was experiencing a rare blank period. Rose looked at Florence, who avoided her gaze, her face still pink. She looked at Joey, whose face bore an unfamiliar beaming smile. Rose could hear everyone breathing during the silence and for once, wished that Ellen Lily would begin to prattle randomly. The silence was finally broken by Florence snorting with laughter fuelled by nervous embarrassment.

'Aunt Rose!" Hissed Joey. 'I have asked Florence to be my wife!'

Rose's mouth fell open. Ellen Lily stared into space and Florence hid her face in her hands.

'But she is worried that she will lose her position in the kitchen!' added Joey fidgeting in his chair.

"I dreamt that I could fly like a bird in the sky.' Proffered Ellen Lily wistfully, causing everyone to stare at her for a brief moment.

Rose, who had never considered that the erratic, wild, eccentric Joey even noticed women, wondered if this was poor Florence's way of rejecting him gently. Joey knocked over the milk jug as he reached for the teapot.

'Perhaps Florence would like some time to consider your proposal.' Said Rose, playing for time and trying not to say the wrong thing.

'She has, she has had a month to think about it and today she has promised me an answer!' Joey said triumphantly. 'That is why I am here!'

Florence remained behind her hands and Rose was unsure whether she was laughing or crying.

'Well! What's it to be?' Joey grinned, jumping up and hopping from one foot to the other.

Rose, believing this was time to give them privacy, stood up and attempted to remove Ellen Lily.

'Please don't leave!' wailed Florence.

Rose noticed tears on her cheeks, so she sat down again, Ellen Lily remained standing, suspended. Joey jumped about with excitement.

'I know she is going to say yes! I just know she is!'

'Joey be quiet, please!' Rose reached across the table and took Florence's hand.

'I don't want to leave my kitchen.' Whimpered Florence.

'See!' shouted Joey, beside himself. 'I knew she would say yes!'

'Shut up Joey!' Rose said firmly. 'And will you please leave us alone for a minute!'

'Why? She is just worried about having to leave, but I told her that we marry all sorts of people in this family and nobody minds!'

'Joey, outside, please!'

'What for?'

'I need to talk to Florence alone.'

'What about?'

'Women's things, now go away!'

Joey skipped across the kitchen, tiny flakes of sawdust falling from his long dark hair.

'I know she will say yes!' he shouted as he slammed the back door.

'Florence my dear, what do you want to do?'

'I want to stay here.'

'What about Joey?'

'I do love him Rose, but I don't want to leave my kitchen.' Whispered Florence, tears rolling down her cheeks.

'Florence you can stay in this kitchen, whether or not you decide to marry Joey.'

Florence smiled shyly through her tears.

'I do want to.' She blushed as Joey, who had been listening at the door, stampeded into the room almost knocking over Ellen Lily who was wafting around the kitchen, being a bird in flight. He grabbed Florence and dragged her to her feet, his amber eyes shining.

'Come on, I can't wait to tell mother!' he pleaded.

He hauled the flustered Florence across the kitchen as she tried to untie her apron and grab her coat. She looked at Rose, her eyes wide.

'Go on!' Rose smiled. 'Congratulations to both of you!'

'Who was that man?' asked Ellen Lily, who had landed and was perched at the end of the table.

'That was Joey, Mina's youngest son, he and Florence are to be married.'

'Oh goody! A wedding!' cackled Ellen Lily and flew off again.

Chapter 48

Young Mustapha, bursting into the kitchen in October, fearing that he had missed the birth of his first child, heralded the return of the ship. He slumped with relief into a chair when Florence told him that Sabia had not yet had the child. Isabella called Sabia, who hurried to the kitchen as fast as her condition would allow and her smile lit up the kitchen. She had willed herself not to give birth until her husband was home.

'At last,' she laughed. 'Now I can have this baby!'

Young Mustapha was alarmed by the size of her belly, inconsistent with her slight, fragile frame. Sabia relaxed to such an extent that at around midnight she woke young Mustapha, informing him that the baby was coming. Bella Mary heard them creeping down the stairs. She woke her father, stoked the bathhouse fires and made tea. Despite her size, Sabia had an easy first labour requiring only a mild potion and at dawn she gave birth to a robust son with the dark hair and black eyes of the Mustapha's. Young Mustapha hugged his father as Sabia carefully inspected her son and was delighted that he was just as beautiful as Bobby, Sophia's youngest. The three generations of Mustapha's left the bathhouse together and Mustapha presented his grandson to the first rays of the watery, autumn sun with a fervent prayer of thanks. By the time they returned, Sabia was in the armchair beside the fire and the sleepy family, woken by Mustapha's enthusiastic incantation, arrived at intervals and waited for their turn to hold Mustapha Sachin, named after his grandfathers. Joey ran to the new house with the news and returned with his mother, desperate to see Sabia and the baby. Mina, despite having lost her husband was very happy. She believed that she could now die in peace, with the knowledge that Florence would take care of her precious Joey. They were to be married in the spring. Esther had measured Florence for her wedding dress, in deep red silk, embroidered with scarlet thread and tiny pearls.

Halfway through December, Sophia shook Tom awake as she struggled from the bed. Her waters trickled across the floor and dripped into the living room below. Tom carried her downstairs and sat her beside the fire. He made tea and added more logs to the fire. Mustapha had warned him that her delivery, due to it being her sixth and that her last birth was only ten months ago, was likely to be quick. Less than an hour later and without the need for a remedy, Tom delivered the baby. His heart leapt when he saw that she had finally produced a daughter. He said nothing and with a pounding heart that he thought Sophia would hear, he wrapped the baby in a warm towel and placed her in the crib beside the roaring fire and removed the afterbirth before the dogs ate it.

Sophia sat quietly drinking her tea, her eyes shut. The baby snuffled and emitted a tiny cry.

'I think Maria needs her mother.' whispered Tom with a huge smile.

Sophia stared at him, dropped her teacup and struggled to get up. Tom reached down and lifted the baby and placed her on her mother's lap. Sophia burst into tears as she unwrapped the baby and saw for herself that she had finally got her Maria Rose.

'Tom!' she wailed. Tom was grinning and her tears soon turned to laughter. The sun came up and shone in through the windows, brightening the room and Sophia was surprised to discover that Maria Rose had deep blue eyes like her father.

For the first time in ten years, Sophia, Tom and their brood accepted Rose's invitation to spend Christmas at the big house. It was a joyous, chaotic time with nine children under the age of ten. Rose commandeered Maria Rose in the chair beside the fire. She looked around the room and recalled the Christmases of her childhood and smiled. Mustapha sat and wondered where the time had gone, between his childhood and his new role of grandfather.

It began to snow heavily the day after Boxing Day and Tom loaded his family onto a cart, stacked with boxes of provisions and headed for home whilst they still had a chance. Once the fire was roaring, he headed outside with the dogs to round up the sheep and coral them in the shelter of the house. There was no wind and the snow fell fast and thick and by evening was already over a foot deep. The shepherds gathered their flocks from the marshes while others built the fences around the village green. Within a week the snow was so deep that only Big Ern was able to navigate his way around the village. The school had opened and housed the families whose cottages were too cold and draughty to inhabit. The women cooked cauldrons of stews and Big Ern delivered hot food to the older residents. The men lugged the sacks of potatoes, onions, carrots, turnips and rice from the barn and there was a constant supply of fresh meat, thanks to the unsuspecting bleating sheep twenty yards from the door and the fresh eggs came from the host of chickens in Elijah's old stable, as well as a fair few chickens fat enough to roast.

Joey struggled to keep the path from the big house to the new house passable. Charles and Aziz kept the fires alight in the stables. Even the big shire horses were unable to plough through four feet of snow. The snow lasted until March and even Sabia and the children became bored with it. The thaw began at the end of March and the ground turned to sticky, slippery deep mud that caked everything and everybody and even Big Ern struggled to get about. Women gave up the battle to keep floors and children clean. The sheep had turned the village green into a quagmire and shepherd slithered about pulling them from the mud and returned them to the marshes where grass was still visible. It was not until the warm May sun arrived that the mud began to dry into sharp ruts that were slowly reduced to dust by the boots of the villagers.

Joey and Florence were married in early June and the entire village turned out in their best, as much to celebrate the beginning of summer as the wedding. Joey and Florence made an impressive couple. The tall Joey was dressed in a dark red outfit designed by Mina, Sabia and Esther and based on a traditional Indian costume. The front of the long shirt heavily embroidered in red and gold. Florence shimmered in her deep red dress and carried a bunch of dark red and white poppies. Her wild chestnut hair brushed loose framed her smiling face. Rose had given her a ruby necklace that contrasted with her pale skin. Hugh and Olivia brought their children, Elsie the cook, Archie and a number of other servants dying to see Florence get married. They all found it difficult to recognise the vision that she had become. Mustapha walked her down the aisle to Joey and later, when he noticed her place her wedding flowers on old Mary's grave, he waited until she had re-joined her husband and he moved the poppies to where they belonged.

The party began in early afternoon and continued all evening. Mina watched her son dancing with his new wife in the light of the bonfire. The pearls on Florence's dress sparkled in the firelight and her only regret was that Sam did not live long enough to see how happy his son had become. The crowd cheered as the fireworks lit up the sky, and just for a moment,

Mina thought she saw Sam waving to her from the top of the tree house.

Chapter 49

Dr Matthew's son John was due to complete his studies at the London Hospital and Matthew was constantly saddened that little had changed since he finished his own training. Surgeons still continued to operate on conscious patients and over eighty per cent died as a result of shock, loss of blood or blood poisoning caused by infections. The conditions in the hospital, designed to care for the poor from the east end of London, were as deplorable as when Mustapha and Sophia had visited and there were frequent outbreaks of cholera. The elderly nurses, largely immune to smallpox and typhus, died at an alarming rate. Efforts were made to recruit younger, literate women with little success. Like his father, John had tried unsuccessfully to broach the subject of potions and cleanliness, and grudgingly accepted that surgery was carried out to improve the anatomic knowledge of the surgeons rather that save the life of the patients and the operations bell was still in regular use. Mustapha was gratified to hear that laudanum was widely available as a remedy in London, a tincture of opium and alcohol, but concerned that is was used indiscriminately and with little regard for its long term negative effects. He was more impressed by the 'microphone,' a long trumpet shaped instrument made from metal, wood or even ivory, that could be used to listen to hearts, lungs and abdominal sounds in a patient. Bella Mary soon discovered that the instrument could be used to detect a foetal heartbeat and promptly commandeered it. Rene Laennec had invented the first stethoscope in 1816, at the Necker-Enfants Malades Hospital in Paris, in order to overcome embarrassment when listening to a female patient's heartbeat.

During one of John's regular visits to the sick house, Bella Mary continued to badger him with questions and demands. She was determined to visit the hospital. Mustapha tried to dissuade his daughter, but she would have none of it. In the end, Matthew agreed to accompany her. John arranged their lodgings near to the hospital.

Bella Mary, made of sterner stuff than her father, did not flee from the stinking filthy wards. She stood, hands on hips and glared at the scene, unmoved by the screams and groans. She watched as the old nurses as they moved from bed to bed, touching patients with unwashed hands, their clothing splattered with the day's stains. The ammonia in the air stung her eyes. She shook her head and marched briskly out of the ward, dragging Matthew with her and demanded that she speak to the individuals responsible for this hell on earth. Matthew told her that would not be possible, that nobody would listen, that it had always been this way and there was nothing she could possibly do. Bella Mary remained undaunted. She stared at Matthew briefly, then turned abruptly and strode off along the corridor, rattling at and opening doors, determined to find someone to shout at. Before Matthew was able to stop her, she had cornered a startled group of eminent surgeons in a spacious sitting room drinking tea. She was a formidable sight. Tall and erect, dressed in scarlet and black, her long white curls swirling around her shoulders and her black eyes blazing. She stared at a small rotund man, currently choking on tea, and pointed at him with a gloved hand.

'Whom, may I ask, is responsible for the unbelievably disgusting state of this establishment!' she demanded.

There followed a clattering of china as several of the men stood up.

'Madam!' It was a voice from the back of the room.

'Well?' barked Bella Mary ferociously. 'Are *you* the one responsible, you should be ashamed of the hell you have the audacity to call a hospital! And I am Miss!'

'Who the hell is she?' grumbled a voice.

'I am from a village and our animals live in conditions better that the unfortunate wretches I have seen in the ward. I make ointments that cure infections and I have potions and remedies that obliterate pain...'

'The damned woman is *insane!*'

'*How dare you*!' shrieked Bella Mary, the angriest she had ever been, as angry as her mother had been when James the lunatic had attacked her.

'Get out!' demanded the tall man at the back of the room.

'A few years ago you would have been burned at the stake!' added another.

Bella Mary's terrible, passionate fury rendered her speechless. She lifted and held aloft a sturdy footstool and with the strength of the livid, she launched it across the room. It smashed the china, spilt the tea, caught one man on the shoulder and came to rest in the belly of a winded individual not swift enough to dodge.

Matthew, who had been hiding several feet away in the corridor, deemed it a good time to retreat. He grabbed Bella Mary's arm and mustered all his strength to remove her from the room. She broke free.

'*You are all incompetent fools! Damned ignorant imbeciles, the lot of you!*'

'Enough!' Matthew said sternly.

He kept a tight grip on her arm, fearing she would start again, until they reached the street. She stamped along the street, her anger clearing a wide pathway through the throng of people. Even the beggars let her pass unobstructed, which was just as well. Matthew followed in her wake and smiled, anticipating the response of her father when he found out about the footstool. Bella Mary was still angry when they reached the lodgings where she disappeared into her room and slammed the door. Matthew left her be for several hours before he delivered a tray of tea and biscuits. He did not raise the subject for fear of stoking her slowly diminishing wrath. He merely enquired when she wished to leave.

'As soon as possible.' Came the quiet reply.

Matthew hired a carriage and they left London in silence. A mile or so from home Matthew took her hand.

'I was so very proud of you today Bella Mary.'

Everyone had gone to bed by the time Matthew dropped Bella Mary home and she retired to bed and stared at the ceiling. Next day she was exhausted from rage and she spent the day in the microscope room making batches of ointment that she intended to persuade John to secretly administer to patients.

Mustapha cried with laughter when Matthew related the incident and John prayed fervently that nobody would ever discover that he was acquainted with her!

When Bella Mary arrived at the sick house the following day, she was greeted with a round of applause. Unlike her gentle father, she remained unscathed by her visit to the London Hospital and set about recruiting two young women from the village and training them to work in the sick house.

Mustapha watched his daughter and wondered what his granddaddy Mustapha would have made of the talented, astute, fearless, diligent and occasionally ferocious Bella Mary. Old Mustapha would have approved and forgiven her for her evident lack of sensitivity.

Chapter 50

Mina, who had remained spritely until the last few days of her life, died that summer, with her sons at her side. She gave her collection of saris to Sabia and most of her jewellery to her granddaughters. She gave her most treasured possession to little Maria Rose, Sophia's long awaited daughter, a long string of pearls ranging from ivory to black that Sam had brought back from China when they were young. To Florence she gave her numerous gold bangles, so that Joey would still hear the familiar jingling. She was buried next to Sam on a bright warm day and many of the villagers attended, remembering the quiet, elegant woman, dressed like a butterfly, who they had seen at the parties.

Tom and Sophia's four eldest, Tommy, Danny, Teddy and Billy moved into the new large bedroom and Maria Rose, who had recently mastered crawling, shared the old room with her brother Bobby. Tommy, the image of his father, was boisterous and confident. Danny was a quiet, serious, sensitive little boy who excelled at school, idolised his mother and loved his little sister and reminded Sophia of her brother Mustapha when he was a child. Teddy followed his father and wanted to be a shepherd and Billy was the daydreamer. They all possessed the searching dark eyes of Sophia's family, but Danny's were the blackest. Maria Rose was a happy baby with an enchanting smile that disarmed the family, particularly her father, who was putty in her tiny hands. The only one not seduced by her charm was Bobby, who treated her with brooding suspicion and the odd kick as she crawled past. Sophia visited Rose each week with the three youngest children. Billy liked the tree house and the woods and Bobby liked Florence.

Ellen Lily's meagre grasp of reality slowly diminished and despite Mustapha's sedatives regularly woke the family with a variety of enthusiastic renditions of hymns in the small hours. Bella Mary increased the dosage that resulted in Ellen Lily sleeping most of the day or staring blankly, unable to respond. Bella Mary decided to shake her awake in the morning and administer tea laced with the stamina potion used in the latter stages of labour. The effect was remarkable. An hour later, Ellen Lily was more lucid that usual and managed to evade the watchful eyes of Mrs May and disappear. Mrs May looked for her all morning, then told the family that she could cope no longer, packed her bag and left to return to the village. Despite searching for her until dusk, she remained at large and the family began to expect the worst. After three days of searching they gave up and began to wait for her body to be discovered. The following morning Ellen Lily waltzed into the kitchen wearing different clothes and leading a small yapping dog. Rose asked her where she had been and Ellen Lily smiled.

'Happy Christmas, my dear.' She said to Rose and patted her hand.

Florence laughed and Ellen Lily joined in and Rose slowly and deliberately creaked her way out of the kitchen and made for the solitude of the tree house with her cup of tea. Ellen Lily suddenly took offence and chose to throw potatoes from the saucepan on the table at Florence, who was disabled by laughter and unable to defend herself. When Ellen Lily exhausted the supply of potatoes she threw the saucepan that glanced off the side of Florence's head. The excited dog began nipping ankles and Florence grabbed the old woman by the scruff of the neck and ejected both her and the yelping dog out of the back door, pushed them into an empty stable and bolted the door. When Rose returned she found Florence with a red bump on her head, on her hands and knees retrieving potatoes. They left Ellen Lily in the stable singing until Mustapha and Bella Mary returned. They sedated her, put her to bed, released the yapping dog and assembled around the kitchen table to discuss the problem. Mustapha was concerned. Ellen Lily's sudden violent episode was disturbing, particularly as there were small children and a baby in the house. Matthew had said that patients losing their minds frequently became aggressive. There were a few imaginative suggestions that made Florence snigger. Putting Ellen Lily on a lead, building a small fenced enclosure similar to the one resorted to when there were four toddlers in the house and making her a garment with no sleeves that trapped her arms. Finally, Mustapha and Bella Mary overruled everyone and decided just to sedate her, as she was too old to worry about her developing a dependence on the potion. So Ellen Lily remained sedated, locked in a web of bizarre dreams in which horses could fly, trees speak and ferrets chewed off her toes. The family fixed a sturdy bolt on the outside of her bedroom and she spent most of her time in bed and meals were delivered to her. When she began to spread stew up the walls and hide food in drawers and in her bed, the family took turns to supervise her meals. Even under sedation, Ellen Lily mustered her strength and pushed the large chest of drawers against the door, leaving Florence unable to get in. Joey climbed to her window and gained entry despite the onslaught of Ellen Lily's wrath. She pulled his hair, kicked his shins and screamed abuse as he dragged the chest of drawers from the door. Florence grabbed her from behind and held her in a vice like grip until Bella Mary arrived with more potions and Ellen Lily spent the rest of the day in which her bedroom turned red and disembodied faces talked to her from the walls. Mustapha felt great sympathy for the unfortunate old woman. He could see the terror in her eyes and he saw it increase when she saw the next potion arriving. He assumed that the sedation caused bad dreams and hallucinations and that Ellen Lily, daft as she was, knew it too. Bella Mary gave her a drink of warm milk, bhang, nutmeg and honey. Ellen Lily became so calm that she was allowed downstairs after the children had gone to bed and she actually recognised Rose. Bella Mary put the bag of bhang into the kitchen and showed Florence how to make the drink, to be administered to Ellen Lily every three hours. Bella Mary added a small amount of sedation to her last drink at night and the old woman was manageable again. Consumed by curiosity, Florence drank a glass of the remedy and spent all afternoon laughing and giggling and completely forgetting what she was doing. After dinner, she shared another glass with Joey and they pottered off and sat in the woods and watched intently as the last of the sun's rays crept in wide bands up the tree trunks until, motivated by a sudden ravenous hunger, they headed for the larder.

Florence found Ellen Lily dead at the beginning of winter and everyone was relieved that she was at peace at last. Her funeral was well attended by a generation of villagers whose parents and grandparents had been taught to read and write by Ellen Lily when the school first opened.

Chapter 51

Young Aziz, unlike his older brother, had expressed no interest in being a sea captain, to the great relief of his parents. He was a cheerful, patient lad who enjoyed his own company. Although he was happy to help his sister in the garden, it was apparent that he had no interest in healing either. Great Aunt Rose captured his attention when he found her reorganising the pages of family history that she had started to write some fifty years ago. He read the memories of his great-grandfather Mustapha, beginning with his great-great-grandfather dying in Afghanistan. He was captivated and pleaded with Rose to relinquish the piles of papers that she was having difficulty deciphering with her old eyes. Armed with pencils and papers, Aziz spent his days with his great aunt and faithfully recorded her memories with the intention of creating a history of the family. Rose enjoyed herself, reminiscing and relating her life to a rapt audience for a change. Aziz visited other members of the family and interrogated them. He spent a day with Tom and the sheep on the marshes. Tom lit the fire in the little old shack that he had lived in years ago and made tea whilst he related his earliest memories. His own father, Thomas had been born in the big house and he had become a shepherd and married Sarah a young woman from a nearby village. They had four children, the eldest of whom was Tom. Tom had only vague memories of his mother who had died when he was ten years old. He remembered his younger brothers crying desperately for their mother, who had been a quiet, kind and loving woman. He remembered his father's grief vividly. He had tried to hide his despair from his children but Tom had heard him sobbing at night and had been petrified. Fearful of letting his father out of his sight, Tom left school and began his career as a shepherd, and avoided the company of women for fear of being destroyed by grief. His youngest brother died of croup and his two other brothers sailed for the America's as soon as they were old enough, in an attempt to outrun tragic loss.

'Why did you marry Aunt Sophia then?'

Tom's face broke into a smile.

'The day I looked into her eyes on the sea wall, I would have given a lifetime of grief just to spend a few days with her!'

Aziz frowned.

'There seems to be a lot of that in this family!'

'What?' Tom asked.

'That knowing instantly that you love somebody.'

'Mmm.'

They drank their tea in silence.

'Memories are strange things.' Tom mused, wistfully twisting a strand of hair. 'I always remember my mother whenever I smell lavender.'

Later that evening, after the children were in bed, Tom watched Sophia as she sat sewing beside the fire and he was overcome. They had been together for over ten years. Tom knelt beside her chair and laid his head on her lap. Sophia put aside her sewing and stroked his tangled hair. They remained like that, smiling into the firelight until they fancied a cup of tea.

Aziz turned his attention to Gabriel's farm and Mary Ellen who recalled such a wealth of information, amusing anecdotes and details of her brother Henry's mysterious disappearance in North Africa, that it was necessary to make notes. Aziz decided that women's memories were far more efficient than men's.

Mustapha and Isabella listened to Aziz's animated plans to continue with Rose's family history. Bella Mary remained unimpressed, largely due to her current obsession with maggots. She had experienced a number of dreams involving maggots. Intrigued, she studied their behaviour as they dismantled a dead seagull. She noticed their enthusiasm for rotting flesh and yet they declined to bite into her arm, no matter how long she kept them there. This fact alerted her to the possibility of enlisting their help in the treatment of the recurrent stinking, weeping ulcers, the result of neglected wounds and infected bites. These ulcers were more common in the elderly and generally on their legs and ankles. They caused great pain and were resistant to healing. The ulcers smelled of rotting flesh and constantly oozed pus and it proved impossible to keep the infected area dry. The ulceration spread into healthy flesh and in extreme cases this led to death. Bella Mary placed small piles of raw meat on the windowsills in the sun, to encourage flies to lay their eggs on the smelly meat until the family complained about the stench and the increased amount of flies. She collected the sodden dressings from an ulcer on the leg of an old man on Lily Lane and transferred a number of tiny maggots from the rotting meat onto the bandages and watched as the maggots made a meal of the pus. An hour later the dressings, although stained, were relatively dry and the maggots crawled away in search of something dead. Bella Mary filled a pot with maggots and dressings and set off to Lily Lane to test her theory. She had chosen old Bill for her first experiment, believing that a man would be less likely to overreact. First, she measured the area of swollen red flesh that surrounded the site. She carefully placed the maggots on Bill's ulcer and told him she hoped that they would eat away the dead flesh. For an hour Bella Mary sat patiently and watched the maggots gorge and then she covered the wound with a layer of soft cotton bandage to stop them escaping, and told Bill to remove the maggots if he felt them bite his leg. She changed the dressing the next day and was impressed to discover that the maggots were significantly larger. She replaced them with tiny ones and covered the area. After a week of the maggot treatment, the area was less red and Bill reported that the pain had eased. The process took several weeks and fresh pink flesh slowly replaced the diseased areas. The maggots took longer to get fat and Bella Mary completed the treatment with two weeks of garlic ointment. Mustapha listened to his daughter's findings and was impressed. Bill willingly showed his healed leg to anyone interested and eventually, sick of the pain, two old women agreed to have maggots on their ulcers but averted their eyes until Bella Mary had hidden them under a bandage.

In the autumn Bella Mary tackled the problem of keeping a supply of flies and maggots alive during the winter months. With the assistance of Joey, a pile of dung, leftover food, a stove, a number of large jars and the stable furthest from the house, her supply was ensured.

John agreed to take pots of her garlic ointment to use in the hospital, as he feared her even more than he feared the surgeons.

Bella Mary made weekly house calls in the village, checking on the pregnant women, vaccinating the small children against smallpox and educating the ignorant, as her great-grandfather had done almost eighty years ago, before the sick house was opened. The villagers became accustomed to the tall figure in the flaming red coat. Her bedside manner showed scant improvement, but she was honest and forthright and commanded their respect and admiration, if not their affection.

Chapter 52

News that a mysterious, deadly contagion from foreign lands was gradually making its calamitous, relentless journey southward from the North of England, reached the village via the pulpit. The disease, known as Asiatic cholera, killed quickly and was soon proliferating in urban areas. Doctors believed the infection was spread by bad smells and parts of London set about cleaning the streets of 'nuisances', in anticipation of the disease arriving. Nuisances included dead animals, rotting food, sewage, rubbish and other unidentifiable reeking objects.

Bella Mary thought that the idea that bad smells carried the contagion was ludicrous, but approved of the street cleaning as she listened to George reading the newspaper. The medical profession was at a loss of how to treat the illness. Doctors were busy administering emetics and purgatives, restricting fluids and bleeding patients, actions that Bella Mary maintained could kill a patient even if they were not contaminated with cholera. She wrote a list of important information and delivered it to the vicar for reading the following Sunday. He suggested she attend the service and read it herself.

The congregation was surprised to see Bella Mary make her way to the pulpit after the sermon. She explained the symptoms of the disease, very similar to the common bouts of severe diarrhoea or food poisoning, accompanied by retching, thirst and excruciating pains in the limbs and stomach. In severe cases the limbs turned blue. Then she read a list of 'rules' designed to protect the village from cholera.

> Cancel all visits to London.
> Accept no visitors from London.
> Limit visits to Rochester and other urban areas.
> Not to eat or drink anything in those towns.
> Avoid ordering commodities from outside the village.
> Report any incidences of diarrhoea to the sick house or to her during her rounds, but not to take the sick person to the sick house.
> Wash their hands thoroughly before preparing food and before eating.
> Cover food to prevent flies walking on it.

Alarmed, the villagers listened and their imaginations ran riot and in some cases this led to panic. Bella Mary promised them, that if they followed these rules, cholera could not enter the village. Preventing it was far easier than treating it.

The rendition of the final hymn was disappointing but the final prayer contained a fervency not generally achieved on a Sunday morning. During the subsequent weeks Bella Mary was inundated with questions and fears as she visited the villagers. She assured them that the contagion had reached no further south than London and should the situation change she would warn them. A couple of cases of diarrhoea initiated a wave of anxiety, but Bella Mary delivered infusions of ginger and cinnamon, with added salt and sugar, fresh sheets and instruction to give the patient plenty of boiled liquids and to burn any soiled bedding. Cholera claimed the lives of over fifty thousand people in England but it failed to reach the village and Bella Mary's reputation soared to greater heights.

Bella Mary was in her early thirties. Her forthright, verging on the stern, manner had succeeded in incapacitating any potential suitors amongst the young men in the area. A farmer's son from outside the village approached Mustapha, requesting his permission to court his daughter. Bella Mary was appalled. She had little respect for men in general, believing them to be the weaker sex and similar to a demanding, high maintenance pet animal. She had no interest in marriage. No interest is cooking, sewing and producing children, all of which appeared to be necessary attributes! She tolerated and respected John, who had been in love with her for years, but knew it was sensible to remain silent. Elias Baldock, the farmer's son did not take the rejection well and made a nuisance of himself at the sick house, based on his belief that women should do as they were told. Mustapha explained to him that his daughter had no other interests outside of medicine and ailments, besides which, she would make an unsatisfactory farmer's wife! Elias Baldock's closed mind, impregnable to undesirable material, failed to absorb the information and he began to follow her on his horse during her rounds in the village. Bella Mary, absorbed in her thoughts, failed to notice. He rode ahead of her, stopped and attempted to block her path. She assumed this was her uninvited suitor and without so much as a glance at him she glowered at his horse and raised her right arm slowly, causing the animal to rear and bolt, almost unseating the unfortunate Elias Baldock. The following week he approached her on foot and introduced himself. Bella Mary took his hand and without a word, fixed him with her penetrating black eyes and he experienced a sudden searing pain in his head and a strong urge to vomit. He staggered out of her path and Bella Mary calmly continued her journey.

William, the clammy curate, hung himself after the death of his mother and Bella Mary pleaded with her father to allow her to dissect the body. Mustapha refused.

Danny, Tom and Sophia's second eldest son asked Bella Mary if he could help in her garden and learn about the potions. She looked into his eyes, so like her father's, and agreed. The cousins, separated by over twenty years, became constant companions. Danny was a bright boy who learned quickly and worked diligently in the garden and the microscope room. He accompanied her on her rounds and carried her bags. Young Danny filled the gap left by Bella

Mary's lack of sensitivity. He knew just the right thing to say to a distressed patient or worried parent. She witnessed her patients relax whilst he held their hand and reassured them, and she smiled. His resemblance to her father, in manner as well as countenance, was profound. Neither of her brothers had shown any interest in continuing in their father's footsteps. Bella Mary believed that Danny was the son Mustapha should have had. Mustapha told him that in a few years time, if he wanted to, he could go to London and train to be a doctor. Sophia and Tom were delighted as Danny had always shown an aversion to most animals, including sheep. Bella Mary was envious.

John completed his studies and replaced his father as the doctor at the sick house, basking in the close proximity of Bella Mary, unaware that his own uncle had suffered a fatal obsession for Bella Mary's mother, almost forty years before. The accession to the throne by an eighteen-year-old Queen Victoria was announced at the Sunday service. Bella Mary, unlike most of the villagers, relished the idea of a woman in charge and hoped that she would change the rules and pave the way, allowing women to become doctors.

Chapter 53

Rose was waiting to die. She did not want to become a burden to the younger ones. She did not want to be remembered as the creaking old lady with faded hair who took ten minutes to reach the tree house and another five to climb the steps. She wanted to be remembered as a young, vibrant woman that danced and laughed without alarming the children. Then she realised that there was nobody left alive that knew her as a young woman. She dragged the case out from under her bed. The old case that held the drawings that she and Maria had made when they were young, before they married. Tears rolled down her face when she found the likenesses of her father and mother. She found some of Old Mustapha before he was reduced to a bag of bones. She hardly recognised herself in Maria's drawing of a serious young girl with long dark hair, bright eyes and a flawless neck. She asked George to carry the case to the kitchen and she sat at the table with Florence and they wrote the names and approximate dates of the likenesses at the bottom of the pages in case they got forgotten. Florence made tea and Rose wiped her eyes on her sleeve as her emotions tumbled and lurched between deep sadness and euphoria. Aziz was astonished to see the faces of the family from over fifty years ago and pleaded to take charge of them for his history journal. Mustapha, with the recall of an elephant, remembered everybody but one, the drawing of his grandmother Ida, and the first wife of his grandfather Mustapha. He put his arm around his dilapidated Aunt Rose and assured her that she would always be beautiful and that in the future she would always be remembered as a stunning young woman, thanks to his mother's drawings. Rose was comforted, everyone in the drawings were young and she was grateful that they would be remembered by future generations as they were in their prime and not in their dotage!

Ever since the death of Mina the new house felt empty. Although she had been a tiny, quiet woman she had been endowed with the ability to flit around and be in several rooms at once, protecting the house from emptiness. A re-shuffle was discussed, as the big house was bursting at the seams with inhabitants. Mustapha and his family remained in the rooms they had inherited from old Mustapha and Mary. Young Mustapha, Sabia and baby Mustapha moved to the new house, enabling George and his family to spread out and create a new larger sewing room for Esther. Joey pleaded with Florence to move to the new house and live inside his imagination, and she loved him so much that she agreed and exchanged her kitchen with

Nellie. Joey was happy but the most exalted bliss was felt by Nellie, who would live in the same house as Mustapha! The new house still felt under populated, so, after the death of his mother, Big Ern, Beth, Eva and their two younger sons Harry and Robbie, moved from the tiny cottage in the village to the strange interior of the large new house. Elizabeth and Sabia became great friends and Beth insisted in helping Florence and the girls in the kitchen. Joey and Big Ern talked about wood. Khalid and Young Mustapha talked about the sea. The house began to feel like a home. At the big house, Nellie made sure that Mustapha never ran out of his favourite cake. Some of the laughter had left with Florence, but Nellie created a calm, warm, gentle atmosphere at the heart of the home and Rose was thankful.

The drought that had arrived in the wake of a wet spring and early summer continued into early autumn. Livestock from the fields around the village joined the sheep on the marshes, where the grass thrived in the moisture retaining soil. The harvest was poor, so George purchased extra supplies to last the winter. Sophia sat on the steps of her house and watched the clamour of cows cropping the lush grasses, their tails swishing to deter the flies. Twice a day the army of milkmaids arrived on carts and milked the generally docile creatures. Tommy, Sophia's eldest was working with Levi and Amos at the forge. Levi was getting old and he was keen to pass on his skills before he died. Teddy worked with his father. Billy was off on one of his walks and Bobby was tormenting Maria Rose with a grass snake. Bobby kept one eye on his mother, gauging when she would intervene, calculated that it was not far off and threw the disorientated grass snake into the bushes just in time. It was late afternoon and when Sophia saw Tom and Teddy, almost as tall as his father, moving across a far marsh, she went indoors, Maria Rose attached to her skirt, and put the kettle on the stove.

The autumn, equipped with biting, icy winds, blew the last of the leaves from the virtually bald trees and winter came early. The cows returned to their warm barns and the sheep assembled around the house for shelter. Joey began stacking wood at the back of the houses beside the woods and Florence discovered that she was with child! She had never imagined she would be a wife, let alone a mother! Awestruck, Joey asked big Ern for some oak and mahogany and he set about constructing the most elaborate cradle since the one made by Paulo over forty years ago. Everybody agreed that Joey should convert a back room into a workshop, if just to limit the sawdust and shavings to one room. The snow began in November. The frosts were severe and some days it was necessary to melt snow and icicles for fresh water. Tom erected the tall fences around his sheep at the back of the house and the family withdrew inside and kept the fires alight day and night. Beth helped Florence and made certain she avoided heavy lifting and Joey shut himself in his workshop fitting dark mahogany inlays of stars into the pale oak of his cradle. He made a removable hood, covered in stars, complete with neatly drilled holes, from which he suspended ribbons with bright woollen pompoms and tiny bells to entertain his child. The oak rockers were carved into undulating waves that little mahogany fish poked their heads from. Florence moved an armchair into the workshop and sat for hours watching her husband's progress. She brought him tea at regular intervals and he would stand up and stretch his aching back, shake the sawdust from his hair and sit on the floor beside her and survey his cradle from a distance. Invariably, halfway through his cup of tea, inspiration would distract him and he would jump up and begin work again.

Blizzards raged and snow drifted up and covered the ground floor windows and Big Ern was the only one not to get blown over by the fierce, unrelenting wind. Everywhere in the village the doors and shutters were tightly closed as people withdrew to keep close to their fires. Charles, Aziz and Harry dug a fresh path to the stables each day to stoke up the fires and deliver hot bran mash to the horses and break the ice on their drinking water. Intrepid shepherds dug their way to the school with their families and remained there, beside the roaring fires, close enough to their amalgamated flock to feed them each day. The sheep clustered together and created sweaty caves and tunnels under the snow. With the assistance of Big Ern, Bella Mary made her way through the chest-high snowdrifts to check on Florence. She had calculated her confinement to mid-March, but after examining her and measuring her belly she decided that either the date of Florence's last bleed was wrong or she was having twins. Without mentioning her findings she returned home and told her father. Joey's father was one of twins and Mustapha thought it highly likely that twins was the correct diagnosis, particularly as Bella Mary thought she had detected two hard rounded areas that felt like heads. This delivery required planning and preparation. It was Florence's first labour and she was in her thirties. Mustapha was glad that the experienced Beth was with Florence and that Big Ern was at the new house. He gave potions to Big Ern to deliver to Beth and instructions to collect him and Bella Mary at the first signs of labour. January and February passed without incident and Mustapha and Bella Mary trudged through the snow regularly to check on Florence. She was in good health, but had begun to struggle with walking and getting up out of armchairs. Joey was reduced to a quivering wreck by an excess of joyful excitement and dread. The second week in March, at two o'clock in the morning Big Ern woke Bella Mary by throwing stones at her window and she woke her father and they hurried to the new house, passing the last piles of discoloured, grubby snow, deep in their own concerns. Beth had sent Joey to stoke up the bathhouse fires whilst she put the big saucepans on to boil in the kitchen. Florence sat by the fire and Bella Mary timed her contractions. At five o'clock she had her first mild potion and Big Ern carried her to the bathhouse, hotly pursued by a panic-stricken Joey. Once immersed in the warm water, Florence's face relaxed into a contented smile.

Beth served tea. Florence's waters broke and Mustapha gave her a stronger remedy. Bella Mary regularly checked on her progress. Just after six, Bella Mary initially thought she was mistaken when she thought she felt a head on its way out. She called to her father and they sat Florence up and Bella Mary jumped into the bath behind her. Florence had a fit of the giggles as Mustapha and Bella Mary helped her to kneel, whilst Beth topped up the water. Anticipating a lengthy pushing stage, Mustapha was untying the rope when Bella caught the baby boy that appeared without warning. Beth took the baby and Bella Mary dripped out of the bath so that Florence could lean back and hold her baby. She lay in the warm water and stared in disbelief at the child who blinked in the candlelight and spluttered his first breaths of air. Mustapha felt her belly and nodded to his daughter who lifted the child, rolled him in a warm towel and passed him to his father. Joey stopped jumping around and sat down with his son in his arms and wept with relief.

'Florence.' Whispered Bella Mary. 'You were carrying twins, there is one more to come.'

'Oh my giddy aunt!' Florence exclaimed laughing heartily.

A few short minutes later another tiny head bobbed to the surface and Florence fished her daughter from the water. It was poor Joey that needed a potion. Big Ern, first baby in one arm, helped Joey to the living room and draped him on the sofa. Beth carried the second baby and Bella Mary helped Florence to dry herself and put on a clean nightdress while her father disposed of the afterbirth. He had expected Florence to have a long hard labour, but then he remembered she was from the same stable as old Mary, Ellen Lily and Mary Ellen, whose babies had been prone to drop out unexpectedly and with little effort.

Nellie, alerted by Mustapha's absence at early morning tea, appeared round the back of the new house, as Mustapha was burying the afterbirth, her face red and contorted with anxiety.

'They are all fine Nellie and it *was* twins, one of each!'

Nellie burst into tears and Mustapha hugged her. Nellie ran in to see Florence, who was in triumphant mood drinking her tea. Big Ern had carried in the cradle and Beth put the babies in side by side. The named the twins John and Rosy. Mustapha pulled the unsteady Joey from the sofa and they took the babies outside to give thanks for their safe arrival. Big Ern ran to the big house, wrapped old Rose in a thick blanket and carried her like a baby to the new house to meet the twins.

Florence made a swift recovery. Joey took longer and it was weeks before he picked up a chisel again

Chapter 54

Bella Mary discovered old Mustapha's notes of the usefulness of bhang. He had written that it induced good humour, aided sleep and increased the appetite, all of which was ideal for recovering patients. Her father had rarely used it and until she had tried it as a last resort, on Ellen Lily, neither had she. She embarked on a series of experiments. Rose's appetite was poor and she barely ate enough to sustain life, so Bella Mary added a teaspoonful of bhang to Rose's tea and honey half an hour before the evening meal and observed her. Rose sat beside the fire and began to giggle as the girls were laying the table. She took her place at the table, ate an unusually respectable quantity and congratulated Nellie on the best meal she had eaten in ages. She laughed and wandered unsteadily to the armchair beside the fire and slept deeply for two hours, oblivious to the children romping around the room. Intrigued, Bella Mary tried the concoction on a number of unsuspecting family members and was fascinated to discover that the results were far more haphazard that she expected. Florence was consumed with uncontrollable laughter. Joey carved a number of birds and butterflies to suspend above the twins cradle. Her mother Isabella drifted into the woods, smiling and touching the flowers. Her father fell asleep. George would not stop talking and Esther could not stop giggling or remember what she had been talking about and Sabia appeared immune due to being raised on bhang. Bella Mary deduced that the potion must react differently inside each person. She had long suspected as much, that the effect of a potion varied according to whom it was administered. Each person's body is different and that must combine with the potion in some way, altering the outcome. Bella drank a glassful and waited. She soon discovered that blue ink is a different colour depending on the colour of the surface of the paper and that if the ink stood for a potion and the paper for a person then it was necessary to study patients in greater depth in an attempt to predict the outcome and the rays of the setting sun appeared much redder that usual tonight and she was inspired and invented a potion for appetite loss containing bhang and ginger and cinnamon to aid digestion and prevent heartburn in the elderly and ailing and came up with the intention of making a series of cards for each patient in the village with the most important information such as previous illnesses and temperament and age and size and reaction to potions and then she was hungry and made her way downstairs and stood in the kitchen wondering why she was there and then found herself in the pantry eating the left-over pudding!

The disarray in the microscope room puzzled Bella Mary in the morning, when she encountered the blobs of blue ink and feverish notes to herself. Then she remembered the new potion and the information cards. At breakfast her father agreed that the cards would be very useful, so Danny and Bella Mary began writing the cards and fitting them in a box in alphabetical order for easy retrieval. Only later in the day did Bella Mary suddenly realise that her new ideas had been the potion at work! Then it all began to make sense. The potion broke through the constraints of the mind, disabled the inhibitions and released creativity. Thinking people thought more deeply, happy people laughed louder, tired people relaxed and gave themselves permission to fall asleep, creative people created and dreamy people like her mother did whatever took their fancy!

Rose drank her glass of Bella Mary's new potion, an infusion of ginger, cinnamon and bhang each evening before dinner. It enhanced her appetite, obliterated her troublesome indigestion, she gained enough weight for her dresses to fit her again and her energy levels improved. Mustapha congratulated his daughter.

Archie and Turnip were sitting on the steps of the imposing ancestral home watching the progress of a spider building its web between the grey stone balustrades.

'Archie.' Piped Turnip. 'Did you meet Thomas when we went to Florence's wedding?'

Archie frowned. 'I met so many people that day, but I can't say that I remember a Thomas.'

'He's not a person Archie. He is a very large stone with a head!'

'He's a what?' Archie was incredulous.

'He is like a rock but he has a little head with eyes and everything!'

'I think you must have had a strange dream, young Turnip!' chuckled Archie.

'No Archie, it was not a dream, I have met him many times and he has four little legs that come out of the stone when he wants to move around!'

Archie shook his head.

'And he is called a tortoise and one of my uncles brought him back from Africa!'

Archie remained implacably unconvinced.

'Don't you believe me?' inquired Turnip, scratching a scab on his knee.

Archie shrugged his shoulders.

'Er…well…I..'

'I am going to ask mother if I can take you to meet him!' announced Turnip and ran indoors.

Archie resumed studying the spider, smiling and shaking his head. He could hear Turnip's running feet as he rushed back to the steps.

'Mother said we can go this afternoon, if that is alright with you Archie. Besides, I would like to see Florence's new babies, wouldn't you?'

'That I would Turnip! I am very fond of Florence.'

'And I, Archie, am very fond of you!' Turnip chirped.

Archie ruffled the boy's dark hair and gave him a gentle shove.

'You just wait Archie! I think you will like Thomas.'

The rickety old George drove the carriage to the big house and before Archie could apologise for their impromptu visit Turnip had him running around the meadow searching for a large stone. Nellie called Archie when she had made the tea and he sat on the bench outside of the front door and watched Turnip running about.

'I think the lad's been dreaming, he keeps on about a stone with a head!' Archie laughed.

'Oh, you mean Thomas!'

'Beg pardon?' Archie stared at Nellie.

'Thomas! Old Ellen Lily always called him the rock with a head!'

Archie's mouth fell open.

'He's by the back door, or was a minute ago, I'll fetch him.'

Nellie left and a minute later returned struggling with a dome-shaped rock of considerable size, paved with geometric shapes and placed it on the grass in front of the flabbergasted Archie.

'He's over here!' Nellie shouted to Richard and he bounded across the meadow to introduce Archie and Thomas.

Archie stared as Turnip raised one end of the rock to show Archie the head. But Thomas, recently rudely disturbed, remained inside, hatches firmly battened. Turnip lowered him to the ground.

'He'll come out in a minute.' He explained to Archie, who began to wonder if it was him that was dreaming.

Archie drank his tea and Turnip embarked on a dandelion hunt, that he assured Archie was guaranteed to make his head come out.

Archie mentioned to Nellie that they were shortly going to visit Florence and the babies and she volunteered to go with them. They began discussing Florence's life and how much it had changed when Thomas decided it was safe to emerge and Archie watched in wonder as the strange decorated creature cantilevered on stubby, scaly, clawed legs and clambered laboriously over his boot. Turnip returned with dandelion leaves and the astonished Archie watched Thomas's head, with beady black eyes, attached by a long gaunt neck, gradually emerge and the large mouth opened and snipped off triangles of leaf.

'Well I never....'

'See Archie, I told you!'

Archie lifted Thomas and he vanished inside with a hiss, exhaling a cold, earthy breath.

Florence was delighted to see Archie and Richard and proudly rushed them into the living room where the babies lay side by side in their cradle. Rosy was asleep, but little John was wide awake watching intently with his amber eyes the coloured ribbons and balls swaying above his head. When they adjourned to the kitchen for tea and cake, Archie was momentarily assaulted by unwelcome, intrusive images of his mistress and the turnip.

Turnip sat on Archie's lap in the carriage as it offered a better view of the countryside. Archie sat thinking about how much his own life had changed and listened with a smile to the child prattling happily about the babies and Thomas.

Chapter 55

Bella Mary and Danny had a busy summer that year. They were accustomed to, and skilled at dealing with the half dozen or so cases of measles that tended to occur in the warmer months. This was the year of the epidemic. It had spread through the villages with an alarming suddenness. Bella Mary and Danny visited the sick children each day, armed with infusions of garlic, honey and cinnamon to ease the throat, instruction to keep the child cool, either by immersing in cool water or wrapping wet towels around their head and mild sedatives to help them to sleep. She taught the village mother's that shivering during illness indicated a very high temperature and on no account should they cover the child with blankets. She also knew that the heart beat much faster in an overheated patient. John had told her that an instrument for measuring the temperature of a body existed in the hospital that took twenty minutes to produce a result. Bella Mary scoffed and continued to use the speed that butter melted on the patient's forehead as the most efficient indicator.

Bella Mary rarely lost a child to measles. She had been appalled when reading the treatments advocated by writers in medical journals, some of which advocated purging and bleeding patients. She knew that with good nursing and plenty of liquids, healthy, well-nourished children rarely died of measles. It was the sudden rise in their temperatures that concerned her most, as she believed that the brain could become overheated and damage may occur.

Plans were being made for the future education of Danny. Mustapha and Matthew chose to send him to the University College Hospital, an amalgamation of the University College in Gower Street and the North London Hospital. It was the first non-denominational university and known as 'the godless college.' He would study under both an apothecary and a surgeon, attend operations, dissect corpses in the anatomy room, attend lectures and accompany the learned doctors during their ward rounds and examine out-patients. Bella Mary was green with envy, and she made Danny promise to inform her of any new ground breaking advances.

Rose had regained some of her previous energy and, thanks to Bella Mary, was once again able to make the short journey along the path to the new house, largely to visit Florence's twins as it reminded her of when George and Olivia were born. John was the larger twin and longer than his more compact sister. They both had dark hair and their father's amber eyes. Rosy slept for long periods but John stayed awake, quietly staring at whatever entered his line of vision. The warm spring with its proliferation of bluebells heralded what was to be a long warm summer with light rains that mostly occurred at night. Rose seemed to sense that it was to be her last summer and with a final burst of energy, she lived it to the full. For the first time in years she boarded the cart and visited Sophia on the marshes, admired the new dining room and spent the day playing with Maria Rose, whose eyes had turned a deep violet-blue and whose curly, dark brown hair shone russet in the sun. Then she agreed to old George taking her in the carriage to see Olivia and Hugh's ancestral home and even agreed to stay for a few days. When she returned home she was very tired and felt out of touch with life, as if she was an interloper in the present. All of her contemporaries had died and she felt isolated, like she no longer belonged to this particular time and place. Rose sat in the tree house and watched the festivities at the harvest party and watched as her children and grandchildren joined in the dancing. This was their time and she felt as though she had been exiled from another era without knowing exactly when it had happened. Mustapha saw death in old Rose's eyes, informed everyone and Bella Mary increased the quantity of bhang in her drinks and she spent her final days giggling beside the fire and saying her farewells to her family. Nellie insisted on sleeping in Rose's room at night, determined that she should not die alone. A week later, when Nellie heard her breathing change in the early hours, she quickly fetched George and Mustapha, and Rose, last of her generation, died peacefully in the arms of her son, with a smile on her face. She had left her drawings and memoirs to Aziz, so that he could continue with the family history.

Aziz had grown into a tall young man and he was of a heavier build than his father or brother. He divided his time between writing the history and learning from George the secrets of the family's finances. George, after consultation with Edmundo and Estavo, purchased a clipper, a slightly smaller, lighter but much faster ship that cost in excess of fifteen thousand pounds. George's investments in the railways paid good dividends and by 1850 there was a new railway line from Higham to Strood, but it would take another thirty years before there would be a branch-line to the village.

Levi Hoare, his joints aching from a lifetime of heavy work, handed the forge to Amos and Tommy. Annie had a daughter and they named her Charlotte, for Amos's mother. Danny travelled to London to begin his training and Teddy took responsibility for the sheep allowing his father to spend more time with Sophia. Little Maria Rose started school and had already announced that she wanted to be a nurse when she grew up. At the other side of the county, Turnip decided that he wanted to go to sea with his uncles. Olivia and Hugh supported his decision and Hugh secretly wished he could go with him. Archie prayed that they would refuse to take him.

Chapter 56

Bella Mary missed Danny, as did her patients. Her workload doubled and she was grateful that it was autumn and therefore less work to do in the garden. Unexpected assistance came from Robbie, Big Ern and Beth's youngest child, a monumental fourteen year old, who took responsibility for protecting the garden from frost, carrying her bags and once carried an elderly patient to the sick house from Lily Lane at such speed that Bella Mary found it hard to keep up. Robbie's imposing size belied a gentle nature and startled toddlers stopped crying once he spoke to them. He resembled his mother, with thick, long brown hair and warm blue eyes and no interest in carpentry. Once the winter snow set in

Robbie moved from the new house, where he had been a wondrous plaything to the small children, to the big house and became the one everybody called when there was anything heavy to be moved. Due to Robbie's size, he had been treated as an adult since the age of ten and the child in him had been stifled beneath a veneer of maturity and emerged at frequent intervals in scathingly honest, albeit inappropriate comments. Bella Mary thought this was an asset, but her father Mustapha attempted to tell Robbie that there was real no need to tell someone that they had the longest nose in the village or that they had the smelliest house or fattest backside he had ever seen! Robbie was unable to understand why and Mustapha explained that people were often sensitive and their feelings could be hurt and he needed to be more careful about what he said to them. Robbie made a valiant effort, with only moderate success and came to be known as Robbie the Mouth to distinguish his from other Robert's in the village.

It was another harsh winter and the children played on the ice on the pond at the bottom of the hill from the sick house, until a child fell through the ice and disappeared. The rest of the children, squealing in unison ran to the sick house. Despite the best efforts of Mustapha, Matthew and Robbie the Mouth, the child was blue and dead by the time they finally fished him out. Mustapha carried the small body home to his distraught parents, who had already received the news of his demise from the other children. Mustapha made tea, laced with a sedative and explained to the trickle of well-meaning neighbours that he would pass on their condolences and they would be welcome to visit after the funeral. Little Arthur had been the middle child of five. A month later, just before Christmas, Mustapha sent a large box of provisions and gifts for the children and a note saying, *'I am sure that young Arthur would want you to have a happy Christmas.'*

The blizzards raged throughout January and Beth delivered Sabia and young Mustapha's tiny daughter, earlier than expected. She was born with thick dark hair and the stare of the Mustapha's and they named her Mary Sophia. Robbie the Mouth carried Bella Mary on his shoulders through the snow to visit her new niece. Little Mustapha, John and Rosy were delighted to see him and rode him around the house until the midday meal was served. That afternoon he trudged to Gabriel's old farm and borrowed the sledge, usually drawn by the heavy horses, and entertained the eager children by dragging them around at high speed and tipping them into the snow drifts, giddy and laughing, until their noses and cheeks turned crimson and their noses dripped. He returned the teeth-chattering grinning trio, dripping wet and shivering and Florence immediately put them all into a hot, steaming bath.

Winter finally gave way to the spring and little Mustapha, driven by internal forces, became a regular visitor to the big house and followed Robbie the Mouth in the garden and satisfied the urgent need to master the secrets of the plants. Mustapha watched his grandson from the window as old Mustapha had watched him as a child and he smiled. It was as though history was repeating itself and children followed in the footsteps of their grandfathers.

Mustapha wondered what the invisible force within a person was, and how it was transmitted from one generation to another. It seemed as though the foundations of the path of a child's life was already laid by the time it was born and it instinctively knew it must be followed. Perhaps it was a luxury to be free to follow the natural path, rather than be forced to follow another, as was the case for many people. Poor children had little choice. He remembered Old Mrs Lyle and her deep unhappiness and deduced that the rich are not necessarily free either. His grandfather's skills and love of healing must have been carried somewhere in his own father, but failed to manifest itself. Perhaps the path that led to the sea overrode it. Edmundo, Estavo and young Mustapha and all followed their grandfathers to sea. Mustapha considered Sophia's children, two of whom were following the healing path that had lain dormant in his sister. Then there was Bella Mary, who had inherited the healing skills and an impatient belligerence uncommon in the family, with the exception of when Isabella was attacked by the mad James. He deduced that this forceful, determined, fearless outspokenness must have come from her unknown mother's family. And now it appeared that little Mustapha, his grandson, had already embarked on his path of potions and healing. But none of this explained Robbie the Mouth's internal pathway. His father was a carpenter and his grandfather had been a farm worker. Mustapha drank his tea and decided that sometime in the future, all these matters would be known and he wished that he could live again and to see the mystery unfold.

Little Mustapha arrived and squeezed into the armchair beside his grandfather.

'I wish I could live here with you granddaddy.'

Mustapha put his around the child.

'But your mother and father would miss you.'

'They have Mary Sophia and anyway I should like to live nearer the garden. Robbie has taught me which things are weeds! And it is my job to pull them up!'

'What about if you stay here some nights during the times when there is much to do in the garden?'

Little Mustapha flung his arms around his grandfather's neck.

'Thank you granddaddy!'

'And, I think it's about time for you to learn to use the microscope!'

They spent the afternoon magnifying various types of plant matter, a hair, little Mustapha's finger and a dead fly.

Little Mustapha returned to the new house in the evening and asked his parents if he could stay at the big house with his granddaddy when he was very busy in the garden and the microscope room and they agreed, just as long as he did not forget about them.

'Can I stay there tonight?'

'If granddaddy says so, but you must ask him first.'

'He already said that I can if you let me!'

'Go on then!' laughed his father.

Little Mustapha hugged his parents and ran off as fast as his legs would carry him and slept in the big soft bed once inhabited by his great-great-grandfather.

Chapter 57

Danny slowly adjusted to living in the mammoth city that was London. The crowds, the beggars, the unpredictable packs of dogs and the eye-watering perpetual stench of faeces and decay in the streets was a stark contrast to the space and the cold, fresh, salty air of the marshes. His lodgings were small, shabby and cramped and the food was disappointing, but the fat landlady was a pleasant woman, willing to wash and press his clothing. After acclimatising to the stink in the streets, the smell of the reeking corpses of the anatomy room was but a small step. The unclaimed dead from the hospital provided a ready supply of bodies to cut open, peer inside of and identify organs of, although Danny was aware that there also existed an understanding between doctors and grave robbers. The hospital wards were still crowded but an attempt had been made to improve the cleanliness and hand washing between patients had become common practice for the nurses and occasionally even a doctor could be seen to wash his hands. The small group of students would stand beside a patient's bed and listen to the learned doctor reciting symptoms suffered by the said patient and were then expected to suggest possible ailments. The responses from the doctors varied, some were patient, encouraging and good-humoured. Others were sarcastic and enjoyed belittling the students attempts at diagnosis and one unfortunate student, who inadvertently forgot to recite his name prior to voicing his diagnosis, was forever referred to as 'Shaking palsy'.

Danny was horrified by the sheer amount of diseases suffered by the urban masses as opposed to those in the village. Most patients were malnourished and lived in filthy conditions. Thousands wasted away from Consumption and Scrofula. He witnessed his first case of Tympany, a kind of obstructed flatulence that swelled the poor patient's body like a tight drum. He was staggered by the sheer amount of people suffering the Great Pox or Syphilis. The disease is highly infectious during its primary phase when there are genital sores, after which the disease seems to disappear. The second stage produces a diffuse, non-itchy rash and the final stage, from ten to thirty years later develops into Softening of the Brain, when there is a general paralysis of the, by then, insane patient! There were always incidents of

Gangrene, a condition that smelled like the anatomy room on a busy day and only responded to amputation of the affected part of the body, a treatment that occasionally met with success. Heavy alcohol use was rife, resulting in Livergrown and Delirium Tremens, conditions from which few survived. Child mortality was high. It was common for workhouses to sell orphaned and abandoned children as 'pauper apprentices', working without wages for board and lodgings. Those who ran away would be whipped and returned to their masters and often shackled to prevent further escape attempts. Danny felt swamped and helpless in the face of such suffering.

Time spent with the apothecary was less onerous. The apothecary made and sold remedies and medicines and often diagnosed and prescribed directly to patients. Danny was familiar with many of the compounds used, in fact he was familiar with many more ingredients, but was sensible enough in the early days to keep silent.

The poverty, described to Danny by his mother who had visited London over twenty years ago, remained rife. The streets were full of ragged, dirty people. The effort made to clear the streets of debris during the cholera outbreak had achieved a slight improvement, but the bad smells, thought to be the source of sickness, remained. Over four hundred thousand tonnes of raw sewage was flushed into the river each day and the stench from the 'dead' river was overpowering. The 'Great Stink' or miasma rose to a ghastly, nauseating pitch in the summers. There were further outbreaks of cholera and ships were moored at the banks of the river to house the sick and infected bodies were frequently thrown into the disgusting, sickening soup that was the River Thames. Danny followed Bella Mary's strict advice. He boiled water before drinking it, avoided consuming anything from the numerous eating-houses and street stalls. He educated his landlady Mrs Moore on the rigours of cleanliness and she followed his instructions to the letter, motivated by mounting terror. Danny was relieved to return to the village when he could, it was the only place he could take a deep breathe without apprehension. Mustapha was greatly depressed by his stories and Bella Mary demanded all the details of the sicknesses unknown in the village and his exploits in the dissecting room. Sophia worried about his health and he assured his mother that he followed Bella Mary's rules and always washed his hands thoroughly after touching a patient.

Danny and his father walked to the seawall, waving to Teddy, who was in charge of the sheep. The estuary of the river Thames, being tidal, just smelled of salt and seaweed and Danny found it difficult to equate it with the offensive brown, sluggish soup that he was familiar with. Later, Tom cooked his famous stew and roasted potatoes and the family sat around the large table, Danny declined to discuss his experiences for fear of ruining their appetites and wasting the delicious meal.

Danny visited the big house and sat in Bella Mary's garden with little Mustapha, breathing in the delicious bouquets of the fragrant flowers and aromatic herbs and dreamed of the time when he could return to the village for good. Little Mustapha went to the new house with Danny to show him how much Joey and Florence's twins had grown and to meet his new sister Mary Anne. Florence made tea whilst Danny was inundated with questions about his training from the family. Later, Danny wandered into the cool, quiet woodland behind the house, busy with wild roses, dappled sunlight and birdsong and was stupefied by the stunning vision that Aida Mina had evolved into since he last saw her. She was walking down through the woods, returning from a flower gathering expedition, clad in a shimmering deep green and silver sari, her long, straight dark hair billowing in the gentle breeze, oblivious to his proximity. Danny was unable to move. Aida Mina jumped in surprise when she saw him and her face broke into a wide smile as she recognised him.

'Danny!' she cried and flung her cool, slim arms around his neck, enveloping him in the smell of jasmine, as his head swam and he tried to formulate a sentence. Unaware of his inner disturbance, Aida Mina took his arm as they walked slowly through the woods and she chattered about trivial matters.

'How long is it since I saw you last?' Aida Mina asked.

'A year or so, I believe.'

'You have grown very tall!'

'And you have grown very beautiful!'

Aida Mina smiled broadly, her amber eyes shining and she elbowed him in the ribs.

Memories of Aida Mina preoccupied Danny when he returned to London until he readjusted to the layers of filth, degradation and death and she became a misty, distant dream and he lost his belief in her reality.

Having mastered a considerable knowledge of anatomy, Danny was assigned to a surgeon and spent his time ankle deep in body fragments, deafened by screams and haunted by the terrified eyes of the patients. Occasionally, a petrified patient broke free of the restraining straps and vice-like grip of their captors and ran off and locked themselves in lavatories, where they cringed and pleaded as the door was broken down and they were returned to the unspeakable terrors of the operating table. He suffered dreadful nightmares, where he was the patient on the operating table and he awoke, drenched in sweat and tears, his heart pounding.

Chapter 58

By autumn, Bella Mary, John, Robbie the Mouth and the two nurses Elsie and Dorothy managed the sick house and little Mustapha was responsible for the garden. Mustapha's hair was streaked with grey, and like his grandfather he was slowly reducing to a bag of bones. He had been relegated, on the insistence of his daughter, to the big house to spend the rest of his days with Isabella and little Mustapha. Nellie cooked his favourite foods, cakes, spicy chicken and beef with pepper sauce to fatten him up, with little success. Mustapha felt as if he was irrevocably evolving into his own grandfather and at odd moments, when he was in the garden with little Mustapha, it was as though the roles had been reversed and he was looking at himself. When Mary Sophia began to follow her brother to the big house and squeeze into the armchairs with him and Isabella, Mustapha was thunderstruck at life's capacity to move in mysterious circles. Sabia was with child again, and she and young Mustapha followed their children and moved back to the big house.

Meanwhile, over at the estate, Hugh and Olivia's eldest daughter Victoria, despite the damning prophecies of old Mrs Lyle had made a very good marriage. Her mother's questionable heritage absolved due to an excess of land, money and violet-eyed beauty. Henry remained unmarried and his twin Edgar had left to become an explorer in Africa. Archie died of old age with Turnip at his side, freeing him to accompany his uncles on the voyage to India planned for the spring and taking to the grave the reason Richard was known as Turnip.

Down on the marshes, Tom and Sophia were enjoying each other's company. They spent their time walking the sea wall and in good weather, riding further afield with a picnic. Billy the daydreamer had joined Teddy with the sheep, Bobby was waiting for spring to sail with the ship and Maria Rose spent all her time at the sick house under the tutelage of Bella Mary and Danny would be home for Christmas.

At the new house, the forthcoming marriage of Eva Violet, the daughter of Big Ern and Beth, to Arthur Smith, the tall, dark, quiet undertaker was announced and Aida Mina was uncharacteristically distracted and restless. The twins, John and Rosy attended school. John was already displaying a talent with woodcarving and Rosy spent her time in the kitchen with her mother Florence.

At the big house, Emily Rose, a master seamstress like her mother, worked at the shop and George followed his father into the field of figures. As three people, George, Aziz and young George, now managed the family finances they split the tasks according to particular abilities. Aziz kept the ledgers, young George was responsible for calculating and paying wages and his father had sole charge of investments and the purchase of major items. Nellie's cakes, destined to fatten Mustapha, had thickened her own waist, requiring moving the big kitchen table six inches eastward. Everyone was looking forward to the birth of Sabia's child, the first since the birth of Mary Sophia five years ago. Bella Mary deduced the child would be born in early February.

As Christmas approached, Aida Mina worried at her mother to invite Tom, Sophia and family. Joey and Florence, very fond of the family supported her request. Aida Mina's odd behaviour increased as Christmas got closer and she spent an entire morning trying on saris and jewellery and demanding that her bemused father Khalid selected the most beautiful combination. They finally settled on an ivory sari, heavily embroidered with silver stars and a heavy gold necklace with a large amber drop to match her eyes and her numerous gold bangles. It was Florence who finally weaselled the information from Aida Mina, late at night in the kitchen, to explain her erratic behaviour. Aida Mina swore Florence to secrecy and Florence hugged her warmly and assured her than Danny was bound to fall in love with her and to stop worrying about it. She suggested that Aida Mina position herself halfway up the elegant spiral staircase that dominated the hallway when the family arrived on Christmas morning. The reaction of Danny, seeing her hovering there in her ivory and silver sari, would be certain to indicate whether or not he had feelings for her. Florence was right. On Christmas morning Aida Mina avidly watched the path outside from the upstairs window, so that she could station herself on the stairs just at the right time.

Danny arrived home to the marshes late in the evening before Christmas Eve, looking exhausted, worn and with dark circles under his eyes. Sophia was alarmed by his appearance. He fell asleep after a bowl of his father's mutton stew and slept for fifteen hours until his mother finally woke him, fearing that he had died. He consumed three cups of tea and a pile of fried bread and eggs and confided in her the horrors of the operating room. Sophia held his hand with tears in her eyes, in awe of her son's strength and capacity to endure the suffering and she could remember the resounding, mournful echoes of the operations bell as if she had heard it only yesterday. The long sleep had brightened Danny's eyes and in the afternoon he walked across the cold marshes to the seawall and stood at the top and allowed the stiff, relentless, salty breeze to fill his lungs and blow away the stench, the blood spattered walls, the desperate screams, the reeking amputated limbs and the spongy excised growths. By the time he returned home to the aroma of roasted meat and potatoes he had begun to resemble the more familiar, smiling Danny.

'Danny, we have been invited to spend tomorrow at the new house, I do hope you don't mind.' Sophia remarked as they ate dinner.

Danny choked as the sudden, vivid memory of Aida Mina in her deep green sari, buried under months of upset and strain, exploded into his thoughts.

That night, Sophia retired to bed early, leaving Danny and his father sitting beside the roaring fire with a pot of tea.

'Father, what made you marry mother?'

'Because I loved her of course, why else?'

'But how did you know?'

'Know what?'

'That you loved her! *How* did you know?'

Tom stared into the fire and smiled, remembering Sophia on the seawall struggling with the driftwood.

'I looked into her eyes and knew I did not want to live without her.'

'Oh.'

'Why?'

'I just wondered.'

Danny tried to avoid eye contact with his father, acutely conscious of his penetrating gaze.

'Have you met someone in London?'

'No.'

'Who is it then?'

Danny looked into the fire and his valiant attempt to appear nonchalant failed. He heaved a sigh.

'Aida Mina.' He eventually whispered, his face reddening.

Chapter 59

Christmas Eve night was cold and still and the first of the snowflakes fell inaudibly. Neither Danny nor Aida Mina slept well and were up at the crack of dawn pacing about impatiently. After breakfast Danny, unable to keep still, went outside to walk on the light covering of snow.

'That lad thinks he's in love with Aida Mina.' Tom whispered to his wife. 'I hope she will be kind to him!'

'I think she will be more than that!' chuckled Sophia. 'Florence, who had been sworn to secrecy, told me that it was on Aida Mina's insistence that we were all invited there today. She knew Danny would be home and cannot wait to see him again!'

'How wonderful!' Whispered Tom, recalling the moment when he knew Sophia loved him.

Aida Mina killed time by washing her long dark hair and she rubbed a little jasmine oil onto the ends and stood in the way of Florence and Beth, beside the kitchen stove, and brushed it dry until it shone like silk. She dressed carefully and applied kohl to her eyes as Mina had taught her and studied herself in the mirror. Khalid told her that she was as beautiful as he remembered his mother when he was a small child and Aida Mina smiled. Then, with a cup of sweet tea in her hand, she stood upstairs and anxiously watched for Danny to arrive.

Danny was annoyed with himself for forgetting to bring a present for Aida Mina. Sophia, who already knew that Aida Mina would be wearing her amber pendant, so she gave her son a ring passed down from Lily, via Rose to her. The ring had a rare yellow-gold sapphire, surrounded by tiny white diamonds. She slipped it into his coat pocket.

'Just in case you need it.' She whispered.

Florence, Beth, the girls and three village women busied themselves basting the beef and the large goose. Florence made the pepper sauce and the puddings. The girls prepared the large trays of potatoes, parsnips, onions and wintergreens. The village women laid the long table, marvelling at Joey's majestic internal tree.

Aida Mina's heart almost leapt from her body when she saw the horse and cart in the distance. She scurried to and fro, delaying her arrival on the spiral staircase until the cart was outside.

Danny's mood swung like a pendulum from ecstasy to terror as they approached the new house.

Tom slapped him on the back as he climbed shakily from the cart.

'Go on in son, a little bird told me that it was all Aida Mina's idea to invite us, but I never told you that.'

Danny smiled, took a deep breath and opened the front door with a confident shove. Then he saw her shimmering on the stairs like an apparition. Danny ran to the bottom of the stairs, arms open to catch her as she descended with as much dignity as she could muster. Which was not much, as six steps from the bottom she launched herself at him and he caught her, swung her around until she laughed and begged to be put down. Tom experienced a wistful moment, thinking about when he had done the same to Sophia and he put his arm around his wife and kissed her on the top of the head and she knew they were both remembering the same thing.

Christmas at the new house was chaotic that year. The twins were still young enough to ride Robbie the Mouth around the house. Following a stupendous meal, with crispy roast potatoes that even the cooks were impressed with, Robbie the Mouth organised rowdy games and poor Arthur Smith, unfamiliar as he was in his line of work, with such riotous, unrestrained gaiety was rescued by Eva Violet, taken to the kitchen and given a hot cup of tea, laced with honey and emergency brandy. By teatime, Khalid had agreed to the marriage and Aida Mina and Danny, both bursting with wild excitement, announced that they were to be married in early spring, before the ship was due to sail, on the same day as Eva Violet and Arthur.

The atmosphere at the big house could not have been more dissimilar. The houses appeared to have classified their inhabitants by temperament. All the boisterous ones were at the new house. Arthur Smith would have been more comfortable at the big house. They had a peaceful, restful, gentle day, interrupted by delicious food and reminiscences. Mary Sophia spent most of the day curled up beside her grandfather Mustapha. Aziz handed round the drawings of the family completed by Mustapha's mother Maria and his aunt Rose. Bella Mary mixed a large jug-full of honey, milk, bhang and hot water and served it in the raspberry coloured glasses. The family slowly descended into a deeper layer of relaxation, with the exception of Bella Mary and little Mustapha, who retired to the microscope room and invented a soft, oily cream for use on burns and a remedy for the downhearted.

The warm, dozing tranquillity in the front room suffered a vigorous flying visit from Danny and Aida Mina, spreading their news and waggling her new ring under their noses. The startled, wide-eyed family offered their congratulations and the ear splitting, rampant whirlwind disappeared as fast as it arrived, with a resounding slam of the front door. The stunned family stared at the shuddering door and then at each other, momentarily shaken. Then they slowly dissolved into silence, intermittent giggles and the odd snore.

'What just happened?' Nellie asked some time later.

'When?' George replied once everyone had forgotten what Nellie had said.

An hour or so later, in ones and twos, the family drifted into the kitchen, slicing off lumps of cold meat and cheese and dipping cold roast potatoes in the congealed pepper sauce and picking at the remains of the puddings and created such disorder that they unanimously decided to shut the door so that the urge to tidy up would not disturb their satisfied belching.

The large snowflakes began to fall softly. Nobody at the big house noticed. At the new house, Robbie the Mouth and the children were already throwing snowballs at each other and Tom was making ready the cart so they he could get his family home before the snow got any deeper. Danny smiled all the way home. Aida Mina sat beside the fire and admired her beautiful ring, absolute proof that Danny belonged to her. Robbie the Mouth and the children were playing hide and seek and Joey was attempting to persuade Florence to make hot chocolate. Elizabeth and Khalid sat and watched their beautiful daughter. The happily vague inhabitants lazing in the front room at the big house continued to belch contently as George intermittently threw logs onto the roaring fire. Nobody had any recollection of the visit by Aida Mina and Danny.

Chapter 60

Boxing Day dawned soundlessly, muffled underneath two feet of virgin snow. Danny squinted out of the window at the spotless landscape, hoping the snow would be thick enough to delay his return to London, where the snow would be grimy, grey and trampled into the stinking rubbish underfoot. In the afternoon he walked the couple of miles to the new house to spend the afternoon with his future wife and ended up staying for three days due to the increasing depth of the snow.

At the big house, everyone was astonished to see both the thick snow and the messy disarray in the kitchen. It was several days before Nellie located her favourite knife and she never did discover how a cabbage had migrated to the bathhouse.

Aida Mina decided that she would like primroses as her wedding flowers and elicited the help of Esther to embroider an ivory sari with a border of pale yellow primroses. Emily Rose made a delicate crown decorated with silk primroses.

The snow finally cleared at the end of January, by which time Danny had reluctantly dragged himself back to University College Hospital and to his great relief he was assigned to the examining rooms to deal with the out patients and their wide variety of diseases and injuries. It was there that he began to use the ointments and remedies supplied by Bella Mary. Her burn ointment was a resounding success, not limited to burns. Danny discovered that if he liberally spread the oily substance onto a clean dressing and applied it directly to the burn, cut or abrasion, it not only deterred infection, it also prevented the dressing adhering to the wound, allowed the injury to heal without scabs and avoided further damage from adhered dressings. Between patients he thought about Aida Mina.

In February, Mustapha delivered his grandson Hassan Salamar in a crowded bathhouse. All three generations of the Mustapha's were there, along with Mary Sophia and, of course, Nellie. Outside, Mustapha passed Hassan to his older brother little Mustapha, who held him aloft and gave thanks, in perfect Arabic, to the sky. Little Mustapha carried his new brother to his mother who was sat beside the fire. Nellie made fresh tea and the family waited for the child to open his eyes. They were as black and piercing as his grandfather's.

Nellie pointed out that little Mustapha was nearly as tall as his father and perhaps he should now be referred to as young Mustapha, promoting his father to just plain Mustapha and relegating Mustapha to the grand title of old Mustapha, not held by anyone for over forty years. Everyone agreed. Once over the excitement of the birth of Hassan, the first new baby for years, attention moved to the forthcoming double wedding. Esther and Emily Rose had finished the sari and were busy with Eva Violet's dress in soft lavender silk with white embroidery. The family persuaded Arthur into an outfit in a soft light brown, rather than his choice of sombre black. Danny let Aida Mina decide for him and she chose a traditional Indian outfit in ivory silk with gold embroidery that came as rather a shock to Danny.

The church and graveyard were packed with family and villagers for the first wedding of the year on a crisp, sunny spring day. Arthur and Eva Violet were first to be married. The monumental Big Ern had lost none of his impressive stature with approaching old age and dwarfed his daughter as he proudly escorted her down the aisle. Eva Violet had never looked more beautiful, swathed in lavender silk and with her abundant hair brushed loose and reaching her thighs and carrying a bunch of early purple orchids. Arthur even managed a smile. Danny waited, feeling uncomfortably conspicuous in his 'outrageous pyjamas' as Tom had called them. He was relieved when he saw that Khalid wore a similar outfit. Father and daughter walked down the aisle, their long black hair loose and their amber eyes shining. Aida Mina shimmered in her ivory sari and

Danny forgot all about his 'outrageous pyjamas' when she smiled at him.

The party was well attended and the bonfire was lit early to combat the slight chill in the air. Arthur was one of the very few villagers who had not made a habit of attending the famous parties. He had been an only child, born late in the marriage and was an orphan at nineteen when he inherited the funeral business. Arthur was accustomed to solitude and would have remained that way had it not been for the forward behaviour of Eva Violet. She had first noticed him when he conducted the funeral of her grandmother, Elsie Richards and she admired his elegant bearing and dark, brooding, lonely eyes. She accompanied her father, who made the coffins, when he delivered the latest order and was saddened by the sparse, cold, uninviting dwelling attached to the rear of the shop. Arthur Smith had made tea for them and Eva Violet had watched his white, bony hands shake as he passed her a cup and saucer. A week later, she arrived unannounced and startled him with a hot meat pie wrapped in a thick cloth. The next week she delivered a fruitcake. It was not long before Arthur Smith began to look forward to the weekly visits from the lively young woman who brought with her the lingering odour of the living. He accepted her invitation to a picnic, then to a meal at the new house and before long they were engaged and now they were married. Eva Violet had transformed his forlorn dwelling into a warm, comfortable home and he loved her with a passion beyond his own comprehension.

Big Ern and Robbie the mouth loaded the last of Eva Violet's belongings onto a cart and the new Mr and Mrs Smith left before the fireworks amidst cheers and applause from the whole village, to begin their life together behind the undertaker's shop.

Danny and Aida Mina danced until the firework display and then he flung her over his shoulder and made for the new house, to a room lit by lanterns, smelling of jasmine oil and a thick ivory silk quilt, liberally embroidered with primroses. It was not until morning that they noticed the primroses stitched along the top of the sheet and all over the pillowcases. Aida Mina wanted to accompany her husband to London and stay at his lodgings, but Danny remained adamant that he had no intention of exposing his wife to the perils of the filthy, stinking city.

Chapter 61

Old Doctor Matthew's wife Anna, who was the granddaughter of old Mary, suffered from a puzzling intermittent illness. Some days she was well and then, without warning she would be unable to get out of her bed. Matthew and old Mustapha were at a loss. Sometimes she would be mobile for weeks at a time and they hoped that she had fully recovered. But gradually the weak spells increased and the mobile spells decreased and after six months she was virtually bedridden. She became so feeble that she could no longer pick up a cup and had to be fed, until her ability to swallow became impaired. She lost control of her bladder and bowel. Old Mustapha helped Matthew nurse her until the end, which came after two days of unconsciousness and laboured breathing.

Matthew's two daughters had married and moved away. His son John lived with his father but spent most of his time at the sick house hoping for the phenomenal miracle that would transform Bella Mary into a normal woman. Old Mustapha spent most afternoons with Matthew. They had been through so much together. The high points of their lives, when they successfully removed their first appendix and pieced together the young man gored by a bull, and the very low points, during Matthew's father's humiliating alcohol withdrawal and the tragic deaths that they had been helpless to prevent. They laughed about the past, about old Mustapha's reaction to the microscope and old Grandy who believed they had given him new legs and old Mary who believed that carpenters always fainted during medical emergencies. They discussed Danny's training at the University College Hospital and how painfully slow advances in medicine occurred. Very little had changed since Matthew's time and operations continued to be carried out on conscious patients.

The ship sailed in late spring, complete with Mustapha, Sophia's youngest son Bobby and Turnip, who could not get used to being called Richard. Edmundo and Estavo were in their late forties and relieved to be able to leave the hard physical work to younger men. The new clipper had sailed around in the English Channel on several practice runs over the previous weeks and everyone was keen to be off on a new voyage. The navigational charts and instruments and the stars fascinated Turnip and the wind and the sails captivated Bobby. They were buffeted by several minor storms on their way to the equator, but the new clipper was more streamlined, lighter and faster than the old vessels and they rounded the Cape of Good Hope several weeks before they expected to. Turnip and Bobby stood in the crow's nest and marvelled at the sparkling turquoise water and waited for the vast whales and shoals of fish that they had heard all about when they were small children. As they moved northward the temperature rose and sea changed colour and they heard the whale's eerie singing during the night. Turnip leant over the prow of the ship and watched the dolphins leaping out of the water beside the ship and wished that Archie could have seen them. They moored off the coast of East Africa and went ashore to find wood and as they were early, they stayed a few days. Bobby and Turnip were like excited four year olds and Estavo absolutely refused to allow them to adopt a monkey as he could still remember the erratic antics of Bill.

Edmundo and Estavo were keen to get to India, a county they had loved since they were boys and also keen to test the speed of the clipper. They sailed east through the Indian Ocean's emerald waters, dotted with tiny islands made of white sand, topped with palm trees and encircled by pale green and turquoise shallows. The water was crystal clear and Turnip and Bobby could see the vivid rainbow colours of the fish, swimming through gnarled underwater trees and shrubs known a coral. Bobby was first to catch sight of land as they sailed across the Arabian Sea to India. The next day, the twins, accompanied by Yusuf, Bobby, Mustapha and Turnip set off inland. Mustapha was impatient to see Sabia's parents and tell them that she was well and had given birth to two sons and a daughter. The cart was met with a jubilant welcome. It had been so long in coming that the people had feared that they would never come again. Sabia's father looked exactly the same as he had ten years ago, but her mother had aged. They hugged and kissed Mustapha and made him sit and tell then all about Sabia and the children and about his parents and about the house they lived in and about the weather over there and had Sabia made friends and did she get on well with his family and did she work hard? Mustapha explained that everyone loved Sabia and she had many friends and she lived in a very large house with a cook and servants and had no need to work hard. Sabia's mother clutched Mustapha's hand and kissed it, tears rolling down her wrinkled cheeks and thanked him for giving her daughter such a wonderful life. Sabia's father sniffed, wiped his nose on his tunic, nodded his head and patted Mustapha on the shoulder. Eventually, Mustapha was able to get up and drag the crate from the cart, full of presents from Sabia. There were two new saris for her mother one in crimson and gold and the other in sapphire blue that caused another flood of tears. For her father she had sent a knife with two different blades that closed neatly away inside the handle when not in use and he fiddled with it for the rest of the evening. There were two large cooking pots and a variety of big wooden spoons carved by Joey. He had also carved a box with a secret way of opening that Mustapha had filled at the docks with enough rupees to stop the old couple from worrying.

Due to the speed of the clipper, they had arrived earlier in the year on this occasion and the land was parched and the temperature was very high and the monsoon was due. They had arrived on other occasions at the tail end of the rains, but never at the beginning. The locals watched the clouds and prophesied when the rains would begin and were invariably wrong. Mustapha got it right and the sky turned deep blue, then changed to blue-black and descended to rest precariously on the palm trees for an hour before unleashing so much water so fast and hard that it bounced back up from the impacted dust and vision was reduced to less than a yard. Everyone was drenched to the skin in a few seconds in the warm deluge that felt like small stones landing. In less than a minute little rivers coursed through the dust and formed great deep swirling puddles. Turnip and Bobby stood, gasping for breath in the cascading torrents that poured from the roofs of the huts and from the fronds of the palm trees. Then it rained harder and the roar deafened everyone as the vast lake in the sky made its way to the earth. Then, as abruptly as it had begun, it ceased, leaving just the sound of the heavy drips plopping from the huts, trees and people. Within minutes the sky cleared and the sun shone and the whole place began to steam. Bobby and Turnip thought that was the end of the monsoon until someone told them that it was just the beginning and would go on for weeks. Next morning the village was already transformed by new growth. By midday flowers were beginning to bloom.

The monsoon slowed down the spice collecting. Sometimes it rained all day. After two weeks the mud was so thick and slippery it was impossible to go anywhere. The women strung up oiled sheets of cloth between the palm trees for a cooking area. After a month the heaviest rain had passed but it was weeks before the ground was dry enough to support the weight of a donkey cart. Mustapha, the twins and Yusuf passed the days lying in hammocks and eating whatever was served to them. Bobby and Turnip spent countless hours chasing each other through the mud and wrestling until they were thoroughly encased in mud. One day, instead of washing in the stream, the boys decided to see what would happen if they let the sun dry the mud on their skin. They spent an afternoon laughing at each other as the mud dried and cracked and they resembled scaly reptiles.

Yusuf and Mustapha went off to help with the spice collection and Edmundo and Estavo lay in the hammocks in a slight breeze under the flickering shade of the palm trees.

'This is the life.' Sighed Estavo.
'Mmm.'
'This is still my favourite place in the world.'
'Mine too.'
'I wonder if we will ever get back here again?'
'Mmm.'

The twins laid thinking and because they were twins they had the same thought.

'Shall we stay?'
'We could if we wanted to.'

'Do you think we would be welcome to stay?'

'I don't know about that.'

Following lengthy discussions, the twins were assured that they were welcome to stay forever. Mustapha gave them gold that they could exchange when they needed money and it was settled. Mustapha sat at the back of the cart and waved to his cousins and felt the same way as when he first left here as a child, wishing that he could be two separate people.

Edmundo and Estavo lived there for the rest of their lives. They made two unmarried women very happy and they were would be reunited with Mustapha twice more before they died.

The ship began its return journey full of spices, silks and wood. It was not until they were in the Atlantic Ocean that it dawned on Mustapha that he had finally achieved a lifelong ambition. Now he really was a Sea Captain!

Chapter 62

The half-naked dead body found on the shore by Teddy and for want of a place to deliver it, had taken to the sick house, was, in actual fact not dead. The unfortunate woman was so cold that her pulse was very slow and her breathing virtually imperceptible. Bella Mary, studying the discolouration on her body to assess how long she had been dead, realised it was bruising from being washed up against the rocky shore. They wrapped her in warm towels but held out little hope for her survival. For two days she lay unconscious. Bella Mary's attempt to get warm tea laced with honey down her throat finally woke her. She remained incredibly weak, disorientated and appeared not to understand anything they said to her.

Several days and several pints of honeyed tea later, she managed to try to get up from the bed. Bella Mary told her to stay there and the woman unleashed a guttural string of hieroglyphic speech that nobody understood. The following day she bit John on the arm and kicked Bella Mary in the stomach. Bella Mary glowered with such ferocity that the woman sat back on the bed and failed to struggle even whilst her wrists were lashed to the iron bedstead. Old Mustapha was sent for. He did not recognise her language and was undecided whether the woman was petrified as a result of traumatic events or suffering from madness. He advised mild sedation and close observation. The women had a stocky build, with pale hair and very light blue-grey eyes and the blank stare of a fish. She spent her days either curled up like a foetus or trying to escape. The collective minds at the sick house failed to solve the problem and John made arrangements for the unfortunate woman to be admitted to the Bethlam Royal Hospital Lambeth, commonly known as Bedlam. Formally a Bishopsgate Priory, it opened as an asylum for the insane in 1337. The woman, erratically aggressive to both staff and lunatics, spent most of her time in a padded cell or subject to restraints until three and a half years later, a visitor from Northern Norway recognised her language. The woman, whose name was Hilla had been dragged on board a ship as she walked home from the market through the docks in her native country of Norway. She was beaten and raped on a daily basis, but the basest pain was the indescribable dread regarding the fate that would have befallen her three small children, alone and abandoned in the remote cabin in the woods. Destroyed by misery, she had gnawed though the rope that bound her below deck and had thrown herself over the side of the ship with the intention of drowning. Sadly, this revelation did not improve her behaviour and she remained at Bethlam until her death fifteen years later. Danny became fascinated by insanity and questioned if the brain of a lunatic could be changed or healed and he became a regular visitor at Bethlam. Licensed jailors staffed the establishment and it would be another ten years before the medical men took charge. The out patients department at University College Hospital provided Danny with a regular source of characters displaying the various levels of insanity, dragged or ushered in by distraught, desperate relatives unable to cope with them. The conditions ranged from the feeble-minded and silly individuals to the ones that believed they were the queen or prime minister. Some heard the voices of God instructing them to commit horrendous acts. They all invariably ended up in Bethlam, some for a few weeks, others for their whole lives.

The heat of the summer encouraged a further outbreak of cholera in London. Although most sufferers died at home a number were admitted to hospitals, including the University College Hospital. Danny elevated his cleanliness regime and thanked God that he had left Aida Mina safe in the village.

After the catastrophe involving Hilla, the sick house settled down to the minor stomach upsets, cuts and broken bones that accompanied most summers. Bella Mary was teaching Maria Rose to stitch using a raw leg of lamb.

'Why are we not allowed to be doctors?' She asked Bella Mary.

'Because the men fear that we would be better!'

'Oh.'

'Times change, one day there will be women doctors!' Bella Mary remarked with conviction.

'In my lifetime?' asked Maria Rose.

'Possibly.'

Danny returned from London following the cessation of the latest cholera outbreak. He spent his evenings and nights with Aida Mina and his days at the sick house with Bella Mary, reporting the successes of her ointments and deliberating his current fascination with lunacy. He was convinced that some individuals were born with defects of the brain, as some are born with defects of other bodily organs. Others, having failed to present with defects during childhood, gradually displayed increasingly bizarre behaviour as young adults. Bella Mary believed that awful circumstances could damage an individual's development, citing the example of a plant or a tree, subjected to noxious fumes, drought, floods or burning sun, would grow stunted and malformed. She had seen the filthy London streets, the tremendous destitution and the wretched dispossessed orphans and was surprised that the poor of the big cities were not all lunatics! Danny believed they could be helped, with the provision of a safe place, good nourishment and shelter, rather than the vindictive regimes of the workhouses that had proliferated after the implementation of the 1834 Poor Law Amendment Act. Workhouses had replaced the old Parish Relief and the poor, having hitherto been perceived as unfortunate casualties of birth, began to be seen as victims of their own laziness and inadequacies. The poor lived in terror of admission to the workhouses. Danny knew that many 'insane' poor were incarcerated in workhouses and only the violent, unmanageable and the fortunate were transferred to the Bethlam Royal Hospital.

Old Mustapha worried about the poor and the social unrest occurring in the surrounding countryside and beyond. The advent of new mechanical inventions was robbing the traditional workers of their livelihoods and riots were breaking out and men desperate to feed their families were smashing equipment. Farmers were ploughing the communal land, traditionally used by workers to grow food. Apart from the seed drills and a horse powered threshing machine, the village farms remained unchanged, nobody lost their jobs and there were no riots. Old Mustapha and George were aware that the importation business and George's investments supported them through bad harvests and natural disasters, a luxury not available to many less fortunate small landowners. Old Mustapha had a bad feeling and wondered how long the blessed oasis of peace could survive.

Bella Mary was not interested in her father's concerns, as she had just discovered that her garlic ointment was even more effective when mixed with honey.

Old Mustapha pottered off to the tree house to join his wife on the warm summer evening. She was not interested either. She found the thought very distressing, was glad she would not live long enough to see the changes, and she worried for the younger residents. Old Mustapha, also depressed by his thoughts, changed the subject and they talked about Mustapha and whether he would write a journal during his voyage. They watched young Mustapha watering the plants, pulling weeds and sniffing the fat maturing poppy heads. Nellie arrived with tea and slices of cake.

'There is no point worrying about the future!' Nellie asserted with a smile. 'What will be, will be. We must be grateful that we are alive right now and our lives are wonderful!'

Old Mustapha smiled at Nellie as she passed him the plateful of cake.

'Well said! Nellie!'

Chapter 63

It was a good harvest and the party, in early September was a riotous affair and the first one attended by Arthur Smith. He and Eva Violet had been married for six months and he was unrecognisable. He loved her so much and he cared far more for what he was in her eyes, rather than in his own. This enabled him to let go of the past and change into a person she could love. She had lifted the funereal atmosphere from their living quarters and placed it firmly in the undertakers shop at the front. She was a breath of fresh air and for the first time in Arthur's solitary, anxious life he could breathe easily. Eva Violet banned him from wearing black when off duty, taught him to laugh and occasionally shared one of Bella Mary's bhang concoctions with him. Then she told him that he was to be a father next year. Poor Arthur began to have difficulty maintaining an appropriately sombre expression and insisted that Eva Violet did not attend any future funerals. Bella Mary calculated the child's arrival to be mid-March. She visited Eva Violet every week and persuaded George to arrange for a bathhouse to be erected in the garden at the rear of Arthur's house. Arthur had never used a bathhouse and watched the fervent activity with mounting interest. Eva Violet, who missed the bathhouse at the new house, got in the way of the workmen with trays of tea and biscuits and constant demands of how much longer it would take to complete. She instructed Arthur to begin the woodpile at the back of the house in readiness. The bathhouse was ready for use in mid-December and Eva Violet lit the fire and refused to let Arthur look inside until she was ready. She filled the bath, added a few drops of jasmine oil and lit a number of candles, hung the towels beside the stove to warm and made a tray of tea before finally allowing her impatient husband access to the bathhouse. The warm, steamy, perfumed atmosphere enveloped Arthur as he entered the room. Eva Violet, her face pink and smiling was already in the hot water, which to Arthur appeared unbelievably deep. It took him a while to accustom his feet to the heat of the water and even longer to manage to sit down. He had never felt so hot in all of his life and feared that he would damage his skin, predominantly in his more sensitive areas. Eva Violet laughed at him, splashed him and poured him a cup of tea. Ultimately he relaxed and began to enjoy the virtual weightlessness that the water provided to his limbs.

Arthur and Eva Violet spent Christmas alone in their own home. Eva Violet cooked roasted meat, potatoes and parsnips. She made a pudding from one of old Mustapha's recipes and Arthur washed the plates and pans and made tea for her. He watched her enlarging belly as she sat beside the fire. He had already felt his child move but struggled to believe that a whole new, breathing human being would soon emerge from Eva Violet's body.

It was a bitterly cold winter with occasional dustings of snow and deep frosts and the new bathhouse was in regular use. As Eva Violet slowed down in her last months of pregnancy, Arthur fussed like a mother hen and took over the fire lighting and even some of the cooking. At the end of February, Bella Mary increased her visits and reminded Arthur to keep the bathhouse fires alight at night and arranged for Jack, who lived nearby, to collect her when Eva Violet's labour began. Arthur's anxiety levels amplified to a frenzied pitch and Eva Violet reminded him that women gave birth all the time. Her pains began at first light. She waited until she knew that Bella Mary would be at the sick house before she informed Arthur that it would be a good time to fetch her. Unexpectedly, Arthur was not reduced to uselessness by panic. He sprang into action, stoked the bathhouse fire, made tea and insisted that Eva Violet sit beside the fire and drink her tea whilst he collected Bella Mary. Ten minutes later they were back and Bella Mary gave her a mild remedy. She had sent Robbie the Mouth to ride to the big house and alert her father and young Mustapha, who she was currently acquainting with the birthing process.

By midday, Eva Violet had volunteered to try Bella Mary's new remedy that contained bhang as well as opium, and was wallowing in the deep warm water and asking for a cup of tea. Arthur was making tea for everyone until Old Mustapha told him that his place was now beside his wife. He explained to Arthur that it would be helpful if he could repeat to Eva Violet any instructions given to her, as in his experience he had discerned that some women were attentive to the voice of their husband above all others. Arthur sat beside the bath with a brave face that shrouded an exhausting jumble of fear, elation and wonder. Eva Violet drank her tea, the strength of her pains subdued by the warm water and the remedy. She suffered bouts of giggling, startling her husband who had prepared himself for groaning, crying and distress. Bella Mary examined Eva Violet and nodded to her father and explained quietly to young Mustapha that the time for pushing out the child was fast approaching. Bella Mary untied the rope and told Eva Violet that she would speed the process if she knelt in the bath and pulled on the rope when she was in pain. Hampered by giggling she did her best, so Bella Mary got into the bath behind her to keep her steady. Old Mustapha administered the stamina remedy and the change in Eva Violet was swift and dramatic. The giggling ceased abruptly and she pulled so hard on the rope that her whole body rose up in the water and she strained and bellowed like a bull with its nose ring caught on a fence. Arthur stood up in alarm, fast enough to initiate a giddy spell. Old Mustapha knelt in front of Eva Violet and told her to let go of the rope and hold his hands. Bella Mary got ready to catch the child. Arthur had no idea what was going on and had forgotten that he was supposed to be repeating instructions to his wife. Old Mustapha talked quietly to Eva Violet, assuring her that her body knew exactly what to do. A few minutes later Arthur saw the sudden presence submerged in the water that Bella Mary passed between Eva Violets legs. She helped her lay back in the bath and Arthur gasped at the first sight of his son, sprawled across his mother's belly. He was a large strong child with a lusty yell. Young Mustapha wrapped the child in a warm towel and passed him to Arthur, who kissed his wife and exited the bathhouse with the men and left Bella Mary to attend to the afterbirth and clean nightdress regime. The Mustapha's carried the child into the garden, with Arthur in hot pursuit, and held him up to the rays of the afternoon sun and old Mustapha chanted the blessing and Arthur bit his lip to avoid a flood of tears. Young Mustapha made fresh tea and everyone sat beside the fire and admired the baby who had ceased yelling and was blinking in his new surroundings. They named him Ernest Arthur.

That night, Arthur woke to see Eva Violet quietly feeding their son in the candlelight and the tears that he had stifled since the blessing unleashed and drenched his cheeks and he sobbed. He had been so fearful of losing the only person that had ever breached his isolation. Eva Violet understood, and with tears welling in her own eyes, she smiled and reached over and held her husband's hand.

The next day, young Mustapha arrived with a bunch of primroses and thanked Eva Violet for allowing him to witness the birth.

Chapter 64

In midsummer the ship arrived home a couple of months before the family had begun to wait for it. The news that Edmundo and Estavo had elected to stay in India caused consternation in the entire village. After a welcome cup of tea, Turnip borrowed a horse and set off to tell his mother that her brothers had decided to live their last years in India and they sent their love to her and her family. He did not stop talking about his adventures until bedtime.

Bobby arrived home and entered with the bearing of a man that had seen the world. The façade soon slipped and it was the adolescent Bobby that related the fantastic stories of the seas, the whales and dolphins, the irritating, unpredictable monkeys, the food, rain like you would not believe, the markets and the vivid colours and smells. Tom and Sophia listened with genuine interest and Tom was very proud of a son able to undertake a journey that he would have needed to be hogtied to embark upon. Tom had never been keen on distances. The far side of the village was distance enough for him. The three sat outside in the early evening sun enjoying the waft of lamb stew before Bobby remembered to tell them that Edmundo and Estavo had not come home and were now living in an Indian village. Sophia was not particularly surprised and Tom failed to understand how they could choose to live so far from their roots. Sophia pointed out that they had never really taken root in the village and had been at sea since they were boys and were constantly impatient to sail away again. Bobby nodded his head, already keen to sail off on his next voyage.

Although Mustapha had achieved his ambition to become a sea captain, he found the separation from his family painful. He asked Sabia and the children if they would like to accompany him on the next voyage to North Africa and Turkey. Young Mustapha and Mary Sophia, devastated by the very thought, declined and stated they would rather stay with granddaddy. Sabia accepted the invitation and Hassan would do as he was told.

It was a hot summer and Danny, in his final year of study, managed to arrange a week at home with his wife. Aida Mina was with child and due to give birth at Christmas. The couple spent their time in the fresh air of the marshes and the woods where Danny could breathe and rid himself of the stink and grime of the big city.

Florence's twins had inherited their father Joey's wildness and were a wilful pair with no sense of danger, requiring the regular medical attention of

Beth. Rosy had no interest in acquiring the skills of sewing and her interest in cooking with her mother had waned by the time she was eight. She preferred climbing trees and capturing lizards and sloe worms to secrete around the new house to scare the women. Bella Mary wholeheartedly approved of Rosy, believing her to be another of the new breed of women that would one day inhabit the village and beyond.

In late summer the ship headed off for the Mediterranean with Sabia and Hassan aboard. Mary Sophia became Old Mustapha's constant companion. Young Mustapha tended the garden and mixed the remedies and Robbie the Mouth fell in love with the Innkeepers daughter.

On Christmas Eve, Danny returned to the village to await the imminent birth of his first child and brought the long awaited news to his uncle old Mustapha, that on December 21st 1846, Robert Liston a surgeon at the University College Hospital had amputated a leg under ether anaesthesia. Old Mustapha hastily made his way to Matthew's home and related the awesome news. Matthew was fading fast but his old eyes lit up and he clasped the hand of his friend and a tear rolled slowly down his cheek.

'Thank God.' He whispered hoarsely.

Danny and Aida Mina's little daughter came into the world on Boxing Day with the assistance of Bella Mary and young Mustapha. She had dark hair and her mother's amber eyes. Tom and Sophia visited the new house to see their first grandchild who they had named Sarah Mina for her grandmothers and Tom was touched.

Several weeks later, during which time old Mustapha and Matthew talked of how the use of ether would fundamentally alter surgical procedures, which could now be undertaken with less haste, more accuracy and less screams. Old Matthew never tired of the subject and died quietly, holding old Mustapha's hand and with a smile of contentment on his face. Old Mustapha knew that patients would continue to die from infections caused by the haphazard approach to cleanliness but had made a point of not mentioning that to his very dear, old friend.

The 'Great Stink' of London rose inexorably during the subsequent few years, interspersed with outbreaks of cholera and typhus. The nauseating odour reached such a pestilential peak directly beside the Houses of Parliament, despite the curtains having been soaked in chloride and lime, that it ultimately choked the government into providing three million pounds to tackle the problem of cleaning up the River Thames.

THE END

Made in the USA
Charleston, SC
27 April 2015